Rama
and the
Dragon

Rama
and the
Dragon

Edwar
al-Kharrat

Translated by
Ferial Ghazoul
and
John Verlenden

The American University in Cairo Press
Cairo — New York

English translation copyright © 2002 by
The American University in Cairo Press
113 Sharia Kasr el Aini, Cairo, Egypt
420 Fifth Avenue, New York, NY 10018
www.aucpress.com

Dar el Kutub No. 7149/01
ISBN 977 424 676 4

Designed by Andrea El-Akshar/AUC Press Design Center
Printed in Egypt

Contents

Translators' Preface

When *Rama and the Dragon* appeared in 1980, it constituted a new and dazzling narrative mode. Since its initial appearance—and it has now gone through several printings—Arabic fiction has not been the same. The impact of Edwar al-Kharrat's aesthetics and stylistics on contemporary Arabic writing is analogous to those of Proust in French and Joyce in English. But al-Kharrat is neither Proustian nor Joycean. He is unmistakably himself: a powerful intellectual assimilating the heterogeneous currents of twentieth-century thought, while remaining rooted in the history and meta-history that surround Egypt, his homeland. Al-Kharrat is deeply aware of Egypt's many cultural layers, from its religiously complex ancient and medieval heritage to its often ambiguous and conflicted status as a modern nation. The clamor of competing voices and opinions and the struggle for liberation have led to resistance and civil repression, and consequently to inevitable challenges to intellectual and artistic life in Egypt.

Rama and the Dragon dramatizes, in a new way, the different strands that, when woven together, help to define Egypt: Pharaonic, Greco-Roman, Nubian, Arab, Coptic, Islamic, Bedouin, and Mediterranean. These influences constitute both a richness and a source of polyphony.

The impact of *Rama and the Dragon* on Arabic fiction comes from its uncanny poetics. It is refreshingly strange as a narrative style, yet renders a thoroughly familiar and intimate reading as it conjures the heritage of classical Arabic, colloquial dialogues, Quranic sublimity, and Biblical intertext, along with mythic and folk motifs. It is a work that makes one feel—with its ironies, dislocations, and paradoxes—the disjointed world we belong to. It also evokes in its meandering text and verbal elegance the richness of Arab literary tradition. The loving care with which al-Kharrat's discriminating pen describes details resembles the fine brush of a medieval miniature painter in its exquisite and painstaking labor. The modulation and exfoliation of motifs in *Rama and the Dragon* partake of the arabesque.

Perhaps most crucially, *Rama and the Dragon* does not proceed along linear trajectories—clear beginning to clear end. Rather, it presents, often abruptly, a series of scenes, memories, and dialogues as viewed through the lens of the protagonist Mikhail, which is juxtaposed to the way Rama, his beloved, looks at things. Mikhail and Rama, though individualized as characters, represent two contrasting modes of living, two worldviews: that of the unifying, obsessive lifestyle whose roots begin with the early monastic, hermetic Christians of Egypt; and that of the easy-going, varied, and cosmopolitan lifestyle born of the city. The novel portrays Egyptian life principally in the 1960s and 1970s while harkening back, via intensely remembered images, to the 1950s, even occasionally to the 1940s. Public demonstrations and their brutal suppressions, underground activities and their deadly dangers, horrors of detention and torture, memories of individuals permanently exiled: these realities and their aftermaths are played out as conversation and meta-conversation between Mikhail and Rama. Egypt seeks freedom and fulfillment, so too do Mikhail and Rama, with results that are inevitably passionate.

Rama and the Dragon can also be viewed as a pastoral hymn in an ironic and erotic key. It is a twentieth-century *fin-de-siècle Song of Songs*—a *Song of Solomon* interspersed with apocalyptic revelations in the manner of St. John the Divine. The novel depicts the passions of a courtly lover—of an 'Udhri poet, to name the Arab equivalent—but with the sensibility of a man molded by the malaise of the age. Mikhail, al-Kharrat's protagonist, is an image of Majnun Layla reflected in a cracked mirror.

Our translation strives to stay close to the original while reproducing its luminosity. Its occasional strangeness in English comes from al-Kharrat's intricate sentence structure and his lyrical indulgences that were, and still are, equally strange and innovative in Arabic fiction. However, the questions raised by the novel are familiar. They are those posed by the ancient civilizations of Egypt, Mesopotamia, and Greece that the world continues to grapple with: questions of how to be in this world, how to cope with an enigmatic universe. Thus the defamiliarizing originality of the novel echoes the deepest concerns of humanity as they return to us in the form of a literary text. In *Rama and the Dragon*, the tension that exists between 'to be or not to be,' between concurrent urges to struggle or to give up, occupies the heart of the novel.

The pleasure of reading *Rama and the Dragon* comes partly from encountering and mastering the challenges of the text. The novel neither tells nor shows in conventional ways. We, as readers, overhear what the protagonists say to each other, also what they say to themselves, often stitched together with the most tenuous of seams. Our sense of Mikhail and Rama arises from bringing into focus these overheard conversations and musings. Composed of fourteen chapters, the novel's structure corresponds to the fourteen bodily fragments of Osiris in the Egyptian myth, an event alluded to in the novel's text. Like Isis, who overcomes the dismemberment of Osiris by joining together the dispersed limbs, the reader encounters then sews these chapters together to arrive at the significance of the novel.

The translation of this superb text went through many versions and corrections, striving to achieve both fidelity and beauty. The translation-in-progress went back and forth across cyberspace for seven rounds, sporadically at first, then intensely, over the course of two years, after which it attained its finale. We have benefited from the close reading of the author—himself an accomplished translator of literary works. His acutely nuanced suggestions have enriched the text beyond what would have been otherwise possible. Also, we are grateful to friends who helped us in so many ways in our task: Abdel-Hamid Hawwas for his guidance in textual issues related to folk culture, Walid El Hamamsy in preparation of the manuscript, Dr. John Cooke, Chair of the University of New Orleans English Department, for generous grants and sincere loyalty to the project, and Neil Hewison, managing editor at the American University in Cairo Press, for his meticulous reading and important feedback.

Thus spoke Husayn ibn Mansur al-Hallaj:

My intimate companion, not known for betrayal,
Invited me to drink as a host would his guest.
As the cup went round,
He called for the execution mat and sword.
Such is the lot of him who drinks wine
In midsummer with the dragon.

1

Mikhail and the Swan

When he entered the narrow square in Agouza where several side streets met—empty, elegant streets shaded by sycamore, mulberry, and camphor trees—his car flashed into that virginal, sunny morning where sprouts of branches basked, joyfully alert, childlike, around the empty square.

Chirping birds, darting through trees and dozing balconies, made the square feel like countryside, as if the Nile Road, with its narrow and crowded banks—with its charging cars, trolleys, and buses lay in a different world.

The morning air, thickening but still taut with dew, gushed inside the car's window as he turned the steering wheel with one hand, draping his other hand across the open window port. He was coming out of a transient moment, a faded-blue moment, unreal, entering crowded streets.

He opened his eyes wider.

I am in the midst of a dream, he realized.

It was the same dream that seized him when he fell asleep at night. Just as when he dozed off, he had just called her name in a grieving, tormented tone.

Or had he?

Rama, Rama, do you hear me? Will you answer? I love you.

It seemed as if he were laughing at himself, tearing himself apart. The walls of his bedroom, unpolished, unadorned except for their fine curved cracks would awaken him, then begin to close in. The room's curtain could not deflect a loneliness thrust from the outside upon him. Neither from the skies nor from the surrounding roofs could anything else enter.

Was love this persistent, unanswerable call that went with him in his sleep—now in his wakefulness too? Was this the call emerging from so long ago—a call without beginning or end?

Every night he died a small death, was resurrected by morning as a ghost.

He was not amused.

I did not suspect such an adolescent in me, he said to her.

In a moderate tone, soft voice as if lined by sarcasm, he said: All this fantasy and pain, all this ongoing talk, this unrelenting day-dream—day after day, hour after hour—doesn't all this seem very sentimental and adolescent to you?

Yet in another sense, in a precise, unsentimental sense, it was quite real. Apart from this dream, from his suppressed call, from this painful yearning, everything else was so much floating on shallow waters.

She said to him: But this is a feeling of genuine life, a good feeling. Two days ago while you were away I sat at my desk and wrote a letter trying to tell you how I too felt. I wrote half a page then tore it up. I found it quite adolescent.

He was silent, choking. His love had become a prison without window or door.

He said to himself: A childish element exists at the center of all this. I thought I'd gotten rid of it a long time ago. Where does the disease come from? Childhood? Or is it in the dreariness we impose upon ourselves because we are children no more?

But this was no relapse to an old disease. It was nothing but life.

He didn't laugh at himself. Not this time.

He said to her: I don't know how to say it. I don't know what to say.

She said: That is why I love you.

He had never told her that every time he met her, he arrived expecting to find not her but another woman saying, Who are you?

He never told her: Don't you feel the weight of prison bars pressing on the open exposed flesh? Don't you feel oppression taking hold of the heart, taking hold of the horizon? Don't you feel the unvoiced scream?

Pride, he realized. He believed the truly significant things were not to be said, were unspeakable. But were there any truly significant things?

He mused aloud to her: What can one say about death, truth, or love? Everything has been said.

Words—no matter how passionate and gushing—embodied treason.

He had told himself once that he was wrong to believe such things. The blight was not in the adolescence of the heart alone. Maturity meant accepting half-solutions, compromises, acknowledging what was your lot, your task, accepting what the world makes possible for you. Maturity meant, as was often said, preserving the freshness of delicate hopefulness even though it could be preserved only through salty waters in the heart of the dry rock of despair.

Such wisdom seemed cheap. Very unconvincing.

He said to himself: It is not a matter of relapse into the adolescent. Rather it is the passionate yearning for life, a passion that

5

cannot be extinguished. It is the solid conviction that a man cannot stay alone, that love is not a lie—a conviction denying all fact, challenging all reality.

Wasn't this exactly adolescence?

He became silent, as yet unconvinced either way.

He said to her: Where shall we go?

She said: As you like, my love, I am at your command.

The Tea Island?

Yes.

She came before the appointed time. From his table he could see nothing but her. Her beauty created pain. Amid Liberation Square crowded with beasts and monsters, did this pain amount to a definition of love?

She was wearing her other face. He didn't recognize it. Yet it was always there, as he knew. A determined longing in her eyes, a loneliness refusing despair. Will you ever find what you are searching for, my love? He saw what others could not see: the blue and green waves of time fixed, not ebbing or flowing. In her eyes, the flesh of seaweed dried by the sun—the flesh of hazel weeds maturing by heat and dryness on a rock untouched by water, though its lower masses drowned in an ancient sea. Her lips, delicate, soft, displayed a neat primitive darkness unspoiled by cosmetic.

My child, how lonely you are. Like me. Lonely in the course of an agitated crowded life.

At the end of the night that dashed her to him by the cyclone of love, passion, tears, yearning, and frustration, she said to him: Tell me a story. Don't leave me until I sleep.

Her childish voice, wounding because so soft, was powerless before the infinite expanse of loneliness.

He felt the warmth of her body, gentle as a child's under covers, filling his awareness completely. He did not know then the value of

6

the treasure between his hands. Instead he was searching, despite himself, for an imagined truth, being constantly pushed backward by a power he resisted until exhaustion. At that time he was still dazzled by the shock of an unbelievable vision, still struggling with himself. Would he ever learn to liberate himself from his fetters? There was no truth except this elemental, naked, and savage truth, the irresistible truth of the collision of two bodies. More than bodies, it was a meeting of two attractions that swept away separation; it was the soldering of the explosion of the cosmic nucleus, the crashing of celestial spheres powered by a compelling law; it was the embrace of an intimate and inseparable union, the kiss of pressing and unlimited yearning, sudden, sweet—a final fulfillment that could be neither denied nor canceled.

But in his fantasy, in his steady inability to recognize reality, he lost a fund of love, of warmth, forever.

She told him once: This frightening physical awareness between us . . .

He could say nothing. Multitudes of feelings, from the gushing of a thousand screams of yearning and joy, from flaming calls and hushed joys, wrestled within him.

A huge, heavy hand suppressed the convulsion while earth revolved, slowly, at night.

He decided to narrate a children's story. As he fumbled through it, he enjoyed yet derided the adventure. His voice fluttered with a passion that he, at that time, was scarcely aware of.

Once upon a time, there was a little Princess who went to the forest looking for something unknown, which, however, she knew was there. The Princess traveled through God's wide world, moving from one country to another. In her search she met trees, clouds, monsters, and children. But she never found what she was looking for. The sun rose, night came. Always the night. And the search continued.

This is no way to tell a story, she said. You should give the name of the Princess. Describe her to me.

Rama. Rama was her name. He laughed shrilly. You should only listen to the story in order to fall asleep.

In a submissive tone that touched his heart, a little girl searching for a tiny refuge, unwilling to lose it, she said: All right. Finish the story, my love.

She said that the Princess found the Knight she was looking for.

He was not about to believe this old, shabby tale. The few salty drops in his eyes remained unshed.

She said: Don't leave me until I fall asleep.

He did not say: What is the secret of this barren world of yours? This infinite desert surrounding you?

He drew his arms around her shoulders, at the same time feeling as if his arms were holding up an unbearable weight. In a private world denied to him, she was drowning. In her sleep now, she groaned, burst out gasping, What a strange man!

He said: Who? Who is the strange man?

She half woke up and said: What? Who?

Then slept.

The strange man? No doubt he himself seemed somehow funny to her, strange. But of course he would never decipher these secrets that not even she could grasp.

The two of them were inside his small tight car—in a dusk ripped by azure quickly fading—when he perceived her warm abundant breath, exhaling her very own fragrance. It surrounded him, an intoxicating sensation both light and deep—a sensation revealing meaning in everything. Her woman's breath bore a fragrance from a secret well running with luxuriant waters from a rich inner site.

She said to him: Everyone loves lovers.

He looked into her eyes, into the intimacy of two salt lakes on the sands of a hazel desert. Even then, the little car was like a playful cat too happy, too gay, though with claws. The delicate blue band by which she tied her hair suggested to him a special softness. He was overpowered by a desire to taste once more her delicate lips. He longed to touch her face so as to experience that rare and strange fulfillment realized only when she raised her arms to hold him. But he searched her eyes, also, for a truth he could not fathom. Why this search that arrested, that froze the running blood of life?

He had not yet known the taste of loss.

Her hand on his in the car exuded peace, redeemed him of his undefined raw worry. The sensation did not go away. It was concrete, organic, raving in its constant presence. Imposing was this feeling: the impact of this hand of unlimited tenderness fixed for a moment on his hand then raised, turning over, under his lips, feeling his face in slow quivering touches.

Calling her by name, voicelessly, covered up all other voices.

He said to himself: When you lose something, you know it will not be replaced. No making up. Yet you refuse the sensation of loss. You revolt against it with all your might, just as a living creature revolts against all that death brings about. You reject it as if you were demolishing heaven with your naked hands, as if you had fallen on the soil of the grave knocking its ground with your closed fists and saying No, No. Yet the pit remains inside you. The loss is there. Something that's been mangled, removed from the very fabric that envelops your life. There is no hope in retrieving it. You must bear it, bear the unbearable void of loss, live with it. In fact, why even live? You see yourself dead. You carry death with you. A dead man walks inside you. A moving coffin concealing a buried man without a lid and without shrouds: you.

Angry, sad, wild nights. Stormy, agitated nights. Knocks demolishing the grounds of the heart by rebellion. Frustrated calls and rejection hiding inside the total silence.

He said to her: I spent angry, sad, and wild nights.

She said to him: Why?

Because I didn't hear from you. You wouldn't talk to me. I haven't seen you.

She laughed. Is that all? All right, I'll speak to you every day. But you'll get bored.

She did not, however, speak to him every day. She did not phone him. His self-mockery was not light, to say the least. The days became an infernal journey into his innermost being. The notebook of the journey had closed covers.

In the light of a winter morning when they were by themselves on the dusty, broad, and black marble staircase she once said: As you wish, my love. I surrender to you.

In his own country he had lived his life as a stranger. But at that moment he knew what it meant to be called 'my love' by the woman he also loved. He knew for the first time, and in her bronze-colored, tender-skinned arms, the taste of dwelling in one's homeland.

What was the use telling her that 'my love,' heard in his language and in a strange land, were sweet thrusts? But hadn't all lovers said this already?

Love and death were unspeakable, unrepeatable. Truth, an impossible illusion.

He did not tell her: My own intuition of losing you has taught me that one loves alone and dies alone. I sense that even death will not obliterate loneliness. After a life condemned to loneliness we die, but even then there's no deliverance. We meet no one. Death folds the book, seals it. And love? Love is a lie, a passionate desire to escape loneliness, an unrelenting rush toward complete melding into a union, a flaring together. But even then it revolves around loneliness. And it ends by consecrating a loneliness more bitter than death. We love alone. Love is an incurable loneliness.

10

In the dark of night he screamed with shut mouth. Not true, it cannot be true, no.

Silence. No response.

She said to him: We have reached maturity. We can control ourselves.

He didn't tell her that convulsions had peeled off his reason, disturbed his equilibrium. He did not ask her which was truer, hence nearer to life's fount: This warm union? This continuous presence at every moment, yes, at every moment? Or these painful convulsions?

He wanted to say: But my love, I live them together, it's a torrent, an embracing passion *and* regression, a rupturing blow, a continuous clashing and separating, a psychological fabric rupturing and soldering, splitting and uniting in constant revolution that fails to distinguish between truth and non-truth. Your love for me is both there and not there, asserted, refuted a thousand times a day in my fantasy.

You said once: I love you.

We were in the midst of blazing fire.

You never said it again.

Your silence. Your continuous closeness, yet remoteness, in whose various paths you defend yourself so well with sharp, alert intelligence. Your life runs in locked compartments, one barred from the other, separated. Desperately you protect each insulating wall. Dear heart, does the real you exist within this maze of ramparts? Behind the fortresses erected in front of my face? In front of the world's face? In front of your own face? Do you exist in the world of these spheres that touch without overlapping? That accompany each other but never join? Do you exist in each lone world that runs strangely apart from the others?

He said to her: Dear love, St. Michael is my patron, my guardian angel. Did you know I was named after him, the archangel? I was told the Nile wouldn't flood unless Michael descended on his name

11

day to the Land of Egypt and wept. One drop of his tears and fertile, red waves pour forth. Cracks of barren land fill with thirsty plants swaying joyfully in the soil.

When I was little, they used to make *fatir* cakes on my birthday, the day of St. Michael, leader of God's soldiers with his two-pointed sword. When I ate the oiled, glimmering cakes decorated with ancient Coptic inscriptions, I saw him—my angel, my guardian, my brother—attacking all the lies with his silvery armor and long lance, all the devils crowded in the dark.

He did not say any of this.

He did not say to her: Truth for me is the demolishing of ramparts, the outpouring and joining of life's waters into a sea with open horizon, where two lovers in a frail wooden bark float upon its frothing waves.

He did not say to her: What I want more than anything—for you, for us—is that you be free with me. Free from the need for self-justification. You, who have met with ghosts in your search through the night, must feel justified simply because you are loved. Love alone needs no further justification. It takes and gives without question. Dear heart, nothing explains or justifies you. Love for me is knowledge. Candor, a burning desire. I don't want to say I accept you. Why accept or not accept? I only want to say I love you, all of you, without condition, without reserve.

So I break the rules of the game. Of course. Life being a game, as is love. But I take the risk anyway. I put my heart, naked, trembling, stubborn in its faith, under the pangs of disclosure, without protection. What happens when the barriers and dams give way, when the imprisoned, anxious waters gush from the fenced compartments and collide carrying stony rubble?

Frightening? Yes.

The warmth of concealed darkness, of preserved secrets—I know these things. But I also know of bitterness and loneliness behind the ramparts. What happens exactly when the Self unveils its intimate disarray? When its incomprehensible and unjustifiable longings are laid bare? Yes, what happens when the drives of its frenzy and hidden demands are finally revealed?

In loving you I find myself. Here is how it is: my love is for knowledge, for total wakefulness in front of every sound, every quiver in the voice, every twitch of the eyelid. That is why I find myself when you are not with me.

A strange and extraordinary thing: the freedom of waves under pale clouds: you away from me. The doors are boulders, rolled tight before the opening.

This too he did not say: Between me and everything, an insurmountable barrier now stands. Alien sky, alien buildings, people making sense no more than muddled things. I am separated. At sunset, from across the Nile, the air pierces my chest bringing no solace, no joy. The sting of noon sun, the silence of streets at night, the inhaling of cool morning air—all this carries loss, as if a veil, transparent yet solid, could not be removed from the eyes, a veil wrapping the heart, freezing me.

I miss you.

He did not say to her: Where is the bliss and peace we knew together? Where is the unspeakable joy in every touch, in every breeze? Where are the outbursts of life gushing, carrying us on the waves of imperceptible pleasures across our magical city? Where are the endless streets beneath our footsteps, their treasures for us alone, lit by bright lamps gleaming from the skies of night and heart? Where is our flourishing city without limits?

Rama, where are you?

She sat next to him, the buzzing of the car engine engulfing them—like stubborn waves breaking on rocks. People hurried by, benumbed,

13

the two of them existed in a private world. He drove on the road of cosmic joy, of freedom, of energy offered generously and potently. Her presence next to him felt abundant, plentiful. His arm crossed hers. He knew the proximity of her bosom, the fullness of her body. It brought him, via a hidden current, on–off, a promise of inexhaustible feminine richness, of sweet water lapping the walls of his soul.

She said to him: If this happened to you, it would doubtless shake you.

Her voice was meditative, a distant echo.

Was that prophecy or promise, my enchantress? An intuition of what will be? Or the first step I didn't know I was taking on the crust of an earth splitting with explosive grumble? Or were you merely beginning the incantation of your mysterious charm?

You say to me now: I am happy that you exist, that I met you.

But you do not go on.

I feel in the tone of these words an inclination toward a coda, a step toward something finished. Your words, instead of delighting, open a permanent wound. I am convulsed, placed in the mouth of a volcano full of lava, melting all the hard rocks of age. How can two bare hands block such a flow? How can they hold up the structures of a world giving in to convulsions?

Rama: name of bitter salty water.

Nobody had ever known such a night. Years—a lifetime—had passed, the sky charged with alarms, the metallic growling rising, along with fragments of exploding sky, then going down in a silence lined with disaster. The quiet locked house at night was fragile, soft-crusted in the heart of the storm that destroyed everything around it. He had been enveloped in an innocent tired sleep, had not yet known the bitter taste that would never go away. The news arrived, while loud shabby music, a song of glory, love with a quavering voice— *yours are my heart and my love*—played on.

14

The clamor deafened the heart, made it bleed. Hollow voices echoed in a desolation where even sorrow lost its meaning. *May you live free . . . May you live free . . .*

Tears, suddenly. His cracked heart could find mercy nowhere. Love had been offered, wasted, even snubbed. Without his having any protective cover, the storm of tears shook him, threw him about in a savage solitude that would not dissipate. By morning, by every morning, the heaviness of stones sinking within himself, drowning him, refusing to let his heart resurface.

That morning he wept. But never again. The strings of final solitude brought their music to him. The notes emanated from hearts tortured by old passions, ebbing through the many years though retaining the fire of buried pain, of world-encompassing sorrow. In a muffled way, while the winter sun streaked through his window, he wept.

He said to himself: My love is always one. Sacred and intimate, yet captured by, offered to, something strange and unknowable.

No, I cannot admit it. She calls on me, captivates me always. Resist as I might, it is in her arms that I find myself. There is a meaning in those arms that I miss in everything else. My hands are empty; my insides, an open pit.

He said to himself: You have definitely reached the age of reason, you are a middle-aged man. So what now? Don't you think this Oedipal interpretation is facile, cheap? Isn't this matter disjointed, neither here nor there, exceeding the proper subject?

He said to himself: Just the same I can stand it all. No matter the price, I can live by it.

He used to think he was tough, did not break easily.

Now he was prey to the melody of tears.

He couldn't believe when he settled down to prison night and called her name, as one might call on freedom, that she didn't hear

15

him. He couldn't believe she didn't know, perhaps even find his situation somewhat entertaining, indicating as it did a most wretched sensitivity. That her life might have other courses, teem with other demands, with other longings and fulfillments, seemed incredible to him. Her name on his lips, the first word uttered in the day, then again during his intimate journeys, he could not believe he wasn't with her, that there could possibly be no response from her.

She said to him: I am torn. I want to be close to you yet also to run away. I want to escape to a forgotten island in some far corner of an ocean, to wake in the morning breathing deeply and peacefully, without tension. I want to say to myself: I'll skip rope in the afternoon! And know that I can do so. Run, play, skip rope.

She wasn't smiling. Only her voice carried any flame. Then she smiled and said: Too bad all the islands in the ocean have been bought by American millionaires.

He had said to her: You make me suffer.

She said: If it's any consolation, I've suffered no less.

He didn't like to pose insignificant questions just to get orderly answers—taut, well-aimed. But now a question he refused to articulate nonetheless refused to disappear.

Why were you suffering, my love?

Could there by a link between that which was torturing me, tearing me apart, and your own suffering? Or is it because you were over there, distant and unconcerned about me, the threads of your pain woven by other hands?

He knew how real, bitter, and unique her suffering was. He also knew she would not allow him to put a hand on it. That with sudden, artificial chatter she would stop him short from approaching this elemental wound. She did not want the wound to heal. In her innermost, she didn't believe it could heal. In her wound she found in fact a wild pleasure.

16

What is the point of cracking with pain when there is no consolation?

He said to her: Don't run away from me any more.

She said: Yes.

The lights on the bridge were flashing, dying out, gliding over
the night's flesh without stabbing it. She pressed his hand in hers, but
was absent. She had entered her private retreat. From then on, she
dwelled behind fences while smiling at him. Sad smiles. After that, he
didn't see her for days—days as long as eternity. By then the tone of
loss had become a leitmotif, a daily entering of his reckless breaths
into an endless series of graves. This leitmotif did not lose—despite its
fragmented recurrences—the violence of the original shock, occurring
time and again, without end.

He said to her: This fancy, this illusion—this running away in the
name of freedom.

He said (without saying): My love, we destroy with our own
hands the structure of our former lives. We bang daily on walls of our
self-made prisons, each wall erected over years, with sacrifices no
one can evaluate. In these walls our love makes a window unto the
sun, a fragment torn from the vast nocturnal sky. Relations rupture,
rules collapse and fall apart. So do the light, essential wares of love
and books. Other fragments lie torn, are left behind: the music of
expectation and anticipation. Adventure steps to the door of an air-
plane taking off, ourselves within. Could my fancy arrive at a stone
house amid olive groves near snow and old cedar trees? At a narrow
road twisting under the second-hand car we bought in installments?
At rocks' surface moist with dew? At the abyss of valleys charged
with the distant blue haze of lofty trees and shrubs?

Such are the outbursts of chaste, innocent beasts imprisoned all
their lives. Such are the fierce joys of fatigued bodies burdened by the
work of erecting monuments to freedom, of creating the impossible.

17

In one heavy blow the false is erased. Tones of muffled voices choke when colliding with the many lights and sounds wavering up, down. You get to know the warmth of dialogue. You, I—become *we*. We: a pronoun purified, no matter how wounded or polluted by bleeding.

Having been defiled—and paralyzed—by the crime of silence my hand is spotted by the color of blood, my own and that of my brothers too. This hand, having not been raised, having remained silent, twisting *yes*, yet dumb, this hand now speaks.

Enough sinning, my soul exudes a foul smell. It's the stink of buried decay. Now you, Rama, in a strange, inverse, and miraculous way have purified me, liberated me. You have freed some of the serene-eyed passionate beasts imprisoned in me for twenty years. If you hadn't freed them, they would have twisted forever behind the bars of my living flesh. For the first time you explore the extended horizons of your world. You come out from that solitary clouded region, half lit, half dim. You live your life as you wish, not from duty. In fact, duty becomes liberation for you, for me. It becomes the unquestionable right of madness and the seizing of one's own life.

Isis, free beneath the fiery eyes of your father Ra, whether by light of the day or beneath the torches of stars.

He said to her: This fancy, this illusion—this running away, this freedom.

On that night she had said: We are not hurting others, we are not hurting anyone.

He did not say to her: The very act of life implies crime and hurt. Either them or us. Or all of us together. Every step on earth, every breath inhaled, partakes of murder, destruction. We choose to kill ourselves, don't we? Aren't we really making a terrifying choice of no return?

She had said to him: Can we construct without first demolishing?

18

He said nothing. The force of things, itself, refutes any possible answer.

When he was in Aswan he sent her a postcard: I remember you and miss you always.

Later, when he asked her, Did you receive my card, a rosy color merged with the brown color of her soft complexion. She said: Yes.

She said: You know that I torture myself more than anyone else. I've been thinking. Something has collided with us. After something collides with you suddenly, unexpectedly, you cry out: Careful! Why weren't you more careful?

He sent her a telegram—from the hot South packed with the vulgarity of traditional outmoded luxuries. He asked her to wait for him at the station. He kept speculating on how to sign the telegram. He spent long hours formulating sentences, choosing signatures, constructing and deconstructing in the spareness of his hotel room.

He arranged everything, prepared for all contingencies. He would arrive two or three days before his official arrival date. No one would be waiting for him but her.

They would go to the magical strange place that had known their steps.

As the exhausted train limped into the station, he glimpsed her. She stood on the platform. His heart raced madly, yearning, excited Among the crowd, not caring about anything else, he drew her into his arms, felt her smooth cheek with his lips. Once again the scent of her erotic, fragrant femininity inundated his face. Mixed with her perfume it reminded him of ecstatic nights. His hand in hers, the two of them in the car, alone, on her ground—which hotel? The Mena House? Shepheard's? The Semiramis? Or perhaps the Fayoum Auberge . . . yes, the desert road at noon, hot, glaring, full of mysterious promises.

At the Auberge we took care in front of the staff and chambermaids to play down our happiness, to be on guard concerning our

19

smuggled love. I had brought you a gold ring. You put it on, gently, surprised for once, silenced. The large room above the broad wooden staircase was dim. As soon as the door was closed, rough waves of yearning threw us into each other. With you between my arms, the barriers pressing the founts of my life fell apart in the delicacy of your flesh. Demolished without sound. I filled my heart with your serene eyes, having known none more beautiful. At last I felt your warmth melting the ice around me. I tasted your hot soft lips. Rama, Rama. My strange and wonderful love. Do you love me? You say to me: Yes, yes. I can hardly believe my hands, my face, my lips. I can hardly believe that such love, such joy, exist. The world becomes compliant, reconciliatory, harmonious. Freedom and meaning become sensuous realities between my very arms, across my own body. I can hold them. And they, me.

Suitcases split apart. Clothes fly about. You rejoice at the presents. I smile. For the first time we go to the window and open it for the air of the salty lake, for its still waters with their silvery glitter shining like dark steel plates. The waters' strong smell drifts in upon hot midday air. The call of a gull in the midst of the void sounds warm, sweet—like the wound of knife in tender flesh. The call falls down from above then goes up again. We laugh for no reason, simply because we are together, in love.

Your limpid virginal rounded bosom—its sweetness eclipses all ecstasy, warm, soft, intoxicating. Your successive hot breathing contains the taste of sweet nectar. This light-headedness, where all things lose their weight, leads us once again to our first steps toward radiant skies illuminated by the sun of your eyes. Then we fall down like predators to the depths, moist with love's dew where wild flowers grow in wilderness gushing with dense fertility and fierce ripening.

The peace of the resolution of contented reconciliation accepts the loneliness of life. Rather it forgets it, negates it.

We went down to have lunch, then we had a siesta, side by side, and we did not stop from talking and laughing. Your eyes were always smiling, amorous. In them no concealing or watchfulness. Beneath them no quick-moving alert intelligence, but rather assurance and glee.

In the afternoon we walked along the fields. The breeze owned a cool touch. We descended to the salty puddles on the soft sandy shore of the lake. We collected handfuls of whitish gray powder that melted through our fingers. We passed our fingers across each other's lips and tasted the brine's sting and laughed. While I was looking at your brown lips, I felt incited by a longing for fulfillment.

None of that happened.

He did not say to her: The fancies of my senses are bitter food that I would not replace with anything else. They are the bread by which I live, the blood-wine that can never satisfy my thirst. Yet I would not stop gulping their destructive liquor.

He did not say to her: After our return, life became pallid, transparent like fancy itself.

Sunset was proceeding on Tea Island. Conversation had drifted into one of those gaps that happen from time to time. Mikhail lit two cigarettes. When her lips pressed on his cigarette at the very place where his lips had left a slight moisture, he felt between his lips the blow of a fleshless kiss, glittering, passing weightlessly.

While she stood in front of him looking at the trees on the far shore, he called to her voicelessly: Rama. Rama, I want to know. Where is the truth between us?

Small Peking ducks in the dark waters stopped quacking. On the pond's far shore the dense trees seemed threatening, dismal, burdened by a mysterious spell.

A drop of salty water fell into the still pond. With its folded wings and craned neck, a black swan glided silently along the water. The

21

Casino lights poured out in hushed blue. Already people had gone away. Waiters sat in the kitchen talking in low voices, as if afraid.

The swan stopped at the iron fence with its slender bars, in front of their table. She floated in place, looking with glassy dark-green eyes. In her rounded body was an invincible, embedded, challenging softness.

Mikhail stood up. He jumped briskly to the pond, his feet plunging into the loose mud. Water went up to his knees. His hands held the swan, his fingers surrounding its long neck, pressing against its slender rounded ribbed bone. The silk black feathers slid over his hands, exciting him.

The swan did not emit a sound. She did not raise a last cry. Her sharp and extended beak did not open. Her wings did not flap or flutter. In her agony she nevertheless kept her lofty neck strong, solid in the squeezing hand in the dark. Mikhail plunged yet deeper in the water, wrapped his arm around her body, clutching it to his bosom. The stagnant water was at his face. He tasted its muddy flavor with its light rotten sweetness. The swan remained towering, haughty, delicately round, floating on the surface of the water without being engulfed by it.

The mud gave way beneath his feet. His legs slipped into soft welcoming tender mud pulling him down with irresistible longing. Inside he yelled out a silent cry of repose in the face of the swan's body sliding, almost escaping from his hold, while he quietly squeezed the folded wings in his arms over the cold rounded flesh.

The mud opened. He plunged in, sucked down by dark stillness. Yet he turned the silent swan that leaned on her side between his arms.

One large circular wave spread out on the surface of the water reflecting a final redness from one torn piece of cloud sinking to the horizon.

All of this really happened.

2

A Boat at the End of the Lake

W hen earth became illuminated and morning arose, I went down to the pond. There I saw a woman, not of human progeny. I shuddered to look at her. Her skin was tender, soft. Her love persists in my flesh.

Light filtered through the world's ceiling—lambent behind white clouds. Behind the clouds lay a low building, the Auberge. The sun's blaze and gusts of salty wind had engraved tiny dots in its gray stone, in the interlaced planks of its wide gates. The glass windows in front were shut with curtains drawn. A delicate fence meandered roundabout, broken here and there. The lake water seemed silvery to his touch, solid with light waves. Small mounds of bricks were pressing against the soft sandy earth, darkened by salty seepage.

A bullet cracked the air from afar. He said to himself: It is one of the Bedouin hunting quails. Then adding: To sell them to tourists and townspeople. Suddenly the sky ripped open with the rumbling of a MiG fighter jet, amplifying its thunders among the clouds. It swept away, the thunders trailing off in the distance.

When he had opened his eyes on waking, he had said to himself: We'll take a boat, go out in the midst of the lake.

He was stepping on stones jutting through the shallow water. The water flowed toward a wooden bridge lofted over it. His feet felt the wet stones' solidity. But with each step, his black cloth shoes felt as if they would slip on the sticky water moss. Small snails sprouting on the stones cracked apart, inaudible in the spacious air. He was hopping from stone to stone, smiling to himself, stretching his arms to balance his quick and precarious movements. He felt new life—an alertness in the air with its pungent smell, its slight chill. For a moment he stood inhaling from the delicate white sky.

Rama . . . Rama . . .

A tormenting, burning yearning to go back to her soft warm arms, to embrace her shoulders, to return to her eyes: an attack of yearning. The suppressed call rises again. Rama, Rama, what happened? Where are you? How do you stand with me now?

He said to himself: This yearning will not crush me; its rising waves will not drown me and envelop me like a wave of tears lifting me up then dropping me down. I will not let these crushing waters swallow me in their depths and fill my eyes with hot salt.

I burst into a scream, blocked by the salty waters.

Strong will and firm intention do not have the last word.

She had said to him: He does not add a dramatic touch to things.

She was talking about a friend of hers whom he did not know. How many friends does she have? What kinds of relationships? Was she accusing him, hinting at the dramatic thread in his comprehension and view of things?

He looked at her as he always did, trying to find out who she was.

He did not tell her: Doesn't it happen in life? Doesn't every moment play a role in a hidden tragedy—whether one is resigned to it or not—a tawdry and voiceless tragedy? This persistent pressure to

24

sink to the ground and plunge into the soul's soil—isn't it sheer pain? The world, of course, is drenched in pain.

Yes, she would have said to him, no doubt: Yes, but let's not add a halo of theatrical light. Let's have a sense of proportion, let's not be banal.

The tragedy, my love, is that our life is banal. And this tragic element recurs. It follows no structure, no formula. Maybe pain is both its form and its essence. But in every moment it has the heat of matchless cruelty. Words have no meaning; naked living flesh can only shiver with the burns of this tragedy. There's no formula here, no word to embody it, communicate it, signify it. This I know—but not how to say it.

Everyone knows what I'm saying, one way or another.

No escape from the siege of banality, no escape from the shabby face of this tragedy.

Desire's unquenchable yearning envelops him in his silent room and it cannot be resisted—no matter how much denied.

She had said to him: In the afternoon, perhaps—but only perhaps—I can come to you. If I can't, I wish you a happy trip.

Happiness? Another story.

He does not add a dramatic touch to anything. But this pointless wait, this intimate tie that enhances his life—albeit through yearning, through silent dialogue with her has been ruptured now. He yearns simply to hear the tone of her voice, to feel the warm tone, the warmth of her breath, of her sound. He does not hear her—as if he will never hear her. His will in all this is necessarily frustrated. Nothing will happen. There are no means. Everything has been cut off. He said to himself: Go down now, go and look for her in the nocturnal streets of Cairo, along the Nile, and at the bridge we crossed together.

I leave the side street to my right—which leads to narrow alleys crowded with fantasies, half-truths, and suffering—going toward the old house that continues to haunt me pressingly, bringing to me the awesome terrors of madness. I go beyond the street for which I harbor useless resentment. I forget it for a moment as I forget many things, or I cruelly push them to oblivion with my hand. I ask the taxi-driver to take me on the nocturnal road. Stopping at a cigarette kiosk, I ask the way to her. I turn into slanting streets and knock at her door.

A thousand apologies immediately take shape in his fantasy, a thousand arguments. The scene of a strange visitor in the late night—as he travels at dawn—and with it, events evolving. From the shade, characters from her other life appear, forming a circle around him. He is confounded by a siege of greetings and welcoming. *Ahlan wa-sahlan.* Would you like a beer? Have you had dinner? How are things? He suppresses his fantasies, squeezes with his hands the blood of clumsy imagination—for none of it will happen.

What remains is loneliness, the eternity of loneliness. The horizon that cannot be reached. When will he exit from this vast, empty loneliness with no need, or hope, for an end?

When the tear-wave came over him—as it comes to him often now—and ebbed, bobbing him around despite his efforts and tearing him apart in its total prison, the whole house exuded the smell of fear. An irrational fear—beyond comprehension and grasp, the breath of something alien and lurking, threatening him in an ambiguous yet sure way, present and lasting. The windows were open onto the night heat—a blank, locked heat closing on the frightful alien breaths inside him. He could not move. His resistance to the fear was crumbling. Despite earlier intentions, he lifted the telephone receiver, pulled himself together as he was once again ridiculing himself; none of this was new in his behavior:

Hello! You there, how are you, *'Amm*? What are you doing? Not at all, I'm leaving in few hours. I wanted to see you before I go. Okay, yes . . . if you can come . . . I'm alone at home . . . yes . . . Certainly, I feel rather lonely . . . if you could come!

A part of him ripped into shreds; he felt the tremor in his voice:

Not at all . . . In fact I'm very lonely and somewhat terrified.

He laughed hesitatingly.

—I don't know, never . . . a fear like this . . . that has no meaning . . . This is not the first time that I've traveled . . . After an hour? Yes, great . . . I'm waiting for you.

Then, total collapse. Everything lost its contours. All measures, useless. Nothing was left but waters of pain and loneliness gushing with difficulty from the rock, sculpting the rock. Nothing left but a suppressed, hoarse howling, the howling of a beastly grief with its sharp, bared teeth, though without resistance.

He said: People repeat themselves. How boring!

He said to himself: And inside of ourselves, we used to think what was happening to us was exceptional, had never happened to anyone before, could not happen again . . . Just this call rising from within me, despite me, with your name . . . Rama . . . Rama . . . stirs the muddled waves of love in this dammed-up sea, making my eyes water. Always, always.

Do you remember the night you came to us; we drank together and spoke of your last trip. You were gay as usual; quick and terribly clever in your observations, full of brilliant, sarcastic yet good-hearted comments on your roommate—how you used to find the toothpaste beneath the pillow, and a piece of her underwear suddenly and without reason in your handbag, next to your handkerchief—and we laughed. You also narrated how you had two drinks yesterday and became tipsy quickly. You said you get drunk quickly, and you told me later that you discovered, at one point, suddenly, that you were about to become an alcoholic. And that you resisted. You

27

said you got drunk with your friends and you sang. You said your voice wasn't at all good for singing, but you broke out in song.

Suddenly I saw you in the desert of the ancient moon, dark bodies of cars, randomly parked at a distance with lights off, winds dry, the taste of soft sand in the nocturnal air. The desert chalet with the door open, people around you, moving about and sitting down, in my painful and awful blurred dream. You singing gaily, not caring. In your singing I detect a tone of despair, as well a call for help, a tone that betrays a challenge sweeping away conventional rules. You, seated in pants on the desert sands.

Was that night the first of Ramadan? Or was it a different night? You had said to me:

I'm once again inclined to do reckless things. I'm back in the mood of the old rebellion. Perhaps the impossibility of recklessness in front of me, in front of us in this story, pushes me to rebel yet again, defying everything.

He said to himself: My heart cries out with rebellion, my love, and I suppress it. I want to break down the world. I want to break the dream's rock with one strike, collect the fragments between my hands in wild joy and throw them in the face of other rocks. I want to plant them with the fierceness of a rebellion that cannot be controlled in the heart of the petrified world, and drown them. And from them make stalks emerging beneath the sun, splendid in their dishevelment. I want to squeeze this yearning that implodes in me—between my burnt-out palms, struck by pain—until my heart dries out, solidifies into a column atomizing unto the impossible. I want to collect you—you, my flying, dispersed enchantress—to my chest, my treasure, my glory, my desire and make you whole. I want to erase with taps of my hand all the freakish disfigured features from the face of the world. I want to tear with my nails the flesh of falsehood that drips as a slow, dull liquid; to strip off the rocky skin, to destroy,

28

destroy, and destroy oppression and savagery—silently, sadly lurking behind its eyes. How dear you are to me! I want to hold in my hands your softly brown face and press your cheekbones, press until their dough is shaped by the bones of my hand, and my empty hands are full in one instant and forever.

The waters fill up with drowning animals howling, open-mouthed, devouring flesh with their long teeth.

I said to you: Yes, yesterday you were at the chalet in the Pyramid neighborhood.

You had not told me where you were; you said in sudden, alert danger as if aware of something: How do you know?

You know how to defend your frontlines, but I too occasionally know something about the art of maneuvering. You related how the straw mat burnt from a cigarette stub or a fire spark. Was there meat grilling along with drinking and singing in this scene? And you told him: Surely man, you are either head over heels in love or numbed.

At that moment I heard in your voice a strange tone whose echoes continue to stab me, each blow more percussive than the last.

On your birthday a car carrying the most dear person in the world turns to the right not following its route—to a crowded street, toward an old house with a dark, narrow door. We are in a taxi, the front-seat passengers jamming their shoulders together. A reserved glance embodying a secret. A song written on a paper scrap. A talk in an accent I know so well—on the phone. A white letter reaching far with the words "Cairo, after midnight" at the top. A thousand thrusts tearing my mind with suppressed bare-toothed howling. How light is the weight of things that produce the fabric of death. How plenty, those things around us.

You said to me, in your eyes that playful, tender look:
Are you jealous of him?
—I am jealous of every man in your life. Every man.

You stretch your finger to my chin stroking a razor's nick: How boyish!

My arm on your bare thigh, the short white chemise rolled high, your belly brownish, round and tender. The light herbage dry. From the décolleté in the nylon appeared swells of your breasts. Full of relaxed, supple tenderness, emerging from your chest, they carry the riddle of love, in repose, invincible, mysterious.

When we went down to the sleepy street, you said to me:

In the last few days I have been remembering what happened in our enchanted city, recalling it a thousand times.

I said to you: Yes, it's as if it occurred in a strange dream, that it didn't take place . . .

You said aggressively: I believe it actually happened.

I said to you: Yes.

I hadn't wanted to deny that it happened. That wasn't my implication. Was there an accusation in your sharpness, in your defensive leap on behalf of this reality dream besides which my world is empty? Even now I cannot believe it happened. I think of it as a dream shared by chance. How can I be certain that the world surprised me, in its last rays, with this mad joy that falls outside the melodic music of the spheres, given its sharp, wild sweetness?

You said to me: Won't you accompany me upstairs?

Our ascending movement stopped. The electric environment of the lift fell silent. Beneath the light, between the walls of this illumined white well, you held my face with your tender hands, turned it to you where I found your lips anew. The beat of cymbals, the rich notes of deep brass echoed in the loneliness of the empty, glowingly-lit box. Our lips come alive, vibrating, turning and squeezing the flesh of joy slowly exploring by touch alone the walls of mutual yearning. The breath of your heaving chest feels warm between my arms. Only by your wind does the world's ship move now; your

30

breath fills the effulgent sails, makes the ship's mast plow the dark, wet sea—in victory.

He said to himself: Where are the happy moments in the story of this love, in the story of this man? There are not many. That was one.

He said to himself: It surprised like a confirmation granted but not asked for. It realized the desired promise, at the same time carrying boundless annunciation. How rare these moments of happiness, and how debilitating.

He did not say to her: O my love, where have the days of annunciation gone? Has the morning of our love touched night so quickly? I detest the night—I detest the night: far face of love's rock, elevated, cutting, massive, and closed in.

He said to himself: I will not allow the dream to crush me.

In his depths lurks an open-eyed solidity. The night neither comes nor goes, and there is no morning. The eyes of a dark sun burn with a mineral black light.

When evening fell . . . night became vast wings of heat. Of silence, closing in. The step of hours falls off. Loneliness has its many long hands and dry-boned fingers thrust into the wet earth, leaving a bloodless, voiceless wound. Each shriek of her name wounded the earth anew.

He said to himself: This is not true. It is not happening to me. This cannot be what actually happens. This unbearable, childish pain. Yet he is not a child, he who is suffering now.

Pointless.

He said to himself: Childhood suffering has passed away. Hasn't it?

He shouted to the dark walls: Mad? Am I becoming mad? Losing my control over reason? This is funny, petty, absurd. But it is happening to me. I can hardly believe what I see once more! Once more? This is happening in front of me in 1971 in a room in an apartment in a building on a street of a crowded city. This is not happening in the clouds or in some dream. In this chair, among these books, papers, magazines, pinenuts, mechanized music from a Japanese recorder, a yellow lampshade with two one-hundred watt bulbs, a glass top of an old desk, wood and stone sculptures, copies of paintings by Rubens, Renoir, and others, pens and inkpots—all the rubbish people possess and live with. This is where it is happening. I stretch my arm, oppressed by a power that cannot be defeated. I supplicate—is there anything else worth doing? I whisper, fearing I might be heard, your name:

Rama . . . Rama . . .

A wild call erupts from my depths, from something alien in me. I myself am alien. I stretch an arm in resistance, in hope of a response I know isn't there. From behind the white ceiling falling on me I supplicate. Yes, I supplicate. Nothing for it but the fervor of prayer, the pressure of nightmare, the agony of beseeching the woman I once embraced, was in love with, hated and loved, whom I took to my heart, knowing her utmost depths: The warmth of her womb, the delicacy of her breasts, the sternness of her eyes, the groans of her rapture, her glory and her defeat, and the taste of her tears. Every day I die. Every day I thirst for this divine woman, this seer and child, this unhappy, serious, laughing woman, the eternal playful lewd and virgin saint. And I don't know her: she's a stranger, even if she's a part of me that cannot be severed. There is no end to her now or ever. An attack of madness? No, enchantment doesn't befall me. Nor is it magic or passion. A thousand times, every day, I decide to end all this, thinking I can make the break. And a thousand times I find myself once again mired in the sludge of your love, immersed in a succulent dream earth, beyond my will. A stone wounds my ribs. Immersed in sticky muck, I say: I shall uproot the dream from the soil of myself. I shall uproot myself from the dream's wet earth, even if it leaves behind a piece of me—severed, red, dripping dark liquid. I want the surface of a vast salty ocean with no horizons—no heavy waves blocking my mouth. I open my eyes seeing the water's thick dregs, the world spread out. And when I wake up I find myself going, always going, to you, invading your world. Which is my world too though I can't recognize it. Hence, I live by you, but not with you. Isn't all this true?

He said to himself: You cannot be sure of what is happening to you. You cannot believe anything while fighting the deadly storm. When death comes, you will deny it, as well. You will not believe: this is a recurring death, an unbearable breaking down, a happening that cannot be grasped.

He said to himself: In the end, is it an arbitrary matter, in fact wasted and meaningless? Even if she knew of my struggle, she would find it unworthy of mention or, at the most, strange, unnecessary, incomprehensible—all of which amount to the same thing.

Could she respond with light sarcasm? Pity? Tolerance and acceptance? Understanding and appreciation, or sympathy? Unbearable . . . All of it amounts to the same thing.

So what do you want? No one needs this drama.

Mikhail was standing on the stone-path winding across the shallow gray-green waters of the swamp. He filled his chest with the brushings of salty air. From the tense, transparent horizon a few distant calls of Bedouin, playing or quarreling, bustled. Their wild tone mixing in the distance with an incomprehensible, suppressed boyish gentleness. Successive bullets buzzed and fell sluggishly from the ceiling of the world: the stones of fragile, tender-fleshed dreams fluttering down in desperation. Bullets tore their offered breasts on the nearby shore, on the fence, atop the mounds of black bricks. A few drops of blood oozed, appearing sparse and round on the brown broken flesh, dark heavy points, all of them red springs, like cruel eyes widening behind white, brown, and gray dream feathers. Tiny, the delicate beautiful wings did not help, nor did the breadth of the vast skies. These heart-birds had flown in a thick wave, fluttering upward, running away with their lives from an overpowering danger that pursued them from beneath. Their silvery bills are closed now. Such tender dreams from the world's ceiling will not find a gravedigger, not here on the salty, sandy soil of the earth. Instead, they are sold in the market place—for a trifle, to satisfy a small craving. Their young brownish breasts hold bones split by the final strike; a little blood oozes.

I wanted to hold you to me: you, the dream and the world together. How plentiful what I used to want, yet how strictly necessary.

His arms swung in the air, balancing the forward movement of his body in small leaps on the slippery stones with their wet smooth faces. The green-yellow tufts of the water-moss thrived and swayed in the salty waters whose wavelets flowed with the sounds of fresh kisses in the holes within the stones.

He gripped the railing at the stairway, the touch of rough rusted iron scraping his hands, electrifying them. He heaved his body up by the oblique rails that shook and bent under his weight. The dried wooden risers groaned as he stepped on them. His eyes fixed on their winding, ascending lines, past dark-green memories whitened by salt and sun, down into slits of water glistening between the uniformly straight cracks ahead of him. The rhythm of the swaying wood beneath his feet produced the feel of easy, flexible resignation, mounting with light rapture in his heart. He takes a long road—stretching along the heavy gray waves—as if returning to a forgotten home. Now he goes beyond the sharp reed thickets around him. Between them: stagnating green froth on the surface of dark, dense water. Between the reed tangles lie discarded, rusted cans, one of a pair of wooden slippers—wet and floating without the leather strap—and a black glistening rubber piece from a tire. This broad, dry board

34

walk—with its very innocence and its spotlessly clean, unembellished, wooden body built above the froth, the tangles, and the scum—compels him toward the vast, high water. At an iron stairway immersed in water waits a boat. In the distance, out of a dull foggy gray line, shimmers the far desert shore. Behind it waver ancient white Roman towers and, vaguely delineated, kilns for brick-baking, massive structures nearly effaced by the distance.

The salty air carries a rare fervor of freedom. His feet obey. Into his body comes something like the lightness of soaring into new spheres.

Close by, a gravid white gull with broad wings expires in silence. Its fall describes the resolution of a blind-intentioned threat.

She had told him: Darling, don't turn off the light. I get frightened at night when I wake up alone from my dreams.

The world has hurt you, my love.

Who among us hasn't been hurt by the world?

We bear it, nevertheless.

Courage did not come to your aid. Your harsh self-honesty, your commitment to duty—like that of a diligent girl—and more, did not come. Your insistence on attacking, all the earnestness you meet others with, all this desperate struggle for acceptance and affection, all this search that never ceases from giving and offering—offering everything until the very end—this search, this search you cannot resist, provokes you, pushes you relentlessly to a kind of a mad desire for peace and security, for belonging and approval, for pleasing others, for the sense of being wanted and beloved. A child searching for the mast of security and a salvation net as she treads a path populated by ghouls and monsters, finds that the leaves of her green dream have withered and fallen at each blow of the wind.

You had come in the morning. When you entered the sleepy apartment its voiceless walls were blocking all the waves of the outside world, the strokes of waters having become light, almost forgotten.

35

You were next to me on the arm of the chair, not wanting to relax and stay still, or to let your body surrender to my room, which was strange to you, a room in fact filled so often with you, without your knowing anything about it. I put my hands on your knee. Your face was a mask, yet fires blazed yellow in your eyes. The cloudy morning sky behind the room's delicate, transparent curtains yielded me a touch of temporary relaxation of wounds throbbing calmly, wounds that have since become that bygone moment impossible to cure and never healing.

The coffee I made for you, after you sat watching me having my breakfast, saying you never eat in the morning and do not need anything. A cup of coffee later, with pleasure, is in your hand now, having cooled without your drinking it. You look around in a room strange to you. Later I learned that it carried a message of rejection and frustration for you. You said that the puritanical inclination in you bars you from many things. You had wrapped yourself with heavy wool and heavy determination. You handed me your first letter without signature, out of context. I read it behind a certain fervor that clouded my eyes:

> I went out in the afternoon alone wandering, seeing my figure reflected in the glass of shop windows. Somewhat lonesome in the crowded street. No one familiar in it. My image in front of me again and again, sent to me by this crowded world; I do not find a thing in this image. I reached Cinema Radio, it was dark and there were crowds. The tumult of oblivion was tempting and I surrendered. And here I am writing to you in the movie's cafeteria, torn by contradictory desires: to run away from you and to come to you . . . I want to tell you I am happy because you exist and I've met you.

36

My darling, I tore your letter in a moment forever repeated, a moment of anger, rebellion. I had been yearning for a certainty that continuously ebbs and flows in rituals of a pathetic drama that both of us enact, playing among others the role of the dispossessed without my knowing the words of the script.

Silence. In my heart the ever-renewed fear of losing you. This petrified, defaced hollowness that does not shake off, that does not slide off, this fear of losing you, hovering and irrational. As if vaulted by an unmotivated will. Don't let me lose you. This is not a supplication or a request. It is no more than reporting on a realistic, essential matter. It is the rock of the earth itself. Don't let me lose you. I shall not lose you.

Of course our lips did not join. I did not recognize in that room the feel of your body wrought in the torments of a mysterious, but non-sensual yearning. You remained inside your other land with its obscure borders. My hand on your knee feeling beneath the transparent nylon hose—a strange land that I love and whose contours I do not know, that are inaccessible, distant from my touch.

Our farewell was hurried, our kiss awkward, perplexed.

On that morning, in that room, you said to me: I want to please everyone. I cannot change my nature . . . I know this, I know the reason for it, therefore I should be healed, but I am not. I thought knowledge healed things.

Why tell you that knowledge is tormenting? And what are your torments? Are they so strange that I can't fathom them? Vulgar tattered maxims? Truths with distorted faces? Shaggy stones carrying inside their marble the spark of green flame?

He said to himself that among his errors, his sins, his crimes, is that when he loves, he names what he loves. Among his defeats and failures, this is one, at the very least. How bitter is this *least!* Just the same, he did not tell her:

My love, pleasing the world is not possible.

She would not have been persuaded. That much he knew.

She said to him: This is part of my psychological make-up, something I can't change.

Another crime—if he wanted to give it a name—was this: I wanted my love—our love—to be a desperate gamble, the torment of gazing with our open, determined eyes at the Gorgon's distorted face that kills whoever gazes at her. But after gazing I wanted it to go beyond killing into the heart of blazing darkness. I wanted—and I still want—to lift with our naked arms together all the heavy tombstones immersed in the soil, to dig with our bare bodies—together—all the hollow bits—in front of the fire of open eyes—in the wet, sticky, earthy mud. This very mud is a rich element that has all the innocence, all the power that goes beyond both condemnation and innocence.

Because you are the dearest to me.

Despite everything, despite having hurt you—I too know this—and you having hurt me.

Your loneliness, your lonesomeness, I know it. I bear its burden on my broken rib with its spearhead, white-bone projection, in the air.

You said to me: There are essential and huge differences between us. Perhaps we have nothing in common apart from loneliness and a certain search.

You were asleep, your wonderfully brown and round face on the pillow. I gaze at you. I am not quenched. In my mouth a dry bitter thirst. The small lamp behind you was shedding light on your arm. On my lips the taste of my kisses on your brown upper arm with its relaxed flesh and with the tender folds between your arm and your full spilling breast. I turned around to put the lit cigarette, propped on its butt, on the shiny wooden shelf in the incarcerated night of the room.

You turned about suddenly in your sleep, raised your head, eyes open. Did you see me? There was no recognition. One instant in the silence of the sparse light: the gaze of a strange woman on a strange man in one bedroom.

You fall back. As usual, silence penetrated by repressed mania does not allow me to sleep. Waiting without end, without arrival.

In the dead silence moans came out from your chest burdened with unbearable weights. A long stretch of moaning—lonesome, strangled, hopeless, not a call of request or expectation. The despair in it was final, complete. An unbearable loneliness. My love, who will rescue you in the hollow, dark region in which the breath of loneliness exhales on you alone? Who can penetrate the boundless stretches of your exile and reach you? This moaning, I still hear it in a terrible dream that never ends.

I wanted to leap toward you, to put my arm on your shoulder, to graze your soft-skinned cheeks with my lips, not to disturb you in your sleep, just to bring you back to me, to take a load off your chest, to embrace you, to remove your fear of loneliness, to warm your lips with my love, to tell you: My love is here.

Everything was shaking around me. I was on the bed facing you, frozen in an incomplete movement. I wanted to reach you. I didn't make a move.

The moaning emitted from your crammed, stifled chest became softer, suppressed, surrendering to temporary oblivion, to the silence of regular breathing, in total distance, in an exile forbidding my arrival or your return. Neither you nor I . . . No one . . . Nothing . . . The world ceases to be. Nothing . . . Except that I turn and put another cigarette, propped on its butt, slowly extinguishing, on the wooden shelf with its glittering dark mahogany color, beside the glasses, the book, the key, the silver and copper coins, the tickets of a play we did not attend, the ends of many cigarettes propped on their butts, extinguished and cold, whose fragile, trifling ashes are still on my lips, feeling dry, bitter.

You had said to me: By the way, don't get upset. It happens to me occasionally that when I sleep I emit a moan as if someone is murdering me or the like. Don't worry. It means nothing.

She was still asleep. Mikhail has wakened from an intermittent, agitated sleep. He has become habituated to this half-awake, discontinuous, sparse sleep during these six days, torn apart by fulfillment and disappointment, by possession and retreat, by anticipation and frustration, joy and mad jealousy, attacks of alienation and perplexity—while all her treasure is within his hands. Her treasure is not his treasure. He has nothing of himself. His objective is to arrive at a different kind of total giving, a state where giving and taking is one thing—nothing is the property of one alone.

He was completing the rituals of shaving. The mirror reflecting his face revealed no message. He felt nothing when the held razor penetrated the skin of his finger. Drops of blood dripped from the wound. He found a piece of white cotton in his overnight kit and stuck the square onto his index finger.

She awoke, opened her questioning eyes, and addressed him in a relaxed drone that failed in masking her concealed, night-drawn tension.

—Good morning.

The voice of a little girl who knows she is loved and wants more love. A voice vibrating like that of a small cat half asleep—its fierce sensuality still very tender and soft. Her fleshy brown breasts glisten and pour within her white, baggy chemise, wafting out a fragrance of sleep and repose as she draws the bed covers to her nude shoulders.

As she slid across the narrow bed, she did not offer him her opened lips. She had once said to him: Don't stir me. That makes me tense all day.

40

She said: What happened?

He said: I don't know . . . I disfigured myself, I cut myself all over.

He had placed his arm beneath her neck. Her head with its fragrant, wild short hair was on his shoulder wounding him with its singular beauty. He stretched his hand, careful not to drop the white cotton soaked with a drop of blood from his finger.

He said: I cut my finger.

She said: My eye!

The words enraged him. He laughed nervously and said: What does this mean: '"My eye"?

He tried to kiss her cheek.

She said, turning her face away: '"My eye" is an old phrase of sympathy!

Again, everything deteriorates stupidly in the morning of the last day. He is spoiling these last few hours.

After an earlier encounter, she had said to him: In a few days you will hate me.

He said now: I love you.

She said thoughtfully as if she were looking for something: Yes, in a way. Perhaps.

But I do love you, completely and totally. I love you: that is all. Without definitions, without conditions or specifications. It is absolute. It is the essence, the complete finale. My love for you can't be contrasted or compared or confronted with anything. I love you and I want you—all of you.

How many times he had said it, how many times he did not say it, how many times he will say it again.

He tried to gather her head to him. She twisted it away. He got up and moved around her other side. In an agitated move he brought his face toward hers. She closed her lips, did not offer him her eyes. He was yearning for a strangely tender gaze. The siege was getting tighter. The stored currents of spontaneous thrust were ebbing. In these few last hours there were only two bodies, stretched out helplessly. Anxiety was no more than failing will. The message that had reached her yesterday: "Cairo, after midnight" was in front of him. A white nightmare and that distant look. She said to him: Don't try to judge our relation . . . What do you expect me to say?

This was another world. She was determined to protect herself with fences. She wanted it to be so. Cycles of waiting. Anxiety. Rejection. Frustration! All of it: Perplexity and interrogation, destructive of all resignation to the pleasures of her body. All this had made of him an unsuccessful lover in the early hours of dawn.

She had said to him: Don't you desire me as a woman?

He said: Yes, yes.

She had looked at him silently yet inquisitively and said:

It seems to me that despite your proclaimed happiness with what is between us, you are unconvinced by it.

Yes, I am. Your soft towering body filled with life excites me, but I don't want you, Rama, as body only. Haven't you figured this out yet? Doesn't this matter to you? I don't want your body as a barrier between you and me. I don't want it as a surrogate or solution. I want all of you. I love all of you, and you alone. I do not want the alien deformations lurking within you. This rich, luscious, eternal body revolving around its astonishingly fertile earth, roused by ever youthful tenderness, blossoming with continuous desire, wet with sweet dew, constantly thirsty, its plowed-over brown complexion never satisfied with tears and frequent penetrations—I don't want that only. I want you, and me, with my shattered dream soldered at last, all together. I want you, Rama, with my love, with our love. I want your cruel earth and skies together. In them the severed head of St. John the Baptist glittering, in the stark burning sun whose sharp edges revolve continuously in this dense purity that I have known, that we

42

have known together in moments of ecstasy, fulfillment, and madness.

She said to him: I woke up with feelings of tenderness for you.

He wanted to cry, to crush with his two tense hands a hard breakable stone in his own eyes.

In the name of what fragile pride, in the name of what anger, in the name of what fear have I rejected your tenderness?

He only looked at her. Can't she decipher his looks? She doesn't want to.

In the station's cafeteria as they were drinking tea before she left, the smooth walls leading to the wide stairway, he said to her as they were a discreet distance apart: Who knows when we will meet again.

Exasperated and impatient, she responded: God knows!

When his face was next to her cheek in the station, as the train was about to depart, he was being forced to leave her. She would be leaving him also. Her imminent departure threatened him with a sense of complete loss, depriving him of self-possession, of knowing what was going on around him. He recognized nothing except her imposing presence next to his body, her full, self-enclosed presence in his arms. It was a moment about to be over, that would be over, never to return, a moment he wanted to sustain forever. He held her tight with his arms, in complete and stubborn despair—her, whom he knew was absent. He embraced her rejecting—at most tolerant—body. He said to her:

I love you . . . I love you . . . Whatever happens, I love you.

She did not answer. She was merciful, giving him, despite everything, a sad kiss.

He said to himself: Whither my journey now? It does not seem to have an ending. Should I learn to accept all this as it is, accept all the demands within me and within her without the need of justifications?

She stood before him on the lake shore. Her legs were planted solidly on the sand's edge, in pale shallow waters, and he was in the boat he had rented that morning from a gentle-eyed, barefoot, greedy Bedouin boy. The distant brick kilns, red-mouthed with their dense slow fires. The ancient wall of the Roman tower, broken at the shoulder with its gray stones behind the sand dunes quivering in noon glare. The small boat was steady, narrow, fragile on the shallow lake's heavy surface, as if it was plowing the waters, though not seeming to advance under the leaden skies. The Auberge Resort continued to look near and loom large behind its thin crooked fence.

He said without anger: What have you done with me?

She said: Don't you know I am an enchantress?

He said: Why did you appear to me just when I was getting prepared for a calm trip to the end of the lake? Why did I fall in love with you? Why do I love you and reject you, reject the unbearable suffering and pain of your love, reject what covers up your spontaneity and gifts? Whoever you are—a goddess, an enchantress, a beloved—why have you kindled the fires of this inferno and started dancing wickedly in them, promising a tenderness never delivered? I was sliding—even from myself—with silent pain until the last rays of sunset disappeared. Circe. Seraph, Siren, your voice—sweet with its suppleness and tenderness—chases me in the solar glare of the night. Rama, from the ripe fruit of almond between your breasts pour inundating waters . . . I hear their gushing between the room's walls. The echoes of the sweet tingle of your words are in my ears. I hear them, I hear them while I am bound by chains in the silence of my room at night. Beasts and leviathans writhe beneath your feet. They open their mouths voicelessly in the faded blue tower. The dry air moves your hair on the skin of your wide soft cheek. Your breath is still on my mouth, fragrant with its singular and intimate scent. I have become fond of you. I know, I know that I will love you. Yet I have never loathed anything or anyone as I loathe you. You said to me once: "I want to kill . . . " But now I want to kill . . . Now I know the passion of someone who wants to kill, to destroy, to close the palms of his hands on the sweet precious face, the only thing he has in the world, the face that carries the beauty, cruelty, and strangeness of the whole world. I know the desire of him who wants to hold such a world in his hands, and press with all his passion, yearning, and pain until it is crushed between his hands. You gave me all this glory, the joys of mad pleasures, all the pain, and the bitterness of disappointment at once, together. All that I have in this world, you gave me. Why did you appear in my life? Why did you come?

Mikhail saw the gull with its wide-spread wings falling behind the tower's stones, but not rising up again; he knew its face.

The oars struck soft white sand, moved up and down without sound. The boat, fragile and caught in the sand, was shaking. The soft-sand and yellow waves roiled with fine dust as they carried the boat. It was not moving though he rowed with all his might. The oars scratched against the two iron rings attached to the sides of the boat, emitting a hushed grating. Plunging into the sand, the oars encountered no resistance, going up then plunging again. He was rowing non stop, feeling neither strain nor obstacles. Meanwhile, the boat progressed nowhere, moored lightly atop a sand body that had no shape.

He looked behind himself and saw a wide, red-colored ribbon, drawn on the surface of the blue lake: a stream of blood poured on the water surface.

When there was light on earth, it happened, as he had foretold. The woman who was not from human progeny met him as he continued oaring, trying to attain the lake's far shore. She came naked with disheveled hair.

3

Narrow Stairway
and the Dragon

Columns of light and dark silence incline his way, clamping onto him in the late drizzly evening. The road in front of them lies open, empty, obscure. Stretches of a clean, charted world, freshly deserted, start flashing in the scant, watery darkness—neon advertisements, towering glass buildings.

He extends his hand to help her alight from the sidewalk. A puddle is in her way. She wears sandals; a slim leather strap passes tightly between her big toe and the rest of her wet, short, fleshy toes. On their nails, a faded red manicure is peeling. The upper curve of her foot seems plump, desirable.

In her response to his gesture there was, for a moment, an imperceptible aversion, as if an old fixed determination were behind it. She always had her fixed determinations. She did not extend her hand to his. She did not walk arm in arm with him—not once during their entire six days in the city, which she called "our city."

He said to himself: It was never our city. Our city is a nocturnal dream of dazzling light, ancient, outside time, cut from the archaic walls of the world.

She had said to him on their first night, some months before:

—I have started feeling this from a number of things. First when you used to put your arm in my arm, and second . . .

In the beginning, when crossing a street—one of those diverse, strange streets they crossed together—he would find warmth and affection in her supple, surrendering arm; he would feel a precious and mutual security. At that time, he felt nothing but a light pleasure, a weightless inner glow.

Later on, he said to himself: The sun, always, rises only once. Not again.

Even now he calls upon the sun. Without interruption. A despair that denies its own existence, a despair that multiplies in ferocity, clamps onto him with a voracity that cannot be revoked.

He said to himself: The sun never responds.

That was their first night in the city she called "our city." She had said to him, I know it is the city of everyone, but I think of it as our city.

This city was his birthplace.

He had come to it across great trajectories of pain, anxiety, spiritual fatigue. He did not know then that she would be coming to him—as usual—from a world marked by warm fulfillment, by multiple victories that she loved, but that she said contained no significance for her. As if that world were a perpetually air-conditioned world, a continuous luxury of glorified elegance. He had said to her: I can hardly believe that we will meet; she had said to him: Yes we will meet unless a third world war, an earthquake, or a cosmic catastrophe takes place. She had said to him, Help me, my love, in choosing a small gift for an old friend, a truly excellent person, the model of a perfect septuagenarian gentleman, whom I have gotten to know recently and

48

for whom I have great affection. I believe he is very fond of me too. Do you think, for example, these cufflinks are an appropriate present, or what? Choosing a gift for such a friend is so perplexing.

He laughed. She said to him with sudden alertness: Why are you laughing? He said: I am laughing at the entire situation. Yes, shirt buttons, not bad. Or anything you like.

She withdrew inside herself all of a sudden then said determinedly, We have to discuss the tickets, darling, I am afraid I don't have the time. The voices around them were loud, the place crowded.

But now, at last, he was on his way toward her. An impending sense of catastrophe kept needling him. He wasn't sure the entire universe had any significance whatsoever. With savage hands he was strangling a din of fierce joy, yet had already fallen into the ruins of anticipating the very worst. Nothing would happen. The train was entering a world silenced by estrangement and loneliness—a world of low gray houses with rain constantly pouring on them. A world enshrouded by an imperceptible fog.

The jolts of the huge diesel engine shake his heart repeatedly, monotonously, imperceptibly. He senses catastrophe. He will not find her, he will know only the shocks of rejection and oblivion.

Here are the two of them in the street. She is now beside him yet distant, lively with her vivacity that never ebbs. Wearing her black and white long dress. Her bronze-colored bosom in the wide, round décolleté of her dress appears soft, slightly pressured against a light dew—the bosom's tender flesh glistening with tiny droplets. A desire takes hold of him: to bury his lips and face in her bosom.

He said to her: I worry about you in this rain. You are lightly dressed. She said to him laughingly: Don't worry at all. Rain and cold don't affect me any longer. In fact, they refresh me. He said: But your sandals. She said: Don't worry, it doesn't matter. She went on talking, on and on about the market and the scenes they were passing

49

through, about the prices and the antiques, about the weather, about everything and anything. He was enjoying, from within, the clever outpourings and polished, gentle fluency in conversation. He was also angry: he could see through her tone, through the attitudes of old schoolteacher, mother, and tourist guide all at once. This tone angered him, made him edgy. He said to himself: Probably this discursive gushing is nothing but a delicate, shapeless bridge over the dark, open abyss in the depths of her anguished soul and within a heart agitated with passions, torments, desires, and madness. He said to her one or two days later in a definitive, cutting tone: I couldn't care less about facts, statistics, and information. These can be obtained from books and libraries. What interests me is something else. This also happens to be my country. Have you forgotten that? It seemed to him as if he were confronting her with his childish pride. Except with a strange and silent gaze of rejection, she did not respond—a huge contrast to her gushing words.

His mind filled with indissoluble, heavy dregs from the last months, weeks, days, hours, as if they were infinitely scattered points of waiting and suspension, of denial and mad expectation, of joy destroyed by basic, intractable doubt, that of the recently experienced moments of loss, that of total and complete despair when he missed her but could not find her. The savage determined resolutions that he undertook a thousand times, had repudiated a thousand times, as he roamed the streets. The curses and waves of destructive hate and aversion. The final resolutions—final each time—not to lose everything. Yet he loses the one thing of value and significance in the whole world, the only thing he loves and wants more than anything else. Instantly he returns to the agony of infinite possibility tossing him in all directions; having lost everything, he loses his bearings. He is burdened with a strain that he feels is inhuman. Then the shock of encounter, unexpected, after he had inured himself, out of bitterness, to an attitude of carelessness. As if his heart, torn, ruined by stabs and fractures, is no more able to feel joy or anything else. Facing the wonder of this sudden event—her appearance in front of him, totally unexpected—he moves with depressed gait. She . . . is beautiful, strange. How beautiful, how strange. As usual, she gushes out her mixture of half-lies and half-truths.

In his mind now are these strata of fresh black mud that paralyze his first steps in this city she had called "our city." She said, I thought it was our city.

His own shoes, tight on his feet, were hurting. He felt uncomfortable about himself—not properly dressed, his clothes not suitable for him, his face shaven in a hurry, washed with cold water. Rainy weather in the summer evening, quasi-hot. Alertness and anxiety make his steps unsteady. Wanting to be finished, he said to her: The first thing I'm going to do is buy a dark gray chamois jacket and velvet trousers of the latest style, of heavy striped black velvet, along with a snow-white polo-neck pullover. He entered for a moment into the game of conversation. Half the game was to escape, to challenge the anguish, burden, and anger he was trying to stifle. The other half was to jocularly present intentions he could not fulfill. She glanced at him, a strange look that continues to rob him of sleep—as if it were permanent, ever present in his heart, this look of astonishment, of distancing and distance. She said: You? I cannot imagine you, I cannot see you in black velvet trousers and a polo-neck white pullover. He laughed, and said, as if talking about someone else: You don't know me. Twenty years ago, here in Alexandria, during my vagabond and boisterous year—

Jokingly, she cut him off: Oh you had boisterous years? Confess. He said laughingly: Not really; it was, of course, innocent joviality when I used to spend all day and all night in streets, cafes, and cinemas. There was a café in Saad Zaghloul Street called Friskadore. We

51

used to spend most of our time in it, and we used to go to the movies two or three times in one day, taking with us small whisky bottles, Craven A or Pall Mall cigarettes, with a big paper bag of mussels. In the darkness of Cinema Metro we used to drink whisky and laugh at Hollywood melodramas, while nibbling on mussels and throwing the shells at the side of the open paper bag lying on the stately red carpet— with some of the audience ready to give us a drubbing. She said to him: I don't believe it. Surely you must be inventing it all? He said: Not at all. In those days, I was going through a crisis. He hesitated before he said: It was the emotional crisis about which I have spoken to you.

Then he spurted forth heatedly about the days of despair, loss of faith in everything, suffering romantic disappointments of which no one was aware. He said: Why do I always associate romance with bitterness and unbearable experience? He laughed to cover up his fear of admitting the old, continuously renewed, striking calamity. Was he sensing it repeating itself now with all its violence and the ferocity of its power? He said, I used to have, in fact, a printed blue silk shirt. It had red, yellow, and white patterns and dots. Also, I owned a pair of black velvet trousers. Those clothes formed a sort of challenge to despair and darkness, a way of dashing into the indifference and derision of everything, but basically of myself and of that which was most precious to me.

She said, with a distant tone—strong, calm, very polite, as if she were on another level, the same tone of reception she reserved for his heated and naïve confessions: I can't believe it. But we will buy for your sake the velvet trousers and the white polo-neck pullover.

He did not tell her how he used to doze on the earth—green with wild grass—and inhale the air of the wet, concealed soil, the yellow flowers filling the eye of the sun—large as it is—and the bees stabbing the open core of delicacy, their hostile buzz receiving an absent reception. He did not tell her about the feeling of the Nile bridge's soft soil

52

in which the bottoms of the feet plunge, so that every footstep finds a slight solidity resisting yet welcoming the print of warm steps. He did not tell her about the splash of rain drops on the jacket and the shirt opened down his neck unto the shivering hot skin and the swarming of a regular, light pouring of water and salt on the face and chest amid wind-blows full of vitality and chill, and the warm, helpless tear-storms. He did not tell her about the cries when running on the street's asphalt among the lonely eyes and the fires of fear, rebellion, amid the anxiety of the wounded falling next to the iron wheels, and the chains gnawing the sidewalks and the lawns of public gardens. No, he did not tell her about narrow, metallic mouth-vents spitting out brief, dry, final bursts. Then the screams of running people carrying across the white stones between the sea and the street amid the indifferent, watching crowd. The cars that had run silently beneath the calm autumn sun—no, he did not tell her of the hands holding to every brick, to every projecting bulge in the seawall, the scraping of knees with the body glued to it begging for help and clambering up with the force of a last, desperate effort, looking with insane hope for the sensual grapes, their minds holding onto the dark, sourish juice spurting from the brownish, sandy, rounded skin of their beloveds' breasts. He did not tell her about the light sea waves drowning the many shoes, filling them with water, plunging them down into the soft sands of final oblivion. The demonstrations, no, he could not speak of them.

He said to her once, at lunch, toward the end of a story, no end as usual, not a real one, as they'd been conversing in a disciplined, calculated way, the way that estranged friends talk to each other:

Yes, the ideal tone . . . The golden mean . . . This is always the rational solution, always logical. It is more persuasive; as it were, inevitable. One has to accept its soundness. This is the issue, in essence. It must be confronted. The Aristotelian solution. That is to say, I am Aristotelian.

53

She said to him: Yes.

He said smiling, self-deriding: I used to think I was Platonic.

She shook her head as she contemplated him with distant light-green eyes in which there was nothing but utter silence, enunciating nothing.

He said: Am I not Dionysian, as well? I used to think I was a follower of Dionysus.

She said: You? Dionysian?

He said: Not even Platonic?

She said: No. Rather, you are Apollonian.

She pointed to her head in a definite final gesture: Everything for you passes through here.

He said smiling: All right. Fine. As long as you are convinced of it. As long as people seem to agree on it. What can I do? Possibly this is true. I have to accept it—God will take care of it. Frankly I am lost among all those Greeks.

She smiled—a complimentary, polite smile. She did not tell him: You are pretentious without the need to be so.

Weeks before, she was talking about her friends: writers and poets. The day before, they had been at a reception in the Soviet Embassy, along with the artistic guests, devouring food, gulping whisky non-stop. She said: These poets, how can they? I can hardly imagine. I suppose it's because they spring from Dionysus. He did not say: Dionysus?

He did not tell her of the shadows quivering in and out of an ancient thicket of trees in deep summer, napping in the midst of a crowded day along whose edges ran the life of the strange city. Nor did he tell her of the pleasant fear while the burden of Being depended on the delicacy of a branch, quivering, warning of being smashed. Pliant, it moved up and down, never separating from the muscles of the hard, firm wood. The dust of upper-story leaves rained down

54

gracefully on the perspiration of sticky dewy hands in the grip of a life that threatened to fall into a bottomless hole. He didn't relate to her the pleasure of rising up among a thousand holes in the blueness of the skies, of the leaf of living wood and green sycamore closing in on its raw sap, of the cries announcing in awe, expectation, and pleasure: the danger of the catastrophe. He did not tell her about revolving in gentle valleys, falling in the embrace of death from pleasure, rising slowly at first, then quickly, then feverishly toward new excitements, new compliant waves with a thousand encircling arms, a thousand embracing legs. My heart fulfilled with two shining eyes, dripping affection. He did not tell her of the dazzling, nocturnal sun in which flames danced and licked the parts of his soul as if a tongue were licking the surrendered, rare milk of compassion. (He enjoys these old wounds as they never burnt the heart.) He did not say: Dionysus? The Dionysus of Scotch whisky and gourmet Auberge Hotel dinners in air-conditioned halls? Dionysus of Berlin elegance bought for the lowly price of blood and rhetorically glorified baseness? Dionysus, where exactly do you come from?

Dionysus of intoxication with the wine of facile cravings, loose sentimentality, and spruced up poems?

Dionysus walking on the roads' asphalt, half-dark and half-lit by advertising neon and turned-off lamps, shouting on the stage in front of the semi-bourgeoisie, semi-literati, semi-progressives, semi-traitors suffering from the guilt of cheap verbal ripples.

Dionysus of washed goblets and china plates on ironed table cloths made in Shubra al-Khayma.

Dionysus of eager copulations following dances played by the plaintive music of recorders whose timbre has deteriorated, accompanied by the rattle of the electric tape player, radio, pick-up, or the electric band, whose name might well be Black Cats, Forgers, or Chat Noir. All of them nothing but a mark on satin.

55

Dionysus of Cairo, Berlin, and Moscow, emptied of everything but bottomless greed and crammed with food, drink, talk, sex—all of it forged, manufactured?

Some Dionysus!

She said to him: I can't imagine you, for example, walking barefoot just for pleasure.

He said to himself: For her I am but a formula, a type, a kind, a mold. She always says: You, as an intellectual; You, as a rational logical person. You as mature adult. He said to himself: Who am I? What am I? Have I really managed to transform myself into a formula and a stereotype? He laughed silently.

Later it occurred to him that her reference to the Dionysians was a kind of provocation to drive him to reveal himself, to spur him to break the coffin crust enveloping his being. He recalled her eyes. Truly she knew nothing of him except the coffin crust. Who could blame her?

He said to himself: There is another story.

She said to him whispering in the last uneasy dawn, as if she were talking to herself:

You don't know how much I need love and how much love and pleasure I can offer.

But I do indeed: I know something about myself.

Yes, darling, but what do you know about me? Do you know the extent of my pain and desolation? The extent of my love?

Infinite, boundless, without end.

He said to himself: When will this pain stop resounding? When will this desolation clear away? An answer cried from the abyss of his darkness. In her arms, in her eyes when they shine, when my face is on her breast, when she recognizes my love, when she says to me, 'My darling,' and I know she means what she says. And that she says it to me. Only.

My darling, you'll never know how much I love you, how much I need you. Answer me. Do you love me?

Desolation, formerly tainted with a tincture of hope, seems total now. Its inevitable face fixes me with unblinking eyes. No way out from this silent horror.

Rama. Rama. How did I lose you? Have I lost you?

What do we know about the suffering of others even if we loved them? You know nothing of it. What then? Do you know the grief of confession? Who will ask pardon for my suffering? Shall I say: My blood has been shed? Shall I say: This slow death with its strangling hands does not remove, raise, or slacken its grip from my throat, holding on until it breaks the last disc in my fractured bones?

Rama. I love you yet I hate this love, wishing like a child to die.

I reject this wish, saying to myself: I am not a child and this love will not ruin me (while it is ruining me).

. . . because you do not love me, and I will never know what love means to you.

You have given yourself, yes, and we have mounted to the climax of pleasure and fulfillment, and fallen embraced, together and naked, unto the soil of infernal frustrations. We have laughed together and you have wept because of me and for me. And I have lived with you for six glorious days. Yet I don't know, I don't know who I am for you.

Silence everywhere.

In his confused exuberance, he said to himself: Then what? Then what, my agitated soul? She does not love you. This is hardly news. This is a daily story, a shabby, repetitive narrative. Nothing new in it, yet how distressful it is.

The world will not break down. What is the meaning of all this? Simply nothing.

He couldn't believe it.

Mikhail had sent a telegram with the date of his arrival. As he was walking, wracked by anguish, distraught with dreams and fears, imagining what he would do if he were not to find her waiting for him, if she were not to honor the rendezvous, how he would avenge himself and his love with a thousand vengeful acts. Then he discarded his fears, and imagined her smiling, welcoming, receptive—the glory and the beauty of the world in her—embracing him in the station. Her image resists despair. He will find her in the corridors welcoming him. The throbbing of his tired heart in an agitated rhythm as he carries his luggage in both hands, rushing in the station while feeling as if he is not advancing.

The first shock arrived, lightly but threateningly, carrying a warning within it: she was not there. He asked about her at the Information Desk. When, with feverish anguish, he approached a police officer in the station's headquarters, the man gave him an unwelcoming look. His worries—dense, heated—had driven him to these police. Did she have an accident? What happened? The officer, who was not busy, began to handle him gently. Mikhail started looking into the register of messages and the index of names: under the letter *M* then *i* then *kh*. One letter after another, as if distilling the letters of his name, one after the other. He was in need of an echo, a response, waiting in vain for a voice. Could she be in that hotel he had never gotten the name of, in Zizinia, beyond Abu Qir Street? She had drawn a small map in his notebook with the address; it all seemed so recent to him, yet distant as a bottomless past. She might be at another address. She is waiting for him. She will come tomorrow or the day after. Nothing. Then he searches for her at the gate, in the station square that seems empty in a strange way, and at the taxi stand. Nothing.

She said to him later: I had barely arrived, only minutes before, from the archaeological site at St. Mina's Monastery. I asked them in the station to write you my message. I contacted the station manager by telephone twice, and I took my precautions: I asked them to put my message under the letters *M, i, kh, a, i, l.*

He said to her with despair, not knowing if any of this had actually happened: I searched for your message under all those letters. I didn't find a thing.

He silently told her: You are the first letter and the last.

The taxi took him to the address. The last moment and the first moment arrived. Now he is here. After he puts down his heavy suitcase and the lighter luggage, he asks about her with a voice that he tries to steady while his chest quivers within.

From that moment everything seemed to be taking place in another world. He would believe nothing of it. Voices were very clear, very distant, as if from behind a barrier. Surprise. Denial. Negation. The moment of loss that does not end. The faces of strangers and the running to addresses given by strangers. No. Sorry. Not here. No, no, nothing. You have come too late, no, we are sorry. The suitcase feels very heavy, the weather has this worrisome mixture of humid heat and cold. The winter sky starts to cloud up in the openings between low roofs and beautiful lofty columns. Empty décor, and the suitcase almost slipping from his hands. A silent, suppressed madness in his boiling blood. He feels the sweat on his face. He has another address in Sidi Bishr and a telephone number. She had said it was her cousin's. Should he go there now? Should he call and inquire? Is she sick? What happened? Not there? Has she come back? No. Indeed she suggested she would never go there unless there was a cosmic catastrophe or a war. At last, he decides to give in, no matter what, to the last address recommended by a stranger. He has no other address. A hotel called Victoria in Zizinia, in a quiet alley shaded by trees. The bell rings. A pleasant face signals to him to push the door. As he starts to ask if—suddenly, in this address that he came across by sheer chance, he hears her saying in a low voice: There you are. At last.

59

She comes to him. In the midst of this incredible derangement. How beautiful she is. How strange her eyes are. How wonderful the roundness of her beloved body that he knows—no, that he doesn't know.

The first surprise was this supple, obedient, alert body that confronts him and attracts him—always as if it were the first time—with irresistible charm, with invisible fine threads that never snap. How she gushes with conversation that never ends: how she waited for him, how she left her new address at the other address. How she confirmed it once and again. How she asked here and there. How she took all precautions, how she called the station by phone. How she spent a night in the Archaeological Rest House at al-'Amiriya. How she traveled and came back, how she saw the doctor and will be seeing him again, how she came only this afternoon by train, how she sent him a message via the station's information desk, how she was about to get up and call again, how she reserved a room for him, anyway—And how are you doing? How was your trip? How she almost gave up hope of his coming today. And where is your luggage? Is that all? Let me help you. I'll carry this for you. No, it's light. Let me. I'll carry it for you. Come. This way.

He's still disoriented from the shock. His footsteps move in a still desolate place, as if he has lost all capacity for joy and wonder.

He climbs the narrow stairway behind her as she mounts the crooked steps. Distraught, he almost stumbles beside the faded red carpet, surprised by the elegance of a hotel he did not know. Her dynamic strong back bends in front of him. She pants as she climbs, exclaims then returns to him, her chest rising and falling, vibrating under his eyes. She says: We climbed the wrong stairway. Not this way. You made me take the wrong way. Let's go down from here . . . Come along.

The yearning for her, the suffering because of her, narcotizes him.

Suddenly his anxious, mobilized footsteps are charged with a repressed and unexpected briskness that he cannot explain.

She told him later as she was remembering: You seemed exhausted, tense, completely lost.

By chance he knew, later, that he had the wrong telephone number, even though she had repeated it twice in front of him when he had been writing it down. He also learned that the other address that he had was incomplete.

Did everything, then, happen by sheer chance? Was she really intending not to meet him? Everything points to it. Could his perplexity reach this point? Did she accept him as he was with his shortcomings when he appeared, as she would accept something that happened by chance, as a fact of life? Did she take him along her way without hesitation since he had arrived anyway through strange coincidence? Is he no more than a stop-gap, an exterior filling for her, not really needed? If he is not totally rejected, is it because he comes like that, without her insistence or rejection? He is convinced neither by this nor by its opposite. He turns the matter in his mind continuously. The unending ravings of perplexity.

My darling. My earth and my heaven. Forever my glory and my defeat. I carry you inside me. When will we meet so that our encounter will no longer carry the crack of permanent separation—when we meet and we stop being I *and* you? Where there is no before and no after . . . When tomorrow becomes a shooting star that our embraced hands will not let go of.

Such were his moments in the city that she called "our city."

When he climbed the last narrow stairway, and she opened the door of her room, he found himself suddenly alone with her.

After she put his suitcase down on the floor, she stood in front of him with all the glory of her presence. She was looking at him with curiosity and an imperceptible smile, waiting. There was tension in his

61

body and soul from jittery and sharp exhaustion, from boyish worries. He said to her: Rama . . . Rama . . . I can't believe it.

He stretched his hands to hold her face between his palms. Her eyes were still waiting.

He dashed to her. In a second, she was in his arms.

He felt her round back and all her chest filling his arms, her face under his lips.

Before suffering had departed from his flesh, a new, heavy sense of peaceful juice was penetrating his body, descending unto the dark region.

Rama . . . Rama . . . I can't believe it.

He could not—even in this intoxicated mood that her presence triggers, in this slow whirlwind of merging and inner chaos—he could not forget as he said to himself: Here she is in your arms, with you alone, what more do you want? He did not forget that perhaps everything happened by sheer chance. That he is only accepted as he is, just as things that befall one accidentally are accepted. Why is love fused with his very being, his physical being, his stature in the world, with the position of his feet on earth?

She said to him: We will meet in few minutes. I'll go to my room; you relax for a while, wash your face. You must be very tired.

He did not recognize the tone of disappointment and forbearing. It was barely there, to the point where he did not sense it except days, weeks, and months later. In the ravings of his dreams that bring back all her presence—her image, her looks, her intonation, her words, her touch—again and again without end, mixed with an indissoluble bitterness.

She was sitting on the narrow bed. The large and small suitcase lay scattered on the floor, on the cushions, on the other bed. She leaned on the smooth dark mahogany screen. Her face was radiant with light tan, the opposite of the light coming from the room's window, half-veiled with a white curtain, revealing cold and strange ceilings, tips of trees behind the glass—green, ripe, sparse leaves hanging on the black trunk with its ripped, hard bark.

He said to her: Wait . . . Wait a little . . . I haven't forgotten.

His voice indicated real joy, dismissal of burdens, a drawing in toward his beloved. In an agitated hurry, he opened the small suitcase and drew out a little green-eyed, green-robed doll.

He said to her: I haven't forgotten . . . Look . . . Look into her eyes . . . Doesn't she remind you of something?

He put the doll next to her face and looked at them side by side. The hazel-green eyes that appear to him in dreams and wakefulness, in life and death, shining brightly in his darkness, always open, always missed. He asked her once, as he was looking at her eyes—spellbound as ever when he looks at that special, non-earthly charm, at that enchantment in which he finds himself falling weightlessly toward a depth he can never reach, with no hope of hitting bottom: Rama, what is the color of your eyes?

She said: Their color changes all the time, as I am told. Hazel, I believe. They are dark when I am nervous, anxious, or sad. In the changing light, they change too . . . Like the eyes of cats.

He said: Hazel, Honey, Green, I don't know . . . They have strange dark rays . . . Emitted from the peripheries of the cosmos.

She said: Hazel? No. . . . I don't think so.

She said to him: Oh, how beautiful. My doll . . . Thanks, my love.

As she was raising the doll in front of her face in the light, she said: How lovely she is. She held the doll to her chest and gave Mikhail a quick kiss of gratitude—with childlike pleasure.

Later, he said to himself: . . . then forgot all about it with childlike cruelty.

Smiling, playful, as if looking for another kiss, he said: Wait, I haven't finished yet.

She said: What else?

63

She said it with the same slight curiosity, as if she were finding him somewhat unusual, while having a good time.

As for him, he was indeed taking the matter seriously even though he was in a light-hearted mood, experiencing a rare joy. It was not a gift, rather a symbol, despite the fact that the distinction was not exactly clear to him.

He removed the light paper and opened the elongated, dark card box and brought out a bracelet and a necklace—modern with an abstract design of unusual patterns in colors of burnt rust, glowing. He extended his hand with the bracelet and she gave him her arm silently, with a look of receptiveness, obedience, and contentment, as is if it were a look of love. For a moment, he could not understand her look, then he remembered and encircled her surrendering wrist with the delicate plates and fastened the bracelet, then surrounded her neck with the necklace and embraced her.

She said to him: Ah, you have learned what I love . . . I love unusual ornaments.

He said to her: Yes.

Her hands fondled the necklace hanging on her full, cozy, soft chest. His heart was filled with desire and tenderness for her. Suddenly he remembered when he gave her a silver bracelet for her birthday. She had given him her wrist saying: Put the bracelet on me. And she surrendered her hand on the table. She apologized for not being able to spend a long time with him, saying that she had relatives and guests at home. He accepted the unfulfilled dream of spending the evening with her, the evening of her birthday, celebrating it with her alone. In the dark car as they were on their way to her house, she had said to him: Give me a cigarette from the pack on my lap. He picked up the pack from her thighs, and was stirred as he lit it for her. When he went back later he found the matches in his pocket with his pack. As soon as he left his car, he saw her turning into the narrow, crowded street, next to the bridge in Bulaq. He said to himself: She is going to the old house of her friend. He is her "relatives and guests." That night, as many nights before, he was torn by attacks of hushed madness, attacks that refuse to lose their claws and whose biting fangs plunge and scorch. Their stings within himself do not heal; they return constantly, again and always. He says to himself smiling: There is not a single part left unbranded. He laughed in silence from the salt filling his eyes.

It seemed to him that she—with her characteristic intuition—knew what he was feeling. She jumped from the bed and said: Come on, let's go . . . I have to show you the city . . . There's still time in the day. They went down together, for the first time, on the narrow stairway. Before they went out, the girl in the hall, with the pleasant face, smiled and greeted her. The streets were calm, silent, unfamiliar. His chest tensely and powerfully bore all the burdens of the old stings, barely dissipated.

On her birthday, she had said to him: I have a command of the art of speech. From my childhood, I discovered that words please people and calm them. But inside, I do not feel a thing.

She had said to him once: Why don't you talk when you are the master of words?

You, Rama, are the first word.

He said to her in the flow of his internal, silent dialogue with her, which stormed him and tore him constantly while he appeared calm among people, friends and strangers, at the office or among crowds:

It is you who master the art of speech. How wonderful your mastery is . . . As for me, I do not know how to talk . . . And when I do talk, I don't say anything, in fact. How many arts do you master? Do you also master the art of body-offering while keeping your heart intact, unconquered, untouched? From within, you don't feel a thing . . . Is it a powerful, irresistible force that pushes you toward such mastery? As for me, I cannot stand this splendid art . . . I want madly and

65

desperately, as well, what is beyond words and what is beyond the body. I want them together: the word, the warmth of corporeal love, and what lies beyond them—the blossoming of the heart. In front of accomplished mastery I am paralyzed, I freeze. Life's waves desert me . . . I watch you admiringly—mad with anger and despair, as if I were an animal in a dark hole.

She said to him once: Don't ever believe what I say. Believe only what I do . . . Lived actions: concrete and real.

What are you doing, Rama, what are you doing? I want to believe you . . .

He said to her once again when they reached the stage in which, wittingly or unwittingly, they were tearing each other through slow torture: For you, I am nothing but a temporary, passing, and accidental event, just like many others.

She did not respond. He remembered that she said once to him: Don't ever have me judge our relationship.

Rama . . . I want to put my two arms on your shoulders, to hug your neck. The tenderness I have for you in my heart fills the world. I want its still, delicate waves—which drown everything—to carry you. I want to bend and kiss your soft forehead, to hold your weeping face to my chest, to get you to relax for a moment between my arms, to erase the pain from your wounded smile. I want you to find with me freedom from perplexity and search, so there are no more questions, my darling. My cheeks open, exposed to the sun of silent dream, the dream of despair, to wallow on the softness of your cheeks. My arms—hanging on the emptiness of tense ribs, thirsting for the suppleness of your breast—demand you. The hard column, taut with the will to plunge into the warm, quivering, moist darkness. Pitch-black waters of the rough waves of tenderness and passion hit bedrock. Multiplied and amplified in their incarceration, the waters inundate and stumble in the enclosed hole of darkness. My lips have suffered dryness for too long. Salt draws

66

lines upon them . . . The torturing yearning for the dew of your lips and the honey of your tongue. My eyes witness a vision that has never taken place and will never take place, like the splendor of raving: Your eyes kissing me without questioning, without probing, without per- plexity, without rejection, without freezing, without despair. A vision not of this world: in your eyes my one and only knowledge. My lips squeezing the taut grapes vibrating with the fullness of their juice, of concealed body wine. My face is attached with gentle pressure to the soft dough. The columns of glory lying on the brown earth under my stretching fingers, containing the whole world. My eyes closed, buried in the supple, round domes. I inhale the scent of elemental fertility. I know by the tip of my electrified tongue the sweet spicy taste. My face in the jungles of your plants wet by the river waters. Their savage scent attacks me. My lips acquire a primitive life in the forests of the body, inquiring, backing then advancing, nibbling and sucking the creamy waters, surrounded by the roughness of the wet herbage, crying in response to escaping cries in the ecstasy of chase and clinging to life. Then the unbearable tension comes and pushes to the last absence, the stab in the open, tender wound of the world, a dance of the last offer- ing where there is no more hunter and prey, sacrificer and sacrifice. Only the flaring glow amid dazzling music of fulfillment, certainty, cos- mic explosion, gushing of astral falls, slumping of burning suns into the heart of the skies' darkness. And I, kissing the sheared-off neck with pleased and pained lips. I hold my slaughtered head between my hands—blood and wine dripping from my mouth. I wipe my lips in streams of hanging, shaking branches of her hair falling on my eyes.

Mikhail had left her after their first night in their city, having satisfied some of her constant and torturing hunger for tenderness and contentment. Half-asleep, half-reposing, she said to him again as he was going out: Don't turn off the light, darling.

In the morning of the following day, when he opened the door of

67

his room, he was surprised to find her—half-surprised as if he had sensed she was there, since he always felt her everywhere, all the time. He will always open his door for her. He will always see her on his path. She will always drop by him; he will always find her waiting for him. She will always come to him, wherever he is. Her presence is a constant fantasy: In the studio in front of his office, in the crowded street, when he goes anxiously to his bed. Her telephone rings, and he will hear her sweet voice, the dearest to him in the world, or he will hear her stiff, dry voice that he hates and whose sternness hurts him. The telephone rings in the silence of the night, before dawn—a persistent, unrelenting ringing. His blood leaps awake in joy and anticipation. Suddenly he is certain that he is hearing the ringing in the ravings of his passion, in total silence. For once, his fantasy indeed had come true all of a sudden. He opened his door, and she was in front of him. The surprise baffled him and paralyzed his heart, making the world boundless.

Now he watches her walking to the hall bathroom, raising her youthful wheat-colored face in the radiating and transparent morning light, in the silence of the stairway. She looks at him with a shy look of obedience, happiness, expectation, and gratitude. She is in a short nightgown of soft cotton, barely reaching her knees, too wide for her strong, supple body. The weak light falls on her delicate cheekbones from above, putting their fine curves in relief. Her wide eyes whose color he cannot see now—with the look that fills his heart—coming up from a different world, carrying on her head the moon, while the python slept.

She had tied her hair like *baladi* women, with a small white scarf. Her plump feet were in the small slippers on the dark red mat. On the stairway, all is strange, profoundly quiet, morning calm. Once again he tastes happiness. Merely her look at him carried with it this rare taste that he seldom knows. He says to her, half-whispering, his chest flowing with tenderness: Good morning, darling. He says to her: I'll come to you soon. She nodded with her head, smiling sweetly, a smile so pure—so rare, as well. Because it was a smile without planning, without staging, without mastery.

In the afternoon, she said to him: Did the scarf shock you this morning? I like to tie my hair with it. I find it practical and fun. Why not? My mother tells me when she sees me with it: What is this? For shame. I laugh. What do you think? Is it shameful to dress like *baladi* women? I said to my mother: What's wrong with it? Isn't it practical, useful, attractive, and easy to use as well? What do you think?

The white fine fabric on her hair seemed to have acquired something of the air, also the dynamism of her hair, something of her body warmth itself. Its color had faded a little; the fabric had shriveled, become compliant and soft with intimate folds from the effect of tying it frequently on her locks and from such a tight wrap. He embraced her head and kissed her. He forgot for a moment what her question "Does the *baladi* scarf shock you?" implied. He forgot for a moment that she always viewed him as a fixed formula, a formula of rigid judgments and conventions by which he is supposedly bound. A shade in the tone of her question persists in his mind later. The cycles of questioning, recalling, and suffering raise him up and down without stopping, yet he does not land on a shore.

They were in the car, after the end of their six days, after the end of a stifling dusty morning—the last morning choked with quarrels, disputes, anger, disappointments. The harsh and hushed sun was dripping heat and humidity. Traversing the distance to the station was long, very long, full of silent gaps and a sense of bitterness. When he put his hand on hers, there was rejection and rigidity in her touch. But they spoke, though she did not care to show her mastery of speech. He sensed her dismal outlook to the coming unknown days. She said to him: You shouldn't have come with me. We should have said goodbye to each other in the hotel. It doesn't make sense for you to insist on coming with me to the station, when you will be making this trip again this afternoon. Twice in one day. Useless. Do you know . . . you have slain the dragon.

He was somewhat startled and said: What?

She said: You slew the dragon. You know in the old legends, in the tales of courtly and uncourtly love, the knight demonstrates his devotion by slaying the dragon. He goes out to the desolate woods after he gives his beloved a handkerchief or a token. Then he departs alone, surmounts all difficulties, overcomes all trials. And endures the hardship . . . Until he slays the dragon; and you have slain the dragon . . . . She quickly emended: And this is neither satirical nor humorous . . . I mean what I say.

He did not say to her: Do I still need to demonstrate my love? I do not want to demonstrate or refute a thing. All of this falls beyond demonstration and refutation. Do you, yourself, need proof and evidence for demonstrating or refuting? You do not cease, time after time, to speak as if you were wondering, as if you were uncertain. Don't you feel that which is breaking loose, day and night, in my inmost? Doesn't it show any signs? Don't you feel that which can never be separated from my life?

A hoarse roar wrecks the chest's rods, an earthquake shakes his insides. Broken, solid stones, cut by nails and claws from the core of his heart, come down. The two hands with their contracted fingers dig ponds dripping blood into his harsh inert walls. The fingers scrape off the petrified heart that beats stubbornly, regularly.

He screams within himself: Agh! Me! He bellows and holds back his parted mouth, agape from the full cry. His scream, never put off, never voiced, fills all the breaches, all the holes, all the wounds, all the gaps in heaven and earth.

I have not slain the dragon. I am living with him. His teeth are piercing my heart in an embrace until death.

70

4

Rama: Asleep
Beneath the Moon

She said to him: Do you know that I want to travel with you to a small, sleepy, rugged island with red leaf trees? Seawater around it to see and feel. Salty air in every corner. Unreachable except by hours of ocean liner travel. Do you know? The two of us beneath a hot dry sun on an old ship—one of those slow, flat ships made of iron and wood? And the two of us living in a white-stone house with fishermen, in a stone harbor where there's only one café and one grocer, who is also the barber and the carpenter, and from whom we buy our bread and provisions every Saturday? Would you like to come along, with me?

The dream that was bright and charging suddenly ebbed.

He said to himself: The stuff of dream, too, is stony.

He said to himself: The islands in our narrow sea have neither bread nor trees. They lie parched, waterless, roasting beneath the sun.

She had said to him: I have stopped believing in dreams, but maybe you can teach me anew.

He did not say to her: You taught me the impossibility of dreams.

True, I believe in them still. But I know better.

Dream, where is your spine?

He said to her as he gazed into the unreflective green of her eyes: You never told me if you loved the moon—the dazzling, strange moon on nights when everything has its shadow, when everything is doubled, a separate yet soldered entity, as if living another life?

She said with neutral voice, as if reciting a memorized, tested, and effective spell: Of course I love the moon, haven't I told you so? I adore the moon. I belong to the cult of moon-worshipers.

She said to him: Did you know that I crossed a thousand kilometers in the desert to go to them?

He said: Who?

She said: Don't you know? They are still there in our desert, the women moon-worshipers, veiled in the enclosed oasis, their ancient rituals still powerful. The adoration of the golden disk and sacred prostitution. You know the phenomenon of temple prostitutes. This ancient historical tradition is still alive, and it is said . . .

Perplexed, having lost patience, he said: Yes, yes, among the Assyrians, Indians, and in ancient Greece, etc., and reputed to have been among our ancestors. All this is well-known history.

With an even-toned, lower voice, she said: I knew instantly, as if possessed of a knowledge spawned in me at life's first moment, that I was their kin. Why are you baffled?

He said: I'm not. She said: It was a strange feeling, as you would imagine. No reason for it, as you know, but . . .

He looked without passion, from behind the somewhat darkened Diesel train's glass, from within the light din and repetitive rhythm of wheels in their successive, hushed beats. The fields, one after the other, flowed by in a different world: A huge mural painted with faded pastel colors in the boring afternoon sun. Her plump brownish arm next to him on the seat's arm. Bare, shining with special sensu-

72

ality. He does not touch it, nor does he want to touch it. Enough for him is the sensation of liveliness radiating from it, enveloping him in the air-conditioned cool air, penetrated from time to time with whiffs of dry heat. Light pours upon them from an exiled day, from the outside, melting in the white, blinding, electric light.

She had said to him: I will be traveling this afternoon. I'll see you in a week.

He had said to her: Do you have the ticket? She had said: Yes. He had said: Will you give me its number? I'll see you at the station and travel with you. She had said: Can you? He had said: Yes, grabbing his clothes and rushing down after a taxi. After the usual effort, he reached Station Square, bubbling with people and cars. He stood, restlessly, anxiously, in the queue, and recalled a dream similarly crowded, though with love and triumph. After exactly an hour, he was talking with her in contrived calmness, joking with her for having obtained the seat next to her in the Diesel train. He sensed she concealed a stubborn feeling of anger and tension, as if he had swept away from underneath her feet a small piece of land that she had meant to keep for herself.

Yet the rapture of this successful, albeit small, adventure had made him forget his embarrassment. The Stella beer bottle in front of him on the rusted metal table. The brown, plump, peeled peanuts. The small, round bottle cork with its black spots. The fields getting farther away, behind the narrow and neat agricultural road with its delicate small trees. The rapture of beer mixed with the strong taste of his cigarette, as he exhaled its smoke from his broad, free chest.

The fronts of mud houses shoot by in the train's hushed beats—solid masses of matted blond straw, their braided hair. The iron waterwheels appear, disappear at calculated, regular intervals, their blackness glowing with water leakage. Electric power pylons retreat with a planned straight slant: conic, hollow, made of shiny white metal, svelte-ribbed, holding their own language and indecipherable code, rising from humble green fields. Amid them the fellahin, with their small bodies, voicelessly bending with their axes that can hardly be seen, digging their earth with the patience of eternity, surrounded and continuously threatened by the desert that envelops everything. The desert: low-lying in the hollow of fixed, pure, unconquerable time.

On the edges of the desert the tremendous, bellowing, metallic tractors with their huge wheels gnawing the sand, turning over the soil with their black curved teeth, next to the geometric streams running in smooth, cement canalwalls. Their water, lead blue, shines in the skinny shadow of the newly planted casuarina trees.

The old enchantress, the brunette with green eyes, stops her Volkswagen, dusty with the fine sand of the desert. The din of the motor that has been rising and falling for hours and the wheels bumping on the stones in the leveled, sandy road fall silent now. The children of the southern desert with their light, white *jallabiyas* on their youthful, dry, black flesh. Their eyes, alert and intelligent; their faces gentle. The men with their lofty bodies. In their slenderness the solidity of sprouting palm trunks. In their swift dialect an incomprehensible finesse triggering an inner and intimate ripple in her womb as she removes the car key in a decisive, possessive, and elegant gesture. She opens the door of the hot Volkswagen. The seats are pushed forward to allow passengers to step in. Few words mix with her untamed accent. A thick and wavy swarm of flies. Where is the Center's headquarters? Here, *afandam*, behind the mosque. What? To the right. Do you see the minaret, Ma'am, beside the Socialist Union? Please come. You honor us, as if the Prophet were visiting, truly. The kids' eyes sparkle with pleasure, curiosity, astonishment. The small, sandy square with its small, yellow-green bushes, carefully irrigated. The continuity of locked-up white walls beneath the palm trees. The room furnished with a single military bed, a mat, a hand-mirror hanging on a nail thrust into dry plaster between bare stones. The group divides off into the two neighboring rooms. She falls into her agitated sleep in her white nightgown revealing her plump wheat-colored thighs, until the blaze of heat succumbs behind the open wood-framed window at sentient sunset, its deep red light freshening the evening's summer air—intoxicating, unbearable in its purity and balminess. Then, a golden lunar disk springs from the sand, glowing with gentle-faced fire, perfectly round, driving her suddenly to total silence and wakefulness.

The hungry veiled faces, with slits for fiery eyes. Bare, firm arms and legs surrounding, contracting, and surrendering. A fluid flows from the heart of drought. On the sand floors covered with mats, there are none of the obscenities of the wet open mouth. Only purity of the worshiped womb—the origin and destination of all things—the purity of the last uprising of death, and the silence of virgin breasts proud in their loftiness and supple resistance. An undissipated silence falling into the deep vales of the brown belly.

Toward waves of dark verdure with black gradations under the mud walls. Toward the breath of sleeping animals and the succession of munching jaws ruminating the fodder of fathers and grandfathers in a corner protecting them from the dazzling silvery fires. Toward the flooding of waters existing from time immemorial, the stagnation of dull ponds, the rustling of dense plantation, the sand wind, the gushing of fear in legs running and shoving. Toward the screams of hushed blood and banging clubs, the luster of the metal helmets and dusty, faded armors, the blows fracturing rough bones and the freedom chants, arms pushing to encircle the chest's rocks, squeezing love and sorrow. Toward the huge column—round, reddish, offensively smooth and bare-headed. Such is the life and resistance of peasants and students.

Granite oppression and terror roll around him. Whirlpools move away then re-appear, breaking apart then joining together in small stubborn rings. Alone in the distant sky, the piercing calls from these rings seem empty, without echo, hitting the stones and the few shining stars. The howling of rubber tires scraping off the earth. The screams of the brakes and the disengaging of the heavy engines with their falling foot soldiers and their fragile, useless armor. The contortions of broken legs and their sudden relaxation under the gripping, tense hands in the act of penetration, possession, ripping off then joining together. And the gushing of white, doughy paste unto the thirst of the eternally fertile, eternally barren earth.

The fusion of youthful bodies. Their blood boiling with bitter, soft mud, free of debris, borne on sweeping flood toward the moon, toward white flames glowing a moment, then extinguished forever. The darkness of lean bodies in shabby, new yellowish uniforms. Hostile, dark innards choking with stench. Savage puppets stepping to hushed commands, exploding suddenly, falling silent suddenly. Blinded by barbarism they dash around, striking out aimlessly in their upside-down terror. The screams, the agony, the calls of love suffered, the curses of deep loathing colliding into one other.

The passion of vengeance, the ecstasy of breaking the chains of years planted in the core of flesh and bone marrow. The turning over of the compliant, terrified, feminine body. The revelation of the inner part of the feet, the stains of fertile mud and light sandgrains clinging to them. Forts of a guarded roundness elevated on the soft hills of the body. Dashes into laps of attacking fever and throbbing resistance, ever demanding, ever craving. The candor of surrender. The worshipful prayers with eternal incantation. My darling . . . My love . . . My freedom. Prayer moans facing the open, violated sanctuary. O sacred and violated land! Bashans, your cruel, horned god will never rape you . . . Your female's ecstasy at being taken, your contentment with the blow, the trembling of your rebellious body, prancing, then recumbent—all fresh and sweet—as if annihilated, yet holding on, solidifying and challenging anew. The whispering of lovers—articulating the wisdom of the torn inner tissue. Pouring savagely their suffering, twisting with warm yearning—never stop, my love . . . O my love . . . My loss and my only light. The fresh mud welcomes the plunging legs, trunk, chest. Arms fold under its waves. The head descends slowly, open-eyed, knowing. He kisses her, the wavelike lips—supple, plump—close over him. The last bubble in the mud bursts, the mud quivering before its clear, sly, firm smoothness returns. A barbaric white light is a cutting edge wounding the bodies bumping each other. They move close, distant, bump again and again, searching in the revolving delicacy the sensations of birth and resurrection. The roaring of hushed and explosive virility in the anger of flood waters. Meanwhile the sandy embankments tumble down. The moon flies into fragments plunging into the dark belly moving up and down in new lust. The cruel god has fallen. Do come, strict Osiris. Love and heavy drops ooze from her luxurious brown skin, throbbing with calling and rapture in the smell of yeast, heavy, sweet with the fragrance of watered soil, as the final moisture soaks the cracks following a dryness of thirst stemming from the Nile's yearly nadir.

Such was the vision of Mikhail.

Rama asleep next to him in her room overlooking the narrow street flowing along waves of thick trees; following his arrival across labyrinths and mazes, his usual fears. The moon sheds its slender light in the room from behind the glass pane covered by gauzy, white fabric. The small electric bulb (of which she will tell him when leaving at midnight: Darling, don't turn it off) illuminated with its tawdry glow. Her new white suitcases, monogrammed, lay between the bed and the faded wallpaper of English flowers. Cars hummed by in the early night. Their tires turning on asphalt could be heard from the third floor. Mikhail popped awake, startled by his position—next to

77

her in bed—after all the traveling, waiting, moving around, after the shock of searching and the anxiety of loss, after going downtown beside her new and strange presence.

The drizzle and the light dinner in the luminous restaurant. Its smooth mahogany and insipid aluminum, the icecream that suddenly fell on his cravat as he was telling her a disconnected story with an enthusiasm that masked his anticipations of the night, the excitement rising in him and making him tense up. Then the return across broad, black avenues kept awake by street lights, then ascending the nocturnal stairway, entering the room speechless, directly drowning in an agitated whirlpool of passion on the narrow bed—half-asleep, half-awake, fatigued, excited, yearning, fulfilled, fragilely tender, then sleep like that of two children one in the lap of the other; her tender, sweet, brown arm on his shoulder.

The existence of this woman, this child-woman now, next to you sleeping under the moon, her scent and her touch, her relaxed, peaceful body, her thick, strong, rough hair—having the fragrance of wild plants. Her body—healed now from its recklessness, its power subdued, her white nightgown pulled away. Her broad, plump haunches—surfaces revealing a gorgeous, tropical, barbaric fruit, having bent its head and turned its leaves inward. Without tension. Calmly. Relaxed. All her existence secure in you, in your lap, surrendering to your love and affection, accepting your anxieties and worries that can never be tamed. This irreplaceable flesh of tenderness on the bed fills your arms. She has come home to you, no matter the reason. She has sought security in you and gotten rid of her voiceless suffering. Hers is the regular breathing of a dreamless night—an invaluable treasure that nothing can cancel. It will not be lost even if its moment passes. And it will pass. It will definitely pass. But nothing is equal to this now and forever—to this feminine presence, with its great richness and fertility that sought tranquility

78

in you. Her head with its slumbering hair, the still surface of her face that registers no waves. She hands herself to you in utter innocence. She is sleeping in your lap. A rare moment of security. How precious. Yet it moves on. It retreats. A moment outside time, but quickly moving away. Going outside your time. No return. It will not return, and you know it.

He said to himself: You know, this is only a night, a moment. What will tomorrow bring?

He said to himself: Her fertile femininity is the only mystery that will remain with you forever. Her gentleness as she sought tranquility in you. The bottom of the wave agitating with love's violence—with entreaties of love—has subsided. But it will rise foaming again. It will sink and rise again forever and ever.

Once he said to her: You, you will never die.

She was taken aback. In her denial, there was a touch of acceptance and confirmation.

Mikhail went out in the middle of the night, descending the few deep-red, carpeted steps between her room and his, having carefully closed the door so as not to scratch the silence. As he was stealing away, a door nearby opened suddenly and a girl came out, about fifteen, slender, her face—in the dim light sneaking down from a high ceiling—pallid, washed, with no make up; her cleanliness childlike. Because he had been surprised by her, she smiled, a smile akin to complicity and plotting. She glanced at the closed door as if she understood and was intrigued by such a nextdoor adventure. She gave him an imperceptible nod. Feeling assured, Mikhail smiled, returned the nod, moving quickly up the stairs to his room. He slept with a smile on his face—one of the few times in his life, as far as he can remember.

Later on, in another time, as they were descending the broad staircase, carpeted with a different red, luxurious in its faded color, and as their boat was drowning without completely plunging, he would say to her: Let's descend by the stairway, not the elevator, and be like Orpheus descending to the underworld.

She would respond: There was no red carpet in front of Orpheus.

He would not tell her that Orpheus went down by himself anyway, and in the end came up alone.

In the morning, they went to have breakfast. The restaurant was on the ground floor. Mikhail was feeling his path down the narrow circular stairway, possessed by his usual fear of all unfamiliar places. As for her, she descended with confident steps, as if she always knew where she was going. Her steps were light, belying the fact that she filled this clean lower world with her striking presence so early in the day. The mirrors were painted with advertisements for whisky, cigarettes, and airlines. The lit lamps exuded a slight energy, metered out in frail, mechanical elegance. The tables were well set with all kinds of well washed and polished commercial silverware. He said to himself: We are not in good old Hades? Surely we are not in . . .

The aroma of eggs came to them compromised by, and mixed with, chemical clean odors. The taps and stoves were making intermittent sounds—gushing and stopping, inhaling and breaking out forcefully with full mouths, with meticulously calculated power. The cultivated and processed fruits had been cut into thin small slices or squeezed into colored juice or arranged after washing and drying; small elegant tags of exporting and importing had been glued onto them, as if their tastes had been thereby sweetened, specifying some numbered position on a scale of prices.

We are in a Hell of organized dining and civilized tearing-apart with silverware plated with ornamental metals from the earth. A Hades of closed-mouth chewing without dirtying one's fingers, in fact as if you—Mikhail ibn Qaldas, who come from the mud of your red-black country, kneedeep in the elemental and traditional glories of long centuries—as if you were involving neither your mouth nor your stomach.

80

Rama gestures him to a table set apart, next to the wall. She selects the light-toasted bread and covers it, all poise, with a layer of creamy butter. She tenders him bread using an intimate, eastern gesture, as if she were a bride, post–honeymoon night, just entering an area of mediated calm.

She tells him stories whose unfolding flows through the waiting for, during, and after breakfast. I will tell you the story of my neighbor who fell in love with me. We were in Heliopolis, and she was a dance instructor. She came from an aristocratic White Russian family. She always wore a black silk *robe-de-chambre* with fringes and tassels, decorated with golden yellow and reddish purple, with large, flashy, flowery prints. When she hugged me, her body welded to mine, she wept from an irrepressible lust. I told her, I am really fond of you and I appreciate your sentiment, but sorry. We remained friends, as only best friends can be. There was also the story of our friend, the grandson of the former prime minister. He was a feudal landowner before the Revolution, and he was enamored of the judo trainer in the Club—a huge man from Bulaq. Did you know when I was very young I ate at the table of Farouk? Yes, he used to visit us at home. In his youthful days, he was slender and gentle, but there was in his eyes a concealed, hushed, mad look. When I lived in one room in Shubra al-Khayma, when I was nursing my daughter, I used to keep a Roneo duplicating machine under the bed. I used to have a sewing machine that I worked at night in order to mask the noise of the Roneo: my comrades were printing secret pamphlets. There were always passersby, coming in and out, at all hours of day and night. Of course, the neighbors suspected me, but none of them could confront me with anything. Those southern Egyptian peasant neighbors of mine were really kind. I used to wear my hair in one long braid, never loose, and I didn't put on make up at all. I used to be strict, serious, with an incredibly slim figure.

In the morning Scheherazade continues her stories as they stroll across elegant, city streets, as they sit in the café at the corner of the Greco-Roman Museum looking for morning coffee again, in the bus and in front of expensive shop windows, as they buy a new pair of shoes for Mikhail, because his tight old shoes were hurting.

Throughout her stories, she exposes her universe—shades of fantasies, memories, actualities, warm desires, wishes—all of which are turning into something: an event, a word, a spell. He will never know the place of myth in her universe with its streets, vast squares, specific darkness, its many unanswerable questions. Even in the period of early innocence there were slender, sharp-edged goads spurring the skin of myths without penetrating into the delicate flesh, only making incision after incision, the traces of a knife raised on the skin's surface with its viscous, heavy juice swallowed back up.

O, my green-eyed brown moon, dim with undying light: You move in your own sphere—with us and not with us—amid engines running and whizzing. Amid the din of jet planes, the whirring of appliances in air-conditioned offices; under the huge, solid stone beneath neon light. Your divine disk embraces the awakened, stretched python forever and ever. Under the primitive and imprisoned spurts of 220 volts and one thousand horses, and the flashes of magnesium reduced to white sand. You, whose charm leaves its powerful effect along the buried wires in cement. Rolls of white linen embrace your haunches, rich with suppleness of dense, undulated clay. Amid the humming of the transistor, the running of magnetic tapes, the giggles—both exciting and desiccated—of the nightclub cassettes in their calculatedly resounding music, with the non-stop dance of images. Their lines and spontaneous forms undulate, infatuated by the changing, out-of-control moments under the electronic buttons—slyly hidden under the flashes of glowing chrome, plastic, and nickel. I told you about the strange jinni of my childhood. I told you how the miseries of that childhood can never disappear. These miseries wake me at night with tears, with sensations of oppression and injustice. In the darkness I realize a wicked jinni has kidnapped my mother, appropriated her form, and come to me from the underworld, from the terrifying, mysterious dark vents of latrines. I told you about my suffering at the hands of this alternative mother with her shaggy hair and bare arms, harboring cruelty, always screaming, dressed in her exact short, light clothes, moist with kitchen waters. She attacks me with her barefooted, oval legs in a paroxysm of physical subjugation, destroying my childish senses and turning them into sharp-tipped, slender fragments, forcing me to lose my nocturnal dream of the good girl that has been metamorphosed by the old witch into a gentle, full-bellied cow, speaking to me as she does in folktales, asking for help in a plaintive womanish voice, pointing to the path under the huge sycamore tree at the head of the well at the end of the field. Hathor on the sharp edge of Bes's crater. I yearn incurably for my real mother imprisoned under the ground by the wicked jinni. I wait hopelessly for my mother's return after chasing away the jinni who violated her body and replaced her authority at home, living among us, the children, and sharing the bed of our father. I have told you about my visit to the Alexandrian Serapeum on a school trip, of stepping joyfully into the land of mysteries. The rays emanating from the face of Isis constituted a revelation, turning the rocky, circular wall under Diocletian's column into a nocturnal sky with bright, bored holes enveloping the ashes of mortal bodies and bones in marble pitchers, after being bleached by pagan burial fires. Alert eyes, star hollows under the yellowish glow of sodium lamps. In the balmy, refreshing, underground air as it blew from the deep vents in the cemetery, I was finding the obscure path of salvation with no known limits. The main well, rock-carved and round, was still deep, dim, and bottomless. We threw a stone in it but never heard its sound hitting the low-lying water in the hollowed earth. We were warned not to step on the wooden planks placed over this well.

83

I was seized with one of those irrepressible desires of childhood. I crossed the lines of life and death with briskness, gambling on life, and I won, as I descended on the other side. The moon-enchantress captivates me with her permanent smile expressing a special understanding that surpasses everything, that cannot be grasped.

You look at me for a moment with an estranged and distancing gaze. In your look there's no love or hate, no comprehension or condemnation, not even astonishment. Nothing, only complete disassociation and negation—negation of negation. The look of a being from another world, neither the upper world nor the lower world, simply a world that doesn't encompass me, does not claim me or negate me. I realize for a moment that it is an exile forever. Yet despite that, no sooner did your eyes flash than they switched off.

Mikhail had brought with him a bottle of Remy Martin. On the night she came to his room, he opened the tight, odd, shared closet where she hung her clothes to the right of his. Her maxi-dresses and mini-skirts—oft-worn, having acquired her very body folds in their fabric. Her blouses and pullovers—light despite the winter. Her pants. All emitting a faded scent of her own perfume and sweat, of traveling dust—not lost despite washing and ironing. Mikhail brought out the bottle from underneath the clothes hanging in the curious, temporary tightness. After the usual stumbling in removing the cork, he discovered he had no glasses. So he removed their toothbrushes, their separate toothpastes, and the shaving brush to the sink. He washed the round glass and another short, transparent, plastic one with hot water from the tap, which gushed out suddenly with a hoarse sound while he was thinking that hot water might deform and bend the plastic. He poured the limpid red liquid.

She said to him: Do you like drinking a lot?

He said: No, no, I don't drink except when I am happy. Wine takes an opposite toll on me in times of worry and sorrow.

Then he said: In days like those I was telling you about, when I

84

was going through the old, long trial of love, I was like someone suffering from a chronic disease. My whole being was throwing up whatever I drank: cognac, whisky, even wine—especially wine. I used to drink with friends of my first youth, whose leaves have now fallen in various capitals of the world; none of them has been spared. But the misery of love, the frustrating fancies, and the silent suffering remain as hard stones in the heart; nothing can dissolve them.

She said: I don't like to drink now. You know I used to drink every night at a set time. I almost became an alcoholic. But I was saved, thank God!

The Remy Martin bottle was on the mahogany dressing table, covered by a slate of glass reflecting the images of their cologne bottles, perfumes and cosmetics, brushes and combs, the lipstick tube—having rolled and settled next to her inflated open handbag—the ashtray, an Agatha Christie novel, metro and theater tickets, the Kleenex box, a bunch of keys and the crowded familiar things—all reflected in the mirror. On the corner of the mirror she had hung a small white piqué handkerchief, embroidered at the edges, washed and left to dry slowly.

His hand on her round, large, resting thigh as she looks at him.

In the clouded morning, she combs her strong, dark hair with a big comb. Every small, plump finger in the intense grip of her hand is like an independent being with its own life. She has these dynamic bursts. In moments of love-making, he recognized such thrusts and tautness in every limb, in every part: stretching and tightening, winding and slackening, the sudden push of her tongue inside his mouth—a voluptuous snake, twisting and standing erect, slowly prying around the open moist space. The elevation of the thigh's sandy bridge, humid with perspiration, beneath it a flood of Ethiopian silt and the roundness of arms encircling it, coming out of the alert nerve center, thick with its charged electricity. She is, then, one and many until every one of her beings reaches a peaceful haven.

She said to him, as if talking to herself: I don't even know how to comb my hair. When I get like this, I must be truly in a bad state.

The small confrontations between them in that small desperate room were accumulating but he did not allow them to explode, as if pushing away a warning charged with threats. The confrontations of love, lust, suppressed jealousies, denied doubts, undefined and diffused anxieties, impediments and failures, efforts of surpassing and tolerance, fall into holes of half-silence and half-articulation, charging glances and gestures with unbearable weights.

Rama is getting ready to go down, while he is putting his things in his pockets, turning around without a specific intention. She takes off her nightgown with a quick movement, drops it sharply on the bed. Her moves are few and agitated as she is putting on her pantyhose and straightening her breasts in her bra, closing the clasps on her wide tight back with sensitive, trained fingers. All of her is challenging, clearly and simply, all preconceived ideas about the romantic feminine body—its timidity, its invincibility, its inaccessibility. She is standing and moving around: her body—a direct, frank, sensual quotidian event—with no poetic spell, no eroticism, not inducing fantasies or fancies. Strictly a body getting up naked in its very odd and very ordinary feminine severity.

This gave him a sense of freedom and liberation from all exertions and considerations. It did not cancel his presence with her; to the contrary, it was fixing it in a special way—on a level open to all options.

She said to him—as she was turning toward him her open back pulled tight by the black bra—in a tone, as if hostile and abrupt:

Will you please button my dress above the zipper?

He smiled as he approached her. He could not hug her from the back, could not join the wealth of her haunches to his taut virility, could not press on her as she was so practical-minded and in a hurry.

His fingers stumbled on the buttons and the buttonholes. He

86

could not find his way in the delicate fabric enveloping the back of her neck. She was patient, but tense, almost hostile in her fixed waiting pose; in the powerful whiffs from her hair and the dew of light sweat on the convergence of her hairline with the back of her strong round neck.

She said to him: Mikhail, Mikhail, the two buttons up high. Kindly put them into the buttonholes on the side, and let me finish.

Her patience was running out, almost breaking through a rather frail crust.

His fingers were one on top of the other, the buttons slipping with every attempt. He became aware of himself, smiled sarcastically at himself and at the whole situation as it was becoming insipid and silly.

She said: All right . . . All right, let me try.

He said, with a voice he recognized as hushed and soft: Good God . . . Just a moment . . . Wait . . . One moment.

A month later, following their stressful days, she came to him for the first time—after trials, after feeling their way along a road that was beginning to branch out—wearing this very dress. He said to himself: What does she mean? What does she want to relay? What does she want to say?

As for me, I talked a great deal—though perhaps less than I should have—without saying a thing. I stretched my arms toward her, holding the love I have for her, but what I held remained buried; she rejected it. How can love withstand the distancing of her eyes? She does not know me. All the bounty of her body stands as an impediment between her and my love. She gives me her body, or part of her body, but she—my sealed black earth of antiquity—gives back nothing.

My hands withdraw from her thigh. I don't know what to do with the rejected gift except let it decay and spoil between my fingers, taut

87

with generosity. Is the fruit of this love green or rotten? Rama, I want to give, but it is as if you were unable to understand me. Your sweet name is mixed in my mouth with gall: I do not pronounce it: I bite it . . . An unbreakable stone. O most beautiful name in the universe, O name created for immortality. Rama . . . Rama . . .

A heat heating a headstrong humor, either hushed when it happens, or hastening in hot whisks and hissing whirls. I am harassed by a hoodoo, hankering for holding it off, hewing the hedonistic heart. Vehement exhortations to hostilities with hesitant hatchets amid the inhospitable horse huddles. Vehement hugging. Hysterical horrors. Whetting the whims and overwhelming the households, with whooping and hurting hooves. The havoc of a harrowing Sahara at home. Downhill through hellish hours . . . Hurdles hovering around me heedlessly. The hurdles lose cohesiveness, behaving like holed hearts. Hoarse humming of helpless whispers. I hover under the hedges of my hazardous house where my hazel whims are halting and hobbling. Horus hovers and halts, hovers and heads down unto the heaths of horticultured wheat. Heaving with honeyed hemlock. Hailing is my haven and harness. Hurling the homesteads, hammering off the handcuffs with horrible whiffs. I hug the hounds in the heat of a horrid hurricane. Hawk-eyed horizons behold me. My heart hollowed by humming whispers. My innermost burns with the scorching howl: Freedom, my only truth; my love for freedom sets me on fire.

Like the youngest of adolescents and the most naïve of them, I write your name. Rama . . . Rama . . . And I want to hail you, to call you. I hear my voice quivering despite myself, tearful again and again. How absurd all this is. I want to say I love you. Do you hear me? I ask you, do you halloo me too? I laugh and make fun of the innocence of all this. A raw emotion? How cheap it is. How banal all this love, these calls and simmering desires to see you once again, to embrace you, to plunge into your earth. How disdainful this blazing yearning to gather you between my arms, to drown my face in your bosom, this constant sense of impossibility—social, emotional, possibly physical. This is a new and odd sensation for me, always and constantly problematic. A dubious matter, it tortures with sharp, nay, dazzling awareness. Is all this a cheap, raw emotion? Isn't this the madness of adolescence, or second adolescence? How come I do not resist, and why resist anyhow? Why this suffering ablaze with constant, unflinching, smoldering embers with white-snow fires? A dazzling point, a solid unbreakable core buried beneath the earth with no radiation. The eye cannot behold it, given its enclosed brightness within bounded limits. A suffering that hurls everything to the four corners of the earth, a suffering that can't stand silence. In the end it shouts, screaming with all its voice, fumbling among the bodies of the planets, closing the open mouths of oceans. It is a suffering that pulls unto itself the pillars of the world, rending them. They thunder and fall in an earthquake or a sandstorm. He chokes, as if his body were being scraped off rocks, moistened with salty water drops. Around him the sleeping hyenas, with ostrich legs, awaken and dig the ground to throw away the open fingers and sharp joints that have never grasped anything. The fish with their meek red beaks nipping then letting the sky's seed fall, the radiating planets that decayed, their over-ripe flesh rotting. The tits of a lioness with discerning eyes, dripping milk, honey, and sweet-tasting blood that etches opaque, thin streams into the luxurious, soft soil. The she-panther soars with her gentle wings—her soft feathers fluttering as they fall down on the angelic prayer of the cherubim and seraphim with their sixty wings quivering in loud flutters, filling heavens and earths. The well beyond the Waqwaq mountains with its smooth, soft, worn-out marble stairs sucks the milky flow until it reaches the deep, rent navel of the earth, still hanging on it the cord of shriveled, transparent flesh that will soon fall off, and a thousand human faces, pale and suffering, are revealed through the ebbing

89

blood, faces gazing but uttering nothing in their voiceless dream. And you, my love, sleeping in my lap under the moon. Your face floating amid the ruins of the broken world around me, on the dark, turbid waters of my love. Your face floats with fixed open eyes: two dazzling black suns that tempt me in this endless night:

When he lifted the telephone receiver in the heart of night, her voice reached him, fervent and intense, almost breaking down:

I want you . . . I want you to take me . . . Come now.

He said nothing.

—I want to sleep . . . Come make me sleep . . . Please.

His voice tensed to speak then faltered. The waters of his heart and body stopped running. Was she crying from lust and craving or searching for support and help?

He said as if he did not know what he was saying: Not tonight. Not tonight.

Without explanation.

Her dry-winded, anxious warmth, like the khamsin, was parching the night, making it splinter, with no hope of healing. Is it a banal struggle between two wills or is it preservation of the gift, the grace, the donation—an act of sparing her from gratuitous wasteful fall?

He went to his empty bed and slept—his limbs relaxed, confident and ready. Was the smile to himself in the darkness a smile of an easy victory or that of a hidden, incomprehensible flesh ritual?

Later she said to him: If you really loved me, you wouldn't hesitate to take me, every time and immediately.

She did not wait for his response.

When they made love for the first time after a long absence, she slept, also, for a few minutes in his lap, in the sweltering night under an almost tropical, round moon shining behind thick glass. Her breath coming out of her relaxed chest under his arms had a child-like regularity. He was careful not to move his arms under her shoulder. Sleeping next to him, strong-bodied, with large haunches and thriving breasts with sweet blood-and-milk-running veins. The insects and worms of the earth buzz and hum in the din of their craving and fulfillment. The beasts in the moon outside have been satiated with their prey. Her face had turned red beneath her luxuriant black hair. Then she woke up suddenly, completely, as if she had been all the time in the same state, unchanged, without transformation. She said calmly, without smiling or apology:

It seems I have gotten used to sleeping in your arms.

He smiled at her with a stoic tenderness.

She said to him as she examined him with her large glowing eyes:

I know I have a tyrannical streak in me, but you too, my darling, have that streak in you.

My beloved, your hunger will be satiated. Your sins will be washed away. Your name will be hallowed.

In the post-midnight light shed by the worrisome, northern summer sky in the partial awakening from profound sleep, replete with confused obsessions, she had said to him: Good morning, darling. Come as you are, quickly. But he had splashed cold water on his face, combed his hair in a hurry, and went to her striding softly. He reclined on the narrow bed. In the dawn, she was looking at him and in her wide green eyes there was an unrelenting question—incomprehensible, neither articulated nor silenced. He was kissing the fingers of her tight, plump hand with its jittery joints, stretching his arm behind her large mane of hair with its strong, exciting, dusty scent. He was feeling the pressure of her head on his forearm, was welcoming it. He attached himself to her grounded body lying on the bed under a light sheet. Inclining toward her, he reached with his hand for her full legs and gripped a thigh's round, non-swaying flesh. He was silent, still—his hands separated, torn from him. His bones were lulled, his lips—no water running into them—hesitatingly explored

91

the flesh beneath her delicate neck. The lips, open and tremulous, went down to the relaxed, slumbering breasts, while his hands were desperately silent, having settled on the curve of smooth, calm soil beneath her light, black moss. The dawn, enclosed and imprisoned in the room, was heavy and restrictive. Rama was now in his arms sleeping . . . sleeping.

You sleep in the arms of your lovers, Rama, in your imprisoned dawn, not reaching the edge of dense light, while anxious wakefulness flows and ebbs at the threshold of your womb, without stopping.

She said to him: Why should I wake up? What pushes me to wake up?

Her eyes shine with reproach and request, not hoping for a response.

The gall in her eyes. Is it the sediment of frustrating days and nights? Is it ambition with wings twisted, one unto the other, in the not completely closed circle of rejection? Is it an aversion to me? I did nothing. I was stranded on her long, narrow bed between the elevated rocks and the sand, as her arms poured toward the lit sea without reaching it.

She said to him: Why do you look at me?

He said: I take my provisions for the lean days.

But of course I am still starved, gazing without quenching my thirst at the salt-watered, green lake.

I am still calling on you: Rama . . . Anima . . . Mandala . . . My woman . . . My haven . . . My cave . . . My Kemi . . . My dream . . . O, merciful Ment, O Mut wife of Amon . . . O Ma'at, my mirror . . . My integrity . . . Maryam full of grace . . . Buried Demeter, her moist mouth rains manna and mercy . . . Her womb greedy for semen and destined by the circle of death and the joys of consummation . . . O mother of the falcon . . . Mother of patience . . . Mother of the swaying golden jasmine on the water . . . Rama . . .

92

When she woke up she looked questioningly into his eyes.

He said to her: You were with me.

She said to him: I am, also, used to taking you with me wherever I am.

He did not say to her: Liar.

But she knew it and accepted it quietly without a move.

He bent over her, kissing her full on the lips. Her kiss was neutral, hiding a great deal, knowing a great deal, not divulging a great deal. Her gaze, as he kissed her, carried a weight of self-containment. Her eyes that continued to charm him—those green, mysterious talismans, very close to his own eyes—were not flinching. Her breasts splay under the weight of his chest. He gathers them with his hands; she does not smile, does not sob, does not hold her breath. He unhands her breasts and goes up. His fingers feel the back of her neck, the ground of the thicket-roots of her hair. He holds tightly her round full neck. She looks at him without flinching, without questioning. The muscular neck under his palms is delicate, throbbing and swaying gently as if it were a wave flowing with gentle breath. He feels he is smiling—a somewhat distracted smile—while his grip is hardening on the body that is acquiring from now a special existence as if independent. Her arms stretched beside her are still. Her belly beneath him: strong and solid. The pressure of his twined hands increases a little. He knows he is not smiling now. He whispers to her, a warm whisper encompassing the world: Shall I strangle you, Rama?

She says to him: Strangle me, my love.

Without challenge and without surrender, as if she were taking a decision on a fact of life, important but not very serious. She neither accepts nor rejects. He can feel now her neck bones, both rock-hard and resilient, between his unrelenting hands, hands having their own will. In the grip of his palm muscles and finger bones, life waters run in the channels of her neck, in the minute veins. The soft, tender skin swells and rises a little at his finger tips. His hand is inclined toward another decisive, inevitable, unavoidable push toward an act of no return. Fetuses are conceived, plants, animals and rocks are created, spring waters gush out, earthly vales open to let the hands plunge in their mire. The face wallows in the sweet mud, kneaded with wild thyme. The torn limbs are seeds planted in the soil, limb after limb, the generous living flesh thriving and growing in verdure. O lady of the green, I pluck with my hands your ripe breasts. I bend and drown my mouth in your open, moist lips. My face turns over the finger traces—light embers—glossed by my tearful kisses. Your arms surround my head buried in your neck. There is no pardon because there was no guilt. There is neither anger nor contentment, only the funeral rites of love without candles or hymns; serious and meticulous, delicate and tender rites, and probably they mean nothing at the end.

Mikhail descends the last stairs carved in the earth . . . The walls, made of Nile mud, surround the oasis that was deserted thousands of years ago. The tender white lotus on the distant columns' conic capitals—their rocky youthfulness does not wilt. The numerous figures in relief are of men rending the skin of the hot sky and breathing in with confidence the sky's pure, dark-blue waters. The soot of love-torches that blazed in bygone days is still black on the walls. The open vent in the wall is bright, drowned by the moon in this room in which the ancient prostitute-priestesses slept. In which they groaned and agonized over sacrificial passions, the roaring of virility attacking again and again with the strangling of the taut burial inside living flesh. The breathing of centuries-long dust wounds his chest. Her abundant hair is a forest untouched by knife—her redemptive ransom, during six days, at the talismanic door. In front of him her face flames with her green eyes, half of it silvery, delicate, soft, the other half pocked, torn, reddish, burnt. Its burns, having healed, leave the skin with dark spots and gloomy veins. Her eyes gazing besiege him with an unending supplication.

5

A Crack in the Old Marble

He was awakened by dream rustle and dawn's agitation. The room abounded with her—sleeping next to him—naked under the light sheet, her breathing heavy. He felt the moisture of sweat on her leg, conjured the ampleness of her brown, delicate thigh, and smiled.

Suddenly he was overwhelmed by desire. He rolled over and put his arm gently across her shoulder. She did not fidget. Who could say for sure that she did not feel him, that she did not know in her deep sleep, in her dark womb, his darkly warm glow of closeness and kinship? Her breathing continued, in–out. Her hair was stuck to the side of her narrow forehead. The wide-open décolleté of her nightgown was sliding off her poured-out breasts. He drew his face close to her neck, recognized anew the fragrance of her sleep, the spice of her lush body. A biting sense of affection, contentment, and rupture coursed through his body.

My darling, you will never know this moment. You suspect nothing—how complete my love was, how unconditionally granted, how

95

hopelessly serene and unified. Purity without egoism, for you and you alone; tamed, hushed without anguish; its despair total and untainted. You will never know that I let myself be immersed by heavy waters, smiling or about to smile, in this still, dark-blue sea of my love. Dawn was, then, this sea. Its shores: the fences of the world. I plunge into it. Its sky is boundless.

He removed the white sheet, wrinkled by use, from her body. He brought down his face from the pillow and put his arm around her hips. He bent his knee slightly in order not to fall from the bed. He rested his cheek on the surface of her round thigh. The roughness of his chin on her tender spot, going down beneath it then holding back. The breathing of the full sleepy body reached him, mixed with the heavy-tasting moisture of the closed, concealed vent.

His tranquility merged with an unfamiliar anxiety about the next moment, from the danger that it had not yet materialized or even been conceived; nevertheless, it was already carrying a threatening element. From day's start, each moment had shrunk while he was still living it. When he lowered his face gently on the spreads of her fertile, sweet flesh—now soft and compliant under his solidity—he also fell in an abyss between two times, neither of which existed. Drowning in her body's tranquility, he tumbled in a vacuum where there was no fulfillment.

She did not join him; she was sleeping. Her hand did not stretch to join his. Nothing saved him. He could not find a thing to hang onto in his fall, not even when she turned to him—in a state between slumber and wakefulness—emitting a faint sigh charged with a sense of peace and contentment because he was there, because his face was upon her. She embraced his head with her arm pressing it tenderly, and said: Good morning . . . Darling, come to me. He said, while his mouth was having its fill from exploring her softness: I am with you, my darling. Where else am I? He amended, saying: Good morning.

From the dense and sweet silt he lifted his face, while her arm pulled him toward her lap with gentle pressure. Suddenly and passionately he was falling on her open mouth.

Still, my love, what is separating us? Why this open abyss between our bodies entwined by the sweat of our early-morning cravings? Why this estrangement annulling our very embrace, when your chest is pressing and buried in my arms and your thighs encircling my legs? Your eyes—two round glittering gems—under closed eyelids, where waters of passion and rapturous quests run. Our bodies not yet merged are hot, moist elements, still separate in their tight embrace.

At the center of this universe, in the trembling giddy heart, at a point on the throbbing, profound circumference, there is an ever-wakeful eye—desolate, and in flames—calling but receiving no answer. It is not death—you will never die—that separates us. And it is not love. You will always love. You are what I love. Is it, then, indulgence? Is a wicked sword—dripping blood, semen, and curdled milk—snipping what's between us? Your gorgeous tongue licks the sword's scorching cutting edge. Your concealed scream is a moan of fulfillment, of pleasure and pain. My tongue—an enflamed parched skin—shrinks like an old parchment and falls. I can find no reviving word after dying from rapturous stabbing. All my body is wilted by dry wind.

Her last quiver was a wave coming from afar. His heart melted, then froze. Her smile between one slumber and another seemed absent, content, self-sufficient.

When he woke up from his little death, the window looked like a rent in the sky, secluded by its partly drawn white curtain from what he sensed to be the outside cold and hostile air. From behind the separating glass overlooking a bare yard, the ceilings—slanting in sharp-edged lines—seemed old, gray with soot. Alone her brownish round face showed from the sheet covering her: relaxed, content in the faint morning light, redolent of past desires.

97

His bones felt light as he leapt from the bed. He looked at the narrow, square court: the stones of its gray floor cracked, clean, marble-like. In the petrified blackish soil of the cracks, no green flourished. The yard was empty. Next to the mute, unpainted stone walls stood a row of huge black round cans, closed with domed lids, moist with morning.

The only tree springing from these stones with its slender yet solid searing-dark wood was crooked and bending, but not breaking. How many winters of loneliness had it borne? How many storms had it faced, twisting in front of wind-blows without breaking? He felt in his insides the aches and splintering of wood.

He said to her as they readied themselves to go downstairs:

Isn't every leaf on every branch, with its minute, faded-white veins in the gentle green flesh a miracle? Isn't this laced verdure, delicate to the touch and winding around strong, soft-muscled trunks, this melodic green with infinite shades—mat green, mellow green, hushed green, whispering green, dazzling green, delicate green, dark green, emerald green—a miracle? Aren't the tiny frail birds flying in the risky and expansive horizon, those animated shooting stars in the galaxies of vast black spheres, a miracle? Hundreds, thousands, countless miracles are repeated effortlessly around us, without the least fuss, without drama. How bountiful all this is, how splendid and abundant! Yet how indifferent we are to miracles happening without interruption. Wondrous is that which cannot be described, wondrous is the silent weave of day and night, continuous forever.

She said: This is what I find every morning when I open my window. I, too, love trees, as you know.

He recognized in his wonder an element of naïveté. His was the wonder of children from back alleys, from neighborhoods denied greenery. His soul was captivated by this excessive bounty, always available, yet impossible to possess, no matter how much he scooped out the riches with his palms and eyes, no matter how much and how long he encircled this ever-renewed sensuousness with both arms and legs. The perfect wealth continued to be untouchable, throbbing silently in the richness of her body: growing, thriving, overflowing. In her cadence was the confidence of a sure world, of life taken for granted. This world was her very birthright, received as such, therefore without much fuss.

He said to himself: When will you finish with your philosophizing, not worth two pennies?

She looked at him with two limpid lakes for eyes. How deep were they? Shallow, the bottom directly under the surface or of bottomless profundity? Under the sun of those cruelly dazzling, sharp eyes, he sensed the aridity of a desert inside himself.

Let us not be cruel, Rama. I mean, let us not be cruel with each other. Can't you see the world around us is overflowing with cruelty, for reason or for no reason. Like walls, people have been scorched by flames and struck by wind: flames of lust and failure, winds of indifference. They are burnt out, shriveled. We too can be cruel—indeed we are. Cruelty is a fragile armor, even if terrifying in form, with its blue, gnarly teeth, its deep jaws open; its eyes unflinching. Have we learned that the only way to stand up to cruelty is through more cruelty? Let us at least not be cruel to each other, if possible, for our strikes are painful and fall on vulnerable spots. We have learned—haven't we?—where the deadly strikes should be aimed. No matter how much we conceal it, these open wounds bleed at times hot blood and continuously discharge dark drops, without ever healing.

He said to himself: These small deaths constitute the very fabric of our life: successive, in fact linked and continuous, every day, each moment. Here we are dying as we gulp life with every breath.

He said to himself: When will you finish with this twopenny philosophy?

99

He said to himself: Again you appropriate her voice. This is part and parcel of your old defense strategy. When will you learn to stand alone, to be self-sufficient without finding excuses, without the need to attack in order to defend?

Fearfully, recklessly, stubbornly, I defend the delicate, throbbing thing, the only part of the body that, if harmed, will turn the body of the whole world into a corpse whose stench will rise to the zenith of immense spheres and make them stink as well.

He said to her: There was plenty at stake, in fact everything. I gambled with everything. The bet was high: on everything.

They were coming together toward the lights of the *mulid* celebration with its clamor and crowds, he holding her arm and she permitting him to do so; she stumbled in a hole on the sidewalk, regained her balance by herself, stood upright and overtook him.

But I lost, I lost before the game started. It was not my game. I gambled with everything, on everything, taking a chance, and I lost. I had to lose. No one can bet on everything and win.

In fact there is no room for winning or losing. The game does not offer turns to start with. All gambling is outside the track. It is invisible and incomprehensible, taking place in the dark.

Her face, amid rough waves of human beings, is a smooth-sided lighthouse, round and calm. They were leaving the warmth of bodies and stones, the large wooden stores with huge gates, the garages with advertisements for car agencies—Ford, Chevrolet, and Nasr—in broad elongated letters, both English and Arabic; they were leaving behind the long, stony fence surrounding the cobblestone stable of the khedive, on its gate the stone head of a horse; they were leaving the balcony with its delicate posts and carved leaves overlooking the marble shop windows of kebab and liver displaying masses of dangling dark-red slaughtered meat, fishmonger shops with bright tins of *fisikh* standing in arranged rows.

Everything here and now is to be questioned. It is not love only, but my very existence, my legitimacy as a human being, as a man. Everything: Truth and deception. Fidelity and treason. Freedom and oppression, both human and divine. You are with me now—not looking at me as if you were, but nonetheless with me. But you are here like the universe—in possession of a firebrand from a sublime and transcendent divinity. There is a cosmic and divine story between us.

They were pushing around, passing among the lupine-seed carts with their conic paper twists made from the pages of schoolchildren's copybooks. The carts had yellowish flames rising from their lamps, almost imperceptible beneath the bright light of the old mosque, detectable only through the smoke dispersed in flying thin wisps. The drone of gas lamps, their strong and constant light falling on heaps of chickpeas, yellow and white with splintered sugar-coating. The lamplight was falling, also, on several red *mulid* sugar dolls, wrapped up in wavy silvery paper and on decorated conic baskets made of palm leaves full of earth almonds.

He said to himself: You have incurable delusions. You think this story between you and her has a mystic dimension. Won't you get rid of this obsession? You are here with her, with her charm and shortcomings. Isn't she a woman? Isn't she special in this unending ocean of people? Isn't she marvelous as a human being and as a woman? She is a poor thing too. She is restless and ambitious. She is jolly and has her own insignificant and significant secrets, like everyone else. Isn't that so? There are defects in her body as well as irresistible appeal. Yes, many have loved her, but what of it? She made mistakes, made sacrifices, became tired, performed duties and more. She did not concern herself with ethical and social conventions, but took them, intelligently and thoughtfully, into consideration. Her passion and her compassion are large enough for everything. Anyhow, you know only that she, a woman who knows how to please and how to

101

enjoy herself, is with you. And you love her. Let it be. Can't you accept that within its own limits?

The lofty minaret—slender, graceful, isolated; alone in the sky. From it, chains of colored electric lights dangle luminous balls of hard candy swaying without touching the millenary stones, whose flesh stands striped in wide horizontal lines of faded red and dusty white.

She walks with confidence next to him, but she is not with him. Tomboyish but with feminine grace of an empowering and daring kind, wearing expensive low-heeled shoes—their leather shriveled and faded by dust. Her wide skirt tightly covers her body; her blouse open, her full bosom moist and glittering with light sweat in the bright night. People are hardly looking at them in the crowded area. She is oblivious of him. He feels her withdraw into her private world.

Above the centuries-old dome is a small crescent, rusty from the powerful rays radiating from below, toward the faded blue skin of the sky. Beneath the deep narrow door the holy steps are lit by electric lamps. They lead to an inner sanctuary seeming distant and apart.

He was stunned by this heavy-edged sensual luxury. She was next to him, alone and happy: full of energy after hours of laziness and apathy that seemed without end; dynamic and aroused, attached to many things and many people, yet singular, secluded. She had performed unknown great things of which no one knew, and in the end she did not do any of the things she really wanted to do.

On the other side were wooden *mashrabiya* balconies and a huge sign bearing the inscription, "Arab Socialist Union." Its doors were of wrought iron with circular designs—their stones carved in splendid imitation of the traditional style, covered by a layer of thick, dingy dust. Western bar chairs overlooked the Nile, retained a 1920s splendor. The advertisements on the mirrors were made of Belgian glass, the sides of their silvery mercury worn out. In the center of the wide street stood a row of carts displaying all kinds of fruits, vegetables,

102

toasted local and Syrian bread—frail, small, stiff, flat loaves—with sesame seeds, radishes, fresh lettuce, leeks with dangling leaves. The street teemed with *jallabiya* gowns, *qibqab* clogs, *malayat* wraps, trousers, southern Egyptian turbans, horns, neon lights, sizzling oil, the heavy and pungent smell of fried fish in the night air.

He came close to her and took her tender arm. How many of your yearnings were frustrated, Rama? And how many joys fulfilled? You are limited, defined yet boundless. Always searching for some lost perfection, as if you were perfect, as if you were immortal. In his swaying heart, both gentleness and alarm are vying. His love knows no frontiers, has none of the unsteadiness of liquid. His love is sharp with wounding projections, sketching deep scar lines into living flesh.

On their first night in Cairo her small dark car was making its way on the Nile Road, under the lights of Imbaba Bridge. The car's smell agitated his senses; a mixture of smelly leather and tin, with the stickiness of old milk and the heat of burning gas.

She had been crying as she drove. Her tears gushed silently, profusely. He felt wounded, profoundly frustrated—why? He was baffled as he gazed at her tears with awakened eyes, saying to himself: What hurts her? What would console her?

She said: Nothing joyful ever happens to me.

He used to say to himself cruelly: What does she want? Does she want a man—a man no matter who? Or does she want *me*? And why my concentration on my own self? Should I continue feeling enclosed and separate? Why can't I join in this strong current, gushing with blood, semen, and muddy waters? Why can't I melt in it, gulp my pleasures from it, heedlessly, anonymously, without identity? She seems to want to drown—every night—in the never-ending waves of this river, allowing her fertile blackness, the mud of her body, to be available for appropriation, free for all, in order to become clean and bright—a blooming, glowing, yellowish-dark lotus, coming out from the mud between the thighs of ancient Hapi of the river without shores, both springing from and pouring into the underworld sea endlessly—a solid sandy island by now.

The car stopped in Sahel Rawd al-Farag Square. In the distance, there was a prickly pear cart on which a gas lamp droned with wild flames in a clipped cloud of tiny, flying, nocturnal mosquitoes. Its peddler with his long *jallabiya* casts an obscure figure in the shade. The Coca-Cola container, with its faded red color, the paint having peeled and erased the Arabic and English letters from its bruised sides. Taxis, old and blue, standing on the Corniche Road under the trees with low ceilings as if dusty, sleepy scarabs. The street leading to open deserted yards in which one can barely distinguish the holes between heaps of stones and bricks. The cafés, bright and empty. The script in their big signs large, colored, cursive. The Quran resounding powerfully from the cafés in confident recitation. Narrow, low, and subdued houses. The traffic policeman, dark and slight from afar, standing as if lost in the middle of the square. She said to him: Mikhail, what if I asked you to leave everything and come with me?

Her eyes appeared mad. But the rest of her was calm, still. She was motionless following the crying spell. By the street light filtering through the mist of imperceptible, minute gases, her cheeks were serene. Her plump hands rested casually on her thighs, lifeless on her old dark-blue short skirt. In her inner, intimate, buried core everything was afire. Deeply, carefully, in this body that was both revealed and concealed.

He said: If you really ask me to do so, yes.

His quivering voice came hurrying, no sign of thoughtfulness in it.

He did not respond simply, instantly, and directly by an absolute affirmation, without conditions since she had not said to him with complete certainty and complete despair, in an absolute way: Leave everything and come with me. He did not say to her: Yes, yes, now

104

and at any time. He did not even tell her: Yes, whenever you ask me to, at any moment you ask me. He knew her question related to a number of different things. In fact he knew the question was not related to him personally. It was not meant to have him leave everything and go with her. He knew she was asking for something else, something temporary, transient. In this profoundly striking question, she was asking him for only a night perhaps, or even part of a night, until the morning. She was playing with the impossible, gambling with what was necessary, with the very necessity of life and death.

She said: Yes, I suppose you love me, in a way.

He did not say to her: In fact, it is you who loves me, in a way. Or does this statement of yours indicate "I don't love you"? I don't know. There will not be a story joining us. What is this then? What is between us? An earthquake, a hurricane, the falling sky? As for me, I love you without limits, without definitions, without reservations; a perfect love that wants you all, completely. Of course, completeness is also impossible. The impossibility is complete.

She said to him: I am myself with you. With you alone, I try as much as I can, with all that I can, to be myself, frank to the point of utmost honesty. Frank in my changing moods, in my distraction and wandering if you will; sorrowful at times and distant; cheerful, of course, if I am in the mood, full of vigor and interest. Isn't it so? But you say I don't love you. I don't know what you want me to say.

Following the crying jag, her face was bright and soft. But now it turned into a mask again.

He said to her bitterly: You are not sentimental at all.

He did not say to her: Does this mean that you do not understand sentiment?

I have never caught you in a sentimental state, stormed by emotions, except when you were talking—and rarely did you talk—about your inner self defensively. You with the multiple masks!

105

He also said to her: You're strict; you don't let go.

Your speculative, silent, clinical gaze that calculates everything, making decisions alone. Your private pleasure in diagnosing, knowing, and possessing. A moment, then you turn away without interest except in satiating your neutral cruel drive to press then relax—given your fear of sharing and your aversion to partnership, given your concern not to give up your very self. You give up your body, yes, but then you abandon this same body—when you want to—for appropriation with no fences or precautions—but only in order to preserve yourself without any scratches or compromises.

She said to him: What is this? Are we performing an autopsy? I hope we don't have already in front of us the corpse of our relationship. We have not yet put it on the slab for dissection. There is something still alive between us, I hope. I know how to be a true friend. Believe me, I know how to be a friend, and I am very proud of our friendship.

She would tell him later: Perhaps what is between us is a romantic friendship.

He said calmly with a repressed voice: I do not want friendship; I don't want you as a friend.

Later on, he used to repeat to himself his response. He never wavered. He did not want this friendship, he wanted something else, larger and permanent. He would say to himself: You are very ambitious and empty-handed, aren't you? His distressful tears fell heavily one after the other, snatching with each teardrop a rib from his ribcage, from the inner wall of his heart. With years, the tears had dried off and become solidified, his suffering become rock-like, replacing the youthful storms that shake and whirl, pouring down pain that turns into rocks that can't melt or crumble. And when these rocks break up under the weight of cruelty, they make blunt, jagged fragments, oppressive and repressive, impossible to displace.

106

He knew she would use everything in order to obtain what she wanted, literally everything: polished arguments and sophisticated ideas that she knew how to manipulate while scrutinizing their various facets; modern values and traditional ones that she mobilized, displaying their core and disconnecting their charges as she pleased. She knew how to plead and implore while she wept. How to play on vanities, how to pacify fears, how to inflame prejudices, how to tap the inflated pride and pat facile arrogance. She knew how to play meek and how to stoop. She also knew how to become a shrew, and harass. She would do everything. She would mold her body, mind, and complex make-up into a living, gushing weapon and attack. She would besiege from all sides, but with absolute honesty. She would use no weapon apart from herself: other than she and you and the relationship between you two alone—a relationship that truly sums up the entire world, though it does not transcend itself. She, her body and her soul, her womb and her intelligence, all of her, and only her; she, herself, is her own weapon and tool. No matter her ways and maneuvers, she is honest, completely honest. The matter is entirely between you and her. Nobody else, nothing else, outside the two of you has anything to do with it. Only the two of you. This is where her singularity and exceptional veracity lie. Only the two of you can decide what you want to do with this pliant and powerful drive, enveloping, immersing, and strangling each one of you with its unbearably soft siege.

She said to him: There is no sense in staying with me in the room, I am waiting for a telephone call. Don't you want to go to the museum or to a shop? You can just go window-shopping. Really, I don't want you to confine yourself here with me.

He said: What? How could this be possible? No, I will stay with you.

She said with irritation, as she glanced at him: Never. I don't want you to be irritated with me and with yourself in this shut-off room.

He said: But, my dear, I don't want to. I want to be confined as long as I am with you.

The confinement in the clouded density of the room was not relieved by the window—looking like an open wound—as if her presence with him, her flesh and her tense body, her nightgown over which she had slipped her faded wide skirt—all were filling the confinement with a panting density.

She said to him afterward: I'm going out for a while. I have an appointment.

He said: With whom?

She said: You know who, I told you about him.

She had told him about her friendship with the former Sudanese prime minister, the good-hearted old man with sharp intelligence and broad knowledge, still preserving the traces of Afro-Arab handsomeness. Out of medical and political reasons, he had opted for exile. She said to him: That man has witnessed the birth of all the children in my family. Whenever he visited Egypt, presents for them were on top of his list. The only time he enjoyed himself was when he was visiting us at our home.

The man had come two days before and greeted Mikhail coldly with his cold palms, indifferent eyes, discerning glances indicating discreet sharpness. They had watched a tennis match together on TV in the somber and bare sitting room with dispersed, unused, desolate, leather-ripped chairs. The man talked with the skill of an eloquent, experienced, aging, weary diplomat about tennis strokes and fate strokes. He went on with elaborate technical details about the game of tennis and the game of politics. She exchanged conversational eloquence with him. Mikhail never stopped wondering over her skillful discourse—calling on her swift, trained hands, her graceful, elegant mind—on a subject she didn't know the least about, but whose general contours she could sense from her interlocutor him-

108

self. Eroticism flowed continually from every pore in her body, mind, and eyes.

What lies between her and those old men, those decrepit remains of bodies and minds, who were once youthful and dazzling, who have left their imprints on the stones of history? She is always there in the background, effective nevertheless. Her erotic tenderness—soft, delicate—envelops those massive, dried out, hard-edged, left-over remains of men, who have experienced bygone masculine glories.

She had said to him: My heart goes to Don Quixote. I love him, I love everything in him.

The old man who does not want to let go of a lance placed in his hand by an extinct age.

She collected Don Quixote paintings, wooden and iron statuettes, metallic insignia etched with his distinctive figure. She also collected his personifications, his wasted dreams. He asked himself anxiously: Do I fight, too, the windmills? Yes, justice is impossible; love is impossible. Can I, then, give up? Can I resign myself?

When returning, she knocked on his door unexpectedly. She had come back early. He was having a brief afternoon siesta. Agitated, he was conversing, half-asleep, with people in his dream. He did not know who they were, but then he did know them. When he heard the knocks he got up in a hurry and opened the door, half-naked, not knowing exactly where the door knob was as he opened it. With a quick stern glance she said to him: Are you doing a striptease or what?

She said to him: What do you think? Do you think I am going to have an affair with you and I will be your mistress? This is ridiculous! I am not your mistress, and I will not be your mistress. We will not have an affair. Doubtless, there is another formula, yes, to be friends; that is all. We have to find this formula. A romantic friendship, perhaps.

109

She said: Where will all this lead us to? Nothing, perhaps.

His silence was, at that time, another treason.

O Rama, my distant beloved, am I simply a number in the economy of your cravings? Am I an equation between two brackets in the accounts of your passion and the pressing demands of your flesh? No, I am not the sum result of arithmetical calculation. No, there will never be an inevitable and neat solution to the problem.

Let it be. Isn't your gift of yourself, your gift of your offered body—even within the calculus of senses—a donation that cannot be substituted for, nor compared to, anything else? Why am I standing helpless before such a donation? You are marvelous in your offer. Yes, this pliant open body is offered to others, to *the* others, offered whenever the night sets, immersing it and baptizing it in the virility of the universe, in the wide, running, ever-changing river.

His rejection smacked of boyishness in the final analysis. He did, and still does, insist on the singular, the absolute, the unique. This is not to be found here, on the shore of a world where the sun rises and sets not for one, not for all, not for anything, not for anyone. The sun is not a constant sculpted burning disk in the petrified surface of the sky. The black night prevails then withdraws from this constantly anonymous mass, made up of infinite units without end and without distinctions.

The car was stuck, unable to advance much in the human torrent, moving mechanically, slowly, along Fuad Street. The exhaust smoke, the intermittent yet persistent honking horns, carbon dioxide, muffled curses behind car-window glass, the unrelenting whistle of the Security pick-up truck, filled with soldiers, hardly stopping yet unable to make its way through the traffic—jammed and creeping slowly, but not silenced. He said to her: What is happening? She did not answer. She was driving the small car, moving it bit by bit, changing gears and modifying speed, her foot rising up and pressing down. Her skirt was slightly above her knees; beneath it her legs showing. On the dusty black mat, partly pulled off from the car-floor, were the remains of a crushed matchbox, a folded and ripped cellophane paper, cigarette ashes, a ribbon of faded fabric. The leg next to him short; its calf tightly round. He could see the interior of the other leg's knee through the grayish, transparent hose—looking whitish because of the reflection of the back light filtered through the car-window. Her legs were two short pillars in a low-ceilinged, secret building. Just the same, they had an extraordinary smoothness, not the sort produced by a sculptor, but a smoothness obtained by the touches of several generations of worshiping hands. The car exuded, intensely, a smell of burning oil and burnt milk.

She said to him: Mikhail, will you open the window a little?

The urban clamor gushes in at once in mixed tones, pitches and rhythms. They arrive just in front of the Ambulance Center, and the clamor suddenly increases. Running toward them—as if attacking the front of their car, then swerving—come a group of boys in *jallabiyas*, pajamas, and loose trousers, jumping between the bumper-to-bumper creeping cars. The boys try to avoid the wheels of the trolley tram which, having raised the mass of its enormous body, stands in a tilt ed position, blocking off half the street. Cars from a suspiciously empty area come dashing at them; they circle and turn swiftly in the opposite direction, almost bumping into the slow advancing traffic. Not too far away, loud explosions and shouts of men sound weak in the brouhaha of automobile clamor.

A demonstration beside the Ambulance Center. Go back. Madam, go back. A demonstration. The police are shooting. Hands point, signal and disappear. Two police officers run—solitary and silent, as if they are running in a sporting event—toward the voices. Glass breaks and flies about. Slogans indistinctly articulated. In a wink—with unusual, exceptional speed—her car moves backward along an

111

incredibly narrow strip, circulating and maneuvering between cars charging from all intersecting, parallel, and opposite directions, amid the moans of brakes and the groans of horns. Her car backs toward a dusty side street with a narrow passageway that widens in front of her. Along open shops and cafés on the sidewalk people are smoking their hubble-bubbles. There is stagnant water in the sand. The narrow wooden doors have leathery-looking layers of accumulated dust. Laundry is spread on iron balconies, round-leaning, seeming glued together in the dark. In front lay odds and ends of things: cardboard boxes, tin cans, pieces of wood, trashy stuff too difficult to haul away by hand—all reflected in shadowy outlines in the light-ponds of street lamps. Huge dilapidated trucks are creeping slowly from a side street whose walls close around them. In front of a car-repair shop—tools, keys, and wheels on its dusty floor—stands a car with its bowels open. Beneath it, difficult to distinguish from the street dirt, stretch two thin black legs of a boy-mechanic, his face buried.

She swerves to avoid the stretched legs and barely misses the monstrous truck blocking the street. They find themselves away from the warmth of the crowds, from the friendly din, from the lights of grocers, mechanics, fabric shops, and vegetable carts. In the vast dusk he inhales the scent of the Nile water. Concrete columns, half constructed, sprout spiky branches of twisted iron skewers. Arranged heaps of wood rise up, pallid as bare bones. Deserted wet tram-rails shine in swamps of gravel and solidified dark cement. From this unusual angle the blurred, not so distant TV building towers. Into the sky of the winter night, lit with a strange glow: red clouds yellowed by the reflection of sodium lamps suggest a fire.

She is confused by multiple directions; he is taken by the spell of this unexpected ruined site in which an incomprehensible and deserted construction has been placed. She stops for a moment; she, too, is astounded. In the darkness, her face is mysterious, lit by a dis-

112

crete light. He says: Let's go back to Zamalek. This way. Abu'l-Ela Bridge is nearby. She says: No. He says: Then to Heliopolis, straight on from the Corniche Road then Shubra. I don't think anything's blocking that road.

A window is an unhealed wound in the massive wall. Behind such wounds the urban blood flows and gushes, himself exiled within. The strings connecting his wounds to those of the windows get snipped apart; nothing links them. The morning light falls on the plain white wall turning it into a dazzling, taut, warm sheet, as if it were a deathbed or an anatomy slab. The living fertile body, the one body, multiplied by thousands—here bloated, uncouth, and over-swollen with ill-gotten food; there emaciated and hollow, revealing yellowish bones thrown out on the floor of hunger and silence. This body of people rushes and gushes in the veins of Old Cairo: the mar-tyred, sullied, patient, licentious, obscene, loud, gilded, somber-faced, breath-choked. This body with its continuously burning eyes. This peopled body stretches, sobs, twitches, flows, swells, explodes, disbands; suddenly burns and screams. The cars speed on silently. "Forbidden. Go back. Go back. Take Salah Salem Road. Forbidden from here." Scattered stones and broken bricks in the midst of the asphalt. Minute glass crystals, their sharp-tipped fragments, are shavings on a black background. Upside down, ripped, and twisted signs. The lampposts inclined and somber with their open shaggy-wired heads.

In the morning, their youthful bodies were glued to each other, inspired by a childlike zeal and innocence. They had wrapped around themselves a rope that gathered them and defined them in the organ-ized outbreak of rebellion, attached to mysterious hopes and ancient, hoarse slogans. The raised, stretched arms are stalks of a tender, tena-cious plant swayed by the winds of hope and youth. The peasant woman, still wearing the long village dress with the gauzy *tarha*

113

wrapping her proud, long-necked head. Her broad, black, yoked *jallabiya* has a long side slit revealing an inner coarse chemise of blue tint, faded from frequent washings. She walks alone with no worries, pleading loudly to God to protect the youth and guard them from all harm. She is moving on, preoccupied with her own worries as if walking on the side of a canal in the village.

Late at night, the streets were silent. The clamor had receded. There were no more dashing shaky chassis with their grating mechanical whirring, emitting stifling exhaust fumes. Trees appeared beneath electric lights, as if for the first time: leafy, tremendous, owning a dense, nocturnal life. The houses became quiet, having closed in their somewhat frightened inhabitants. From behind locked doors, dim lights could be detected around window crevices.

Beyond the ever-present Nile, unseen and unheard in the darkness, he heard the crashes of other currents, blocked for a long time. The surging of masses in distant successive waves in the stillness of night, coming from the other shore, rising and falling in a rhythm that inspired him with awe. At a distance he cannot distinguish the strong, packed, frequent whiffs that the repressed volcano is stubbornly emitting. The grating deep voice of hundreds of throats threatens the night, the sky, and the shut-off, walled-in houses. It has an appealing and alarming echo that makes his eyes water despite himself. The echo brings back glories of his expired youth with its frustration lying in the deepest layers of his heart, muddy with aches and regrets.

The granite of this haughty body-of-people comes from youth challenging death and atrophy in the early afternoon. No blemish in it, smiling mysteriously as always. Powerful in front of the gods because this body is one of them, pulled from the distant giant polygons of the hot south, pulled from the dimness of candles and the awe of stillness in the distant past, so this body-of-people can rise up with invincible pride. Get up in the provincial, shabby, crowded square amid dusty long shells of trains twisting as they creep imprisoned within their rails or else deserted in parking lots, resigned to a rusty death. And yet he is among his folk, among his people. Around him circulates the non-stop traffic with its wheels and wires, buzzing as if it were a trivial game of the lowest level. The panting sirens are triggered, the red and green lights seem commonplace in the floodlight. The rock-like body-of-people is permanently youthful, its power will not pass away. But the world will pass away, leaving the scars, one scar atop another, thickening around the flesh of the heart. In this crust, the heart's blood beats with an endless pain.

Theirs are shriveled bodies, disappointed, torn, hermetic, that do not know how to glow with vigor except in the daze of hashish and the quickly-extinguished passions for female bodies. Theirs are unwatered bodies. The dirty desert sands are crumbled grains of rock. Their holiness comes not from the body or the sands. Within this undying body-of-people inflicted with wounds are the sorrows of these perpetual monks across deserts of generations, overcoming their powerful lust. They step over the ardor of their flesh with steadfast, spiritual feet, now rough and cracked. The living slender limbs are alert inside the hard rosy granite, unconquered by time. On the chests, crosses and vessels with crescents and sails made of delicately wrought gold and silver, as if they were lamps extolling the glory of God, illuminated with olive oil in marble niches, carved with the names of the Almighty. Limbs, growing and flourishing, as if they were plants and flowers.

Baffled heart-shaken groups become separated from the city-body as they wait and anticipate with anxious but controlled curiosity. In the thin, fatigued faces confronting the wind and sun with their inner concerns, and under the films of somber eyes—swollen from lack of sleep—veiled dreams and defiance glitter. The sun is like

115

an open eye with a fixed gaze, neither scorching nor responding. The metallic faded helmets glitter in the sun. The poorly-dressed, agitated, yellowish rows are falling from the freight wagons with discreet thumps over slender legs supported by the effulgent, coarse, new shoe-leather. A commanding yell, faint, abruptly cut off: "Go back. Go back." The huge rubber tires running then coming to a halt, loom high. In their grubby blackness is a beastly determination. In front of white clouds from low-voiced explosions, groups disperse with uncontrollable fear. The horses' hooves plunge into the soft asphalt. Towering broad shoulders under the pale faces that cannot grasp anything except the excitement of blood, the agitation of the people, their charged silence alternating with shouts. Desolate, tense, and lonely figures , close to each other, and throngs running with a thousand feet stepping on stones and stumbling on bodies, melting away into safe neighborhoods. Melting away in supportive alleys with broken warehouses, between always-opened doors, as they do not have locks. The dark and narrow stairways becoming safe shelter that cannot be touched by murderous explosions. The dirty, coarse, waterproof, faded-yellow covers dangling on thin skeletal rails, oppressive with their smell of wood and shoe-leather, of iron and stinking gun oil. The spray of bullets echos in the sudden stillness. The rustle of many running feet can be heard in streets emptied of the daily clamor of non-stop nocturnal traffic. Open eyes cannot grasp and will never grasp what has happened. Moans and bell-tolls from a distance. The flames in the winter midday light have ferocious and healing heat. Their light is the color of imperceptible sunflowers. No votive offering—impossible to fulfill—can undo their vengeful, full-throated, hissing voice. The flames lick the yellow government buildings constructed in old-fashioned British style with bare walls and criss-crossed rails on their broken-glass windows. The fire spreads to the cotton stalks and the alfalfa roots on the canals and drainage

116

ditches. It flares up in the barns with heavy black smoke. The death lowing of the slaughtered male buffalo, with blood spurting out silently from its hefty neck—nothing can stop it. The dark-red density flows out onto the crumbling soil with its half-black, half-yellow grains. Columns of black smoke, entrenched, lofty, acrid in the dry mouths, gyrating and going up amid the tongues of flame flying and whirring with wicked glow—colorless in the sun. Crushing of doors, crackling of glass, rending of walls, running with lean, shabby spoils; and calls no one can listen to. The hooves of the horses slam the black basalt rhythmically, emitting repeated echoes in the street emptied of traffic and familiar noise. In the swaying body of the city new and solid, obstinate knots are formed that soon dissolve and melt in mists of tear gas. In front of slim phalanxes of armors, clubs, and helmets, other small knots are formed. They bulge slowly, with outcries like the eruptions of an old painful disease. An outpouring of stagnant water, confined by oppression, by suffering, by daily toils that have neither explanation nor solution. The howling of the Tommy guns with their intermittent echoes, seemingly insignificant, leaves in front of it small bodies that fall suddenly as if they were insignificant piles of sorrow and worn-out clothes. They get transported quickly by hand to the sidewalk in the hope of a mercy that may or may not come. Slender-figured plants bend beneath the blows and collapse. These flowers that bloomed only for the course of a day and then were smashed, will they leave behind them regenerating seeds? The fiery and bitter flowers are quickly put out.

As if Mikhail felt the wounds, the cracks, and the burns in his own slight body, his other body lay buried between desert waves and the belly of soft soil. The dragon fidgeted from the stings of the sharp cuts left by stabbing spearheads. If only it had risen with its blazing eyes and wide-open, flame-blowing mouth with a thousand teeth. If only it had raised its strong firm back, balancing itself on

117

the huge tail covered with scales and taut muscles, then the pillars of heaven would sway and rock the nether world on which the black earth is mounted.

There, amid these bodies that derive—from their closeness—warmth and inspiration, pouring and overflowing the narrowness of their monotonous, packed life. There, amid these bodies that have assembled, do assemble, and will always and forever assemble in endless and arranged droves, shouting with a voice that is not simply the aggregate of their voices, but a voice coming from another realm. Gesturing, there, with hands that are considerably greater than the sheer number of actual hands, raising to the sky a pharaoh, the ancient one, with renewed faces, offering themselves, their blood and their soul, as sacrifice for him, looking for redemption, presenting their oblation to the pharaoh—he, the glory-maker—he, who makes the blood burst out; he, the caller to peace prayers. The bodies supplicate in front of Amon, the all-powerful, the almighty, the donor of bread, love, and pardon. These bodies make their way toward freedom, toward the sun with its mighty and merciful fingers. They know vaguely, but with certainty, that their sun is hidden inside their hearts. There, with them, is Mikhail's place and freedom. There, with them, he knew the intoxication of a wine not of this earth, of which she, Rama, is a part. There, with them, he knew this heat flowing into his blood as if resurrecting him from death. There, he did not realize that his voice had died out, and that those rhythmic slogans for which his ribs are swaying are theirs only, that he alone did not have a voice. There in 1946, the hand that threw the bomb was distant from him, yet it was his hand too. He did not hear the explosion and the British military vehicle that turned over suddenly, like a struck hawk, not far from the stern-looking, dark bronze statue. The soldiers with funny yellow shorts, a bit beneath the knee, jump down. In their hands a Tommy gun with short muzzle, drawn but not firing. They run inside the encircled wooden kiosk before a deep clamor follows them. In the following desolate nocturnal silence, the bullets have amplified echoes with a deep hollow ring to them. The bodies falling under the wheels by invisible shots, no one knows where they come from, as if they are suddenly the bodies of desert hermits—emaciated, thin, wasting, let-down, forgotten, no paradise awaiting them. When will the Kingdom of Heaven come? Without glory, thrown about on pebbles and sand, the hawks roam around them for a short while then suddenly attack from the heart of the white burning sky.

Yes, I love you. But in my love there is an inevitable betrayal.

He said to himself: This internal combustion is meaningless. This silence, too, is betrayal. You, alone, voiceless with no love of your own. Yes, I love you, and in the heart of this love lies a silence, a nucleus of inevitable betrayal. Nothing is inevitable. Crimes are forgotten, pass away, are probably pardoned. Nevertheless, in passing they leave no trace. Even the bones of victims and martyrs dissolve without being avenged, without justice, melting in the sand and dry soil.

But the flowers of rebels stay with open claws.

He said to her: Rama, we hardly know each other. There are entire regions in yourself, in your life, of which I know nothing and will never know. And there is a kind of entrenched, profound, and discreet intimacy between us as if it were there from before the beginning of time, an intimacy which overcomes all estrangement, and which needs no recognition.

When they returned in the early morning, the car stopped at the traffic light in the small square that had the smooth sculpture, the big cat with smooth sides. Its face was vacant, withdrawn—the hand on its head seems weightless, as if it were not there—the cat kneeling in almost obscene gesture. The old traffic policeman stands bored, almost dozing. The police officer with his transparent plas-

119

tic helmet and dark, tight clothes amid the cars, moving his head slowly and haughtily. A man calls out, without warmth, without rhythm: "Dustrags for ten. For ten, dustrags," holding in his hand a spread-out, clean dust rag that he swings monotonously while no one looks at him.

On the sidewalk next to the tall light post, beyond the thriving, thick trees, suddenly rises next to him this bare and dry tree, as if life had withdrawn from it. It is no longer waiting for spring. Impressive with its dark wood and black veins, its limbs intertwine sternly, as if the tree had long forgotten the pain that had caused it to split, to become tangled, distorted, and to fold upon itself. Its scream is frozen and mute with shrinking arms, stabbing the sky with twisted, slender, trailing long fingers, without hope, without despair.

6

A Broken-Legged Pigeon
beneath the Pillars

She leisurely opened her eyes. The morning, locked up in the room, was a satiated, quiet monster. Her relaxed body emitted a sigh of pleasure when stretching its naked, contented limbs. She said once more: Good morning, my darling. With a stolen kiss—a quick alighting of two delicate lips, having the gentleness of a soft-beaked bird pecking at a grain not out of hunger, but out of affluence. She stretched her arms around him, her body becoming taut with rising wakefulness.

Her eyes, two glittering rock-lakes, had in them this permanent open question, neither admitting nor accepting anything; knowing nothing, surrendering to nothing. She said, inclining her side toward him, as she gathered the faded-white sheet around her body:

Mikhail, you left the window open. Look what you have done.

—What?

—The morning air has invaded my shoulders. May God forgive you, my darling.

Her plump hand coursed over his rough cheek. In her eyes

121

something resembled a smile, and everything in her body lay calm and relaxed.

She said: Will you rub my back a little?

She turned over, giving him her back. The vale of her waist plunged down as the hill of her soft buttocks rose up—the line of their circular cleavage indicated beneath the shriveled white sheet.

This body, all of it, is a mask in its beauty, its strangeness and sleepy stretches; it contains nothing, has no message. Its warmth is generated as if from behind a smooth metallic surface that slips from hands. Its curves are deliberate, geometrical, foreign. He does not know their language.

The roundness of her bare shoulders: two solid, supple rocks on the sides of the elongated elevation of her back, surrendered to his hands. He caresses the soft vale with deliberation. His hands possess knowledge, elicit a special infatuation of their own. He senses a large feline's open eyes in the darkness of the old cemetery buried in the mountain. The sighs of deep, tender pleasure coming across times that do not pass away, under the scorching sun of the Valley of the Queens. His hands move to and fro with the rhythm of flagging funeral rites. He inclines his face without impetuosity, inhaling the sharp scent of the rough hair at the back of her head, aware of her smile taking place then disappearing. Under her right shoulder is a light, longish scar: trace of an old wound? Of a child's fall? Or a cut by claws made in an old lusty battle?

He said to her, from behind her head: There is an old wound on your back.

He did not go on; he came down with his lips touching the thin line as if trying to heal or erase it; clearly it was too late, much too late.

She said to him with her mouth buried in the pillow: Mikhail, what are you doing? Are you rubbing my back or caressing it? Beware.

Her laughter was faint, tense. His extended fingers moved faster; he pressed with the surface of his two palms, knowing they would never be filled. In one motion she turned on her back and opened herself to him: breasts pouring; the other face of her body, extended, rich, demanding suddenly, on display. She emitted her faint involuntary sighs. The merging of the two bodies, the joining of lips was instant. His virility fully awake; he felt in his eyes and in the tenseness of his figure the fierceness of attack.

She said to him in a plaintive, pleading, desiring tone: Mikhail, don't hurt me.

The world's rock collapsed. The column broke and fell; everything withdrew.

The contractions that followed announced failure. He joined his face to her shoulder: a pressing touch of failure and frustration that asked no pardon, a touch of hurt pride that neither apologizes nor asks for anything.

Her request "Don't hurt me" had reached him as words from a practiced professional. How many times had this exclamation been repeated with the same precision? The white light of a letter she had received only the day before flashed in front of his eyes. She had concealed the letter with an intimate, secretive gesture. How many— besides he—had hurt her? The repetitive act cancelled him, made him anonymous, a number in an unknowable mathematical progression, a nameless member of a certain class. He stopped being Mikhail and turned into an element, among others, in a recurring code whose symbols had been entangled and disentangled a thousandfold.

He broke down, knew for the first time how the old marble cracks. She was surprised by his failure. Her eyes vented cruelty, anger. He was not there.

He said to himself: This surprise is nothing new for her. She's expert at this game. For too long she's been living at the gates of Astarte, against the pillars of the Ramasseum that never collapse. The lives of others, the presence of others, is always within her. Who are

123

they? Who is *he*? She is aware and calculating; she is open-eyed even in the sigh just before reaching climax. This awareness isolates me, exiles me; it makes me, too, one of the others.

God can separate a man from his own heart. But why this cruelty from myself, from her?

He lay down, silent, withdrawn. Then he got up and sat in front of the window. The wintry dry tree was without flowers or leaves. The room around them was hostile, the morning dismal once again. The window was still cracked open, issuing cold air.

She said to him: Anyway, I will get in touch by phone at 5:30. If I don't call you then I'll see you at the Club.

He had said to her: I missed you a lot. I really missed you. It seems as if I haven't seen you for ages.

She said: It's wonderful to hear this from you. It really uplifts my morale.

He said: I never hear anything of the sort from you.

She said: You know I don't say such things. I assume you know them.

Her voice was tight, dry, on the verge of breakdown.

He said: There is never ever anything assumed in such matters.

She said: I hope you'll wear the white pullover, so you can remember me.

He said: I don't need it to remember you.

He said to himself: Wasn't it nice that she had told him such a thing before—that she'd missed him—despite her claim to the contrary?

He went back to his *idée fixe*, recurring to the point of boredom: This romance is sullen, stern, overwrought. Even now I cannot believe it. It's as if it were a badly-written romantic novel, with ready-made clichés. Does all this talk mean anything? It's a struggle with words, isn't it? Tiring to the utmost. There is neither victory nor defeat. Will unity and fusion be realized? Is it the struggle of Jacob with the angel on the staircase that does not reach heaven? Is it a stumbling, awkward Hamlet without tragedy, and no stage? Have I ever considered my life, taking into account the defeats and victories? Not at all. How many defeats have fallen on my soul and body? How many victories? How many miscarried intentions, burnt out dreams, black suns?

He said: Why these blue sunglasses? The sun is not so strong right now.

She said: Don't they suit me? Look. Too big on my face? What about the color? Darker than it should be?

He said: That's not the point. They suit you very well. Everything you put on partakes of your beauty.

She said: God bless you, my love. You always compliment me.

He said: No, it is true. But why the sunglasses in the late afternoon?

She said: To erect a wall between me and the world.

He said: Oh, please come off it. What wall? No wall can ever stand between you and the world. You, yourself, are a cosmic force.

He said to himself: This cliché is very suitable.

He said: Forgive me. I am happy today, an irrational happiness: a strange receptivity for no reason. Alertness and openness toward everything, all day, after your telephone call this morning. Once I knew I would be meeting you, the rhythm of the day became more dynamic, more refreshing, livelier and larger than life itself.

Her large, round, bronze earrings were swaying under her ears in a gypsy mode. Her arms, their downy hair barely visible in the sun, ended with broad silver bracelets holding the wrists in tight confinement, inciting an erotic mood.

She looked at him with scrutinizing eyes, a look that freighted contentment and something else, as if she wished he would be easier, simpler, happier, and more direct than he was. Of course, she knew she was dealing with him, himself, as he was, and that such wishes were sterile and pointless. It was as if she were saying: Doesn't he go

125

too far in the seriousness of this love, doesn't he go too far in his anguish, his pride, his rejection, his devotion, without ever actually moving in one of two possible directions?

Long spells of torment and misery had gotten hold of him. Now there was this lively and joyful tremor shaking his body after a period of depletion.

He said to her, to her person that he kept within himself, but while physically looking at her, yet as if he were not seeing her: Not bad, not bad at all. I was expecting all this, or half expecting it. It has become a completely familiar pattern. No, no, let me finish what I need to say. The fact is, I don't admit such things. I must say that I have made a fool of myself, the perfect image of the fool in these matters. Just the same, I am not sorry. But I hope that now you are content, whatever the reason is behind your contentment. No, don't give me good justifications and arguments, exact and logical reasons. They too are possible, even facile. I want the real reason—if there is such a thing— if you are really ready to put it forward. We have reached now an implicit agreement to avoid the issue of the real problem and the essence of the real question. Real? Is there ever anything real? Well, I have in mind something, and you do too. But I know that my version of the real is different from, even contradictory to yours. One cancels the other. But what would I know? Do I know the implicit agreement, which is not to answer the genuinely important questions, not to ask them even, and that that is the crux of the matter? Here we are now. Do I love you? I ask myself this question a thousand times and I answer in the negative a thousand times—no, no, no. Yet I love you. Even now, my love is a rock that cannot be displaced.

In the twilight that always carries with it an ambiguity not to be resolved, the bite of yearning for your arms gets hold of me suddenly. Lonesomeness is increased, becomes unbearable when one is in love. I am tormented by a desire to meet people, to drown my lone-

126

liness in words, in chatter, in sarcasm, in a glass of whisky with water and ice. With sex too. Easy solution? No. There are no solutions. Sex is passing, an act of emptying tension—mechanical and organic, mere penetration of flesh. I am in a car creeping through crowded and noisy streets, helpless and defenseless, when the silent light of a car comes from the opposite direction with incomprehensible and hidden power. A stab in the pallor of sunset.

He said to himself: Childish torments are painful for grown-ups.

I am alone in the taxi, when a whiff of your perfume reaches me from nowhere, from the burning Nile sky in the evening, from above the crowns of desolate trees on the island soil of the other shore, between high-rise buildings, wires, trees, columns, the ancient obelisk and minaret, emerging from a land I thought I had left and forgotten. The pale moon drips blood in the sky. The falling of blood on earth has a subtle effect. The dry sand and the green grass are soaked with blood. The stabbed sky-flesh still drips blood. I love you, though I curse you and resent you a thousand times. A thousand times my heart inclined in devotion. Yes, this is your old song.

He bent over her in his room. There was this whiff of body scent. He had made coffee. He bolted it while looking at her, smiling because he was with her. She left her coffee to cool. She sat on the armchair, open-legged, steady in her low-heeled expensive shoes. The shoes looked old, dusty, soft, carelessly put on, as if they were an extension of her feet's strong flesh. Her eyes were heavy, her body exuding its lustful melody.

How beautiful she is today—after a month's absence? Impossible? Not really. This long night of wounded pride, of buried desolation, of the usual love-sickness, seemed incurable. But now he is cured, his heart awakened and flourishing. How gentle her gaze on him, yet what a stranger she seems to him.

A soft and supple sense between two old friends in middle age is

127

like the touch of figs whose skins have thinned, almost breaking and falling at the last stage of ripeness, yet delicious in the last moments of their tenacity. He said to himself: As if I had not known her before yesterday, yet as if I had known her all my life. His sharp desire quivers, flashes, glowing steadily on a calm fire. He feels indulgent as he approaches her, as they join together. He closes his eyes to the faint traces left on her face by the fingers of time—the imprints of birds on a sandy shore. The slight heaviness of her hands, their exciting tenderness. The intimate affection between two embracing bodies, without complications, with erotic yearning coming out of him now—without frantic flaring—flowing in a steady current of tenderness. Her clothes lay dispersed on the armchair, on the clothes rack, on the edge of the bed and the small table. The sides of her black bra adorned by lace are dangling, the clasp made of silvery thin metal; between the cups a tiny rose of red fabric, somewhat wilted, shriveled. Her long, beige, transparent panty-hose is on the armchair: one of its legs swings free without reaching the floor. Her spread-out skirt on the wooden bedstead seems ample, strange, empty, though its tightly-woven fabric feels warm as if it retained a dark intimate spot of her sweat. He feels secure, trusting in this feminine presence that surrounds him now, as if it were a signal along a somber road whose ending is unknown. Once more, he recognizes the sharp, rich womanish smell, that of every woman. The whiffs of powder and sweat, the taste of honeyed saliva, the scent of worn, diffused perfume, the warmth of the barely flowing juices. He is surrounded by the fragrance of light, pungent whiffs, by the aromas of love in this female body as he buries his face in its folds, in its pleats and tucks. The body that gets endlessly recreated, always renewed, surprising each time, yet still the same body. Suddenly he feels strange, the object of an invasion. In the moment of intimate merging, she steals away. There is only this tight, tender entity, nameless and impersonal even though possessing specific features—familiar yet without identity—which his hands

128

know and plunge into without difficulty or effort. A familiar body yet unknowable fills his arms now. Her hard surfaces soften with the fresh moisture of assurance. The last silent kiss, as she looks contentedly and quietly at him, reveals her small white separated teeth. A tangle of rough hair sticks to her narrow forehead, as if waiting. The two of them fall into a quasi-slumber, almost oblivious of each other. He ridicules himself a little, contentedly though, since he senses his power and confidence in the usual masculine triumph. Her obedient, subservient body with its bright skin, the color of sand, undulates one last time, its waters flung on the shore in an effort for final consummation.

This gift that is never the same: each time it is something unique and extraordinary. So what worry of his is eating him up?

She had said to him: Yes, I love you. Haven't we spent six days together? Isn't this an expression of affection?

He said to himself: As if she hates the word love, no sooner does she mention it than she withdraws it. Isn't she simply being truthful though?

She said to him: I sacrifice myself for those I love.

She had said to him: You . . . You have not yet reached this stage.

She was scrutinizing him, without provocation, without hurry.

On the inside wall next to the window, there was an amulet, a folded square of animal skin, hanging with a triangular string from a small nail—a charm made to counter adversity and bring about love. Next to it sat the mummified fetus of a small crocodile of solid yellow with open, black eyes.

On my shoulders I carry dreams and a bundle of frail but heavy reeds. I shall sing to you, Rama, the songs of my ancestors, as I walk to Memphis the capital, carrying my burdens, carrying my dried up dreams. This Nile is my wine and Memphis is a bowl of soft ripe figs. I fear my grip will be too much for them. In the reeds of the river, I shall find Ptah of knowledge and truth. My trajectory along the edge

129

between the reed and the wine is endless. Ancient waters flow between you and me. Their waves are solid, fixed beneath my feet. I feel your body as an amulet and charm. Your breath scorches at times, like the desert; at others, it moistens with the scent of earth and of watered greens. From a distant death you revive me, and my body flourishes. You open your lips and I am intoxicated. You say: Don't you want to pass your hands over my legs? I say: Thirsty I am, my love. Then you say: Here is my breast, drink, my beloved. Your eyes, Rama, are two fallen birds and it is not in my hands' power to save them from snares.

Considerably later than midnight, having left behind them the tremendous Imbaba Bridge—which seemed intricate to him, as if vaulting huge circular arcs, layer after layer, through a frozen movement of time—they reached her house. The car stopped in an open yard near the sandy road—everything indistinct at night. She opened a small wooden gate in a low fence constructed with sun-dried bricks and whitewashed with lime that glowed pale in the dark. Among the fields and narrow roads, in the heart of the cultivated areas, there were small, awkward, broken-sided buildings amid the trees. Her four dogs barked with welcoming excitement, then made plaintive cries that were not only welcoming but also freighted an organic and physical yearning. They wallowed on the soil and jumped all over her, throwing themselves at her legs when she bent down. They nibbled gently on her hands, licking them, whimpering affectionately in what goes beyond welcome and longing, becoming a kind of adjoining and joining. Their soft paws were feeling, touching, and hanging on her hands, legs, and face, while she was babbling affectionately with them, as if addressing them in their language, using soft sounds that had the same whimpering and plaintive tones as their own. They formed a mass of five bodies, all one with multiple limbs, expanding and contracting in the intoxication of reciprocal infatuation.

She said to him as she raised her head from this sensuous drama

130

that nevertheless had no obscenity: They have been waiting for me. I am the only one who gives them food, no matter how late I might be. I am the only one who trains them, takes care of them.

She called out: Mabrouka! Ya Mabrouka!

A woman's voice came: Yes, Madame, right away. The voice was saying to someone inside, Madame Rama has arrived. From behind the vague darkness, weak electric light, pale and yellowish, was snapped on. She said: Bring the dogs' food.

From beyond the open yard that looked lighter among the dark squares, the fields in the night seemed silent, hot, depressed. In them stood the bodies of crooked old machinery, small tractors, agricultural implements with tremendous, vast, blunt teeth. Their outlines merged en masse in the darkness now soaked with faint morning light. The old trees with their enormous twisted trunks and their packed, profuse, thick branches seemed like good-hearted, strong-muscled guards breathing deeply in their nocturnal wake. The trees possessed animal powers. The dogs howled and whirled at each other, at her, at the food. In front of them were boiled heaps of bones and scraps of offal and bone joints in chipped, dark glowing pots. The dogs took their mouths away from her hands, as if with difficulty, then went back to her, pushed by hunger for food no less organic than their hunger for her. The cracking of bones in the dogs' teeth was mixed with the supple sounds of munching, of tender smacking, of voiced swallowings.

In the tiled corridor under its stony unpainted ceiling sat a long Istanbuli sofa covered with an embroidered peasant fabric and small rumpled, stuffed cushions. Asyuti armchairs with their long wooden backs and a tightly-woven plaited mat exuded a pale bronze sheen in the faint morning light. The mat was glued to the ground as if sprouting directly from it with ferocity and power.

He glimpses a female figure through an open window: she feels with trained, sensitive hands the teats of the buffalo—full and painfully

131

swollen with milk—employing slight and comforting pressure that emp-
ties from them the toil of pleasure-giving. The milk trickles intermittently and hits, in light sprays, the walls of the black earthenware pot
lined with foam the odor of fresh hot cream. The two hands have their
own skill in releasing pleasures. They feel about the taut column and
press on the back of the neck. They encircle the green shoots of arugu-
la just above their roots and pull them with their moist mud out from
the edge of the small canal under the upright, steady, reddish flax stalks.

She had said to him: You know, Mikhail, I am not difficult at all.
This is just a sip of water for me, a mouthful of plain fresh bread. I
can climax in a minute, I know how to give myself pleasure.

I do not see myself except beneath the murderous, solid light on
Cairo's cement, among its ancient stones, amid the clamor of asphalt
and the whiz of elevator buttons, amid hoarse groans of metallic cars
that possess none of the elegance of earthenware pots, nor the freshness of plants plucked with their roots from the soil, taking along knot-
ty grains of earth's dark moisture, almost breaking up, grain after
grain. I bury my yearnings in the soil of the old earth and forget them.
You are a field full of clover flowers and flax; on your bosom are the
fruits of love. Do you hear the twittering of my birds perfumed with
the pungent scent of myrrh, the quacking of geese amid reeds in the
night of my childhood on which the sun never rose? I long no more
for the sun-bread that is instantly cooked, without yeast or oven, on
wooden boards under the sun of Akhmim on the roof of the elevated
old house whose staircase rises in the shaded, fresh midday darkness. I
long no more for the thick, white crust enveloping the cooked doughy
core that melted in the mouth with a fertile, erotic scent. My sympathy
for earthy plants—tender and fierce at the same time—has dried out.
Nothing excites me any more except the flutter of transparent feminine
fabrics on the shining body folds, the skillfully intelligent coloring, the
embellishment of brilliant, sly, undulating music of metallic surfaces

and polished plastic, reflecting in their roundness and sharp lines the echoes of distinct glittering images. When you say to me that my love penetrates your body like an aimed taut lance, my bird fumbles around in the wind; when you come to me, you are joy itself. The hawk has steady wings in the heart of the sky; it neither dives to attack nor rises up. I recall the dark-red lipstick with small mirrors, silver-striped with aluminum frames on ready-made corners; I recall the blue turquoise eye shadow on the eyelids, full of hot painful fluid. I recall them when I wallow my face in the embers of cool grass close to the earth's soil, the nearby waters of a canal the color of light coffee, with eddies of sluggish water swiftly whirling handfuls of shaggy grass and other innocent-looking trash toward the hand-dug openings to fields having the color of your bosom and its fresh nakedness. I feel no more than a slight yearning for the other Mikhail, as if he had achieved manhood in a bygone world. I stretch my hand to him, but it doesn't reach any-thing. We are strangers. I and the other I. We know each other totally, invisible barriers of estrangement stand between us, refusing passage.

She narrated to him:

This relation between me and him is very special. Not in the sense that may come to your mind (his belief in her was on hold). I will tell you his story with me, but promise not to tell it to anyone. Never. Do you promise? The question of privacy is not related to me but to him. It is a matter of his security, possibly his life, I am not exaggerating. Don't say 'Rama and her stories.' No one in the wide world knows this story except three, and I am one of them. I am the only one who did not actually partake in the story. It was on the first dawn of 1959, when Nasser imprisoned them. Do you recall?

He said: How can I not recall? How truly strange all this is. How small the world is. In the morning of that very day, I drank cappucci-no with him. I was in Simonds and he entered. I wished him a happy new year and we talked for a while when we were having coffee.

133

He lit two cigarettes and handed her one. She grabbed it with awkward, tense fingers.

—Were you friends?

—I knew him, but friends? No. I have very few friends. I used to follow his writing and I respected him. He had a sort of dynamism, alertness, broad-mindedness. Has this turned awry now? I wouldn't know.

Definitely his escapades have no end now, and no logic of course.

—So you two were friends, on the one hand, and, on the other hand, he and I were friends or something of the sort. Years go by and we don't know these things . . . is this your proof that the world is small?

As if she had listened neither to his childlike wonder nor to his sarcastic tone at this very wonder. As if she couldn't care less for his discovering in these intertwining trajectories a mystery and significance which he barely tried to clarify. She accepts effortlessly his obsession with finding links, relations, meanings—this chronic but not so serious ailment.

—On that night he came to me in the early evening. We made a crucial decision. The discussion went on all night, but thanks to this decision, he was one out of three or four who were never detained.

He said: That is correct. It was Hashem who left via Libya—wasn't it on a camel? And Abdel Ghani . . .

She said impatiently: Of course. If you have some money and some connections, you don't need a passport or a visa.

He discovered once again his naïveté. He felt that despite his immersion in the past world of revolutionaries, the virginal days, he had always remained on the margin. The practical details, that is, the most important details, had always been strange to him. His experience with that world was passé now, indeed carefully forgotten, as if it had been the experience of a person he had heard of. How many persons had lived or died beneath his skin?

She said: For almost three months he didn't leave the seaside

134

apartment I rented for him in Sidi Bishr. He was with Hasan. Once a week I used to take them what they needed. I used to wash and cook for them and also entertain them. Hasan was arrested later, as you know. It was not possible for Hasan to travel: he wouldn't accept it. He took a political stance on the matter; or was it perhaps for my sake?

—How did *he* travel?

—He traveled with me to Port Said. Since 1956 I'd had friends in that port: courageous native seamen who still remembered the time we were subjected together to British bullets. We went together in the Ismailiya train; Hasan wore a native *jallabiya* and I donned the native *mudawwara* to cover my hair, and the castor gown with yoked bodice. He, of course, could not handle at all the ferrymen and the bum-boat hawkers. But you know how I love people and how people love me. Behaving gallantly means more to those people than anything. Yes, money may be important, but, for them, what is truly necessary is generosity, valor, honor. This is true. And since the days of 1956, they have never forgotten Fatma—the freedom-fighting journalist who crossed with them from al-Manzala. Mikhail, where have those days gone?

With a faint voice touched by timidity, he said: Such glorious days get forgotten, but in some sense they stay forever.

She went on narrating her story as if she wanted to finish, in a matter-of-fact, practical manner.

—From the boat in Port Said, then out to the Italian cargo ship far from shore was easy.

He said: He is indebted to you for his freedom, for a change in his entire life.

She said: Mikhail, come off it. Why dramatize? Who knows who owes what to whom? Who knows how life's trajectory will change any of us?

He did not say to her: All these stories—narrative weavings of chases and conventional adventure plots that cannot be imagined

135

except in fiction and films—happened yesterday, in this place. A good-hearted friend was murmuring some words—inarticulate, insignificant as usual—talking to me in the midst of the New Year crowd with the joyful festivities on the stage at Simonds coffee shop, as we were sipping the lip-burning cappuccino with its light-colored foam, exchanging good wishes for the New Year. "May every year find you well." "You too." Anxiously said, yes. With hope and concern, perhaps. But without knowing the seriousness of the blow that was destined to befall him, befall us, that night.

What a wealth of details lie in hiding, in anticipation, in disguise and bargaining, in traveling third class in trains, entering ports, crossing borders with small boats on rough waves. He said to himself: There is nothing strange at all, no more tension in all this than what you would find every day, at every step, in every direction, with any intention or hidden purpose. These details, no one knows; they are your own concern, and no one else cares about them. In them alone lies the drama. It is something between you and yourself. No one knows the tension except you. Daily, practical life that moves on and stops for nothing immerses you in its swift current just the same. Who cares to know whether you are a highly-educated revolutionary pursued by the State, or a simple traveler with round face and a jacket covering your native *jallabiya,* struggling to make ends meet for your family? Who cares to know if this woman with the *ouya*-embroidered *mudawwara* head-cover and the old overcoat worn over the gown is a militant mistress, an affectionate friend, or a housewife traveling to her family in Port Said? Throngs of people circle around each other, bumping each other for a moment. Their bumps are calculated and limited, having recognizable conventions and rituals to which no one pays too much attention. All encounters are practical, clear with familiar patterns. The important thing is to have with you the money for the ticket and to stand in line with the people, to know

136

the door you knock upon and the man you greet, the café in which you will find him and smoke *shisha* with him, or drink tea with him. As for the paths, they have been charted and are open, teeming with footsteps—their codes well known.

He said, as if continuing a dialogue with himself: Really, Rama, do you know that death, love, and freedom are all abstractions, illusions, and *idées fixes* that no one sees and no one knows? The contraction of the heart muscle, the expansion of the chest, the storming of the brain—no one knows these things except from inside one's self, in one's own experience. All that others know of me is abstraction, approximation, impression. The important thing is the steady hand, or at least the one whose shaking is not evident, as long as it grasps what is needed. Pray for the leg that knows where to set its foot, even if on the inside it's wobbling. Be satisfied with the familiar tone of voice that knows what's required and pays the price. All this is not trivia.

She said: You move quickly from one extreme to another. Freedom, love, and fear are surely not abstractions. You are, like him, a Copt and a southern Egyptian, and you know it.

He said: What? He a Copt? I never knew it. He didn't seem so.

She said: Of course he is. What do you mean "he didn't seem so"?

He said: A Copt? Don't you mean, of Levantine origin?

She said: A Copt, a Copt from southern Egypt.

He said: Then he is a kin of sorts—from my part of the country!

He laughed, enjoying this new face of kinship between himself and the old revolutionary who had exiled himself.

She said: His mother had a strange and decisive role in his life—of course. And he's still a Mama's boy. He was married, had children, divorced, but he continues to be madly devoted to his mother. Twice he failed in marriage, because he conceived of women as facile harlots. As for the wives, he saw in them a sacred mother for whom he would always yield. But then things always got turned on their heads.

137

Unhappy in his intimate life, he doesn't feel quite right except with a one-night woman. In the end he's very much torn apart.

A question flashes in his mind suddenly: Whom is she talking about? Whom does she mean?

Later she said to him: Mikhail, I think you viewed me as the evil dimension in your life, the dimension of corruption, decadence, and unethical pleasure. Your conceptions drove me mad, but I hid my feelings from you.

He was surprised. For the first time she surprised him genuinely. In fact, he was alarmed. It had never occurred to him that she saw him this way. So little did she know him. She saw in him the chaste puritanical man who drops the primness of good behavior once he's with her, surrendering for a wicked moment of pleasure.

He exclaimed: What? Is this possible? Strange. Very strange. Impossible. Can't be true.

She was silent but not convinced. He was honest but not convincing. In many instances honesty is not convincing at all. But why was he alarmed?

He thought anxiously to himself: Did she know how to be the woman with whom he felt the absence of taboos?

He knew that she, herself, did not give a hoot for sexual conventions—all of them put together—not matrimony or fixed special relations between a man and a woman, or all other varied financial–sexual institutions.

He said to her: It's not important what you narrate and what tale you tell. What's important is that you are the narrator.

She said: I don't know what you mean.

There was, however, a look of understanding in her eyes.

He did not comment.

They had been walking in the broad elegant streets looking unsuccessfully for a cup of coffee until he despaired and gave up. They sat

138

before the museum on a solid wooden bench with rounded back in the slow, late evening. The light of dusk tarried at the edge of the sky, stabbed equally by adjoining lofty towers, with stretched arms, and by triangular roofs whose dark red tiles have faded. The wide, marble, ivory white staircase, lofty but slightly worn down, rose in front of their eyes with an entrenched, steady, and soft dignity. The staircase rose beneath the elegant, skillful Greek columns—blackened designs in their capitals—that faced a row of self-contented, old, and dignified houses. Their longish windows, resembling each other, had lowered curtains. The street was empty. The few cars passing in it were quiet, a depressed light falling on them. Large, heavy, gray-breasted birds jumped around late in the day on the marble staircase and on the columns' capitals. These pigeons suddenly alighted from house roofs in the early dusk to pick up imperceptible grains under the thick, leafing trees of the small yard.

Neither of them said anything as there was nothing left to say. But they were together inside this silent spell. The light of dusk revives strange yearnings that he cannot understand: nostalgia for youth, dreams of the adolescent years inside his small room in their old house in Ragheb Pasha. The noise of the living crowded neighborhood has quieted down now. His window overlooks an inner skylight in a wall seizing a slice of Alexandrian sky whose blueness deepens in the twilight, soon disappearing. He would have been reciting youthful poems with their regular beat and childlike sorrows, bittersweet, rocking the dazzling, innocent, first wounds. Tears were sweet then, and gratifying. The yearning of this adolescent, not yet knowing how to be mature, seizes his heart within the old grip—tenderly wrenching the hard, deep sorrows. Across distances of time, the piercing sudden cries of the sunset curlew reaches him, ripping the invisible sky as if with a knife—without answer. He sees a lead-colored pigeon with swollen breast, slow, jumping up with one flattened leg, sprouting light white feathers, on the marble of the staircase, lifting up in vain the other leg from

139

the floor, for it is broken. Doubtless it knows where it is heading with its unsteady, patient, and obstinate steps. He said to himself: Don't be so considerate. Leave off this sentimentality. It is too facile. A broken-legged pigeon, so what? I guess you find in it some naïve allegory. Won't you stop making metaphors and similes? You stopped writing poetry a long time ago, didn't you?

Sparrows and pigeons, gathering in rings, circle and flap their wings then dart off like arrows to the column capitals, to the tangled leaves. He can see no longer his full-chested, heavy pigeon.

Rama was singing in a low, hoarse voice neither beautiful nor melodic, yet of ambiguous appeal nonetheless. The verbal rhythm was faint amid the marble columns under the summer sky: *A white pigeon, how can I get hold of her? Oh, mother, a white pigeon flew away with her partner.* Her small mouth hardly opened when she sang. She was humming the song as if she were alone: *Oh, mother, he knew her language.* It seems to him that he does not know, nor does he want to decode, all the phrases of this language: of the lofty columns, of the pigeon cooing hopelessly with hoarse whispering *aloooone, aloooone,* of the marble sky and of Rama extending her hand without expecting help. They went off looking for a cup of coffee or an apéritif before dinner, under dusky clouds now darkening, their deep redness fading out.

An ambulance siren wails like a nocturnal lament. In his agitated sleep, he recalls the lonely cry of the curlew. She turns over in her bed, says with a voice coming from the clouds of slumber:

Good grief, that sound at night is foreboding.

He said to himself: What a woman! She too has forebodings and premonitions from incomprehensible portents—she who uses reason, logic, and ruse as intellectual tools!

He stretches his hand, pats her hair. She shrinks from him then presses her head on his chest.

When they go down to the restaurant, taking the round, narrow

140

staircase, there is, in the midst of the warmth and vapor of boiling water and in the hum of kitchen tools, a hole of loneliness from which the two of them cannot figure how to extract themselves.

He said to her: Do you blame yourself for something? Maybe you've not forgiven yourself.

She said simply and affectionately: Mikhail, don't be silly.

He said: I am not asking you to forgive yourself. I want . . . how I want to remove the first cause of your misery, to remove from you the burdens of others.

She said: I don't know exactly what you're saying or what you want. But can't you accept that I might need to live with these burdens. You have to take me as I am.

He said: Truly I can't imagine you changing.

She said: We all want several things simultaneously.

She is now spreading the butter on the toast in front of her in a detached manner, without looking at him. She does not bother to spread butter on toast for him.

She continues: Isn't this natural and normal, and shouldn't we accept it?

He says: I don't know how to accept things. A meaningless fact, I'm aware. But I don't know how, believe me. I always reach dead ends.

She says: It's your nature to be skeptical for no reason.

He says: This is my darkest side. I'm not able to do this—just accept things—with anyone, not at all. I was hoping, for no reason, you'd continue nevertheless to care for me, as you say. I was thinking I might possibly get healed, might justify my existence. About this particular point, yes. I can't get rid of this childishness.

She said: It's not childishness. Don't blame yourself. Do you enjoy feeling guilty?

He said: I know you've stopped caring for me already.

She said: Mikhail . . .

141

He said: I don't know why you cared for me in the first place. Was it a sumptuous gesture of yours, a crush, a generosity, simple curiosity? Or was it a supplement to an installment in some series?

She said: You are needlessly unfair and cruel. Not to me alone but to yourself, as well. Can't you see there's nothing making me listen to all this from you, except . . . Can't you see this?

He said: Yes. Yes, I see it, and I am thankful and grateful.

She said: Don't ever say that word.

He said: You are very complex. Yet very primitive—simple like first elements. Aren't you? I don't know. I don't know you.

She said: No one knows me better than you. Don't you know how to speak simply on anything without anatomizing it?

He said: I don't know how to speak. I don't play with words, nor do I select them and embellish them. I am in front of something very intricate yet very simple and stern. I am trying to reach this something in you, this foreign yet terribly intimate thing.

She said: I won't say that I pardon you. There is nothing to be forgiven or forgotten, as they say.

She said to him all of a sudden: Mikhail, how old is your mother?

He was baffled but told her.

She said to him: I'll see you on Wednesday.

She did not come but called and said: I'll see you today.

But she didn't come then, nor did she call.

Their hippie friend goes ahead of them with his girlfriend to the next table. On his chest are metal chains clinking and "Make Love Not War" buttons. His messy beard reveals a smile like those of children, and moist dark lips. He wears an embroidered black Indian jacket with slits on the side, over a thick, soft, ripped, leather vest and heavy-fabric, faded-blue jeans. His wide belt is perforated with ornaments, embellished with silvery, round nails.

He says to her: Good morning.

142

7

Isis in a Strange Land

They agreed to meet at the door within ten minutes. Her
voice on the phone was cheerful, gay as an adventurous
little girl's.

He shaved, washed his face, put his hair under the cold water tap.
Then he changed his mind, took off his clothes hurriedly and chaot-
ically, throwing them here and there in the unfamiliar bathroom in a
manner quite unlike himself. He got into the shower. The water came
down on his body splashing and abundant, quickly, as he breathed
deeply. He emerged from the shower glowing. A current of renewed
youth flowed through him.

The elevator came up for him without delay—a good sign. In ten
minutes exactly, he was standing at the door. He noticed, with a sense
of self-tolerance, that he still found good and bad omens in little
daily things, finding in them signals and warnings.

She came out slowly and gently from the double glass doors, like
a large heavy bird, and he smiled at her, a serene smile.

Once outside they found delight in centuries-old buildings,

143

their partly ruined, high fences surrounded by entangled trees. The branches were crooked, dense, dark green, tender, tumbling down. Delighted too by the old shiny tram, with its rails chattering between the black basalt strips of pavement in streets with few passersby. Delighted by lit windows of closed stores and bookshops, with terrace cafés and their leather and aluminum seats under large umbrellas with colored fabric, leaning under steady neon lights. Delighted with stairways, with marble columns, old and luminous beneath the animated lights seeming to dazzle with their own intelligence. They laughed at the good-hearted faces of old ladies with emaciated bodies. As for the younger set, they turned around together looking at the elegant steps of bare, curved legs beneath miniskirts. Their attention was drawn to the effective simplicity of a church below street level with its old medieval style, devoid of ornamentation. They noticed the boring pornographic film signs and the dimly lit vestibules of their entrances. Their footsteps were light as they walked through large squares with fountains sprinkling clear water beneath towering trees. They went down narrow and deserted streets between high, massive walls with no vents. Red traffic lights stopped them at wide boulevards packed with huge, lofty department stores as the crowds of the evening mixed in a calculated pattern, with a succession of cars and engines pushing and rising suddenly to hoarse roaring, then soon enough falling into a regular whirring. At the intersections he took her tender hand, which felt small in his. Whenever they crossed streets to the opposite side she put her arm in his with spontaneity and a sense of assurance as they watched the intricately decorated and packed-up shop windows—the dark ones and the ones with sly, rotating, colored lights. They conversed freely with the joy of discovering a new city and a new friendship. His eyes were gazing at her with admiration, affection. Her eyes in that rounded, soft face of hers were

144

stealing speculative glances at his eyes without any indication of danger or threat.

He said to himself: The beginning was quite innocent, childlike, not even recognized for what it was.

They descended a few steps to a cafeteria and a restaurant decorated with marble and tin plates, lit by cheap lights, choked with warm odors of food and coffee, with whirring and whizzing sounds emanating from mighty stoves and bright kitchen devices. They ate off small round plates on top of carefully folded, frail, paper table mats of light brown color with a sketch of the Coliseum, the restaurant's logo. They drank espresso coffee, he felt its unusual pleasure, its aroma alone, erasing the food's fatty taste in his mouth.

They ascended back to ground level and walked beneath dark arches supporting solid buildings, walked amid huge columns around which so many signs were glued that no vacant space on the flesh of the curving black marble was visible in the dusk. She clapped with her hands as she ran up other stairways that seemed without end. No sooner did she sit on the large marble upper landings than she jumped up laughing, saying that the marble was cold, having sat on it with her light skirt and been bitten by its chill. Over them soared the Four Horsemen of the Apocalypse, made of white stone, looking in the night lights somewhat worn out, their edges smoothed over. They discussed whether to enter the narrow street that went up suddenly, ruggedly toward a huge fence that blocked its end. They wondered whether it was a dead end or turned into some surprising way out. They decided to venture climbing up. He said to her: Aren't you tired yet? Doesn't climbing bother you? She said: And you? He said: I am ready to walk on, to go up and down in this strange city until morning. She said: Me, too. Their shared sense of adventure brought them together in the late evening advancing on this bright, magical city, its breath cooling, its alleys

145

leading to closed fences—a city protective and tender with its gravid columns inelegant but solid, with large, tarnished buildings on which advertising lights were attached, closing and opening their electric eyes in mechanical sequence revealing a shabbiness that had stolen into a side of the city's ancient glory.

They came all of a sudden onto the vast Station Square. The breeze was cold, piercing, making the sides of her skirt fly about her fleshy legs. He felt the wind both invigorating and biting in his chest. They joined their arms into each other's as they quickly went down toward the straight and broad street. He asked her: Shall we take a taxi? She said: Goodness, no. Are you sleepy? He said: Not at all, and he laughed happily. Then he said: I've never been as alert as I am now. Coffee is not the reason, at least not the only reason. She looked at him again as if with admiration and astonishment, without denying or rejecting. She said: Are you always so precise, adding reservations and clarifications in every statement you utter? He said: The pleasant company in the first place is what wakes up everything in me. She laughed—a very small laugh—but did not comment. He felt, however, her arm pressing his ever so slightly, signaling that she received the message, or thanking him for the message.

As they walked down the street in long strides, she told stories, how there were three boys among the youth of Munira neighborhood who all loved her at the same time, and she used to go with them to the movies and to the Gezira Club in its bygone days of splendor: I was very young, ten or eleven, still a little girl, and there was nothing. She said it while passing her other hand lightly over her round erect bosom that seemed to glow in the lit night beneath her flimsy blouse in the cold breeze. She emitted a hushed short laugh: When I went to boarding school in Alexandria, the three of them used to send me letters secretly via a common friend who went weekly to Cairo. I didn't travel to Cairo except once every two or three months.

146

You know my father was busy with his many unending stories, responsibilities, and affairs with the Palace and the Army, with politics, art, women, and businessmen.

She said, suddenly, in a context all her own: I am ready to give up my life for those I really love.

She questioned him with a look. His sense of her was permeated with tenderness, affection, admiration, as he smiled at her stories, getting to know her world.

She said to him: Aren't there such stories of love in your childhood? All young people at that age have such stories.

He said: I never knew the meaning of childhood.

She laughed: Come on. Don't be unreal.

At another time she might have said: You are still a child of sorts.

He said: You have a point. I have what resemble love stories, but they are not stories. They have no external drama or events. They are rather fantasies of love, dreams of love, both torments and splendors of childlike and adolescent infatuation—hidden and held back. I used to be very shy and introverted, living mostly with myself. Probably I still do.

She said: It's true to a certain extent, but we cannot say you are an introvert—though possibly reserved and sedate.

They laughed. She said: But I love in men this reserve and calmness. Words and things from them have a value because they are rare.

He said: I too have mad escapades.

She asked in an incredulous tone: Really?

It never occurred in his mind that he was tapping the thresholds of love's realm that would open up for him hours of joy he could never have imagined—no more than a few hours but enough to fill an entire life with an inextinguishable glow. He would also fall into an anguish of torments he thought he could never have known—persistent, invasive, inconsolable anguish, seemingly without end, with

147

no hope of crossing its vast, shaggy, prickly labyrinths. It never occurred in his mind—not for a moment—that in these first hours he was beginning to fall in love with her.

There was not a single policeman to be seen in the vast city; it was bright, pleasant, empty. It received them in its bosom with open arms, as if it were meant for them only. Like Hansel and Gretel, like the Sultan's Daughter and Clever Hasan, in the land of fairy tales, they did not know they were at the intersection between *the way of regrets and the way of him who goes and never comes back*—about to face a she-ghoul whose questions are unanswerable. Their footsteps took them in a thrall of discovery and release toward a summery dawn.

Holding his hand, she was talking as they descended the narrow staircase in a hurry toward the small old yard where the light of a lamp shaking in the breeze fell on the closed door of a small hotel. In the midst of the yard was a white statue of an elegant, naked boy surrounded by rings of densely green flowers. She said: You know I can fabricate a million white lies and half a million rosy lies, really, but in crises you will not find any one to depend on better than me. Try me.

He smiled and didn't take the matter seriously then. It was more appropriate for him to forget it. Her mind, like her body, was quick moving, constantly jumping around with an inner force. She liked to formulate intelligently worded phrases to surprise her audience. In fact he was not surprised, nor did he want to respond to her game by feigning surprise. He was not interested in splendid words and skillful performance but in what lay beyond them: the experience that seemed to him unusual, at times exceptional.

She said to him: Do you know what time it is now? He said without surprise or astonishment: Yes, around three. She said: Look, look Mikhail . . .

148

The sky above the lights of the sentient, nocturnal city was becoming pallid, not yet luminous. He felt its texture getting lighter, more transparent. In the trees, something was worrying the birds—perhaps they sensed the shades of dawn? Not yet awakening or bursting out with chirping or twittering noises, they nevertheless moved here and there from above—a listlessness before waking, a lonely stirring, then quiet again. Something fluttered, or else leaves rustled in the air beginning to cool, as they hurried on without feeling anxious to get back, yet looking forward to a warmth that had nothing to do with the warmth of the heart; the hearts were plenty warm. Small cars with their lights extinguished were crowded, parked beneath deep red, huge, old buildings. Suddenly, she gently pulled her arm from his and lingered a step behind him, bent down on the ground of the sloppy street—unevenly paved with black basalt having been smoothed and made glossy by multiple and successive generations of footsteps and wheels. Rama was purring to herself in a low voice—oooh, a little cat—as she lifted from the ground a gray kitten whose crooked small legs were moving weakly in agitation. Rama was mewing in response to it, holding it to her chest moving it up and down with the keenness of repressed tenderness. When he turned, he was truly surprised. He felt somewhat worried. She said to him: Look Mikhail, the little cat. What is it doing alone here in the street? He said: Doubtless it is looking for its mom, in a nearby shelter. Rama, leave it, so it can return. She said: Mikhail, my heart won't let me do that. How sweet and small! Let me hold it a little. He smiled but his worry didn't cease. She gently placed the kitten on the ground as if despite herself, but her hands didn't want to let go of it. She moved down and sat on her heels next to the kitten, her skirt going up to her upper round thighs, lit by a golden brown glow in the late hours of night. The kitten ran with its shaky legs—purring with the excitement and joy of salvation and, with what seemed to Mikhail, sorrow

149

as well—behind the row of parked cars, toward a dark window with metal bars opening no doubt onto a hole leading to a cellar or a basement under the aged, huge building.

It did not occur to him in the elevator, or next to her room, to kiss her goodbye. They shook hands—her tender flesh a little moist with sweat caused by the sudden internal warmth right after the cool dawn air. Her hand relaxing in his was slack, flaccid, not pressing. He saw in her large, alert eyes affection, tenderness, and contentment. He said to her: Good night, or rather good morning. She laughed. He went back and slept right away. He was genuinely free of concerns, his body feeling peace, opulence, and happiness.

In the morning, she was wearing a button-up dress and a short-cut wig the color of her hair. She said: The wig is made from my own hair. At first he did not understand and he looked at her puzzled. She said: I had my long braids cut and made into a wig. Can't you see? The same color, the same texture of my hair. He exclaimed: That is true! Around her neck she was wearing several necklaces holding small amulets alternating between silver and leather. Their tiny bells jingled and tinkled gently. She said: These are amulets made by an old priest from our town in Sharqiya, written in Coptic, Arabic, and Aramaic. He said: Amulets? Of what? What's in them? She said: I haven't opened them. The priest asked me never to do so. Does this surprise you coming from me? I, the scientific materialist, the old Marxist, the believer in Socialism? He said: No, it doesn't surprise me. I know. She said: I only need them to bring me luck. I am really in need of luck.

Months later, she was wearing the same dress and the same amulet-necklaces. It occurred to him that this had some meaning. He said to her: Remove these ugly sunglasses. She laughed—a rare and surrendering laughter. Then she said: Oh, you never liked these glasses. But she did not remove them. He said to her: Rama, remove these glasses, take them off. She removed them silently and put them in her huge, large, always-open handbag. She never wore them again.

She said to him once: I imposed my will once. So, yes, I am something of a tyrant. You told me that, I know. But you are also a tyrant of sorts, my love.

He said to her: You move freely from one caprice to another.

She said in bad temper: No, I did not mention caprice. I said I loved the freedom of moving about—moving from one moment to another. But I don't move from one whim to another. In fact every time I move I have with me those I love.

She said: I am used to taking you now with me wherever I go. For me this is friendsh—This is love.

But he'd heard the change. He said to himself: Is this what's called the well-known Freudian slip? Is this then the whole story? Friendship?

Later she said: Friendship is a truly precious thing. If only you knew it.

Later, in the anguish of his agitated torments, he said to himself: This is foolish, useless. Ours is a mere cycle in a series of relations, friendships, affections, and infatuations. So what? I am to blame, of course. First by rejecting, then by entering into a game with rules I did not abide by, followed necessarily by failure. Then I raised the issue to metaphysical levels that have nothing to do with anything. Then I abided too by the social norms and counseled commitment to them. Shouldn't I have entered into the game as it should have been played? The commitments and conventions are matters one can implicitly subvert without confronting, without challenging, without admitting. Furthermore, I lacked shrewdness, experience, and begrudged time—this is also a kind of self-sparing and constriction. Add to all this my regression when facing images of ruin and destruction. Gambling at the price of total loss is also one of the rules

151

of the game. Why acknowledge defeat before even entering the arena? Wasn't all this abiding by the rules of the common, bare, shabby, pleasant game, exactly what was required? Wasn't there in the game a diversion and distraction of sorts anyhow? Wasn't it necessary to have at least a measure of initiative, intelligence, generosity, and discretion? And tolerance too?

He said to her: Not on the bread of dreams does man live, but rather, with it he dies.

He said to himself: Man? What arrogance! Not on the bread of dreams do I live myself. That is all. In fact, with it I neither live nor die.

The salon was cozy: its chair cushions soft, submerged in quasi-sexual repose beneath their seated bodies; the arms of the chairs returning to their elbows a gratifying sense of firm relation to the rest of the body. The walls were inlaid with sculpted marble, with wrought iron that formed flowers in relief, complete with taut slender branches. In the larger, ornamental fish tank, black speckled carp, mischievous looking, passed among wild, flourishing water-plants. There was also an archaeological column of old marble perforating the ceiling, around which the walls and staircase had been carefully erected. As for the old crystal chandeliers, they illumined from on high, dazzling and distant.

They asked for Campari. The elegant waiter with shiny hair brought the red liquid in crystal glasses, the ice cubes gently shaking and carrying melted tangled fluid-threads of deep red.

He had entered to find her with the Finn, the same man who had met them at lunch. His thick, light blond hair reached his shoulders. His colored shirt seemed expensive. His face did not have the bland complexion of northerners; it was full, slightly rosy from a previously ordered Campari, or from heat, or from his persistent project of flirting. His eyes, which had a clever, blue glow, seemed narrow in his broad, heavy face. They had some sort of insolence and indifference,

152

yet managed to focus sufficiently on his discreet courting, which she was encouraging—or at least not discouraging—by the way she sat with her skirt up, revealing in the light her upper thighs' soft bronze. She had thrown away her shoe, one of the pair; her toes—short, plump and pressed to each other—were painted dark red and kept on plunging up and down into the thick fabric of the carpet.

Mikhail looked at the familiar little drama. He was not interested, but felt somewhat hard pressed nonetheless, wanting to come out of this situation, in some way, rather successfully. He didn't know Rama, not really, nor did he care about what adventure—whether one kind or another—she thought to delve into. Their stroll in the city until the dawn that morning had confirmed friendship and pleasant collegiality—not more in truth, but no less either. That was why he could not immediately excuse himself and depart before an appropriate time had passed, whatever the measure of propriety was. Anyhow, he couldn't know the measure.

He noticed the Campari had given her face a rosy flush. Inasmuch as he was in the end an easterner and a southern Egyptian, he felt that he had an obligation—which no one had assigned to him— to take care of her, even if from afar.

The Finn said: I am captivated by stories of Egyptians. The pyramids, what are they? Aren't the Egyptians the ones who consider cows sacred?

Mikhail did not answer. He found Europeans—educated or uneducated—somewhat boring. He didn't feel the need to deliver a lecture, to meet a challenge, or present an apology.

He said to himself: Finn, your world is not mine, even if its contours match mine exactly.

He said to himself: But what is my world?

Rama said: Mr. Qaldas here is the best person to tell you the story. The ancient Egyptians were his direct ancestors.

She was enjoying the entire situation. Mikhail was angered a little. It was not his intention to sally forth upon a venture or to win any prize. He always felt above this competition to appeal to a woman, as if he thought the prize was his right, *a priori*, and his cause was taken for granted. Or else he would give up at the beginning through abstinence or by conceit, choosing for himself total defeat, though treating it like a victory upside down.

Mikhail said to her, talking in English so the foreigner would hear: True, yet no one has any direct ancestors. We also have a strand of the old Greeks, and possibly of the Romans. Of the latter I am not sure. Probably not. The Romans were soldiers and masters. One thing is sure, we do not have Arab blood in our veins.

She said: What about Arab civilization and Arabic language? Don't they transform the very make-up of men and reformulate them?

Glowing, he said: Yes, the civilization and the language mingled with our blood. But even so, I am not so sure about their effects. Certainly their language penetrated; as far as their civilization is concerned, that is another story. I have forgotten my language or I have let go of it. Besides, my infatuation with Arabic is a kind of traitors' infatuation—ambivalent, like the infatuation of one with his strangler. But it has become my language, mine and yours, our language. You and I spoke in the language of our ancestors when we first spoke. This much you know, don't you? We still speak a sacred language of sorts, a hieroglyphics under a different wrap perhaps, beneath a new mask. This is the magic of Egyptians: they transform everything, literally everything, to their own special gold, their own special soil, their own special form. This seems to me primitive and naïve, but I am sure of it. I have faith that needs neither proof nor evidence. It's somewhat mystical.

She said: As for me, family stories relate that we came from

154

Spain, crossed the Delta and mixed with the Bedouin of Sharqiya. I am thus a hybrid, as you see.

He said: You are hundred percent Egyptian, no matter what you claim. No one has this face but an Egyptian. Isis too came to Sharqiya.

She laughed swiftly and quietly, but Mikhail had become excited by the provocation.

He said: Our blood in Egypt is always the stronger. I am not a racist and I do not adhere to the supremacy of a race over others. But I do insist on the uniqueness of Egypt which you call hybrid, and I call a melting pot, one of its kind, because of the purity of its flames and the strength of its fire. Even the ancient Egyptian gods are the saints of yesteryear and the holy figures of today. Our people, whatever faith they belong to, find a depth, sense, and significance in religion that no other people does. Horus might be called Mar Girgis or Sayyidna al-Husayn. Isis has many names living among us in every home in Egypt until today, tomorrow, forever and ever.

Rama lifted her shoeless leg, as if unawares, and put it on the luxurious seat under the other thigh in a comfortable position, revealing the lower part of her thigh with its pleasantly suggestive folds.

The Finn had been isolated from the unfolding discourse, even though he was passionately following it, trying to understand these two Egyptians. It was obvious from his face that he was getting confused. He said:

Isis? Isn't she the goddess of love who came out of the sea in an open seashell?

Rama said with a touch of both sarcasm and affection: No, you mean Aphrodite. I think Isis too was a goddess of love. Should we ask Mr. Qaldas to explain it to us?

The Finn asked with naïveté and cunning: Do you know her story?

Mikhail said: I have, of course, forgotten the details.

155

Rama said: Please, Mikhail, tell us.

He lit a cigarette then redressed himself and offered the Finn a cigarette, which he declined, and offered another to Rama which she accepted. He lit it for her. She put her hand on his, circling the tiny flame, drawing in the smoke through her rounded lips with pleasure. The elegant waiter was passing by with the tail of his black jacket swaying in a graceful rhythm, cognac glasses in his hands. She was settling down in her seated position, one leg without a shoe under her thigh as if she were sitting on an Istanbuli couch.

He said: Yes, Isis, the ancient, the first and forever goddess of love; the virgin, the mother of Horus, the mother of Christ, our chaste Lady; Astarte, Persephone, Hera, Demeter, Aphrodite, multiple Marys; the multicolored, receiving, fertile, immortal essence.

The Finn asked: But how? What happened?

Mikhail had forgotten the story. It seemed to him that he would not know how to narrate it, but he wanted to. By the second glass of Campari he was narrating it as if it were a family story that he had heard from his grandmother, or had read in the yellowed papers in one of the drawers of the marble desk in the hallway of their house when he was a boy probing into family documents hidden under receipts, bills, and photographs of faded colors, along with the heavy, large Bible with its black leather cover.

Bereaved Isis, with her hair down, had gathered all the torn-off parts of Osiris, the martyr; she gathered everything except his phallus. If she could not find it, drought and death would befall the brown, fertile land of Kemi, the gentle, warm heart of the world, but blocked in its left ventricle. The box, bed, coffin made to the size of the great god and on which melting lead was poured is in Qift, the city of dispossession and mourning. It has been carried by the scanty waters of the Nile coming up from the vales of the nether world, lit by an inextinguishable sun, sending it to the Mediterranean Sea. The

156

unruly *khamsin* is deranged. The loathed storm of dryness and fine sand eclipses the moon, blackens the face of the sun. The first Cain with his violent animal force is the descendant of the ancient, gigantic prince of darkness, the ally of the black queen of Ethiopia. Here is winged Isis fluttering on the massive leaden shell. She is the millenary phoenix; from her wings waft the perfume of seasoning, the fragrance of spices exhaling ambergris and astonishing balm. Her two wings are spread-out sails on the face of the sea waves, legislating life and death. She is the goddess of land, sea, and sky; the protector of ships until the waves throw them upon the heart of the stump of the old Phoenician cedar tree, a column's pedestal in the house of the king of Byblos. Thus a tree grows on it again, flourishes and surrounds him with its invincible body, protecting him from oppression, dryness, and dearth of soul. Isis is the sister and beloved of Osiris; they loved each other before they were born, and they were married when they were in the womb of their mother. Osiris with innumerable eyes, the Light of the World, the imprisoned Light, born on the first day of Genesis, living until the ninth and final day that has no end. I still see him; no food for him except a head of onion and the green stalk of the fern at dawn, with the wounded head wrapped by the large handkerchief whose greenness has faded from ancient dust. Music, skills, plants, and laws are imprisoned with him in his leaden floating grave. As for Isis, she nurses the son of the king of Byblos with her finger in his mouth. She places the little prince every night into a celebration of baptism by raging fire, conquering death and bringing him into the hallways of immortals. The queen mother loses her mind as she sees the blazing fire consuming the body of her son. Then Isis, the divine enchantress, reveals her glory. She splits open the ancient cedar, which pronounces the secret in clear tongue, and she hands her dear charge to the Egyptian, she who always brings plentiful good after the drought. I still see the prolific

157

tender cow with udders that will never dry up, with her elevated haunches in her full black *jallabiya*, carrying her earthenware jar on her head, svelte, her figure undulating amid the fields suckling a thousand thousand Horuses endlessly with the milk of pride that does not ebb despite the famine of times. The dark land under the mud of the valley with cracked shores flooded by water turns into the giving, eternally youthful body of Osiris. The sun springs out from the lotus flower and the black bull Apis is continuously renewed, having glowing skin. The fertile moon rays have parted, revealing Horus, the falcon. He will be brought up and he will defeat the scorpion armies in the exile of eastern swamps among frail reed stalks, with the power of his mother's all-potent amulets. He will grow up and stab the vicious hippopotamus and distribute its meat to the dispossessed. He has thus avenged his torn-up father, great martyr buried in Busiris. Each part of his dismembered, most holy body is a mausoleum and a shrine along the canals, the waterways, and the banks of the Nile, now, as it were, ruler of the kingdom of the living dead, in his white attire and handsome ebony face, open-eyed forever and ever, maintaining justice by the scale of Ma'at, and next to him the monster 'Am'am, the god of retribution who gnaws at the hearts of unrepentant sinners.

He emptied his glass. When he went back to his room, his estrangement was not painful.

Isis is not one of those ancient myths, but on some level living and present in his life, permitting neither denial nor confirmation of his acceptance of her or, should he rather say, his belief in her? His is an elemental conviction, not a matter for questioning or answering. It is a given, a condition—for that which amounts to more than his own existence and comes *before* his existence.

Shaken by the telephone's ring, he rushes and lifts the receiver, made anxious by the surprise. He hears her voice: Can you come down now? Confused, he answers thoughtlessly: Now? What time is it? She says: What does it matter what time it is? Are you busy? He says with hesitation: Not at all. She says slyly and tenderly: I am seeking you to save me from a critical situation. He says: A critical situation? His thoughtlessness lingers. She laughs: Our friend Peter.

He was perplexed a little, then he said: Ah the Finn. What about him? He felt himself becoming a bit hotheaded. She says: He persists on calling me, inviting me to go out now to see the Church of St. Peter, saying it is beautiful at night.

He says: A church after midnight? She says: Indeed! He says it's the church of his namesake and patron and that it's open all night.

He says: And you want to skip out? She says: Exactly! Can you be ready in ten minutes? He says: In two, the time it takes to get to you.

He had the sensation of southern Egyptian gallantry and the joy of a small adventure. She said: Then right away. I'll wait for you at the front door, outside in the street.

They went into the magical night city, rediscovering it, recreating it.

Centuries old marble stairways and squares: buildings with dim doors, old fences, fountains with water smoothing with its constant fall the sides of the stony bodies with their handsome muscles bursting with blocked vigor, the doors of small restaurants with old-fashioned lanterns and elongated classic windows with curtains drawn and the hyacinth bean trees strangely green in the artificial light in the small square.

Later, he said: Thus was the beginning—long, joyful, and innocent, not knowing it was the beginning.

What happened was neither in the past nor in the future, but carried by the moment's lightness—delicate as down from a sparrow's feathers blown by the lit nocturnal breeze, whose light is

159

equally distributed, neither keen nor blunt, across the quiet walls, buildings, and across a sky without depth.

He said: Even the meaning of what happened is a matter of inquiry. I mean, simply what happened on the physical, concrete, sensual level, without search for motivation, cause, or goal. Simply, what happened is alone real. As for its meaning, who can know?

She had said to him: I loathe self-pity. I loathe betraying a trust. I loathe incompetence.

He said: Your truth has a thousand colors, but it is your own.

She said, looking mysteriously as if scrutinizing an uncharted land: You are worried and not sure. There is nothing strange in this. In such cases this is the nature of things.

She did not continue what she was about to say.

No matter how much you say to yourself that the seed of truth in your fantasies is fertile, impregnating the future, you will never be cured of your bad dream. My days and dreams are weighed by the wine of your name—Rama, Rama—radiating with the dark glow of my never ebbing yearning for you. Your name has become once more a magical incantation. Do you—he spoke now to himself—want to hold the sun in your palms and embrace the wind? No, you don't know how to say it. Your language is neither correct nor precise.

Rama, you are in truth the image of all things that shine in the heart. You come, bidding to your lovers in dream, and they cannot ignore you. You are the desired, the holy of world holies. But the world is not holy; it is polluted. The Nile waters come to you from the nether world and flow up to your chest, making the rocks mellow, and this according to your will, you the seer, the woman with the crescent necklace, lunar earrings, and silver python bracelet.

She said to him: You call yourself a man of ethics, puritan and upright.

He said: No.

He said: The lie, the intoxicating and common ambiance of the lie. Whatever dragged me to this stifling ambiance, I the "ethical man"?

He bought her a doll. The doll's eyes were green and in its face were the same roundness and softness as Rama's. Its dress was full in its miniature measure, made of red velvet, a deep, warm, heavy burgundy. At its waist it had a yellow ribbon decorated very elegantly with fringes at its ends. The doll's short arms were stretched in front of it, powerless in a frozen gesture that utterly fails to reach the embrace it seeks and desires; its shoes soft and extremely well made triggered a sense of tenderness. Rama was delighted with it. She held it to her big bosom as if the doll was closer to her than her own daughter, and said: Oh, how beautiful! How small her mouth is! She patted the soft yellow hair made of tightly woven nylon threads that momentarily deceived the eye and the heart, calling for a gentle touch.

He said to her: You have no separation between the two worlds, that of reality and that of childhood. This quality in you charms me. On the other hand, you are also realistic, pragmatic.

She said with an obedient look: The world of reality and the world of fantasy, yes, you know a lie is sometimes the only truth.

Are the seven masks of Isis a personification of the truth? A road to a destination, stage by stage? Are they ritual stations in a pilgrimage toward the permanent element that will always be? Or are they talismans and amulets under which the ever-changing, revolving, and throbbing truth is concealed and disguised—the truth that renews itself endlessly even when death approaches it?

When he saw the collection of dolls in her bedroom, he looked for his doll but couldn't find it. He said nothing. He had been expecting yet denying it at the same time. His realization made him shut up.

161

He said to her: Rama, isn't it in the ABC of Love that the lover gets rid of his worries, becomes liberated from uncertainties?

She said: I don't know, Mikhail. Since you raised the question, why not answer it?

He said: While I'm so uncertain? He laughed.

He said: Are you ready to confront the moment of truth? Is each of us ready to do so?

She said: I have already told you as much as I can, all that's within me.

He said: And everything that happens with you? Everything? Rama, everything for you is half-and-half. There is hesitation in everything; half of anything is silence. Isn't it? No escape from this. It's inevitable. In everything there's half an adventure, the other half a step backward.

She said: I am fed up. You tire yourself with these half truths. Isn't this quest for complete truth in itself a half truth? Mikhail, the moment we are in—one moment after another—which may or may not be renewed, as long as we live it honestly and completely, this is all I know and all I need to know of truth.

He called her on the phone, on a whim, without knowing whether she would be there. Her voice came to him permeated with joy, confidence, and peace: Hello!

This joy—this forgetfulness of him—stabbed him. Clearly she did not recognize his voice. Nor was she waiting for him.

After recognizing his voice she said in a hurry, amending: Oh, Mikhail, I'll talk to you right after lunch.

He said: I think when you talk to me in this decisive tone you mean to say something of this sort: We are mature, old enough, knowing the facts of life, and we are handling this relationship accordingly. It is a taken-for-granted issue that has its limits and its end. In other words, emotions have no place in it.

162

She said: Yes.

Self-reflecting, he questioned himself: If this is true, why do you want to have tenderness, affection, and compassion declared at every moment? Is this possible? Is it honest? No, it cannot be honest at every moment.

He said to himself, though affectionately addressing her in one of his exalted apostrophes: This delicate tone, can't you know it except in the act of making love?

He instantly felt that he was deceiving himself. The moments of feminine softness and tenderness in her voice were not rare. They were not frequent, either. True, but then the sky itself dons a velvety scrim on which he manages to rest his face, right?

She said: How are you? How has life been with you?

He said: I am coping.

She said: You are doping?

He said: No, no, not doping. Coping.

In the longish, low keyed, elegant station packed with crowds, he was hurrying, looking around, his heart beating fast. They had already said goodbye in the taxi that had then darted off with him. She had already alighted and gone down the stairs with her small suitcase, wearing a light blue hat. Even earlier they had rushed together in the dark, early morning, before the train's departure, to a secluded shop overlooking the side of a square ebullient with busy traffic; he had bought her the hat she said she liked precisely because it was a useless thing—it was simply a lovely plaything of no use; wasn't this the salt of life? Wasn't this what made the day turn into something special, saving it from being lost?

She had said all this when she saw the intricately designed hat, elegant in a subdued way, in the shop window at night beneath the light of a lamp.

So today she was departing from him, after the cycle had com-

163

pleted itself. They were concealing from themselves—or they seemed to conceal—what had happened because it was precious, valuable, and intricate. It could be examined later, slowly and with care because it was very delicate and significant; thus, it should be enveloped in silence. Regardless, there was, from now, a continuous rapport between their bodies that could not be broken, even when they were separated—a rapport in sleep and wakefulness, when alone or when in the street with people. From now on, and for the first time, their eyes would have that special gentility and tenderness known only by bodies that have embraced and joined in the erotic moment outside time.

But he had gone back to the station. He was breaking their agreement to let her leave by herself, to spare themselves the distress of farewells in the station, the repetition of formulaic statements whose trodden roads have been smoothed by wayfarers with crowded hearts, so as to spare themselves the tense last moments, wanting the train to leave so the ordeal can be finished but also wishing it not to leave, to delay departure at least a few minutes more. He had told the taxi driver to turn around, hoping to meet her as she was about to depart.

He saw the blue hat from a distance. He hurried, running fast toward it. He could see nothing else from a distance in this clouded blur of intertwined people and luggage carts rambling amid platforms, planted trees, newspaper kiosks, cafeteria chairs, and the white faces of big, round clocks.

Her eyes picked him up. She emitted a sigh of surprise. For a moment her face remained slack, as if she did not recognize him. She held his hand with her two hands. She said: Mikhail, I was writing a letter to you in my head. I'll send it to you as soon as I arrive.

He never received the letter.

The church dome from above the roofs asserted itself from the

164

side window, flattened to some extent, not complete in its arch, though perching with repose and calm weight. Its paint had been scratched off, revealing the light gray color of its limestone. Bells hung silent in the tower. Their greenness inside the morning's shade was that of a dark rusty bronze. Around them flew gulls with spread-out, white wings against the pale blue, swerving and straightening as one mass.

In his daydream he was next to her soft face, hearing the chiming of bells.

Later, he will come to this room and look from the side window to the outside scene again. The sky will seem empty and still—within him—after her dense presence has departed and the place with its walls has been deprived of her teeming energy. The surface of the wallpaper, decorated with small flowers, seems delicate, warm, and tight; not stifling when the agitation of the anguished soul with over-lapping concerns settles down.

Wearing blue—a dazzling blue blouse, her hair with a blue head-band—her image was painfully beautiful and distinct.

He said to himself: Every image, every dream, every passing word of love in the music that flows like turbid waters without stopping, every yell for love—a word that carries no weight—in a well-made song, every shrill, popular tune in its mechanical sorrow coming from the transistor and the microphone—all of it scorches my soul and inflames its inner lining with an unbearable fire. Does this make sense? Does it make sense to find myself in love, in flames, with the sides of my heart collapsing without resistance amid the market of ready-made sorrows, bought and sold, pushed about as a non-stop torrent into air-conditioned studios turned into a thousand thousand commercially marketable commodities, popular and far flung?

She said to him in her detached, clinical tone: Mikhail, you did not have a difficult childhood as you claim. That is, based on what

165

you told me. To the contrary, you were overprotected more than you should have been.

He was taken by surprise. He used to think of himself as neglected, lonesome, wretched in his childhood. He used to tell himself that his childhood was not happy; in fact, he did not really know that childhood that was said to be innocent. But at the moment, he could neither negate nor confirm these thoughts.

She said: But I am happy, happy for you. You have really attained a remarkable maturity, even within the period in which I've known you. Rarely do people keep maturing at this age.

She lightened the matter by saying: As for me, I will never attain maturity.

All this was new for him and different from what he thought of himself, so he kept silent.

8

The Amazon on White Sand

S
he said to him: There was almost a brawl between two ferrymen on Raswa's dock in Manzala, each in his boat and the
two boats practically glued to one other. Each man held his
long oar like a threatening weapon. Each one insisted that he alone
would take me to Port Said, wanting to serve *Sitt* Fatma joyfully—
"from the bottom of his eyes." In those days I entered Port Said regularly under the name of *Sitt* Fatma. Once I came with a duck, another
time with a couple of chickens along with peasant bread, eggs, and
oranges, from the presumed house of my mother to the presumed house
of my husband in Port Said. Of course, I was also carrying coded
letters; once I carried, under the eggs and bread, a small load of disassembled revolvers and their ammunition, all of it bundled in a piece of
local cloth. The center was in Manzala behind the Mustafa Shahin Café.

I was very convincing with my black *malas* overdress, my
mudawarra head cover, my thong sandals, and my castor *jallabiya*—
so much so that the Irish sergeant at the checkpoint got used to me
and trusted me. We became almost friends without talking.

The cold weather had settled in. Don't forget it was December 1956. At the dock, the boats were swaying on the shallow water as if about to capsize. I was standing on the wooden planks steaming with anger, trying to mend things between the two boatmen so my journey could get underway. The sun had set. Other ferrymen had gathered around, trying to settle the matter. Night was thickening, time was running out. All the ferrymen knew *Sitt* Fatma, were all comrades to some degree. I said to myself: If I allow this brawl to proceed, I'll never deliver my message tonight, and I know it's urgent. No point losing your head in such situations. It was obvious neither man would yield to the other. They'd figured out who I was, a journalist so they thought, covering the action surreptitiously. They never charged me anything. As you know, things go this way in our country. So I brought them small gifts saying they were from home: "The Prophet himself accepted gifts, so don't refuse me." After first declining, they took what I offered: a basket of oranges, eggs, a pair of pigeons, whatever was handy. The trip took the entire night; we reached the shore of al-Qawati at the peep of dawn. There we crossed a thicket of reeds and sea plants. Those boatmen know all the paths. By day, the journey was dangerous anyway, with the French bombing the lake.

He interrupted her: So you spent the night in a lake, among reed thickets, in a small boat, just you and the ferryman?

She shot him a glance and said decisively: Yes.

She went on: I had to find a way. You know the gallantry of country people. I shouted at the two of them: Is it proper to leave a woman all alone on the platform while night is falling? I went to the elder of the two and I swore: By my God, by my Faith, I am not leaving except with you. Are you content, Captain?

She paused, then said: One time the British entered to search my house. In fact, the house was in a dead-end neighborhood, and they came in the evening after the curfew—had I not been there, the rebel

168

Egyptian officers would have been lost. You know how they were: young, full of enthusiasm, polite and proper, and very brave. But at the end of the day, inexperienced. They kept their military uniforms in this house, whether by instruction or tradition, I don't know. When at home they wore *jallabiyas*. When the British banged on the door, I was the countryish woman inside her home in her plain nightgown at her kerosene stove engaged in frying up a dish of green peppers. I had made one of the Egyptian officers lie down on the room's bed. Then I opened the door looking at the British as Fatma should look, utterly surprised, but following every word as they talked in Cockney. They and the sergeant leading them with his pistol were definitely from south London. Throughout, I remained the country woman Fatma of Port Said. I slapped my chest in lamentation, I pulled my *tarha* over my disheveled hair. There I was, in my nightgown, with my sleeping husband on the mattress of a bed without sheets. The rest of the Egyptian officers were hiding under the stairway with their guns. At any moment, disaster could have happened. I yelled at the bum-boatman who had led the British to my house, translating for them in port English: Tell them, O brother, may the Prophet's name protect you. This house harbors no harm. By the Prophet's life, why don't you tell them? What have we to do with the disasters that befall us? I broke down in tears. I only realized the intensity of my weeping later, once they had left. When the Cockney sergeant saw this 'family,' he unloaded his foulmouthed Cockney curses on the boatman–informant who had claimed there were Egyptian officers to be found in the house. They withdrew and all was well, after a quick search *pour la forme*.

She fell silent for a moment.

—As for the bum-boatman, he disappeared after that night, leaving no trace. Corpses would float in the canals and the port every day. It was impossible to recognize the identity of a corpse. Oh . . .

169

ugly, but necessary. Isn't this the logic of warfare in the end? You cannot close your eyes to it, no matter how torn and contradictory your heart feels.

He said to himself:

What price treason? Yet the person who falters is human too. Murder in all cases—even in these cases—is unforgivable, cannot be compensated for. Murder whether inevitable and necessary is still murder. To recoil from that fact for whatever reason is another kind of treason, another unjustified murder.

He said to her: Yes, this logic cannot be escaped. Necessary murder is inevitable, whatever the direction is. Everything maintains its own grip that cannot be undone.

He said to himself: The nocturnal boat, you and the boatman in his prime, amid the reed thickets all night. You and the young intelligence officers in the distant house at the periphery of the city. You and the bum-boatman, murdered in a way nobody knows how. What is the price of treason? The price of patriotic struggle? Of freedom-fighting?

She had said to him: Do you know that I am writing a novel?

He said: No! A novel too? Isn't there an end to your talents? You are a great actress, a nurse, an archaeologist who can read dead languages, an old revolutionary, and now also a novelist?

She said: A revolutionary, period, if you please. They say it's the search for the self. Personally I find no self. It happened to me once that I dropped everything. I stopped searching. I fell into a stupor of indifference. Didn't talk, eat, or sense a thing. I lay here on this old sofa for a whole nine months. The official diagnosis: clinical depression. The danger of never leaving this indifference was real. Something was inside me that I didn't know about. I was sectioned off from it. Nor was this border, for good or ill, ever closed down decisively. I don't know . . .

He said anxiously, also inquisitively, half-believing: Why? When did this happen?

She said: I don't want to talk about it. Don't ask me, please.

He said: Yes, no one really knows the extent of such suffering. Indifference and separation are never a blessing. Does any person truly understand his or her uncontrollable, inner torments?

She didn't answer. She became oblivious of him, of the whole thing, as if all of it was senseless.

He said, trying to call her back: So what is the story of the novel you are writing?

She said with an enthusiasm born of fantasy that he knew so well: It's the story of an Egyptian girl who wants to realize her dream completely, in its splendor, without blemish. But in the end she accepts what is available to her.

He said: À la Chekhov?

She said: Not the nocturnal Chekhov. The midday version, in light and sun.

He said: And what is her dream?

She said: This is the topic, the novel's problem. Does anyone know his dream? This girl knocks on many doors, meets a lot of men, she is also looking for herself.

He said: And she has plenty of relations with them?

She said: Of course. This is the only way a woman can know men, and possibly know herself. A woman may go to bed with thirty men. But only when that happens to her can she reach happiness and fulfillment of an incredible sort, beyond description. When it doesn't happen, she feels bitterly disillusioned. And it rarely does happen.

Later, she said to him: This happened to me with you once, the first time.

He said to her: You are sociable, extroverted as the expression

171

goes. You are also self-enclosed, extraordinary, unusual. This is true, not a compliment. I am not trying to woo you.

She said: I know, my love.

He said: More than this. You love people, you love men, this is your nature. But isn't this self-love?

She said: I love people and I fall right on my face. How many times I have fallen!

He said: People? All people? Without distinction?

She said: Yes, every person has his own distinctiveness. But I love the complete man, the total man. He might be broken on the inside. But this is not important. In fact, I think it is necessary. The important thing is that he is total, complete, while carrying the crack inside him. I also want him with a sense of humor, the kind of man who attracts attention, in fact the man who calls forth attention instantly, the one who attracts as soon as he enters a place. He's the man to whom the waiter comes directly when he enters a restaurant. He's the one with personality, overwhelming and commanding, even if he never opens his mouth. But the first and last thing should be his honesty. Essential honesty, honesty with himself.

He had said to himself: In other words, everything I'm not. In the end, she's saying she doesn't love me. Then he noticed his silliness.

She had said to him: I sacrifice myself if need be—as you know—for those I love. She looked at him and said: You have not arrived at this stage yet.

Or does she want to say: You will arrive at it. Or does she want to say to the contrary: That is what you are! Despite the cracks. He had said to her: You know that I am not sociable and lack a sense of humor. She said to him instantly: To the contrary, you can dazzle at times when you want to.

He said to her: I wish I could see what you write.

172

She said, chasing the thought away quickly: Later on, maybe when I finish. Otherwise, the very act of writing is ruined.

He said: Or aborted before it's born.

She said, with the tone of someone deciding on something already given, without the quiver of a confession: I love particular human traits in you. Because as a human being, as a man, you have particular human traits.

He said with the tone of someone philosophizing, objectively, while the wound in his voice bled: One does not love another because of certain human traits. One often loves because the other has a weakness, even loving this weakness, this shortcoming, this failing. One loves first because the beloved is the beloved. This is not accepting the beloved nor is it a kind of mothering. What's essential is the will to merge, that there is no self, no other, no twosome, but one: total reciprocal giving and total reciprocal taking.

She said: Even if it were possible, it is very dangerous. It demands more than one can bear.

He tenderly patted her honey-colored hair, as if he were a paternal lover—a soft, combed thicket of thriving plants with the force of primitive, elemental life. Her hair was long and intertwined without being tangled, as if tightly plaited by itself without the interference of anyone, and yet so delicate. It was the hair of a beautiful animal, a repository of irrational powers. Her head lay on his knees; teardrops remained on her serene face, no longer running in an undulating stream after the storm that ripped her handsome facial features. She was relaxed, tired by the fatigue and yearning of an exhausted soul. The luxuriant eyelashes were like shades for two oases in a desert lit by a tranquil sun; the flesh of the eyelids, like leavened dough, slightly swollen as if just awakened from sleep, offered new temptations. The flimsy blouse, décolleté at the breast cleavage, the tightly pressing black bra, full, almost bursting out and

173

overflowing with its luxuriant contents, having a fleshy feel from behind the warm, skillfully woven lace. As she lifts her arms, her breasts stretch backward toward him. She brings his head gently toward hers, so that his mouth falls on her moist lips. His kisses are quick flashes on her lips, cheeks, neck, and chin without distinction, but there is hesitation in his closed eyes. The small silver earring with diamond-like stones is glowing in the half-light with imprisoned and penetrating rays of changing colors as he touches the lobe of her ear in an erotic tenderness. His hands reach to open the buttons of her blouse and find the clasp of her bra with confidence. When the clasp is undone, a delicate, very light metallic bursting is voiced in the silence of his room. Her broad back has been liberated, his hand wide open plies its firm soft curves. Without a goal his mouth still explores her surrendered face. The sighs of the little cat dying are very faint and weak as if coming from a distance, yet very clear, pleading without hope.

Suddenly, she says with a slightly tough voice, hoarse after silence, after weeping, and their fever of the brief corporeal intimacy:

Let go of me. Let go. What are you doing?

She lifts to her chest the withering cat now mewing calmly and says to him: You don't love me.

He says: I do love you. Simply. That's all.

She said without enthusiasm, neither accepting nor rejecting: I know it.

He had become bored with this word that now meant nothing. Verbal barriers had closed all exits. He felt annoyed.

The dialogue was broken.

Rama, you broke it.

Nothing is left but one continuous scream of longing, its wave rising continuously toward the sky, shooting up and turning over. The silence and foam of its waves drown me.

He says to himself: Let go of the poetic phrasing. It might be entertaining and somewhat consoling, but it is weightless tin.

There is only this terror of losing, incapable of being measured by weighty words, every time she is late for her appointment, every time she fails to show, every time the telephone remains silent with none of its anxiously promising rings.

I have lost her. Indeed I have lost her. It is over. The cymbals of finale and the uproar of the large resounding drum press upon me announcing the end, the closure.

At night he struggles with terror. Fear stretches its long soft arms, drawing from a well that's deep, dark, with wide-open mouth. Invisible arms lurk for him. He turns his head on the pillow, saying to himself: What is this childish terror? You are much too old for such fears.

The cracking of something in the stillness makes his nerves jump, and he, in his bed, becomes alert. Under the window, a faint crying voice of unknown character, the crying of a murdered girl years ago in the street demanding a revenge that is not forthcoming. He says to himself, whispering: *Afreets*? Is it the ghost of the murdered girl? Can this sort of thing actually occur?

Wishing to get up and put the light on, he says to himself: Shame on you. He holds himself from moving, looks for the oblivion of sleep. The house is large, empty, airy as if open and unprotected unto a somber, threatening, empty space.

He calls her with his closed mouth: Rama, Rama. In the echoes of his calls there is something frightening. The faint light reaches him from the glass window of the bathroom door. It seems as if it has come from an outside and foreign world that cannot be reached. Yet it is very familiar: a faint radiation of light from the vents, with invisible contours, as if it possesses the living energy of a botanic species that creeps and steals in, presently quiet, falling on the tiles of the hall outside the open door of his room in a waiting posture.

175

The voice of rational questioning quiets down and the horrors of open-eyed, waking nightmares have taken hold of him as he lies on the large bed, alone now in the clutch of terror. His entire body wails without voice or tears, as if he were drowning and twisting, hushed and breathless, strangled; as if he were beating with arms and legs on a semi-solid earth, only partly responding to his bangs, responding only by its being beneath him, neither going down with him nor plunging him into it.

His body is torn in fourteen fragments, thrown about in the open space. The wailing of Mirages and Phantoms spirals up, becomes louder, eventually explodes as they smash into the sand. The successive rumbling of fire feels like a solid, sharp-edged rain penetrating the unprotected innermost. He buries his head in the semi-earth with a violence born of despairing of salvation and a violence born of its continued search. He risks everything looking for deliverance but none exists for him. The nightmare lid has been locked down on him by the magical, melted lead seal. Tight darkness descends, totally. His body, blocked and breaking out, cannot come up with any movement. Fierce alertness and attempts to escape, wallowing and turning over in fetters made to his size, paralyze his every sound, his every tremor completely, leaving him breathless. Out of hopeless animal fear nothing in his body—constricted by such an evil spirit—obeys him. Dry, repressed weeping shakes him without the moistness of redeeming warm tears. A wild wailing like that of madness: Rama, Rama, Rama.

She said to him: The military camp was in the desert behind the Pyramids. We went to it in an old car, then stayed for three weeks. I completely refused anyone's objection to my joining the military barracks because I was a woman, that the camp was for men volunteers only. I rejected all talk about training me in nursing, or needlepoint, crochet, or knitting for the soldiers—all the womanish fare that's neither here nor there as they say, the fare that takes place outside the battleground. I participated in the training on equal footing with all. In yellow overalls, I was stronger and quicker to learn than any volunteer. I crawled on my knees, I learned the panther crawl and the monkey crawl, as they call them. I jumped over barriers and climbed rope ladders. I memorized the parts of the Mauser and Kalashnikov better than any old soldier. Soon the glances of doubt and sarcasm and the insinuations disappeared—replaced by gestures and statements of collegiality and equality. I did not allow any encouraging or even admiring words. I asked for absolute equality, received it, then went beyond it. I was stronger in hand, more accurate in aiming, sharper in seeing, more forbearing, quicker in walking, firmer in getting footholds, than any other volunteer. Even the guard from the regular army soldiers who stood outside the fences could not distinguish me from the others.

He said: Who was with you in the training camp?

She said: All of them, from Reserve Officers to Intelligence, from Communists of all shades and factions, to the Muslim Brothers, from the National Guard to the Popular Resistance, from the Misr al-Fata Party, to the Old Wafd Party, to Trotskyites and Independents. Also, there were the usual lot of visionaries who later died at Port Said, or were wounded and maimed by the bullets and bombs of the British and the French, or who later died or were beaten and humiliated in the prisons, in the desert detention centers of the Revolution. All of them, the core, the elite of the country. And where have we gotten to?

He said: The struggle continues. It does not die, not from thousands of years ago on to eternity.

She said: Oh, do please leave off the romanticism.

He said: Who would have believed it? Those days stormed our hearts with joy, with the ecstasy of sacrifice. But we soon returned to extended silence and perplexity.

She said: It was three weeks when night joined day. I've never known a time more difficult nor more pleasurable than this period

177

among men. Soft sand not only filled my pulled-back hair under my khaki cap, but also clung onto my eyelashes and in the crevices between my toes. I invented a device for taking a shower from the scant drinking water: a bucket hanging on two blocks of wood, going up with a rope attached to a pulley, another rope bringing the bucket mouth down. The water, having the smell of rust, yet refreshing, flowed down in small, slight, miserly gushes, then it would pour down all at once. I sucked in my breath from surprise while standing naked behind a single curtain on one side strung on wooden pillars and made of tenting—the other side open to the winter sun.

He said: You were a true Amazon. In fact, I think you have always had this Amazonian side latent behind all your femininity.

She said: The Amazon is a female first and a fighter second.

He said: Fortunately, today's Amazons do not have to fight with bows and arrows.

She looked at him, the two of them laughing at the same moment. He was not late, not for a second, but his laugh was tense.

He said: So that they don't have to cut off one breast.

She said: No, both of mine are here, safe and sound.

He said: You're telling me! I know they are there. May they sleep tight.

She said: This hard training was very helpful when I went to occupied Port Said. My name then was *Sitt* Fatma of Manzala.

He said: I can imagine your enthusiasm for the exercises. You are tough despite your delicateness.

She said: The basic exercise was shooting. But there were other endurance exercises: withstanding thirst and hunger for calculated hours, handling scorpions and snakes, exercises like that of the Lightning Brigades, but to a lesser degree, and also Japanese wrestling. No one could ever throw me down on the floor. These were the most enjoyable exercises.

The defiant Amazon storms men, breaking fences of their forts, wrestling with them in an unending hardy embrace in dazzling nightmares, riding horses toward horizons that can never be reached; her quiver is never emptied of arrows.

She said: What were you doing then?

He said: My battle ended early, before that. I came out of the detention camp and I cleared away from both revolutionary and political work. The abyss of despair paralyzed my heart for a long time. I got to know Cairo streets by night. We were constructing public housing. Then the iron and cement ceased coming. The buildings became standing vestiges before they were constructed. Some of them were used as assembly centers for the youth of the National Guard and Popular Resistance. Guns were distributed to them in front of me with live ammunition, even though they did not know how to use them. I was the first person to show up on the morning the British and the Israelis landed in Port Said. I and those southern Egyptians, then the rest.

She said: We should have met there fifteen years ago. Imagine what kind of change would have taken place in our lives if we had been together in the military camp.

He said: I'm sure you were very beautiful even in the yellow overall with your hair under the khaki cap.

She said: Fundamentally, life was very beautiful then. Promising. Hope had no limits.

He said: As for now . . .

She said: I am happy with what took place between us.

He said: It is, in itself, the most wonderful thing that has happened to me, whatever the reasons or justifications.

However, a tragic seed of perdition had entered the very foundation of what happened, whatever its results were to be.

The tragedy happens and moves on. What does 'what happened' mean? It happens, and that is that.

She said to him: Why not? Let me make people happy. Inasmuch as they want to be, no matter how. Let me give it to them. What do I lose? Even if I fail to bring myself real happiness, for what is happiness?

She hesitated for a moment and said: Whatever it is, it is a good thing.

He said to himself, once again, repeatedly, endlessly: This talk is exactly what I cannot fathom and what I don't understand. It cancels me, classifies me in a category of an anonymous and common base, not aiming at the unique, singular goal that cannot be repeated, but toward an element in me which I feel is common and dispersed even in its most intimate special moments. No. There is none of the glowing particularity with its unique and extraordinary sharpness in all this philosophy of hers.

He said to himself: How foolish we are, how miserable. Can there be a fundamental uniqueness when we dismiss our identities and become instruments, yes instruments, performing a function. Even if that function is wasted in the clutch of a cosmic fever?

She said to him: You have attained a stage of maturity that a man your age rarely manages to reach.

He said: You mean that competition—assailing my foes and fighting for the prize—has ceased to have great significance for me? You mean a kind of inner liberation that you are happy with, for my sake, since I have stopped believing that I can hold the universe in my fist, hence cannot possess it and refashion it, as I used to think in earlier times?

She said: However, you still respond harshly to people.

He said: I?

She said: You can't stand their company. In the end, you are a satirist and a mocker.

He said: This is not true. Who am I to satirize people? I believe I know their suffering, their defects; even their crimes I do not condemn, let alone satirize. Even those who are full of themselves and are conceited I do not mock. They simply amuse me and I enjoy them!

She said: Why this faint smile that never blossoms completely? Of course you do have a kind of a giggle. But . . .

He said: Hasn't it occurred to you that it's a small trick of self-defense? But of course, you would have thought of that. Maybe my smile represents a kind of ethical decision.

Annoyed, she responded: There is something else I've not put my hands on.

He said: Yes, ethical. As you always say, I approach people treating them according to preconceived ethical judgments. Perhaps so. Yet it's also true that in the context of ethical judgments I accept them on the grounds that they are people who act rightly and wrongly, suffering perpetually, searching despite themselves for their pleasures and joys, whatever they are. True?

He went on: Not at all. All this is not true. Who can claim for himself the right to make ethical judgments? How unhappy people are and how fierce as well! To the contrary, I cannot judge anyone.

She said: Precisely. There is always a frame of reference even when you deviate from its rules. First of all, ethical judgment is present as an issue, then you reject it or you don't. This is another matter. Even when you reject it, it is still there, overshadowing your entire behavior and life. That is why you enjoy it and smile sarcastically at people.

He said: Possibly. As for you, you are fortunate enough not to have ever had this. You accept people almost in a physical way. You enter with them in a direct relation, an organic one, even a spontaneous one, without ever entering into your mind the possibility of an ethical judgment, without ever having any ethical criteria in the first place. There is nothing to condemn in all this, there is not even anything disgraceful about it. It's simply that people and men are an extension of you, yourself.

181

The canon of her faith is a full life at every moment.

She once said with a touch of jealousy: Svetlana Stalin got married six times. What a woman, what a cyclone. And no one can count the lovers of George Sand.

He said: We too have had our legends: Amina, Samia, and Tahiya.

She said: I am my father's daughter. He lived his life well and fully, by length and breadth. Indeed, he filled his life with everything: love, adventure, politics, women, wealth, bankruptcy, beauty, bullets, people of all walks of life, with glories and frustrations. He lived a full life.

Thoughtfully, he said: No doubt you are your father's daughter.

She used to move around other people's tables all morning in the Auberge garden. The waters of the dark-colored, vast lake seem to melt away in the sand amid the stones under the cement fence, looking out of place on the moist sand. The swaying shades under the umbrellas gave her face a special luminosity. She laughed softly and faintly as she raised the foaming beer mug, and as she ran after the big, colored ball, while yelling and leaning on the shoulders of Mahmud so as not to fall.

She said to him: Mahmud, in the end, is insignificant and silly. I had to put him in his place. I am sorry. He wasn't acceptable.

He said: What did he do? What did he say?

She said: Nothing in reality. Trivialities. No reason at all to make you jealous of him.

He said: No reason?

She said, going out from Mikhail's place at high noon, as she was closing the door behind her: I am the one who is beginning to be jealous—something that has never happened to me before. I was trying to trigger your jealousy all day.

She closed the door in a hurry without waiting for a response.

He did not tell her: Because I worry about you. Because I am concerned, in the end, with the immediacy of your responsiveness toward them, concerned by the easy companionship you grant them.

She had said to him: You don't care about knowing people. This isolation of yours and your solitary inclination . . .

He said: Not that. I do care about knowing people. I'm fascinated by them and I yearn to know them. Their ideas, dreams, calculations fascinate me. But who can claim to know people genuinely in this confused marketplace which has nothing but buying and selling? There are no people in it, only instruments. They have turned themselves into instruments. How do we know them? I mean, the burning knowledge, the knowledge of those we love: For this is knowledge. What are you thinking about? How do you feel? What do you read? Of what do you dream? Even, how do you breathe? What are your discourses, your visions, your concealed ravings? What is in your handbag? This is not meddling. To know is not to possess or to dominate. Knowledge, alone, is Truth; it is love.

She said: Haven't I told you that you are Platonic?

He did not say to her: No, this jealousy is simply an irresistible inclination toward possessing love alone. Nothing else. Not your life nor your memories, not your past nor your future. But only this love–eroticism–knowledge, filling all the gaps of the past and future, making it one massive body, no matter how heavy and stifling, nor how crushing and unbearable.

He said to himself: No, the issue for me is ambiguous. Doubtless. Furthermore, these are the ideas of the market place exposed at every corner. So why are you tortured by such vulgar, common, and trodden ways?

In a hoarse voice, she was humming a song to him, making him feel as if he were on a ship without mast or sail, deep within its somber inner hold, as it tracked across still waters toward a vast blue sea whose light foamy waves poured onto a sand of green slopes from which grew lofty, ancient cedar trees.

183

He said: I have not heard you laugh loudly, burst into laughter, at all. How does your laughter sound?

She said: Maybe I am more inclined to be tragic, somehow. Like you.

He said: There is something tragic in you, it's true. Not melodramatic; something inevitable, as if fated despite all your surprises.

She said: Yes, written on the forehead.

He held her hand.

He said to her: I really want to know who I am in your view, my image in your mind.

She said to him: As you wish. I have two images of you. One is that of a rational man: the image of a man who lives by a set of rules and conventions concerning what one should and should not do; the image of an ethical man or at least he who views everything in an ethical light. This, in itself, is a good thing. The other image is that of an emotional man: the image of a donor. You know my well-known distinction between people. For me people fall into two categories: those who take and those who give.

She gazed at him for a moment then said: You are in the category of those who give. Of course, you also take like everyone else. But giving for you is what you wish for, in my opinion.

He said urgently: Where are you situated in this split image?

She said: I am the wicked side of you; that is the way you see me. The side in you that dismisses rules, conventions, that which should be done, which is correct, permissible; the side that does away with social and psychological fetters. This is what I am for you. This is what drives me crazy almost. This is what I hate in you.

He was baffled. The surprise was such that he could not respond to it at all. Her words had never occurred before in his mind.

He said to himself: You are extremely self-conscious, you ramble too much about yourself. That is why you don't know yourself, and

184

you don't know her, and you don't know what goes into her mind. With all this babble you say nothing in the end, and particularly you don't say anything about yourself.

He said to himself: Also, in everything you say there are these familiar, ready-made formulas available in the marketplace. Her body is hers alone; she possesses it and she has never turned it into a commodity; it has never been an instrument. She has made love with you and others, but she has not compromised her body or cheapened it; she has never turned it into a thing. This is a way of speaking, a discursive formula. Granted. She is the only one capable of giving or not giving her body. You cannot take it for granted, doing with it what you please. It is not an object. Between her and her body there is total unification. She is, contrary to you, seeking multiplicity from within her unargued unity. As for you, you are searching for a divided, fragmented, lost unity.

He did not say to her: I am not holding you accountable, nor is it within my capacity to do so. You have absolute freedom, and this is not a donation or a gift from me. I know—it seems to me I know—the wretchedness that pushes you and provokes you toward your madness as well as the wretchedness that keeps you within the fences of your moderation. My eternal wise child, the enchantress who cannot be seized: Because I love you, I want to know who you are, what you are. I want to plunge my naked hands into your innermost being without wounding you. And I know that it is impossible. Don't say this is sadism. That would be easy. How difficult it is to tell you that the inundation of this love brings along self-loss and self-discovery in the same act. This is another formula: to cross in dignity the space of unbearable humiliation. A formula, formula, formula. Where can I find the redeeming word? When can I finish with the suffering of faltering and muttering? Don't tell me it is simply the wish to possess when I really want freedom, not my freedom, but freedom . . . with you, as a

185

crown under your feet. Yet I am unable to reach its threshold. You and I continue to be bound by fetters when I want to reshape the face of the world after your face. This is my freedom. *What insolence!*

He was silent.

Why?

He said: Surely words impoverish, because they put fences around that which cannot be enclosed.

He said: Because there is the act. Acts alone can give silence its meaning.

He said: Acts too can contain ambivalence. In fact, they are mysterious in themselves. They are the thing and its opposite. They are limited too, and they set limits.

He said: Therein lies their value.

He said: Whither escape? An act is more than one thing and less than one thing.

He said: Words too are acts, acts-in-words, their tone, warmth, allusion, spontaneity, reserve, inarticulateness are all necessary, inevitable, vital.

She said: You make my head turn. Isn't all this absurd?

The old-fashioned kerosene lamp fell with him, with its plump belly, its long glass neck, as he dropped down on the floor without a sound. Is this the old yellow mat that used to be on the floor of his room in their house in Ghayt al-'Inab in the years of his childhood? His hands were hanging onto air while the glass belly had broken and its fragments flown about, mute on the mat, as the kerosene flowed slowly. An elongated circular spot darkened over the slender cords of the delicately woven mat, flattened by successive footsteps and the pressure of cushions and soft, sitting pillows. His face bumped across its soft cords. A sudden pain stabbed his chest as he was opening his mouth that had smashed against the floor, but no sound was emitted. Wide stretched wings with firm feathers flap on his body, but he does

186

not hear their flutter. They hit the walls that contract and enclose completely on him. The slow spreading fire has the color of light red with dancing fringes inclining toward the color of orange peel. He shakes off a nameless pain as if his limbs are cracking and dropping shaggy-sided, like sharp stones, and ripping hooks plunge into his living flesh. He strikes with both fists on the floor without the slightest sound or echo. The successive, random pounding does not help him. The windowpane shudders, and suddenly from it comes the sound of continuous convulsion. It is the first sound he hears after a long silence. He falls at once into a wounding, resounding, successive clamor. The huge wings flutter roughly around his head and rap with tight armor and rattling iron clatter. The tall spear plunges into a muddy sky. The trumpets of heralds resound at a distance in despairing lament. Stars fall and crumble between his fingers. The smile of pleasure on her beautiful face appears in a rusty brass mask that stretches out and is crushed by armors. The waves of the oceans of the universe cannot erase the bitterness in his mouth, nor wipe the pain bursting in his ribs. A tremendous earthquake hurls him. He is tossed about by the walls of the confining room that contains heaven and earth, having all become a vast ruin in which the wind blows. The braids of her honey hair are drooping from the sun, and the green-eyed moon is dripping blood. His eyes shed pebbles of tears. The seven seals are locked. They are not opening in the clamor of the earthquake nor are they broken by his fist which continues to fumble with their locks. The black steed rips the ceiling, escaping with the fast beat of the rumbling thunder of its hooves. The guts of the Dragon are open, throbbing and welling out a bloody flood, gushing in the glow of fires in the dark, which is then swallowed by the wasteland. The two great olive trees have dropped their fruits in the roar of outpouring waters. The six wings are not broken in a war that ends in either victory or defeat. Heaven's towers are collapsing, but

187

the supple feminine body in his contracting embraces is pure. It has not been touched by the flood of water replete with corpses. The large sunflowers with their rounded tips and dark-colored centers are up, thriving and swaying among the flames, and he has fallen.

He calls out voicelessly in the clamor of the earthquake: O Mikhail! O Archangel! O Centurion!

His arms desperately and heroically encircle the legs of the old desk—where he used to sit studying and dreaming, during the years of his childhood—seeing with unblinking eyes its marble, oval slab, and holding onto its carved twisting legs of old black wood infested by woodworms making small irregular holes in it. The desk is staggering, almost falling then straightening over his head. The tongues of fire rise up with elegance and precision, licking the lower, rough, gray side of the white marble. Her cold, soft arms, as if they were weightless, were embracing his neck above the rapping of wild wings, blowing a breeze of repose and ease. He longs to wallow his ripped face in the freshness of her temptation. But he does not say the words of the final incantation that consecrates his fall and repose: "O my enchantress, I surrender to you." No words can be pulled from his innermost. A destructive, ardent, scorching, cauterizing flame, touched by pain monsters, has lived with him for a long time. He cannot live with them without retribution.

9
Craving and Reed Stalks

W ater drops fall from the long, rusty wound in the stone of the centuries-old statue. The murmuring water flows cheerfully, without quivering, under the light poured from a strong, high-pitched, firmly radiant lamp. The iron surrounding the fountain is low, circular, presenting an island in a street gushing with two streams of shiny cars—one in each direction—hurrying with their noisy, exploding, fluctuating emissions.

The new friends, Mikhail and Rama, having come out of the cinema, are overlooking the statue from behind a broad windowpane inside a large modern restaurant practically without customers. Their comfortable seats were mounted with ribbed, black plastic resembling leather, Formica armrests dappled with splendid cunning to imitate wood. The hollow, round aluminum, resembling commonplace silver, emits hushed echoes whenever a leg accidentally grazes it.

They have been to the cinema. Her warm and subdued whispering—unfolding vague images that possess distinctly erotic features—draws the side of her face, radiant with captivating appeal, near to his eyes. He glances at her as if she were part of the film itself, his arm in his short-sleeve shirt touching her soft, bare arm whose fullness increases as she presses it on the rough woolly armrest cover. Between them stands a kind of physical affection, a warm, undeclared sensual understanding.

After the disappearance of the last traffic wave over the crosswalks used by the nocturnal crowds and the dispersal of the last show viewers gathered in their intimate circles, the lit city became theirs, as if its empty, clean, wide streets were welcoming avenues into the mind for a gentle night wind that promised unlimited good things. Having left the restaurant they passed an endless series of dazzling ponds of light, gravely empty and quiet, choosing to amble toward islands of still shades with tree leaves fluttering harmoniously.

He said to her: I have known streets of many cities in almost all hours of day and night. There is nothing more beautiful than empty streets at night with the city lamps lighting them in a practically useless way. Public lights fall on buildings and on the black asphalt—vast, shiny, free—which can be crossed and walked on without penalty. Despite the heaving danger and the unknown, the city seems as if healed forever of hidden evil and violence, from the wrangles of a herd of mechanical and electrical armors gushing without stopping. How beautiful is this city!

Just before their walk, they had ordered hamburgers and beer; she said she liked beer. They ate with an appetite for everything. She spoke spontaneously and heatedly about her fear of death, though not her own. She said that death was horrible and unimaginable. He said: No one ever believes inside himself that he will die. Death is simply an abstraction, something that happens to others, and does not happen to me at all. It is the only thing that no one knows, for I think that even at the very unimaginable moment of loss of consciousness, no one knows, no one believes that he will die, nor would he know the meaning of death even if he knew and believed that it would happen. For a person remains convinced, intuitively certain, that he will live, until he crosses the boundaries. And he is right, for even in crossing he lives. After that no consciousness, nothing. Yes, death is the only thing that can never be known, neither before nor after. What is known about it are things related to it, associated with it, that precede it or surround it, but not the reality itself. Death—simply—does not exist.

She said in a bout of strange passion that this was exactly what she had been thinking about all the time without saying it, for no one would believe it or be convinced by it. She said: The frightening thing is the death of a loved person. And she asked: How can someone live if his truly beloved person dies? She said: This is the death that a person feels and knows intimately through a loss that cannot be made up for at all. This is the diffused suffering, gratuitous, filling the corners of earth and heaven. And she asked: Why? Why? The flowers of such suffering are so thorny.

Her eyes watered. She was swept by terrible fear, provoked, maintained by the fact that her loved ones were still living, that they had not died. She said that she was ready to die for the sake of those she truly loved. She said that she prayed, never knowing whether she was a believer or not, but nevertheless pleading vaguely and daily to a divine power to protect and keep alive those whom she loved.

He said to her: As if you were talking with my voice, expressing what I sense without having given it a form or a definition!

Their happiness in this rare, enabling articulation was complete and untarnished. They celebrated in the refreshing, faint glow of the beer mugs, in the light meal, and in the warmth of the sensuous closeness in the cool night air blowing from the open window, open onto the wet statue and fountain—gushing in geometrically intricate trajectories; its drizzle radiating on the husky, muscular male body in

191

a challenging position, entrenching his exploding legs in the earth, two tree trunks of undecaying stone.

He saw on her bare arm, as if embroidered on her skin, the trace of the cinema armrest with its rough woolly cover.

She said to him: I always need human warmth, human relations. I cannot stand for any substitute. I can't live in a furnished apartment, day in, day out by myself, cooking on Fridays for the week, washing my pantyhose on Saturdays, going to the hairdresser on Sundays. I am not this kind. I want to meet people, talk and live with them, get out in the world and encounter new types of men. This is why you find me looking for inspection trips in my job, so that I can embark to any place without hesitation.

He said without complaint, without disapproval: As for me, I am a loner. I can—and at times I love to—stay in my room for a week without seeing streetlights.

She said thoughtfully: Yes, that is possible for you. You can be cut off from people.

He said: No, no. I need people badly, especially those I love, even if at a distance. The most important thing is that they are there. Being cut off, like monks are, troubles me and gives me insomnia.

One day, he said to himself: Was her interest in me in the beginning simply to pick up a new type of man? A new naïve type that seemed uncontaminated, simply for the hobby of her collection? How does she best get to know new types of men? Is this an accusation of cheapness I'm launching?

He said to himself: Why does the traditional reaction of an Eastern man, of a southern Egyptian, persist in you? Isn't it an outdated and medieval sensibility, no matter what philosophical and contemporary views and positions—existentialism, Marxism—are involved?

It never occurred to him to answer the question, which, in the

192

final analysis, constituted a process: admission of the fact, then the doubting of it, then the admission of it again: an endless cycle.

He said to her: The need for human warmth triggers your many friendships?

She leaned toward him, in the fervor of an opening up between two new friends. The pressure of her breasts on the bra beneath the light blouse was evident. She pushed her face close to his unintentionally, relaxing her bosom on the Formica table next to the empty beer mug on whose lip a slight white foam was attached, and, on the other side the shiny metal box from which white paper napkins come out, also the small ceramic hamburger plate with its brown color and traces of dark red, dry ketchup.

I don't know how to maintain relations with women, she said. There's nothing in common between us. I can't, I really can't, enter into a conversation about fashion, recipes, types of make-up, problems with servants, or gossiping about others. I don't know how to put on half a ton of powders and creams every day, tarnishing or beautifying my face with them. As you can see, I don't use lipstick. There is something masculine in me. They say I am a policeman, an old guard.

He laughed and said: You are sheer femininity.

She said: May God bless you for the compliment.

He said: No, I mean what I said.

After dinner, when having coffee, she said to him: I have an appointment with a Sudanese friend, an exile visiting this country. He phoned me this afternoon and invited me to an unofficial diplomatic soirée. These invitations usually bore me, but I couldn't refuse. I haven't seen him for a while, and he is a dear friend, an elderly gentleman. I ask you for a favor. Kindly take me in a taxi to the Clock Square. You are not so busy, are you? This request humbles me, but I have to say I don't dare take a taxi alone at night.

He said: Is that all? Your wish is my command, my lady, from the bottom of my eyes. I shall apologize and delay my appointment for half an hour.

She said: O my God! You have an appointment? Then no need.

He said: No, no! It is very simple. I'll take you.

No sooner had the taxi moved away with them—in the intimate, private darkness typical of narrow spaces, while he was gazing at the city, with its people and lights disappearing soundlessly behind the windowpane as the engine roared softly with its hushed, internal, mechanical power—than he had stretched his hand to hers at the same time her hand was moving toward his. The fingers touched, clasped firmly. He felt blood rising to his face for the first time in their friendship. Her voice quivered as she called on him pleading and anxious: Mikhail! He said: Rama, what is happening to us? She said: Mikhail, Mikhail, I don't know. This was their first and last mutual confession, then a charged silence fell upon them, pregnant with all possibilities.

She tried to pay for the taxi, but he refused, laughing. The driver hesitated for a moment in front of the two different hands, each extending a large sum. Then as a matter of male solidarity the driver quickly took his money. She said to him: Go back in the same taxi, so you can make it to your appointment. He said: No, I will walk you to your destination and enjoy the air. She said: But your appointment? He said: I have time.

He stepped down, they walked together. She clung to his arm with new familiarity and spontaneity. She said: I'll phone you when I get back. I'll talk to you; at least wish you good night. He pressed her hand as he parted from her and stood watching as she entered a residential building full of quiet windows. He walked aimlessly, a bit distraught as various scenarios filled his head. Under his feet the streets felt like waves. He was plowing their waters, sailing with spread sails pushed by abundant and prosperous wind.

194

He said to himself: No, she will probably forget or else it will be too late. She will not call tonight. Tomorrow, she will talk and I will hear her story.

It was one in the morning when he went to bed. Exhausted, his senses were yet alert. A lightness and joy fluttered within him. He had not known such feelings for a long time, and as yet they were vague, without content.

Suddenly, in the profound and enclosed silence the telephone rang loudly. He stretched his hand—alarmed, anxious, not fully awake—as if knowing it was she. The light, he discovered, had been left on and shone brightly. With an unimaginable effort he responded with an awkward but alert voice: Hello!

Her voice came to him, unsteady, low, and womanish: Hello, Mikhail! Have I awakened you? He said: Not at all. I was waiting for your telephone call. How was your evening? She said: Horrible. Let's not talk about it. I miss you. He said: I miss you too. He looked at his watch. It was after 2:30. She said: Mikhail, I need you. I can't sleep and I want to talk to you. He said: Now? She said: Yes, now of course. I am in an unbearable state of anxiety and I propose we talk.

Having had the matter slip out of his hand, he said: Do you know what the time is? It's 2:30. She said: What does it matter what time it is? I am resorting to you. He said: I don't know. There are certain things we have to take into consideration: we are Egyptians, after all. We'll talk as you wish, surely, but tomorrow morning. He did not comprehend what was going on. He was frightened. She said: All I want is to talk together, talk, t-a-l-k, like two mature, rational persons, one to the other. One person who needs the other. I need you. That's all. Her voice was shaking—drinking more than she should have? Sweat oozed from all the pores of his body. His face blazed. He fell silent, didn't say a thing.

She said: All right. I understand. You are right. No doubt. I am mistaken.

195

Her voice began to crack. No resistance could stop its breakdown. She said: Please forgive me—as the tears gathered, amplified, exploded over the phone—I apologize, I didn't mean—the words got lost, buried in her unbearable crying bout, in the pain and sense of rejection and loss, in the night and in the loneliness without hope of comfort. Sweat continued dripping from him without stint, without resistance. He said: Don't cry. Please, please, Rama, don't cry. She said intermittently: I am not crying, I am not crying. He said: I will be with you in minutes. Please. I am coming. She could not get her tears to cease flowing, as she said with a tired, surrendered, thankful, and grateful voice: No, no reason to bother yourself. I understand. I am better now. He said: No, that's enough, Rama. I'll come right away. I want to come. I wanted to come all along. She said, while the last hushed sighs were making her voice present in his own room as her femininity enveloped and embraced him in its soft, captivating tone: I'll wait for you.

He changed his night flannels, as they had become moist with sweat. In few moments, which he took to be hours, he dressed. When he went out, he was confounded again. First, he went down to the dark lobby: in his agitation he thought the appointment was there. He was surprised by sleeping chairs, extinguished lights, a detained nocturnal emptiness. He went back perplexed and self-questioning.

He entered her room. But after she opened the door in a hurry, she did not close it herself. Instead, she said to him: Close the door behind you, Mikhail. A single wall window was their only sky, their only light. Agitated, his eyes were slightly blinded in the darkness. She said to him: No, don't turn on the light. I don't want light now. I cannot stand it.

The bathroom was lit behind the glass of the closed door. The light was stealing in like trickling water.

She said to him: Come! Sit next to me on the bed.

196

She was under the white sheet while preparing a place for him on the edge of the bed with her hands. He sensed the bronze color of her bare arms in the faint darkness. The church dome in the window frame seemed to him heavy and flattened.

In her face, the anxiety of the tearful storm lingered. Her cheeks and eyelids seemed round, slightly puffed, adding to her appeal.

She said: We will talk now. Nothing but talk.

This was followed by a belated tearful sigh. He leaned over and kissed her under the eyes. He patted her cheeks and eyelids with his hands in a silent, comforting gesture. She raised her arms and slid his glasses away from his eyes in a deliberate, slow gesture, putting them down next to keys and a cigarette pack under the shade of the turned-off table lamp.

She said: Come, let's talk. If we analyze the problem objectively and logically we will . . .

He put his hand on her lips and said: No, no, Rama. No need for logical, objective analysis or for a non-logical, non-objective analysis.

She said: From the dialectical angle, we can look at the issue from the point of view of . . .

Smiling lightly and affectionately, he said: I don't want to discuss the issue from any point of view.

Her lips held on to his: the appeal of the lightly fragrant wine breath of her mouth was immediate and sudden. Their first kiss was sudden, unexpected. His lips came to know the freshness of the open, slow-moving, and clinging mouth. In her mouth was a light sugary taste—the sweetness of a mature fruit plucked from a mother tree.

He leaned to take her between his arms, and he felt on his chest the weight of her naked breasts under the light nylon, white gown. The music of the spheres was grandly mellow, and heavens resounded with glorious, lofty melodies. The juxtaposition of chests was a fulfillment, a realization of a deep primordial demand that could not

197

be questioned. His arm behind her shoulder held the magnificence of that which he did not know the world could contain.

She said to him: Come next to me.

His move was quick, without thought.

She said to him: Put your hand on my breast.

He felt the virginity of her blooming bosom, its strange innocence while she looked at him with gentle ecstatic eyes. No present, no future, and no past. The moment that does not end is everything. There was no discovery, nor the rush into new recognition. Their knowledge of each other was as old as time: entrenched, having its own principle as if eternal. This determined voracity, this burning desire, this distilled eroticism devoid of the weakness of humane affection. The boat of craving rose with them above deep waves with quiet surface amid the reed stalks. His hands knew their way to the wet and rich jungles as he sailed in no time between the two full and soft legs that he could not see: his face was buried between her breasts.

She said: Tomorrow you will return, and we will talk formally as required by good manners. As for now, we have a few moments together.

She said: We will wait for our pleasure together, one after the other: each in its turn. We will not hurry.

There was nothing between them except a joy with steady music— its uproar controlled by a strict, spontaneous, uncalculated rhythm.

She said: Wait, till we come simultaneously together.

The waves were lapping between their embracing bodies. Her full thigh on his leg was a spread-out sail of heavy fabric filled by the blowing of joyful wind. Just the same, he was listening from afar to the fluttering of vast wings filling the blocked sky, in a frame of radiant but faint fire, above the joyful bells twinkling: the annunciation of the coming of a new resurrection. Death, where is your darkness? Then the dams broke after their soft rocks trembled under the unbearable anxiety of pleasure. The roaring of the last waves broke out: her abrupt cry from the pain of pleasure was sharp and hushed. The boat that carried them together was shaking in its final shudder in the jungles. It staggered and drowned in the warm pond whose waters streamed off, and on which the breeze collapsed amid the soft reed stalks, burnt and dried up by the sun.

They were traveling once by train when she said to him unexpectedly: I seduced you. Had I not cried when I phoned, you would not have come.

His friend Ibrahim once said to him: Ah, Rama. This woman is incredible. Everything with her goes through there, from below, everything. What a loss! Such intelligence, education, brilliance, self-sacrifice! All of it passes through there: all her mind, her work, her play, her archaeological expertise, her radicalism—all are in the service of the lower part. He added: She used to be, indeed, very beautiful in the past. When she went to Port Said, she became a legend, but now . . . Who would look at her now?

Mikhail said to himself: For the cynics, everything spirals into a repetitive cynical mold. Is this the story of a woman-nymph, like any other? The flesh of truth is something alive, gentle, soft. It cannot be reduced to a cynical formula; it cannot be a mold among other judgmental molds—ready-made, cheapened by hands, made commonplace by gossip.

He said to himself: I, I look at her and I fully see her. I know a beauty in her that no one else can see: a gentleness that hurts the heart, a childish weakness, also a rock-like force, a hunger not of this earth. I know through her a woman's body pouring into my arms as well as a stony, harsh wall that cannot be possessed. She has both indescribable affection and absolute indifference—an indifference not even aware of itself. What does it matter if the feet of conquering armies have stepped on the fresh flesh of your truth, endless times? The rock stays, the

199

fertility of the flesh is renewed in the jungles of Manzala swamps and down to the drowned cataracts. The hippopotami, with ugly mouths, gobble tons of dry grass of shooting stars. The Nile waters disappear behind the great dam, and the earth cracks, opening up a network of wound marks without blood. Ghosts, ghouls, and monsters surround me, surround you, you, nymph, you, dark river houri. Phantoms in the gardens of Circe disappear in the burning noon sun on the mountain of Aswan. The crooked tree trunks are laid bare, black, leafless. These are not her sins; they are not her sins. She has no sins. It is my sin that I did not know how to teach her my reality. I remained for her without substance, a chiaroscuro. What, then, is my reality? Do I have any? If so, why do I wish to see it reflected in her green mirror alone?

She said to him: I love you this way, when you are gentle and sweet; I don't love your fierceness.

He said to her: I want you to open up for me all your inner life, even those things that shock, torture, and frighten. I'll live them again with you. I will share with you the mad frenzy, if that is what it is called. Perhaps I shall be wounded deeply. Yes, but the wounds are open now, anyhow, and they might never heal as it is. What I mean is that I am ready to live with you. I am capable of it. A shared healing might be in this. I don't know. What I know is that you're staying alone inside your loneliness, a relentless loneliness within loneliness, each with its own flavor of cruelty. Your solitude is made by your own hands inside a self-enclosed planet. When will it end? Is this what you want? Or is it that you possess nothing but this? It is not, and it cannot be, your will. Nothing is forced upon us from outside. You know this. There is no need for me to say it.

He said: You share with me all the moments of my life . . . I want complete sharing.

She said without accepting, not even for a moment: Total sharing is very demanding.

200

He said: Yes.

She said: Haven't we agreed that perfection is not of this world? It is enough that we get what we can, if we can.

In his fancy, it was possible to arrive at this absolute love within the prison of conventions that people erect for their lives. In the heart of such impossibility, he wanted to reach her totally, and to give himself totally.

He said: Knowledge for me is love.

She said: What do you want to know? Nothing. Void and emptiness.

He said: You? In the midst of your crowded activity?

She said: The worst kind of void is that in the midst of crowds; in the midst of people, urgent issues, successive problems, and everything emptied on the inside.

He said: It is not emptiness then, but escape.

She said: I want to escape from you.

He said: Isn't there a kind of escape forward through confrontation?

She said: Last night I did not sleep because of the heat.

He said: You told me you slept well.

She said: I slept well, yes, but not enough, only a little.

She yawned and put her hand on her mouth, looking at him with a half-apologetic glance.

He asked himself, he doesn't know how many times he has asked himself: Was that an act of self-destruction or an act of self-liberation from the rubble of a previous, repetitive, and unending destruction?

She said: I leave matters to unfold on their own. I take things as they come. Most things do not ever get completed. How many things around us, inside us, are half-made things, partially completed, thus partially incomplete!

Of course he did not tell her: Do you know anything about the long, long hours passing by in which I think of you, for you, in you— talking to you confidentially and at length, with utter bitterness? I shy from such naïveté, from the fact that all this is half-cooked, half-raw, half-crude and wasted, of no interest at all to anyone.

He said to himself: Music tortures me these days. It invades me without resistance, a sort of sensual conquest on the level of blood and guts. It possesses me instantly, opening up all locks and flowing heavily into my veins, as if it were a poison of a very deadly kind, absorbed by every cell in my guts, welcomed and demanded. Music's indefinite language is a resounding cry. Where are the music of the mind and the spell of its pure geometric lines?

He said to her: You are fortunate, at least for not being romantic at all. I don't know if you resort to certain escapes from romanticism?

He meant escapes into sensuality, the continuous, diligent search for relaxation of organic tension that can never be quieted, escapes into a non-romantic absorption and drowning. At times, he was surprised and shocked by her calmness, her acceptance, her surrender, and immobility. The morning would stretch into a slow, alienating rhythm, as if it would never leave off. Even the taste of her kisses changed, lacked sharpness and responsiveness, lacked the slightly sugary taste.

With the absence of certainty, numbness creeps into him. His mind falls into a heavy stillness. Even his heart gives up on expressiveness.

She said to him: When someone loves, usually one's energy gushes at every moment. Creation, creativity, and discovery spring out, even as you drink your cup of coffee, as if you are remaking the world.

He did not mention to her his confusion in the perplexing waves of unanswerable questions: Small waves, turbid and block-ing the horizon, without hope of reaching the vast surface of the sea toward the unlimited and extended borders, melding with the open skies.

Sorrow lies in your eyes while cool air and pure blue radiance fill the November sky. This Sea City is my city, diffused in the high noon of its paved road. Your stabbing eyes carry a weight, which cuts the surface of my self to the very bottom, while I am a step apart from you in the high noon of the road. And you, my love, so distant—more illusory than my love fancies. What do I observe in your glances? Is this look, with its alienated depth, yours or my own fancy? And this love that troubles me, possesses me, murders me—is this love my own delusion? What is in your mind, Rama? A depressing, fragile sorrow or a void? The void of a November noon? I don't know, I don't know anything about you, my enigmatic love. I don't know the meaning of your glance. I don't know who I am for you. I don't know who you are. The winter void of my taciturn noon. My city escapes me: Fancies, people and their cars, traffic lights and horns, the rattle of trams and the eyes of the people buried in the secrets of their troubles, all silent on the road. All disappearing in November clarity, in distant white clouds hanging on the city ceiling in al-Raml Station. Nothing is left but your gaze—a secret I will never decipher.

The curtains had been lowered on the picture window in the Auberge. The room was dusky as if it existed inside a glass pond whose water had been removed, but whose air remained humid and heavy. Visible through the window, placid Qarun Lake felt heavy, distilling some of its presence into the silent room. Its salty breath blew from behind the wood; the piercing cry of the gull reached them from its distant niche in the secluded sky.

She opened the door for him and stood next to the bed—her lofty body under an Indian blouse, of light green with dark gold flowers and designs, reaching above her knees, leaving her legs bare. Her protruding breasts under the blouse lifted a little the front hem. Her loose hair was flowing in a dry rustle, like a subtropical plant whose softness masks the presence of multiple saps.

She said: After I came down from the train at the station, the porter bumped into my back. He was carrying a suitcase. It seemed— God knows how—the lock was open; you know, the small sharp metal tongue. I sensed it scratching my back. There is a cut there, and I can't reach it.

Suddenly she turned and lifted her blouse up with both hands.

Under the blouse she was naked. He was taken aback by the love- ly bronze back—a dark marble—yet soft, slippery, gently flowing, powerfully sculpted. He found the scratch: thin and sharp, almost imperceptible. For the first time he saw her buttocks in a standing position: steady, smooth, and full of curves.

She said with the voice of a calm interlocutor in a parlor room full of people: Do you see it? Is there blood in it? Feel it with your hand.

The whale swims in the depths of the dark still ocean. The lines of its tremendous body have the smoothness of a slope. And Jonah remained fasting until sunset.

He touched his finger carefully to the scar. It was a slight cut in the gentle flesh of her back, no bigger than half a finger's length under the shoulder blade. He smelled—or thought he did—an electric shock triggered in his skin, from tension and anticipation. His blood was throbbing, but the inside air was paralyzing his responsiveness, and keeping him numb in a way he could not understand. His voice was obstructed, he was worried that if he talked it would rattle. His gaze seemed the only thing alive in him.

Without moving, he said at last: Yes, it is slight; nothing, in fact.

She dropped down her blouse. The sound of silk falling on her body, ending suddenly at mid thigh, was that of frustration.

She said while turning toward him: You are tired from the train. The trip was exhausting. Come, sit for a while.

She turned in a hurried move and bent to straighten a pillow on the bed and to draw a seat for him near her. Caught in a quick glance the vale of her split haunch stirred him, but the moment passed, as if her body had taken a decision to encircle itself, locked, rejecting any touch.

Later, she said to him: You don't love me.

He said in disbelief: I don't?

She said: If you loved me, you would take me every time.

He mused: Did you want failure to come about, though? Was it your very desire? At will and from within, doing what would not lead to fulfillment because you felt a risk, a threat, because you were not willing to undertake the final gamble in a game that went beyond the rules? Because you knew intuitively, without thinking, that there was in this relationship that which goes beyond the usual, repetitive, lovemaking? That such a relationship is not simply the sum total of stabs searching for an oblivion that never takes place?

He said to himself: What to do? How can I—how can we togeth er—challenge that which I presume to be her authentic desire, to genuinely end this fluctuating, continuously dynamic relation in failure, despite the usual repeated successes? How can we undertake another deep craving toward final fulfillment or toward the finality of fulfillment?

He said to himself: She was talking to me about love, truth, and freedom while we were overlooking the statue wounded by water gushing on its chest, and looking above its legs, at the raised arms, muscular with masculinity that had reached its apex and was about to fall, but now will never lower no matter how many stone grains the flowing of water scrapes off its edges. Then at night, bright and empty, her words and her eyes were reflecting in a wonderful clari-ty what was in my own mind. Her mind is a sharp-toothed instru-ment, reaching to the depths and penetrating easily all the levels of

205

reservation, guarding, and secrecy. Was she talking only in order to extend her arms toward me, with a powerful net, soft-knit, so as to captivate me? I was not the hunter. Or had the hunting journey for me started a long time ago?

They were standing at the top of a street stairway. A loose iron chain with thick rings extended between two ancient columns. They stood waiting for a taxi on the first stair, smooth-edged from footsteps. The sky was the color of pale gray pearls: clear under insubstantial white clouds, having the same transparency as that of the morning following the night he had met her. Her face was calm; his heart was quiet and content in that extinguished light beneath the slow, stretched clouds.

She said to him: Mikhail, is this the first time you have broken the chains and liberated yourself from repression?

Later on, he reflected she had not said to him that his love-making was romantic, but in fact pure and purging, in a certain sense, founded on tenderness and sensuous devotion verging on ritual worship, that his hands, lips, and tightly taut body were unravaged by use and vulgarity.

He said: Yes, it is the first time.

She said: That pleases me.

Without any quiver in the tone of her voice, she decided something that had importance but triggered no excitement. As if the matter had not been, for him, a stunningly beautiful discovery, an earthquake that shook the walls of his life, breaking and piling the rocks into the split and cracked yet clean-cut and pure-edged.

How can she be so closed to communication when she chooses, or when her taste or distaste chooses? She rebuked him by her sheer presence. Alone, it denied him, negated him, voicelessly and effortlessly.

After six days, she told him: You slew the dragon.

And she said: Thank God we are traveling today and moving on.

206

He said to her, obstinately: Thank God in any case. But I cannot say, here and now, and despite everything, "Thank God," were it not that for Him alone one offers thanks.

She said to him: Of course, you are free in what you say and what you don't say.

He accompanied her to the station, nevertheless, and he embraced her, thinking it was farewell, but he knew in his innermost that it was not farewell.

From the dragon's teeth planted in my heart, bushy dark-green twigs of reed flourish and sway.

In his mind he saw her on the roof of their old house in Ghayt al-'Inab. She was distant and up in the raw morning light next to the low roof fence with its unpainted stones. She had the obedience and the bronze coloring of his thin, gentle sister Aida, with her southern Egyptian features and dark eyes. She had Aida's secretive face while also Rita's briskness—Rita, the Greek girlfriend of his youthful days who dropped out of his life without him noticing it—with her light blond hair. She had also the daring of their Jewish neighbor—in their house in Muharram Bey, a long time ago. She had the creamy body of his neighbor with its penetrative openness and cleanliness, with its special glow that excited his precocious sexuality. She had his neighbor's joyfulness in the mornings as she hummed intermittently a song, happy with her opulent body, rested after sleep. As he was on the unlit stairway, bending and gazing at her from below, he saw in her something of all the women he knew. On the stairway, he recollected dispersed earrings, shirt buttons, shiny metal rings, safety pins, and large, round mother-of-pearl buttons. He recalled his hands rubbing the sand on the stairway as he searched, finding these spilled-over things, as if poured out from the sewing box that was originally a round cookie box decorated with an image of an ancient European city, which his mother kept when he was a child. He would collect them in his hands, finding difficulty in holding onto them and keeping them between his fingers. All this took place as she was descending from up high. Our footsteps on the stairway were silent as we went down into the dark night, for once without being surprised and without the need for explanation. The steps of the stairway were twisting around us, their wooden fence shining darkly from blackness and age.

I knew then that everything was ready to move to another house. The big horse-driven cart was at the door. Packages and parcels were tied by thin cords; wooden boxes and palm-frond cages for chickens and vegetables were filled with household odds and ends, covered with old rags that used to be white sheets, and tied with twine. The cupboards, chairs, and tables were arranged carefully in a row in the cart after having been disassembled, and having their nails and screws placed into a special drawer on the cart's side.

The apartment door is unexpectedly open. I realize the place has been robbed and emptied. The tiles are bare; there are dark traces on the wall paint where the removed pictures have been hanging for a long time exposed to the sun and air. The kitchen door slams and I see the thief stealing away in the darkness. His grating presence triggers in me a frightening shudder, as if he were coming from another world with its own laws. I see him from his back—a strong, tall, agile youth—as, wearing shirt and pants, he is descending the stairway, running and escaping—as if he were carrying with him everything in this world. I feel a sense of final and complete loss that can never be rectified. The resounding cry in my throat does not come out: it is stifled. I want the world to shake, the walls to crumble down on the open, nocturnal sky. The cry of help and the call for aid in the final moment of life gets no response, no relief. Despair is an unbearable blow, but the cry is not realized.

And the sigh is open and frozen.

He was walking on Sa'd Zaghlul Street, hurrying on. The air coming from the sea was humid. A light drizzle was falling on his head, hitting his face gently, when he heard his name on the side-walk from behind: Mikhail, Mikhail. As always he could not believe that it was possible to have someone call him in any place at any time. The asphalt was shining, and the cars slipping by seemed warm on the inside, in the afternoon light. He turned around, as if unintentionally. Rama appeared walking hurriedly toward him under an open, colorful, transparent umbrella, smiling and panting a little. Water was dripping from the umbrella's edges onto the side of her shoulder. They exchanged a quick kiss on the cheeks, somewhat unintended; she was not expecting it publicly in the street. Suddenly, raindrops, having accumulated from the side of the umbrella as she leaned slightly with it, were pouring on his face. Laughing, he shook the water off. She told him she was sitting in the Trianon Café when she had seen him through the window. She said, in a hurry, that she had spent two days already in Alexandria and was leaving early the next morning. She was staying in a nearby pension in the Shatby quarter, overlooking a vast, lonesome Christian cemetery with very white, fragile statues and tombstones. The drizzle struck the tight umbrella fabric rhythmically as he entered beneath it, alongside her, for protection. People were dashing around them indifferently. She said that her friend Alphonse had chosen this strange, depressing, and stirring pension, close to the sea but also close to downtown. Her face was shimmering with a warm bronze glow in this dry circle, detached from the world yet in its very focus—a circle he felt was theirs alone, together. He laughed without pretext. She looked at him; her smiling, questioning glance preserved its distance. He said: Come on, I will have coffee with you. Won't you invite me to a cup of coffee? She said: By all means. Come, let me introduce you to Mahmud Bey. He is the new Director of the Archaeological Inspectorate. Yesterday, we passed by Kom al-Dikka and the Serapeum and the new archaeological digs in Mareapolis. He is great fun. Very old, very polite, and very humble. He depends on me and needs me at every step, whether related to inspection or not. Come.

His heart dropped quietly and he became depressed: They had thus returned to the world of people, friends, colleagues, compliments, and social conversations. He had been hoping, as he usually did, for a special encounter. She had frustrated their privacy. He drank his coffee with neither enthusiasm nor eagerness. Their farewell to one another was lukewarm, polite, indecisive—as usual.

10

A Copper Mask
with Gaping Eyes

I t was happening yet again: his fancies were circulating around her. He was daydreaming of her, addressing her in his mind. He heard light knocks on the door, opened it indifferently only to find her standing there. He could not believe it. It occurred to him that something miraculous attended her presence at his door, as if he had established her there by his fancy, something inside him magically becoming embodied.

The expression on her face, a beautiful mask collapsing in embarrassment, confirmed the moment's strangeness.

She said to him: I rang the bell but never heard it sound inside.

Tension was in her eyes—threatening imminent dissolution, however—and something resembling shyness.

She carried in her arms, next to her chest, a small living creature swaddled in a white towel.

Perplexed and dazed, he said: Come in, come in. Welcome.

She sat on the divan under the window with open curtains. The sun behind her—the light morning rays behind her head with her hair

211

pulled up—turned her bronze color into an old, soft, dark tableau set within a halo of fluid light. In this dim tableau, her eyes blazed. His heart once again fell into passionate, adoring admiration and anxiety. He instantly saw in the towel a kitten, gray with yellow stripes, gazing just above the folds, with fixed eyes, emitting no sound. He almost laughed, but her expression stopped him.

—Excuse me, Mikhail. I could not go down without her. She's feverish. Look! Bring your hand; yes, put your hand on her. Do you feel her high temperature? Isn't it so? What shall I do, what shall I do? She is quite sick. Refused food and milk, even water. Sniffed it then withdrew her nose.

He was overwhelmed, had no idea what to do. What could he tell her?

She said: Do you have lukewarm water? Can you warm up a cup of water? Never mind, I'll do it. May I? I'll give her some water. She doesn't want milk or food. I tried to tempt her. Nothing works.

Her voice was beginning to break down, and her anxiety and worry were contagious for him.

He took the wrapped-up kitten from her and placed it gently in the adjacent armchair under an armrest, as if to protect it, and he tried to make it drink. It wouldn't open its mouth, and its eyes didn't move. Its frail body throbbed, visibly and swiftly, while its slim, long front legs hung limp, with paws folded under.

He put his arm on her shoulder and tried courageously to raise himself to the level of the task, even if he could not stop feeling something akin to sarcasm, irony, and vexation while simultaneously acknowledging that something was happening that he did not understand completely and that it was not at all a matter of sarcasm. He approached her face and kissed her lightly on her cheek saying:

Don't be concerned. Don't worry. Isn't it a cat? Cats have seven lives. It will return to its own self, lovely and healthy as it was.

212

She accepted his kiss and looked at him with an appeal for help, but also with reproof. She said while patting the back of the kitten so gently that she barely touched it:

Is that true? I'm scared. She won't die; she can't die.

He said: No. It won't die. Of course, it will not die.

She said: I will not accept her death. Promise me she will not die. Promise me. I want you to promise.

She broke suddenly into a crying fit. She wept profusely, agonizingly, in a hushed voice. Her tears, spherical and limpid, one drop after another, each separated from the other, dripped down the smoothness of her cheeks, while her bosom shook with crying that would neither stop nor dilute the torment. He took her in his lap without a word, patted her hair, pressed her slowly toward him, as she went on in her stifled crying fit. With no sign of dejection or reluctance, she sought refuge in him, yielding to his embrace, delivering over to him her weighty chest. She felt secure with him as his hand pressed the arc of her ample bosom from the other side, affectionately and gently. He turned her face toward him and wiped off her tears against his mouth without lust or hurry. He felt on his lips a sweet taste mixed with a light, salty flavor. It came to his mind, lovingly, that this light sugary taste was very strange. His lips sought her open, moist mouth in a sort of consolation and slow rhythmic, erotic appeasement. Then his hand descended to the back of her neck, under the hair, firmly touching it; his fingers went down to the zipper in the back of the blouse and opened the bra's clasp easily, with agility. The muscles of her strong back lay calm beneath his spread-out hand that circulated around to her bosom, feeling its weight and plumpness, embracing it toward him. Under his lips, he felt the sharpness of her small white teeth. He rubbed her back above the narrow waist, and in his hand he felt the heat of her tight, taut skin—youthful and soft—on the side of her plump strong haunch.

She raised her weeping face toward him as the clear drops, pure and

213

welling, clung to it. In her rounded features no convulsions of crying or contractions of pain were visible. There was anticipation in her eyes, as the rough waves of the storm were quieting down. Her face—of how many masks?—resolved into the one real face, with tears, tears craving and calling for men's affection. The clarity of this face and its roundness without a blemish, the two strangely fixed eyes having dripped the pure waters of grief, provoked pain and distilled his affection. They exchanged kisses; in her breath the traces of her weeping, now mixed with another tension, in the throes of which her body shook. She raised her hand weakly. Her fingers were almost unrecognizably strange as they pressed his face toward her. Her bare breast was now fully in his hand. In all this intimate closeness, there was no blazing desire to complete a sensual act or to satisfy a lust. She was seeking refuge in him from the evil, from the imminent travail, as if she were performing a magical act. He received her in his arms, in his lap, rather protectively, to confront together the invisible blows, partaking helplessly in the process of childish surrender. He said to her: Why didn't you talk to me on the phone and relieve yourself? Why didn't you tell me?

She said: Would it have been all right? Would you have been satisfied if I broke down crying on the phone? I was agitated and had no idea what to do.

Then she said to him as she was wiping off her tears with the back of her hand, as if she were a little girl: Sorry; so childish. It's a childish thing. I'll take the kitten to the veterinary doctor. I know a clinic nearby.

When he asked the next day: What happened?

She said: What? What do you mean?

He said: The kitten.

She said with an indifferent voice as if she had forgotten, and in a decisive tone as if she wanted no sequel, explanation, or commentary: She died.

Despite that, he said: Do you know that in southern Egypt when a person dies, we wash his clothes in the Nile. We also throw into the Nile the first childhood lock of hair.

He asked himself: Is that in order to place the end of things in the Nile waters, to entrust its flow with the mystery of beginning too?

She didn't say a word, as if what he had already said was more than necessary, no need really. As if they were sharing in a crime. That's how it felt. Was the sharing of a grave sin a feature of love or a sign of distancing and separation? His feeling of guilt could not be explained at all by this silly, insignificant death in which he'd played no part. He said to himself: No death is insignificant; none is silly. And he said: Did I really play no part? He said: Now I understand the induced guilt that happens in love, what's meant by "crimes of the heart." I could have never imagined it—this guilt that manages to emerge from a destructive fit while questing for the impossible.

He entered the small bedroom, before dawn, felt the fields and the Nile behind the unpainted walls. At the door the dogs were still whining in the aftermath of their meal. From behind the open window, he caught sight of the large palm trunks with their dusty, curved, and cracked surfaces standing in a square, lit by a single bare electric lamp. She had said to him: This is Manal's room. She is spending the night with one of her girlfriends. The bathroom is this way. Goodnight. She left him for her room. He did not have his pajamas, but the summer was merciful. The blue sheet was light and gentle on his body, feminine with its embroidered edge. It exuded the aromas of a sleepy girl who has not yet become a woman: a very slight fragrance of a feminine body not yet bloomed. There were large posters on the wall: Che, Elvis, two European horses with heavy, short legs running on a sandy seashore, water drops flying around their manes and open mouths, frozen by the camera's eye in a luminous, melodic pattern. A study desk, one end flush against the wall,

215

had on it an old-fashioned phonograph with a collection of discs, some black and bare; others in their colorful, torn covers. Amid text-books, fashion magazines, French novels with yellowed pages, English hard covers, and dictionaries lay small and large dolls in faded-color fabrics, twisted bead necklaces thrown about on the shelf, a very small plastic doll with one arm cut off—the kind that infants in their first months play with—which she had kept. He felt he was violating a child's sanctum. He put on his trousers, slipped his bare feet into his shoes, walked carefully to the bathroom, feeling wakeful eyes and watchful spirits in the sleeping house. Without a gush, a weak stream of water poured from the tap. He wiped his hands with his handkerchief, felt the roughness in the small *kilim* under his feet. He went back to bed, covered himself, and plunged his head back against a soft pillow which he had to fold twice. He picked up an English book and read a few lines about Cromwell's revolution. A gentle and strange mewing which he could neither locate nor com-prehend made him get up again. He looked around and picked up from the lower bookshelf two newly born, frog-like kittens . Their slight bodies, almost boneless, clung to his hands and to the edges of the bookshelf, mewing weakly, pleading. He opened the door and put them in front of it, returned, closed the door, and turned off the light.

He enters into a narrow corridor between two rows of successive, unending, slim columns, and he puts his offering on the awesome altar. He hears the cry of the black goose at night under the priest's knife and hears his prayer: *In the name of the Father, the Son, and the Holy Ghost, O God give us patience when afflicted, O angel of mercy, O angel!* The tingling of silver in the round, dark, shiny, ceramic pot, the living offering with its flying feathers shrieking between the hands that will set its body on fire with rising incense and the aromas of grilling, of cinnamon, and of aged musk. In the darkness, men pass between columns into the temples of priestesses nude beneath white diaphanous

216

gowns, performing their votive offerings and fulfilling the right of Isis-Astarte for six days and nights. Around him rise walls of entrenched millenary stones, up to the dark clouds in a distant, engraved ceiling, open to the sky. Around him huge, lofty, rounded columns spring up—the arms of ten men insufficient to encircle a single one. The capitals of these columns' fully rounded, three-dimensional circularity are almost invisible. They are topped by granite lotus and mysterious petrified sugar canes in the light of stars that he touches without burning his fingers. On large marble tiles, smoothed by the touch of bare feet and by bodies rolling in unending suffering—in the grip of unrelenting oppression, amid the steady columns that never shake or fall down, scratched by the fingernails of those who are dying in agonies of passion, injustice, and famine—the columns never fall. Children's fixed eyes, dimmed by dispossession and devoured by inflammation, fasten their power on the columns, but they never fall. Below the steps of the columns the fields are covered by still, reddish waters from the Nile's flood season, taking in the fertility dough, reaching the depths of the silent, black womb. 'Amm Tadrus under the row of thin, outer columns bends at night with an adze on two *qirats* of earth, having wrapped his hair with a striped, dark red, large, Mahalla kerchief, with sweat drops hanging from his taut spiked cheekbones, and a long row of men who neither talk nor look at anything, standing up and bending in formulaic rhythm until they reach the farthest field beneath the mountain slope—when will their suffering end?

And Rama sleeps beneath the moon with her marvelous, plump, lightly bronze, wheat-colored body, which has ripened and matured beneath the soft skin covering its flesh. Diaphanous, deep red muslin silks fly about her arms that reach without claws, but rather with gentle nails, from fluttering wide sleeves. She arises slowly, deliberately, dancing in a fire in which her stretched body does not burn, but grows, flickers, and shimmers with its inner fire responding to the flame

217

tongues. The two fires embrace in a rite accompanied by slow music emanating from the white ground marble and the bluish hues of combined, transparent levels of an invisible fabric that has neither warp nor woof. The bronze color of mature breasts proceeds gradually from the tan of the plump, flat belly to the blackness of the small, bushy elevation with its dense grass. Her abundant corporeality is soft and earthy, desired and loved, thrown about in the divinity of lofty rising columns. Her legs are silently collapsing columns beneath the tight embrace of ritual ceremony causing the oblivion of this world in which the taut, erect cobra has been slaughtered. Its head has fallen with undermined pride, and its dispersed blood drops have dried and frozen on the white stone, polluting it. He stretches his hand and takes from her neck the large necklace of multiple hoops, with large lapis lazuli and sapphire beads, and the reddish, gold cross chains. The moon burns with an imprisoned yellow fire between the horns of the haughty bull holding up the weight of the sky. Her large eyes with their deep greenness gaze at him while performing the votive offering, paying the price, contemplating him in a voiceless hymn beneath the trembling light of tall candles, lit within several high niches constructed into the sides of the stony walls. The coal-black hue of her broad eyelids is harmonious, for the first time, with her rich red lips shimmering like creamy waves. They penetrate his heart, encircle him, goad his tension into a harmonious, unhindered gush. There is no invasion, only arrival at a planned destination—paved, cozy—as the two bodies roll over and over in the dance of relief and contentment. This painful mask of beauty on her face—the ever recurrent copper mask of his dream—the mask of pleasure as she dances, as she loves, is the same pleasure-mask as when she talks, smokes a cigarette, or writes a letter, the same mask of the last moment of love-making in all its modulations. There is a will and a formless determination behind this mask with gaping eyes. It is the mask of the woman with eternal

218

experience in both love and pleasure: it is fixed; behind the quiver of ecstasy lies calculation and planning. By a kind of a predestined faith he continues to seek protection from the ever-tense and threatening risks at the corners of the road. The amulet has never been put to the test. It has neither failed nor confirmed its magical power. His wakefulness at night is anxious, the smoke of his cigarette flavorless.

In the very early morning, he drank Turkish coffee—*sada*, bitter—with her on the low roof. From there the gray public square could be seen with its trees, refreshed by their slight verdure. In the morning air, the palm wreaths were dangling with their ample arching leaves. Amid the lolling trees was a warm, reddish glow emerging from clusters of ripe, green dates—the short, swollen, finger-like fruit—which he used to buy as a child from the wrinkle-faced, gentle-eyed southern Egyptian peddler. He used to pay him a big, red coin: a millieme. The dates would break up in his mouth and he would feel them there, sandy and soft, their pungency making his tongue contract.

Below the roof, the dogs were circulating, sniffing something near the old tractor, its red paint having peeled and partly erased a set of black roman numerals also painted beneath slits cut into its metallic side. He looked around and listened. No trace of the kittens, no sound. Had they been part of his long, agitated dream? She looked at him and said: I heard you at night as you opened the door and removed the kittens. I too did not go to sleep for a while. Did you find Manal's room reposeful? He said mechanically: Yes, yes.

In another time, I saw you, I saw you incarnated in Manal on the sand of al-Ma'mura: youthful and aging simultaneously. I held onto myself, for our time had passed. Her narrow forehead and the roundness of her gentle cheekbones; her round, short, muscular legs bare beneath the flimsy summer dress, inspecting with her feet the hot sand in an absent-minded gesture under the leaning umbrella; and the eyes—not yours yet so much yours—with their dark green color penetrating

219

the heart, as usual. She—this you-in-Manal—was alone in the midst of white sands at the shore polluted by summer's frail, wilting trash: sun-dried reed stalks dispersed by the wind, ripped plastic bags flying about and indestructible, fresh skins of watermelon with their green halves buried in the sand. I did not recognize in you this adolescent, girlish body. I only imagined it under the flesh I had contended with and filled, thus dispelling the years and fulfilling the cravings. I know this rough, abundant, strong hair under the sun with its pungency and wildness, its smoothness and provocation. Traces of its touch remain on my fingers and on my lips. This girl in whose empty, virginal bed I slept once, a bed preserving the impression of her physical fragrance. This unique dual presentation repeating a past and persisting as a model in an eternal world: its dark passions and breathtaking love shake me. She was cut off from the summer world of sea and sand, from the triviali-ties of a bored and boring bourgeoisie who spend hours on al-Ma'mura beach under multicolored umbrellas on wet cotton chairs, amid the noise of cassette players—hoarse but lost in the sea air's larger, contin-uous din. The children were sloshing around plastic pails full of salt-water that quickly soaked away into shallow holes in the sand. Peddlers were selling newspapers, salted seeds and nuts, candied peanuts, thin sweet wafers, seashell necklaces; supplying the trashy domestic needs of summer vacationers: cups, plates, plastic tablecloths with ludicrous colors. The harsh midday sun pounds the bodies lying about on the sand and in the shade, moistening themselves in the water and getting tanned slowly—bored, neither relaxing nor enjoying themselves. And this dual person was alone behind the sea coast and the row of umbrel-las, away from the crowds along the shore with sands corroded by foaming, turbid waves. Having become domesticated, the throng had lost its power and prime. So this person was occupying both a new and eternal context. Around her was an invisible halo from a hidden sun separating her from the world, yet making her the focus of that world, because she was there incarnate, returning to my heart and coming out of it; embodied alone without delusion, thus invulnerable; in fact, unattainable. How painful love can be!

She said to him: My emotional life is neither troublesome nor complicated. There was only one man in my life: the first one. I was his student. We were engaged but never succeeded in getting married. I told you his story in detail, didn't I? He is still my true love, my first love. Never mind my marriage; that was not love. As for this first man, he was quite another matter. We spent an entire week in bed without going out. We ate in bed. I have never known anything like it, not in all my life.

He said to her: A friend of mine told me that when you were in Port Said, during the Occupation, your code name in the Resistance was Fatma. You told me that the Egyptian officers quarreled over you, using revolvers—didn't you?

She said: They were very polite.

He said to her: What is the secret behind your insistence then? Why do you insist on calling all these relationships "friendships"? Why not simply end that nomenclature?

She said: Is that what you want?

He said: This obsession of yours to offer everything in order to attract, to please, to make others happy. I know I was not—nor was it possible for me to be—the only one. But you go out of your way to please first this one, then another, and so on. Does this benevolence fulfill an irresistible need you have?

She said: You could have refused what you call this benevolence of mine. Why do you think I come to you, Mikhail, if I don't love you—whatever that word means?

She said to him on their first night: Tomorrow I shall call on you as I would on strangers, but tonight these hours are ours. For as long as these hours last, I'll call you "my love."

221

She said to him: Dearest one.

He said to himself: Is this a term of endearment or a formula?

He said to her: Or is it a tendency of yours for vengeance, for getting even, for settling old accounts? Is it possible for me to step on grounds that might hurt you?

With glowing eyes, she gestured coldly and in stifled anger.

He said: You are neither child nor woman, but a woman buried in the heart of a slim child with long braids, with thin and slender face, and hungry eyes. Aren't you seeking revenge as a result of your first and last lover—the first column on which the monument of your world was erected, and whose tremendous roundness your slim arms could not encircle?

She said, half objecting: Perhaps.

He said to her: You have passed your early years, half your life—maybe more—engaged in revolutionary work: a world with its own rules, calculated ventures, concealment, secrecy; where the principle of safety is the principle of survival, and yet you long for a lost sense of security. This path in a dark, labyrinthine cavern, without hope of finding a luminous exit, of finding the aperture to lead you out of your endlessly sensual world . . .

She looked at him contemplatively, half-convinced, and said: I . . . don't know.

He said: Then let's just say you're searching for unification with a primal scene that can't be replicated. A diligent search, with trembling and longing fingers that never tire, for the ever elusive *ka*, your spiritual double, ever present in front of your eyes. Yet you never arrive at this much-desired unification that could calm all this zealotry.

She said nothing. Her eyes were gaping.

He said: What frightens and provokes me is the ferocity and ruthlessness of your eagerness for pleasure. What hurts and isolates me is your submersion in a completely silent, locked-in depression.

222

She said: What's the use of this dissection? Stop tormenting yourself, Mikhail.

He said: Is it the irresistible yearning to quench a sensual thirst that can never be satisfied? A search for security and protection, even if for a fleeting moment—the moment of attachment, of doubling, of complementariness, if you will allow such a term? You are, in the end, loved and truly wanted at this moment of total, deified love. The final proof of this moment is its realization, endlessly repeated. Or perhaps we're all instruments in those hands of yours whose fingers we kiss? You don't know the bitterness of putting myself, that is, finding myself put, within a group, within a herd, within a legion of men.

He said to himself: Your wild Freudian interpretations aren't worth a dime: facile, naïve, possibly fake, and deceitful. The truth you claim you're after is a star you'll never graze with your fingers.

She said without cruelty: I don't know what makes me listen to you. Don't you possess your own strand of masochism? Why not look into that?

He said: In fact I do look, and with wakeful eyes. The eyes are not a weapon for amputation. The time for miracles has disappeared. The light hopefully will add flames to the fire.

She said in a dry, decisive tone, interrupting him: It's better not to discuss the subject.

She had told him before that she used this statement whenever she felt annoyed with a disagreeable interrogation. Was he not now in that area? So be it.

Stubbornly and childishly, he said: In fact, it is better to discuss it.

She said: All right. Logically, dialectically, I am with you until the end. Haven't I left everything, everyone, in order to be with you for six days and six nights, all alone? What does this mean? Do tell me. And you say I don't love you!

Suddenly he realized the absurdity of his endeavor, the very

223

effort of speaking up. Words. What were they? How could he emerge from the dilemma of this lie that has the face of truth, at the same time wearing a thousand faces?

Feeling his masochistic impulse and unable to escape it, he said to himself: Hamlet.

He laughed anxiously, trying to find strength within his defeat.

—A thousand times a day: Hamlet. Without glory, without ghost, prison, or sword—a unique Hamlet who shuns his individuality in the herd. Poison—what a commonplace. Yet we learn to adjust to it. Whether I like it or not, the sand raised by the herd's hooves fills my mouth. I deceive myself: either the unique, the rebellious, the leader, or nothing, or none. It's not true I've laid down my weapon. I can't help but be in the beastly, competitive, fighting army.

She had said to him "Dearest one"—that is all that he still possesses, all that's left, provided she meant it. If she meant it for only a few days, a few hours, if only for a moment! Are we in front of a still body lying on an autopsy slab? When the relation between us dies, there will be no need for an autopsy.

It will never happen.

He heard the sound of God's fluttering on his submerged head in baptismal waters. No annunciation was in it, only the portent of the angels' trumpets on the Day of Judgment.

He was one step ahead of her. They were coming back in the quiet, dim street under steady silent trees that resembled witnesses. He stopped suddenly, turned back, and kissed her without a word. That was what he had wanted to say to her. She responded, affectionately and receptively. Her lips opened up obediently—she, the wild one, who never obeyed anyone or anything. The bells of a distant church tolled. He heard the silvery bells three times, drawn-out, as if announcing a funeral. A large tanker truck, silent and sealed, passed by with its huge round belly full of diesel.

224

On the night of January first, the Balloon Theater was packed. Within the fluttering fabric of the tent, it was a mixed crowd excited in its rush toward a familiar entertainment. Amid the brouhaha, they were waiting for the musicians, singers, and dancers, anticipating the small wrangles, the calming requests prefaced by "Praise the Prophet," and the moving of chairs to the front rows on the floor covered by sawdust. Some civil servants of the host organization, the Union of Arab Workers' Syndicates, had donned the Palestinian *kufiya*; their women wore black *milaya* wraps. The orchestra sat in its pit under the stage, with the curtains down. The confused sounds of tuning up, of mewing and howling—the gushing and ringing of wind instruments and the banging of drums—mixed with the rapping of Coca-Cola peddlers on their soft drink bottles and the calls from peanut and melon-seed vendors. At first, he and Rama sat apart, then he asked permission from his neighbors to let her have a seat next to him. She settled down silently on the narrow bamboo chair, while a vendor of bean and *felafel* sandwiches extended his hand between them, his commodity wrapped in oil-soggy paper, toward a family with several boys and girls sitting behind them. A long row of boisterous soldiers wounded in the October War dashed in. They exchanged greetings and laughed, calling out to each other by name and supporting themselves on shiny metal crutches. They were limping and leaning on each other with half arms and amputated legs. Under the military caps some heads were still wrapped with bandages. Some were pushing wheelchairs occupied by motionless soldiers wearing long, clean, white *jallabiyas*. They crowded the first rows, carelessly and with self-assurance, taking the middle and the sides of the stage. Proud of themselves, they were also proud of the people making room for them affectionately—a little irritated but tolerant—while not betraying pity for anyone. A tall, slender soldier blooming with youth jumped on the stage, threw his crutches on the ground in a loud, deafening bang and stretched his leg in the khaki trouser

225

folded just under the knee, pinned with a large safety pin at the place of a leg that was no more. He leaned against a back wall of the wings, stretching himself out in preparation for a long soirée's merry-making.

Under the excessive stage lighting a tallish singer was mewing, her dress's embroidery of spangles and beads shimmering in alternating colors. On her face was a carefully applied, smooth, glossy, heavy makeup, including a considerable amount of kohl on her bright eyes. She was swaying back and forth on legs concealed by a wavy maxiskirt, lamenting in an affected tone, swaying with a persistent artificiality that sought to support her whining. The soldier in the wings of the stage clapped his hands, shouted in a voice of loud, confident rapture: Allah! Once more, lady; by the Prophet, once more . . .

She gestured to him with her memorized, professional moves and pointed to the orchestra to repeat. Beside himself, he shouted, "May God guard you!"—demonstrating that he knew how to live proudly and joyfully with an amputated body. In the streets, he would always encounter his likes on the pavements, spread there with books and newspapers next to traffic lights, pushing themselves along with severed arms, beseeching each car window with their faces. Their flesh having healed at the joints, become tight and swollen, smooth and red in a raw way, dead or almost, they moved their half-arms up and down skillfully, knowing how to use them—without shame—performing a task, going through a routine. At least, they were not ashamed of their bodies, even if they no longer took pride in them.

In the folds of such a rejected, wrecked, and slight body Mikhail feels an identification, latent all along his own body, spread out amid the touches of gentle waves and the roughness of deaf rocks against which red waters crash and rise. The tremendous body explodes in hushed, concealed anger and in the ecstasy of self-mutilation. The body wounds itself and stabs its guts with nails and knife, pressing with determination on something he does not comprehend. The

226

swellings break open, in search of an unattainable cure. The fracturing of bones and the falling of stones and glass join in a single rhythm. The heartfire burns suddenly within walls painted with colors, obscured by Cairene dust, in the rude and insolent wood.

This inner dragon lets me down, slips free from me. I feel him as an Other, a stranger, close and clinging to my innermost. How often I have tried to deny him.

Mikhail said to himself: When the cock crowed three times . . . He laughed. Who hanged himself? Who was Peter, and who was Judas? Regardless, I ignore and forget this other, inner person. A slender, sharp razor slices his finger until the bone is electrified and his knee scrapes on a stone in the soil, somewhere. The knee's wound doesn't heal, a crust forms that he removes over and over, yet it keeps re-forming.

Mikhail said to himself: Do I know how to live a full life, with his person in me? This stranger who doesn't obey me. He knows me, but I do not know him. A matchstick burns in my hand, my foot stumbles in a hole I can see clearly from a sufficient distance. This other man does not know submission; in his inner darkness he's a tyrant: lofty, granite-like with a mysterious smile. His eyes are locked open though lacking pupils; he is ancient, steady as a rock, silent. His inner agitation never slackens. I gaze at him in a black mirror, which is the dream itself. I do not avert my glance.

I knew him, this Other in myself, in the flights of erotic passions, under political torture on the edge of death, and in the harsh grip of love, becoming a mere subject matter, a mere instrument, a mere something banished with no life but retaining the endlessly stubborn beat of mechanical determination. The soul ebbed from him a long time ago; his sister separated from him; he's become isolated. Nothing is in him but the current of thick sap with its flow and ebb, a wiped rag that possesses sheer mechanical movement from within. I see him with an external eye. There is no more unification, only

227

dualism and the torture of banishment, a resignation that can hope for no consolation. He moves and throbs with a determination that I'll never understand.

She said to him: I have a gift for you.

He said, with a yearning that stirred him out of utter stagnation: Really? What is it? Where?

She said: It will always be with you, though no one will see it.

He never received her present. He never recognized having received her present. Did she ever give it to him?

He was attentive as she told him about herself: Back then, I used to be slender, in fact skinny. Tahiya Karim painted me nude. I was modeling, yes, naked. My tableau is now exhibited in the Guggenheim in New York.

Smiling and without conviction, he said: When I go there, I shall make a point to see it.

She told him how poets had dedicated poems to her, composed in colloquial and classical Arabic, and how she took under her wing a young poet who came from the farthest south of Egypt: a violent-tempered, unpolished young man, touchy and ignorant of Cairene ways. He would break a whisky glass and the drink would flow on the carpet, leaving a mark on the armchair. Appetizers would fall from his fork on the tablecloth and on his lap. But the radio and newspapers made of him a knight, because he had written new *mawwals* in the classical mode during his detention.

He saw now a sculpted bust positioned at the side of her hallway in dim light on a low side table between the door and a wooden, open-shelved study with neglected books, crammed-in newspapers, magazines, and bibelots made of ceramic, glass, and cheap metal.

She said: Ah, you noticed it? Do you recognize me in it? A young sculptor, whom I used to see and entertain at my house occasionally, made it for me. I put up with what he thought was his love for me,

228

his "only love." He was so pathologically sensitive, I didn't want to turn him down. He died thinking he loved me. Look how he sculpted the *mudawwara* kerchief, putting it on my head like a *baladi* girl. I used to be very thin-faced then. Isn't that so? He died from TB, young and unknown.

He said anxiously: Who is it? Sultan? Gamal Sultan?

She looked at him trying to dodge the question.

Instantly the tip of a thorn, an old pain stung him. This sculptor whom he was so fond of, whose purity and spontaneity he knew! He had met him for the last time in al-Mubtadayan Street in a dusty, crowded, noisy, Cairene noon. That was in the period before cars swept the streets, drowning them in their incessant circulation. He was having his lunch: a cheese and felafel sandwich wrapped in the newsprint of *al-Masa*.

He had said he had to go home—a two-room apartment on the top of a high-rise building that he pointed to—and wait for the Acquisition Committee at three o'clock. He said he was doing something that he thought would be important, and anyhow, he was selling a work of his to the Alexandria Art Museum. In his hoarse voice, he expressed hope for the future, though he was critical and tense with life—his last gush of life, as it turned out. He too was resentful about the political and artistic state of things, yet he was jolly. He said his health was improving, that he had left the hospital in good health. His face was dark and warm; his protruding cheekbones soggy with the flow of sweat drops—a continuous stream without breaks. They agreed to meet. He embraced him and felt the dry and hollow ribs of his chest under the not very clean, short-sleeve shirt. It was an embrace of unfulfilled brotherhood. The agreed-upon meeting never took place.

She said: Did you know him?

He said: Yes.

Your green eyes—their wavy surface whose depths I do not

229

fathom—sing to me of loss and estrangement. I am warmed in those dark eyes. My repose lies in their thick, burnt honey. Deep, yet I know how deep; I plunge confidently into their depths, whose taste was in my mouth since weaning. As for the eyes in the soft mask, which make me slip into estrangement and repudiation, they are planted on a hot rocky land, blasted by a sun I do not know.

In their last private encounter, she will open the door. She will be wearing a light homely dress without sleeves that falls carelessly on her desirable body—a body he had known so well, a body he had undressed and experienced in both successful and failed erotic duels. She will welcome him casually, without ceremony. She will apologize for her looks, then rush inside to change her dress, as if he were a stranger. Despite everything, he will experience the least possible measure of bitterness and sarcasm at himself, at her, at the whole issue. Thus proceeds the endgame of love and loss. He will enter the elegant, open, modern kitchen with its polished, clean instruments, its silent-flame stove, its futuristic tap mouths bursting out with water that gushes forth in sudden, intermittent blasts—dazzling and quickly disappearing, mechanical, like magnesium flashes. She will beg him in a formal way to relax as if he were at home. Then she will tell him in a quiet, disappointed tone: I thought you were going to take off your jacket and shoes, and actually relax. The light lunch will be made up of artificially-flavored canned food, carefully and hygienically cooked, served on small, colorful, plastic plates that will stand next to stiff-edged paper napkins. She will talk to him, in ready-made phrases extracted from the commonplace treasury, about the constantly renewed Arabic music, about colloquial poets, about politics, about art books that have become exorbitant and thus a matter of mere fashion and display; she will talk about the October victories of '73, the predicament and glory of Egypt, the absence and funeral of Nasser. He will drink two beers, feeling lethargic and slow. He will not care for the ice-cold beer out of the square-sided, white, small fridge of hers. When he leaves, she will plant a kiss on his cheek. He will embrace her for a moment, recalling in his heart a lost affection that will never return and he will feel, in contrast to his dried-up body, the freshness and power of her familiar body beneath the loose-fitting, black *jallabiya* embroidered with silvery threads. In his arms, she will be like a stony relic, softly throbbing with the memory of timeworn yearnings; in her voice will be a warm quiver, self-reflexive, now hopeless and without regret, as she says to him: So long. After that, no encounters except chance crossings: amid plenty of people, whether in offices or stations.

She said to him: I worked in theater, as well. I was an actress at university, which is not all that important, I know. But we formed a troupe with the prestige and dedication of a professional troupe. Beside my other talents, I discovered I had a knack for acting. My performance is natural, spontaneous in a trained way.

He said: I don't know what's staged in your life and what lies behind the stage.

She said: I also worked in nursing, as you know, after three months training, after the attack on Port Said. The wounded soldiers wanted me specifically to change their bandages. They appreciated the detailed care I took with down-to-earth bodily functions, without resorting to hollow words that meant nothing, that amateurs and the inexperienced think will mean so much when it comes to nursing. I am not turned off, nor do I feel disgusted, nauseated, queasy, fuddled, or lacking in discretion when faced with the details of life and death. When bodies are troubled and deranged, throwing up their contents or anxiously craving to ingest bodily requirements, when body juices are decomposed, or when heavy, gluey excretions flow out, I don't find it disgusting or incomprehensible. I accept it all, acknowledging it and dealing with it in a spontaneous way.

He said: I don't care who you are, what you are, what you do, or

231

why. I just care for you. You, alone. But you are something else behind all this, besides all this. And *that* part is you.

End of my unending desire.

He said: The precious thing is scratched, in fact broken, by lies. What are lies? What is the precious thing?

He said to her: Yes, lying is the foundation of all human relations. How can a lover manage with his beloved, a man with his wife, friends with enemies and ninnies, without a lie here or there, white lies, possibly gray, pink, or black lies? How can we say that such lies are insignificant, in fact irrelevant? Lies are the lubricating oil without which people would be scratched and fractured in their encounters, confrontations, and in their comings and goings. It is so, even between man and himself. I, on the other hand, want innocent, rigorous, and completely honest confrontations. I want an attachment with the purity found in lead. Do I thus conceal a terrible lie? My hands want to remove the mask even if they rip apart the flesh of the face beneath it.

The predatory bird—the length of two stretched arms—whose body is an open-breasted corpse collapsed beneath the weight of collective guilt and lies. How terrible are obituaries: draped in black on stiff, hard cards. The final seal. The loss that you suddenly recognize with definitive knowledge, that it cannot be made up for. In the sky, the stabbed corpse with silent heart. The eyes, in the aftermath of every agitated rebellion, strike or blow with two wide wings cleaving the clouds and breaking the sky's layers. On his hands now, following the shock of falling down, the corpse is dry, arid, shriveled. Even the traces of decomposition and decay have disappeared. So has the putrid smell and fermentation. The corpse has undergone the last stage of death. The blazing sun has whitened it, rendering it stiff and rigid. It seems to him fragile: no sooner is it fingered than it crumbles and flies away in a vast coppery horizon. But no, it remains between them. So it will always be: a loved corpse that death cannot efface or wipe out.

232

11

Diocletian's Column

The long narrow street was craning upward with force, filled with repressed but ready energy. They were going toward the sea below, sensing from afar its fervor, glory, its unassailability. To their left, the ramparts of Mustafa Pasha camp rose high and massive. Its huge stones embodied exceptional rigor, reminiscent of the Spartan spirit of Imperial Roman army corps in the old Necropolis, or the severe discipline of Bonaparte's soldiers, or of British cannons or Italian detainee camps—not to mention the inscrutability of Egyptian barracks. They continued running beneath the ramparts toward the sea. The road was imbued with a nocturnal light making their way long—with its moist air—as it climbed upward toward the night's few stars and a dazzling half moon. On the right, the gardens of locked villas with stony balconies, solidly constructed in the neoclassical French style, shone white in the moonlight. An English-style church tower surprised them. Amid the thicket of camphor and royal Indian palm trees with slender white trunks and amid the foreign mallow plants with luxuriant green leaves flung on iron fences elegantly wrought, flashing with dew as if capable of inhaling the garden's wintry, verdant fragrance, the high, disciplined lines of the steeple seemed out of place.

Suddenly she bent down panting. When he turned back, she was below him. He caught sight of her ample bosom. Its bronze flesh was glowing and rounded, imprisoned in her décolleté dress. She pulled off her shoes, held them in her right hand, then straightened herself up and resumed climbing toward him. She insinuated her arm into his and pushed him gently. Off they went, running again. She was laughing—a special laughter, almost soundless—in a joy that had no pretext, a pure joy of the moment. In the moonlight, the dark nail polish of her toes gleamed then disappeared. Her plump toes contracted on, then let go of, the black asphalt as she dashed along in confidence.

She panted happily, saying to him: I haven't run like this for years.

Their ascent was effortless, without resistance, as if plunging through an immaterial element. From below, unseen, came the gentle roar of the sea—an invitation, an unformulated promise.

They reached the road's pinnacle where it sloped down beneath their feet. In front of them, from below, shone the tops of the Corniche street lamps. With their whitish bulbs they resembled radiant fruits, one next to the other, sprouting from iron boughs, surrounded by bright, round halos of seaside mist.

Suddenly she pulled him toward her as she was sitting on the sidewalk, on the slightly moist, grainy, black basalt stones. Her knees went up as she seated herself: round and bare, their flesh taut on bones of living, pink granite. He looked at her at the moment of pausing before he sat down next to her. Her hair was pulled back, combed flat on her head, surrounding her delicate face and fine eyebrows. Her eyes looked up at him with innocence and contemplation: A chaste, cleansed, white expression as if gazing out of something welling up from within—splendid and vast but indescribable. Dark, very large and round, her eyes. Her delicate cheekbones made her face resemble a girl's: virginal, milky.

She put her arm on his shoulder and brought her face toward him in a gesture of love, incomparable for its simplicity and intimacy, for its deep connectedness.

She said: Are you tired from running?

He shook his head. Tenderness, gratitude, and a gentle craving arrested his words. He kissed her quickly and lightly on her cheek with warm, dry lips. She looked at him in a quiet, speculative gaze, keeping her visions and dreams to herself. She was contemplating him in her own context—that of possession. Already it seemed she was gazing alone into the realm of the future. Knowledge, not communication, filled her gaze.

She began to sing, not apart any longer but from within her relation to him, in a hushed voice—her breathing still fast and controlled, with a slight hoarseness:

O, sea captain, take me with you,
It is better for me.
Learning a trade enlarges the mind,
It is better for me.
Take me: a sailor to pull the towline,
It is better for me.

Her hands were firm leavened dough in his; her subdued cooing song stabilized his breathing. His unsteadiness came not from running but from his flare-up of physical longing.

235

The wind of passion
Passes by,
Coaxing us.
We lean toward it,
Our braids flying.
The wind of passion
Passes by,
Inclining us to stray.
Let the world stray;
We will not stray.

A patrol policeman with his tall figure and old-fashioned gun came unexpectedly from a dusty side street. The moonlight on his dry southern Egyptian face deepened the shades and protrusions of his noble cheek bones. The rhythm of his regular footsteps did not change, and they could not tell from his facial shadows whether he was looking at them or simply straight ahead. She whispered in his ear: By God, we've been caught, Mr. Courage. Even though his heart was bothered as usual by distant, childish fears, he whispered: Don't worry. No one is kinder than a patrol-man, especially these southern Egyptians transplanted to Alexandria. She continued whispering: Chauvinist! Then she added, in one breath and in a loud but gentle voice, which, when joined to her pleading tone, her confidence, haughtiness, and sovereignty, was of the kind that only women of aristocratic background can come up with: Please, Sergeant, is Rushdi Pasha Station on the left or the right side of the sea?

The policeman stopped for a second, said with an honest voice, with the tone of a man who ultimately knew his position on the social ladder: On the right, Madam. And he continued on his way with calm, unhurried steps. They looked at each other furtively, barely able to conceal their laughter. Instead, it roared inside their chests—an implosion. Their eyes dampened from the surge of with-held mirth.

The sky above him cleared off and appeared to drop down upon them, turning noiselessly over in front of his eyes as if it were break-ing apart.

Did all this happen? Did such joy really happen to me?

He could not tell if he was recalling an experience or conjuring a daydream.

Clinging to this transcendent experience he said: For the first time in twenty years, no, twenty-five years, death seems attractive. I see it, feel its presence. My hand is reaching for it, but I stop it. My hand feels tense under an irresistible pressure that pushes it to cling to death and its awe, just as it would cling to a rescue jacket, even if clinging for just one moment, away from that which is unbearable, unbearable, unbearable. Not since distant youth has death seemed so close, so seductive, as with the interface of love and its double.

In the darkest hours of silence, when I stumbled at last on the rubble dreams of justice, crumbling under the frustrations of wilted yearning for the dawn of wishful utopias on earth . . . When libera-tion-visions of the poor masses, humiliated for centuries, became dis-credited . . . During the long years of despair and solitude in front of the tyranny of the world, and the silence in front of the drawn fangs of repression . . . While floating like a wreck on the turbid waves and the confused noise of glory . . . Even then I desperately defended in my inner self, in some corner in me, the basic right of counterattack. But now . . . !

Did she say in a neutral voice: Haven't we agreed not to consid-er the significant themes? Not to pose the great questions and not to articulate the real answers?

This is his secret, intimate inferno. It locks him within gates that

237

will never open. Are these his first steps in the land of insanity, through the scorching winds of loss? He doesn't know what she said to him, what she did not say. He doesn't know what has happened, what he fancies has happened. Is it an act of recollection to save this scene from the void of oblivion? Or is it an illusion extracted from the claws of reality?

He said to himself: Reality has nails, teeth. He asked himself: Are you insisting on intoxicating yourself with words, words, words with capital letters? Then he said: To be sure, my blood's been poisoned. Knowing this strange geography where dream and reason intermingle is not a comfortable thing.

They were standing under Diocletian's column.

He said to her: Look at this beauty! How can the rock become a lofty, unbending rose and the granite possess the voluptuousness of a rounded youthful body?

She said: Isn't it easy enough to say it's a phallic symbol?

He said: Yes, it's easy, and meaningless. Pedantry and sophistry if you wish. But no, I am thinking of the magnitude, of the horror, and of the inevitability of thousands, hundreds of thousands, of my ancestors' bodies on whose bones this column stands. This beauty with all its cruelty was the bait that the martyrs' bodies fell for—my Coptic forebears with their arid stubbornness, or should I say glorious stubbornness? But what is the point either way?

She said: Pure martyrdom seeks no use.

He said: As for us—who have not yet been martyred—we are searching. We are those whose suffering is neither engraved on a stone nor mentioned in a book.

The violence of his response was a blow, but only against himself.

They took a taxi, an old Fiat, a yellow Alexandrian taxi with small folded seats. Its antiquated glass barrier had a round hole that linked the front part of the car with the back. She had purposely

238

slipped her fingers under his thigh knowing their effect. They passed what remained of the old Alexandrian quarters: Karmuz, Bab Sidra, and Kum al-Shuqafa. They passed through the streets of his youth, once a network of large and leafy boulevards with a tram clanking merrily on its middle ground, the road beside it paved with clean, shiny basalt. Now he saw crumbling houses, squeezed next to each other; a clamor of bottleneck traffic crowded with cars, horse-driven carts, trucks overladen with cotton bales teetering slowly toward Mina al-Basal and al-Qabbari; collisions of mixed processions of men, women, and children wearing shirts, pants, pajamas, *jallabiyas*, a few *milaya* wraps, dresses, light creased nightgowns, local shawls, *mudawwara* kerchiefs, turbans, skullcaps, slippers, wooden clogs, high-heeled shoes, and thong slippers that made crunching noises when walking. Only a few donned with pride and confidence the bulky, puffed, black, Alexandrian *sirwal* pants.

The bony-faced archaeological guard with his faded yellow jacket and narrow, questioning, bored eyes looked at them from within his dark green booth whose paint had peeled away from the tough old wood left from the time of the British, a hut with a pyramid-like ceiling whose dark red roof tiles had fallen down. He gave them two tickets, saying in English: Tourist? Good, good. Welcome, Sir, welcome, Madam. Need one guide?

He said: No, my good fellow. Praise the Prophet, we are from here.

With a slight disappointment, yet also with true joy, the guard said: *Ahlan wa-sahlan*. You honor us—as if the Prophet were visiting us.

Supposedly she was making an inspection, in secret, without prior announcement. Later she would report what she found to her department boss.

Inside the grounds, she said: Can you imagine? This column used to be an obelisk of Aswan granite, constructed by one pharaoh in an

239

endless chain—I can't think which Seti he was, the First or Third.

He said: How did our ancestors manage to smooth down the cutting edges of an obelisk and produce this perfectly smooth roundness—perfect in its elegance and magnificent roundness?

This capital of the world, his magical Coptic Greek city with its monks, merchants, and clowns; its actors, singers and artisans; patriarchs and prostitutes; its mob, its coquettes, its soldiers; its one-of-a-kind, interminable library and thousands of public baths; its churches erected underground and its glossy marble columns in the temples; its tortures and festivities—the circus, the lighthouse, the theater, the temples of Jupiter, Zeus, Amon; its public massacres, ghastly incinerations; its wine presses, its golden grain silos; its sailing ships, its anchored ships attached by ropes in the eastern port; its routed priests of the ancient cults; its martyrs from the new Christian heresies; its Jewish philosophers; its geographers and botanists; its poets still composing in the lifeless, ornamental diction of the ancient Greeks; its people people people, nameless, teeming, making a living, eating, giving birth, relishing, moving on to break apart under legendary misfortunes, dying without significance—no one knowing them, no one ever knowing them. He said to her: Here in the capital of the world, they erected this obelisk on top of the bones of youths and atop the horses of Caracalla's cemetery.

Bringing her body and face close to his, she said: You fanatic Alexandrian!

He said: You know that here in the Serapeum below, about forty years ago, I—as a child—jumped over an impossible well, a bottomless one, and crossed toward a brightly lit square. I often entered the rock-hewn tunnels and felt a kind of freedom in them.

She said: Yes, you told me.

The guard said: Sorry. Descending into these ruins isn't allowed. The waters have overflowed in them again.

He said: The sewers?

The guard said: God knows. An engineer went down there two months ago, and didn't make it back.

She asked: When will it open again?

The guard: When God makes things right.

Later she said to him: My office knows nothing about this. If any report was filed, it's bogged down in our ministry. Or got sent to another ministry altogether.

He said to her: Well, it may still arrive. May God speed it.

The column—a layer of dust coating its large square base—seemed smaller, shorter than he recalled. The dwarf sphinx at its foot seemed wrongly placed, as if it had been abducted from the vast, lonely, extended desert where it belonged. They were circling around the base of the statue, on large pieces of ancient, broken marble, trying to avoid stepping on the rubble and small, sharp, scattered stones that hadn't been touched by hands in centuries. The column's capital, with its adumbrated Roman and Byzantine carving, swam above them in a patch of flimsy white clouds that streaked over a clear blue sky that appeared and disappeared. In the pure moist air hung a dusty fragrance emanating from the crowded, vast, Muslim graveyards nearby.

Your body is a delicate yet firm papyrus, a field in which hieroglyphic flowers bloom. My bones relax in the soil of your soft body, O Isis, Virgin Mother. My legs embrace your gravel-strewn delta. In my sleep the polygonal obelisk—bursting with imprisoned blood—falls down on me. It catches fire under the sun of your eyes. I hear the singing of your soft, sandy dunes as they entomb the vestiges of my temple. Falcon feathers scatter in the wind, O mother of saints. With my lips I graze the stones of the ancient pyramid's stones in the walls of your mosques. I enter Memphis victorious and I fall powerless under its fortifications. I am knocked down by a yearning for your deep dark vale where slender reed stalks sway and ripple, soughing hymns and heavenly laws, the words of philosophers, the suffering of martyrs, the prayers of God's pious saints. My forehead is smudged with the tomb dust that lies beneath Diocletian's column and I listen to the merciless wailing of the stoned, the slaughtered, the burnt. I embrace you, wrapping my arms around the columns of ancient pharaonic temples with their deeply incised designs, surrounded by incense rising from monks, deacons, priests, and archpriests under the deep, husky voice of the patriarch—hoarse from fasting and long silence. O lady of the apostles, sister of Osiris, I fling myself into your currents of hair whose braids gush green waves. Rust-red waters spring from your underworld. The wells of Fate supply your arteries as you shudder with the fulfillment of desire. Waters geyser forth from the controls of giant turbines, purifying the greenery and choking with the tough leaves of water hyacinth. I kiss you on the forehead and dream of your kisses. I call on death as I turn over with the agony of my sacrificed heart on your white, soft sands. I hear the sound of death in my final rapture and I leave, on the large, cold marble of the column, perfectly dry, perfectly round drops from my blood.

He used to fear night's fall, firmly sensing what it would bring: This delusion in which events are mixed up and in which he was called to address his fantasies—fantasies now familiar, nightmares domesticated by human faces—in a dialogue of give and take, question and answer. His nerves would leap out and shatter from the jingling of his phone that had not yet rung. Yet he had heard it echo in his cluttered, tranquil room, here at nightfall. The fish-like dream slipped out of his hands in the heavy waves of half-sleep, half-wakefulness, as he wallowed in the lap of the sacred harlot, turned back by the witch-seer who read the unknown, plunging deftly into knotted events, possessing an ability that went beyond the empirical field of sense. The professional, aristocratic belle ceased to speak to him, and the boat that the priestess of Isis steered—casting spells on the scorpions in the marshes of Kemi—upended, sank. He ran away from the police with his utopian radicalism. Around him rose the bare iron skewers of buildings and massive columns supporting no ceiling. The phoenix, with its tremendous wings, emerged from the flames, fluttering into empty sky at its violent peak.

He addressed her casually, but with an agitated heart: I saw Mahmud yesterday. We talked about you.

She answered with the old folkloric phrase: That must be why I choked and almost died.

He said: May the evil eye stay away. Our talk was benign. Mahmud is a true friend and I am fond of him, but he has a streak of wickedness along with his intelligence and stubbornness, not to mention his bizarre attachment to Samia.

She said: Bizarre? Love's never bizarre, or strange. There are no conditions with love, you know. Mahmud is kind and helpless.

He could not bring himself to say to her: The kind friend, of whom both of us are fond, is the very one who said of you, not maliciously—he doesn't know what's between us, or does he?—that in the end you were nothing but a nymphomaniac, and that he knew this right after he met you for the first time, that he could have very easily slept with you but chose to run away from problems and complications, as he knew your type of woman too well and never got close to them.

He said to himself: Was that all? Is it only a story of a sex mania? And for me? What's my role in this story? Instrument? Prey? Or hunter in whose lap fell an easy victim? How painful this is! Is it the story of a middle-aged man saying oft-repeated and memorized statements about himself, an oedipal victim, an eternal adolescent, a loner and recluse, mystically involved with eroticism? These Freudian and neo-Freudian abstractions and terminology recur on the lips of all. Clichés like these are repeated in every age, varying perhaps, but

243

meaning what exactly? What's the troubling fervor behind them? How can one express it? It cannot be expressed.

He said to her: We also talked about how intelligent and cultivated you are, also about your beauty.

She said: God bless you!

Unlike death, despair is not a mode of repose from worry. It is a modulation on suffering. Indeed, it is a total loss, unacceptable. A thread of wily hope remained intertwined with his despair. A sharp pain, it burned while turning over endlessly. When, when will he be done with it? At every moment, despair was growing teeth that plunged into his flesh with new stings.

He said to her: Don't you resort to a kind of Machiavellian love?

She said: You know I forgive such thoughts of yours. Otherwise, you wouldn't dare say them.

He said: I don't know. I am not looking for forgiveness or anything.

Then he said: I miss you. I feel lonely without you.

She said: Me too.

He said: I don't believe it.

She said: Don't believe it then.

She said this in her cold, decisive, final tone, in her special, unromantic way of finishing with something that needs no further argument, as if to say that she would not match him in his facile, running emotions. A major decision for her . . . what there was between them was more entrenched. This thought calmed his infatuated heart for a moment, returning an inner smile to him.

In this world where the Amazon's struggle never ceases, where the Amazon never steps down from her winged horses, she is perhaps avenging the glories of her father Ra, triumphing alone in her inner world, with her special truth, with no accounting to anyone, in the midst of a displacement process that never reaches its goal.

The toy sheikh in the shop window looked as if mean circumstances had thrown him, a stranger, among all the dolls holding tight plastic fists to their immutable eyes and with fixed smiles revealing delicate mouths like pomegranate seeds, with ponytails made of yellow thread, wearing small embroidered dresses. All of them stood among can openers, oriental perfume bottles, poorly made ballpoint pens shaped like pharaonic obelisks, colored cups, amber necklaces with large beads, and imitation gold earrings handmade of copper. Behind them hung Kardasa *jallabiyas* of gaudy colors, trophy jugs encircled with sickly orange and blue spangles, and a thousand and one types of trashy trinkets produced by tourist souvenir factories, light in weight, exorbitant in price and taste. The sheikh looked at him with two bright, black beads. He had a hollowed face of gray cloth, a beard made of shaggy, spun cotton wicks, a native gown falling down in fixed folds, hands dangling next to it in loose sleeves, and a low Moroccan tarboosh with a black tassel, around which an elegant white turban was wrapped.

He said to himself: She will be delighted with it. A rare sheikh: dignified, lonely, and miserable in the midst of this festivity.

He said: She'll add him to the procession of disjointed, frail-bodied dolls and ghost dummies she's so fond of embracing.

She had said to him: No one captivates me more than Don Quixote. I just love him! He stumbles, stutters, fails, sets forth all solemn, without an inkling that he's a washed-up has-been, that his values and manners have long been gone. Perhaps you didn't know that I follow the Quixotic creed and its eternal rituals.

He said: You? You can relate to the creed of old age and failure?

She said: It's true that I hate incompetence in all its manifestations, whether it's daily work, militant activity, archaeology, transportation—not to mention that I hate it in love.

He said: When did love become a matter of competence or incompetence? The issue's not love-making, but love itself.

245

She said: No emphasis on the making? Come now, my darling.

Certainly he had no answer for this.

She said: Incompetence, no. But Don Quixote, I die for him. I have various first editions of *Don Quixote*. I am learning Spanish to communicate with him in the original. I also collect paintings and statues of him in all the variations. Have you noticed my small iron statue, hollow with longish limbs? Quixote's ancient nag Rosinante has protruding bones. His towering lance has fallen beside him, gratuitously and pointlessly. His pale, sunken, metallic face hangs in dry hopelessness. I just love my darling Don Quixote.

Why did he suddenly realize that Don Quixote was also a certain former prime minister of the Sudan? That suave, elderly gentleman had passed his glory days without knowing it and was now exiled among windmills, his lance become a tennis racket smacking balls that neither came nor went.

And what about her comrade Alphonse, with his shriveled face tanned by the suns of southern Egypt, his deep wrinkles like archaeological sands? At this point, he was nothing but the fruit of a doum palm with a hard pit, his white flesh containing a slip of aging water in it. She always ended her encounters with Alphonse by kissing his dried-up cheek. Then too, look at Ibrahim, her tall friend who used to be a soccer star in the thirties, currently a hunchback, all hollow-eyed, his hair still jet black even if nothing but strings. She goes drinking with him at bars, engages him in intimate chats, thrusting forth all parts of her soft, feminine body dynamically. He could see her alert face while she held her cognac in a childlike way, as if every part of her ripe body was prancing unconsciously with joy, longing to dash off into a new game. What kind of a child had she really been? Naughty, adventurous, daring, unconcerned with grown-ups, not awed by their world? He remembered there was also her boss, always calling her at home, basically asking for free nursing, complaining as aging people

246

do. Her boss used to incline his head toward hers as they read together a demotic text in sloppy handwriting. He could never have enough
of her competent affection, her delicate sense of responsibility.

He said to her: You have a peculiar soft spot for men whose pale
suns are about to set.

He said to her, as he was hiding behind his back the small box
wrapped in silvery paper tied with braided, multicolored string: I
have a present for you.

She said: My God, is that so? I love surprises.

He said: This surprise has hidden meanings.

She said: You silly man!

She smiled blankly in expectation, as if he—not to mention she—
had simply disappeared, while at the same time her fingers tore
through the package's richly plaited string.

She drew up the sheikh for inspection, its eyes answering her
smile with the same sorrowful, blank gaze. Her hand softly patted its
beard automatically. She said: Oh, my God! She glanced at him and
said: Thank you. All my life, I have wanted him in my apartment.

She replaced the lid on the box, shoved it into her large, plump
handbag with its puffed, expensive leather belly—perpetually open,
zipper undone. And forgot it, in fact both of them, just like that.

Rama: Her legs are two open sea rocks, two Assyrian columns
with white-foamed waves of desire crashing down between them.
Mad hounds of Circe howl, run open-mouthed, gnashing their jagged
teeth without taking any prey. Rama, I know you better than anyone
else. I may not be the best of your lovers, nor the most competent,
nor the most active, but I am the one who has loved you the most,
the best, or so I believe.

He said to himself: What is this? A vulgar old folktale? Story of
a nymphic woman obsessed by sex, craving the security of random
accidental love, which she then expects to be renewed ad infinitum?

247

He said to himself: No, that may be what's going around about her. To be sure, Shafiq, her old friend, pointed it out most casually: "In her prime, this Rama slept with whole street blocks!"

His friend's recklessness and cynicism had tied his tongue from responding, had dried his heart and made it crumble like an incinerated leaf.

He said to himself: Have I in fact hurt her?

He said: During certain moments that just went on and on, I wanted to kill her. I hated her as I have never hated anything or anyone. I forgot the unbearable, nameless torment of love. Is that possible? Then my resentment and hate ebbed at the center of my lonely heart. It's only now that I remember that dimension of her love that flows and gives, and I miss it, long for it.

She said to him: Are you an architect working in archaeological restoration who has wandered into politics, poetry, and philosophy? Or are you a poet, a revolutionary, and a philosopher who wandered into architecture and archaeological restoration?

He said in calm admission: I am a middle-aged Copt, getting on in years, who never got over his childhood.

She said: Don't turn this conversation into a drama. You know I wasn't fishing around for such sentiments. Anyway, what shall I say to you, Mikhail? Don't you see what's happening around you? Can't you see that this poetry or mysticism or this *je ne sais quoi*, whatever it is, chops off and mutilates your self, the world, together with this Egypt to which you are tied as if by disease? I mean, can't you see reality?

He said: I see, I see; I cannot but see, of course. What I see devastates me. I don't want . . . to see. But despite myself I am open-eyed.

She said: You who protest of honesty again and again, don't you find fakeness, deviation, and lies—intended or unintended, white or not white—in this poetic embellishment or mysticism, in this *je ne sais quoi* of yours? Don't you beautify, embellish, and make up?

248

Don't you see hunger, fanaticism, dirt, greed, falsehood, pauperism, deception, and formless chaos? Can't you see the coarse physicality of faces with their rotten flesh, all hollow, pulled back with cunning, poverty, sorrow, and ugliness? Aren't those figures also people? Aren't they Egypt? I too love Egypt enormously. Who doesn't love Egypt? But I want you to see it as it is.

He said to her: Please stop it. Do you really think I don't see? Look, I don't want to quarrel. I raise my hands up: I surrender!

She said: No, don't surrender, love. You are a fighter too!

Mikhail and Rama entered the hotel from a side street shaded by trees looking indistinct in the weak light of morning. Beneath the platform of the entrance, their feet grated on spots of yellowish sand that were scattered on the asphalt descending toward the sea. They were both yearning for a refuge to shelter them from the cruelty of the small world and its exhausting beauty, a world moving along its way, not paying any attention to them.

He was holding her hand in the taxi that took its time—interminable—in its way across the desert, across Tahrir District, the new villages, the model farms, the chicken hatcheries, Lake Maryut, and the oil refinery that had been relocated there from Suez. One other passenger rode with them, sitting next to the Nubian driver, who silently tended to his job. The passenger was young, exhausted looking. He was, he said, a Palestinian returning from Lebanon to resume his engineering studies at Alexandria University. Unlike most Palestinians, he owned a cool voice, talked without fervor about the war in Lebanon. He spoke non-stop about the various militias clashing in Beirut. He explained, dryly, how entire families in Shiyah were obliterated, how a relative of his had fallen into the hands of a militia group. They raped her collectively, then murdered her with a Tommy gun.

The casuarina trees stood in long lines on both sides of the road, lit by the gentle heat of an early autumn afternoon.

249

He said that Beirut's streets were rotting with corpses and rubble, covered by a rancid smoke that stuck to everyone's noses and mouths. Nothing could wash it off. The rats increased and grew big to the point of attacking homes, adding to the terror. Walkers of the street like himself were finding men castrated, their cut-off sexual organs stuffed in their mouths, pushed with coagulated blood between their blue swollen lips and broken teeth.

Mikhail said to himself: Ramses the Third, the Assyrians, medical doctors of the Byzantine Cross and of the Swastika, sultans of *The Thousand and One Nights* did this too, each in his own way.

In the reclaimed lands stretching to their right were newly-planted trees and bushes with shades of varying intensity, the lands rolling on flat. The tresses of weeping willow and sycamore trees hung short and dark, reaching the straight canal running in its trough made of cement. A small flock of white and gray geese were floating on a pond the color of café au lait, as if they inhabited a world sketched on stone. The geese were opening their bills, but from inside the roaring car, no sounds came to them.

Killing on the basis of identity, he said to himself, without question or succor, becomes our daily bread. The ID card determines life or death. The militias and the small armies, the generals and the chiefs, the gangs and the patrols, the guerillas and the buddied-up goon squads are beyond count. Alliances, allegiances, and confrontations change from day to day, hour to hour. The say-so of bearded youth with guns, bombs, and rockets carries the day. They don't know any more whom are they defending and whom are they killing or what they are smashing and destroying, and at whom they are aiming the muzzle of their cannons, rockets, and tanks in neighborhood streets. Their weapons pop and crack in every direction, day and night. The war of open spaces and deserts now takes place in alleys and streets.

Her hand was under his on the vinyl taxi seat. The seat's color was worn out from desert dust and time. Her hand felt calm, surrendering. A slight numbness had penetrated his entwined fingers. So he spread his hand to squeeze her short fingers and passed his index finger along the tops of her nails painted in a subtle but glossy gray. Suddenly, their tiny taxi was speeding in vain behind a huge oil truck with rounded belly, a wide rusty line cutting its side from the effect of hardened spilled oil.

The passenger said that pregnant women were aborting as they died from thirst in Tall al-Za'tar, their bodies drying out. Tommy guns faced the children, delirious from starvation and lack of sleep, whenever they strayed from their destroyed shelters. Despite this, he said, Palestine will not die.

Mikhail said to himself: Tall al-Za'tar and Abu Za'bal, the arenas of the Colosseum, the graveyard of Caracalla, the dungeons of the Inquisition, and the helmets of the Vikings. The hounds trained to mangle the blacks in Rhodesia, the power of the papal bulls, the instructions of political bureaus and central committees. Spartacus, Jesus, Husayn ibn Mansur al-Hallaj crucified with thieves, rebels, and fugitives. The cells of the Bastille, the swords of the Crusaders, and the chains of the Saracens. The harlots of Saigon, the victims of Black September, Black June, and all the black months. The Devil's Islands, no matter how their names differed: Sing-Sing, Tura, Robben Island, and those in the Aegean Sea. The floating corpses in the Nile in Uganda, the bodies stabbed by poisoned spears in Burundi and Rwanda, the crushed ones in Chile, the squashed ones in Bangladesh. The snows of Argentina and the ovens of Dachau. Quartering of limbs, guillotine blades, execution blows. The Khartoum of Kitchener, the Victorian factories of Manchester, the Commune of Paris, and the fields of sugar cane and cotton in Mississippi and in southern Egypt. The huts and putrid wounds covering the face of the earth, and the

251

ghettoes of Harlem, Odessa, and Warsaw. The barbed wires of Siberia and Saharan oases, and the electrodes in women's breasts and men's genitals in Algeria and Haiti. The caravans of the Qaramatians and the fall of Baghdad under the blows of Hulagu. The pyres of witches, and white soldiers harvesting jungles and valleys with a wide-mouthed cannon. The slave ships from Guinea and Zanzibar, the whisky, syphilis, opium, and bullets for Red Indians and likewise for Black and Yellow Indians. From Beirut to Guernica, from Berlin to Leningrad, from Sinai to Dayr Yasin, from Carthage to Constantinople, from Jerusalem to Shanghai, from Buchenwald to Munich, from Bombay to Dinshaway, from the Huns to the Mongols, from the Hyksos to the Mandarins to Vietnam, from the Mamluks to the tycoons. Isn't this the story of every day? Of the first day and of the last day? Isn't this the principle and the rule? Isn't this the story of this wise, productive, dreaming, upright, articulate, intelligent, ravishing ape? The bruised living limbs, stamped and torn, and the wounded spirit behind the stifled, concealed eyes; the anguished mind starved by oppression and paralyzed by degradation; all the cards and the values, all the gods and the systems; all the beasts and the preys; all the heroes and the sites, all the epochs and the masks; all the victims and the freaks. The lists do not and cannot end, and the dragon is one, unslain. The lance of St. Michael is blunted, but it is still brandished among the stars.

Their taxi reached the Nuzha grounds, trembling over a pair of railroad tracks. It passed beside a tattered banana tree and entered crumbling streets harboring a group of fenced, small factories with graffiti sprawled across their outer walls in outsized, pathetic penmanship. As the taxi sped along, they could read occasional snippets, lit by the street lamps: *Elect . . . The First Detainee of Centers . . . Hero . . .* They motored past dusty white tents of army guards erected amid dry grass and bushes that would never grow. They hurtled beneath the steel arcs of a dark bridge whose arched stone piers had blackened, and, passing quiet graveyards and gardens planted around racing cataracts of fresh water, they reached the sea, its balmy air redolent of salt and freedom. The Palestinian got out at the Cecil Hotel and said goodbye. Spindrift from the Mediterranean was lashing the Corniche wall, falling on the large broken-up riprap consisting of old, white flagstones. The Corniche highway was empty except for speeding cars under high Zizinya hill that overlooked the dark sea whose surface foam frothed, soundlessly, in successive incoming rows . The few winter nightclubs looked deserted, cold, their red and blue neon signs having lost a few letters. Then, as they proceeded, the silent, shut villas appeared, one after the other, the rust from sea mist having corroded the iron of their tightly closed windows and doors. They felt as if they were entering a city of the dead, empty, of forlorn beauty.

Along a side street lined with silent trees, in the middle of its asphalt surface, sand had been scattered by the constant sea breeze. The taxi driver put their two small suitcases behind the hotel's glass door. No one stood or sat at the reception desk, where big bronze balls of room keys were hanging out of their pigeonholes. A shaky light from a neon lamp softly hissed in the prevailing silence. They stood looking around until a young Nubian of the new generation arrived wearing an impeccably white shirt with elegant black tie. He glanced at them and was won over. Mikhail said: Good evening. Would you have a room with a bath overlooking the sea? One night, possibly two. He said: Most welcome. Do you have a passport or identity card? He quickly took Mikhail's passport while she fumbled in her handbag. He said: One passport is enough, Madame. So, I give you a deluxe room. Mursi, he said to the bellboy, take the luggage of the *bey* and madame to number seven. He handed the bellboy one of the keys with a heavy, polished bronze ball. Over here is the elevator!

The elevator's wood was old, shiny, of an expensive type like that of the reception desk. The polished parquet floor was something from Alexandria's glory days. The elevator flapped along its transit upward, emitting a metallic rumbling that seemed to come from sudden, repeated jolts.

Her first kiss that night tasted of sand, salt, metallic rust, and nostalgic search for a peaceful haven.

He glanced from the side window, above a narrow lane planted with naked trees, at an inhabited building with lit windows. His own window curtain was not yet drawn, so he tried to pull it closed. Something was holding up the curtain's metal rings where it normally slid along its bar. He selected one of the room's chairs, steadied it beneath the curtain, and climbed up on it. Using his two hands, he pulled the two parts of the curtain toward each other. They grated along the white metal rod with a rusty sound but refused to close all the way. He said to her: Rama, do you have a safety pin? She said: What? Ah, the curtain! She could not find what he requested in her swollen handbag, so he felt with his fingers along the back of his jacket collar, and found a pin. Using it, he attached the two sides of the curtain together, but even then, a voyeuristic triangular slit remained, high up on the curtain but wide open nonetheless.

He pulled back the cover of the bed and felt the soft pillow. His hands relished the ironed fabric. He took off his jacket and stretched out lazily.

Another window on the bed's side of the room presented a group of panes foggy with sea mist. Nevertheless, a long chink of sea shore and winter lights was available. He watched the waves hurl what seemed to be handfuls of water, splashing with minute drizzle, upon the low Corniche fence. Some of the sea wall's stones had fallen to the pavement, and lay inclined on their sides, looking tiny and insignificant.

She said to him: I'll be back in a moment—and started toward the bathroom. He said: Rama, can you let me get in first for a moment, please? Aren't you going to open your suitcase? She said: No, I don't want anything from it.

He dashed in, splashed water on his face, and within minutes had run his electric razor, showered, gasping in cold water. He stepped out in his pressed pajamas—the folds still evident—and felt glowing in his newly bathed body. Then she used the bathroom. He heard water pouring over her. The bedroom felt warm and closed, welcoming and sheltering; he took off his pajama top and slipped into the bed. Suddenly she was out of the bathroom walking toward him naked. He said: Rama, wait a moment. She said: I am still so shy in front of you. But the next moment his bare chest felt her breasts while they embraced: Darling! He smelled in her body a whiff of Sudanese sandal perfume, and he felt the passion of love raising them up and bringing them down in the wonderful excitement that they knew so well. Yet they could never stop exploring this world of flesh with its quiet herbs, gentle warmth, and dew.

She will be saying to him as they return the following day: You know, Mikhail, I am a woman and need love. Women dry out and wilt if they are not loved, if they do not make love. Yesterday was the first time for many months. I feel an equilibrium again in my body and in my soul. It's a good feeling.

And he will look at her but not respond. It will occur in his mind, afterward, in the pangs of silent, slow torture, that she was exaggerating a little, and that there was no need for such a comment. He has forgotten about her life and needs in their love mist, in an act that might be voluntary but only vaguely so. Why then does she remind him of those things?

He said: Where shall we dine?

She said: Your call, love. I don't know. It's your city.

In their desolation apart from one another, they knew few hours of intimacy, the peace of the senses, the banishing of anxiety monsters that followed such a brief wintry squall of love.

They walked to the Corniche: the sky was immense, the waves knelling deeply against the sea wall. The restaurant was empty, its glass front covered with a layer of mist from the sea against which a reflection of lights gently played, a swerving of red and blue rays. The grilled shrimp and dry white wine tasted crisp, fresh. They spoke sparingly but without tension or watchfulness. The crashing of waves on the huge, square, cement stones below the restaurant came to them as a muted echo, repeated with intermittent persistence, slightly intoxicating. They watched pine trees swaying in the night breeze on the other side of the street and felt they were alone, in need of nothing. White clouds were on the move above the sea's dark surface. Suspended behind the distant citadel was a half moon. The citadel seemed small, black, looking like a bit of old tin.

He said: I haven't known the ecstatic joy that makes the heart fly and goes beyond the senses, since the days of our early discovery—days that can never return. That was when the old locked doors opened and revealed whole zones of light-headedness and intoxication, fiery and wakeful, that I'd never known existed. Remember when we were walking together in the empty street at night, and you kissed me on the mouth all of a sudden, nothing but spontaneous affection and gratitude? It sealed something inside me, completed it. We started a journey then with no idea where it would take us.

He held her hand and said: Shall we go back?

The column seemed distant at that moment, the martyrs necessary.

12

The Phoenix Born Daily

I t is just as it happens in his dreams: going out and coming in; doors, elevators, stairways—a constant searching for her, an agitated and perplexing trajectory of muddled numbers and directions. At night when he knocked at her door, the face of a taut-skinned man, awake and tired, in his underwear, with disheveled hair, appeared. With two large, wrinkled hands, he held the door cracked open and gazed out with a lightly sarcastic smile. Mikhail mumbled an apology—her door was the next one, he realized.

It was unlatched, swinging inward when he tapped on it. At that very moment she was getting up for him. In the early morning light, she was in a gown coming up to mid-thigh. She raised her arms to embrace his head, showing her light brown underarm hair against the brown flesh of her body. She kissed him on the mouth— a quick kiss—then turned and closed the door.

She said to him: Mikhail, did you drop your keys somewhere?

He patted his key pocket then passed his hands through all his pockets. His mind started wandering in all directions, wondering where the keys might be.

He said: Did you find them somehow?

She said: You know, about an hour ago, in the early morning, maybe at seven o'clock, I heard a knock. I sleep, as you know, with nothing on, naked.

Swiftly, it occurred to his mind that he did not know this fact.

She said: And the door was open. I don't like to lock it on myself at all.

He knew that much.

She said: I was half slipping into my gown when Mahmud entered. He said good morning then asked for small change—at that hour. He wanted to go shopping and only had large bills. Imagine. As he was leaving, he bent down and picked up a set of keys. He handed them to me without a word. I think he knew whose they were.

So they had fallen from his pocket the night before, when he'd thrown off his clothes before entering the bed with her.

He was not yet acquainted with her world whose corners were interlocked with other well-knotted relationships. He laughed, covering his anxiety and lack of immediate comprehension.

Later will come the hours of love that resemble treason, not fulfillment. Cold physical anger will push him to make love, lying to himself. The one act will exist adjacent to the other—intimate physical penetration while feeling she is foreign, a stranger on whom he is thrust despite himself. Pushed with a violence from which no salvation is possible. Without affection or tenderness. Simply the raw body responses, a riot in the flesh that should be repressed. Then suddenly the awakening: dripping cold sweat from a nightmare. A scorching, dazzling awareness in the darkness. The horror of the inevitable and definitive discovery that the lie has come, not to be forgiven or erased.

258

In the midst of his rush for her—in a restaurant, in a café, in a movie theater, at home—he offers her his severed head on a burning solar tray. She yawns. Words wilt in his mouth; he falls into a stupor. Has she taken him for granted to this point, so carelessly? When she saw the look—wounded, no doubt—in his eyes, she said half apologetically, as she was twisting the knife in the wound: Haven't you always told me you wanted me to be myself? Here I am being myself.

In a third course of time, at the end, his greeting to her in a crowded station resembled a final farewell. He wanted a break with the unresolved, effusive suffering, even if it meant delivering an uncalculated blow that wrecks the heart. So be it. He saw how that was scaring her, how she shrank back the way a sunflower leaf will do. He said to himself hurriedly: this is because she can't accept rejection. These reactions are deep-rooted, entrenched. Her little doll, no matter how varied its forms, is forever in a locked box, never thrown away, nor given to someone, nor taken for granted; it always remains in some corner. This is the crux of the matter.

She had said to him that her childhood dresses were not at all elegant, not even properly cut. Her stepmother had said to her once: Come my little one, what is this trifle you are wearing? Let me fix your dress for you. She got hold of the hem of the dress and cut it off while it was on her. It was as if her stepmother had cut off part of her body.

As for me, I am terrified by rejection too. I sense it in every gesture. I cannot envision myself left in a large, barren square, nor can I feel, with gaping eyes, the rough plain walls or the soft, feminine, and neglected dress.

In a late stage in this relationship, when I kept missing my chances, kept deviating from the rules of the game, when I failed to live out my predetermined role, there was not even sexual interest. The interconnections became burdensome nightmares, complicated

259

but clearly with a pattern. Wild, angry, lonely nights, stormy nights in the heart of silence. Her name mixed with tears. Her body thrown into an open space attacked by wolves beneath a sky of melted lead. Such is the price of defeat.

Should he admit that he betrayed her, simply by his silence? By his cracking up? By his sterile childish tears—ashamed as he was of these tears, and knowing the futility of shame? Or is he, like all betrayers, unable to see his treason?

He said to himself: Who cares about other peoples' pain? Or even their deaths? No one. Not even their closest loved ones.

He said to himself: The act of life itself is selfish: a fundamental egoism that does not diminish. It is concentrated around itself: a hard pit that cannot be harmed by anything. Give and take? Granting and accepting? Conferring and consenting? Not at all. Never, never. There is only the open mouth that chews and mangles, taking and taking, paying attention to nothing else, in the process of sheer appropriation and total possession, with teeth and lips.

He responded to himself: Why do I get so upset about this simple, basic truth that cannot be argued? We live alone, die alone. We suffer alone. Basically we enjoy ourselves alone. Other people are instruments. Sharing: dream of the defeated.

He said to her: Love is the endeavor in which loneliness should dissolve away. Correct? Yet I ask you. I ask you and you must answer: Does the lover really know the anguished torments of the beloved? The inner dying of the lover? Or is the sharing of this suffering, even if granted, no more than a revolving around the self? I want to know.

She said sorrowfully and with belated knowledge: I have tormented you a lot. I know. But this has passed. We have known some beautiful moments. Isn't that enough?

No, it is not enough; it is not enough, even in the moment of consummation of love itself, that merging forgetfulness in the flesh.

260

Even at that moment, is there anything but the confirmation of the self? At best it is binary and reciprocal, but it never becomes one entity. In fact, this merging confirms a fundamental separation, which can never be soldered, never, never, never.

Once she said to him in deceptive simplicity: Why this merging, which you search for with such ardor? You act as if we don't possess human rights, his or her separate sovereignty.

Then she added, trying to lighten the tension: Or have you become a Sufi? And you, dear sir, whom I thought to be so rational and sedate.

She said to him, narrating, her lips pursed around a cigarette he had lit for her, enjoying the telling of her tale:

This city reminds me of Algiers right after the War of Independence. We were part of the Egyptian mission to study and restore Greek and Roman antiquities. We had an Algerian friend whose friendship I valued. I don't know what has happened to him. I received the last of his letters before Ben Bella's dislodgment. We used to go out in his black Austin. He had simply confiscated it from a French colonial settler who fled. Yes, a car like Nasser's. Why are you smiling?

He said: Revolutionaries everywhere behave the same.

She said with a dreamy, almost erotic look: Ben 'Ammar was a revolutionary of the pure type; able to forget bygones completely and start from scratch each time, after each failure, without regrets and especially without bitterness. This bitterness is what I cannot stand. It is a sure sign—I'm not saying of weakness—but of something worse, of hesitation and confusion. He knew how to welcome life and its pleasures, taking his fill without excesses, without squandering, without false abstention. He also knew how to put up with blows. He was dismissed from his army committee after Independence, and he started anew. He was entrusted with planning the decentralized, self-managing

261

economy of the *autogestion*. He took the task seriously, tried his utmost, and called on his imagination. But they removed him to the cultural committee in the Liberation Front. His responsibilities included antiquities. He used to come out with us wild bird hunting—what are they called, sandgrouse? Anyway, that was in the northern swamps, a few hours away from Algiers, near the sea. It was just like Manzala, over by Port Said: reed, brush, and clear shallow waters over solid sand. The strong black Austin knew the way. He was always in a good mood, and his shot never failed. He never added a dramatic veneer to anything, no matter how dramatic the situation was.

He said: A man of many talents; a man for all seasons.

She said without blinking: A man who cannot be matched. He was a brilliant conversationalist. He was not fluent in Arabic, but I learned from him the Algerian dialect. At moments of emotional excitement he forgot his French. There was a potential writer, an accomplished novelist, in him; but he never wrote a word. As for me, I do not love nature. I wouldn't lie to you and tell you, for example, that I love opera. I simply don't love it. Just like that. All intellectuals in Egypt love opera, say they love opera.

Interrupting and with a sense of honesty and duty, he said: I love opera.

She said: Nor will I say that I feel ecstasy when the sun sets or rises in the fields, or that I find in it a symbol for *le je ne sais quoi*. Or for that matter the chanting of birds. Do birds chant or sing? They make noise; that is all. They twitter, titter, or trill, as they say. But sing like 'Abd al-Halim Hafiz?!

He said: You are right. Most people resort to ready-made molds for their so-called aesthetic judgments. They select among prefabricated groupings of canned emotions.

She said: I don't deny that perhaps a few have genuine feelings, virginal and intimate, in front of nature. I think you're one of them.

He said: But does this "nature" exist? I believe what people do is a constituting part in making nature. I don't believe in another nature, separate, imaginable without interference from man or his existence. This is particularly so in Egypt. Do people who speak about nature know it? The pallid imagery they believe in is taken from translated poetry and from the clichés of innovative though not especially inventive literati. As for me, nature in Egypt is entirely made by people's hands, with one exception of course: the desert. After you go beyond the telephone wires, telegraph wires, and the new electricity towers, you'll find the terror and the magic of pure desert—its complete immunity from human penetration.

He was pleased she saw eye to eye with him. At every moment he was discovering they met in areas where he formerly thought himself isolated, sequestered.

She said: When Ben 'Ammar spoke of a sunset, of a hunting expedition in the mountain, or of a political struggle in a committee, he was able to make me forget everything else, to make me live with him, to love nature and hunting, to be a partisan in his political struggle.

He said: He is single-minded then in every project of his, having one overriding purpose.

She said: Yes. But not quite. For example, he did not claim that he abstained from non-marital relations, because it would have been a lie. He simply didn't want to wreck his marriage. He looked as if he were twenty-eight when in fact he was in his forties. His wife seemed in her fifties though she was probably in her thirties. You can count then how much older than him she seemed. But she was dear to him, and he was intent on her as one would be on that which cannot be replaced.

He was trying to overcome his sudden jealousy, which he felt was out of place. She had not missed the slightly sarcastic tone and rejection in his response to her story. She had simply chosen to ignore it, if only for the time being. He became silent, waiting.

263

She said: Yet he was able to come back, if need be, to discuss an issue, after several days following the end of a violent polemic around it—a polemic worked to his advantage—to tell you that you were right, that he had thought it over, and come to see what you wanted to say. I mean by that, he was not self-centered. He had no need to negate the other.

He said: He was not a man cut out of a single mold. He did not have a single god.

She said: He might have been torn on the inside, but he was whole at the end of day. Perhaps not the ideal model of perfection, but integrated. Everything in him—even his inner fragmentation—complemented his other dimensions. In no way do I mean he was tepid and calculating. His exuberance and passion matched his prudence and careful weighing of matters. He called things by their own names.

Naughtily, he said: How difficult it is to know the names of things before we name them.

She said: Yet the thing remains the same, no matter how it is named.

Later, he said to himself: Of whom was she talking? About a man she really knew with an intimate knowledge that went all the way? Or was she talking about a combination of lived experience and lived illusion? Doesn't this man have some of my own features? Rather, isn't he the way I should be in her dreams? Isn't she talking to you about yourself, using an alternative image?

He said to her in a voice that he strove to make clear: What a man! As if he came out of a novel, rather than Algeria.

She said: It is true. Rarely does one have the chance to get to know a man like him. I don't know how to explain him to you. He is at any given moment a single, integrated human being, aiming at one goal, moved by one need. But the moment is not something imposed, fixed, frozen. The moments change, and every change brings a new man, also integrated, unified. Yet the moments that pass by, and the ones to come, exist in every moment. They do not pass away completely. They do not pass away at all; they form a concealed and luminous fund in the depth of his oneness.

He said: This I understand.

She said: Without drama. Have I told you? No drama. And he does not feel pity for himself, or at himself. This is what I love in men, first and foremost.

He noticed instantly that she did not use the past tense: "This is what I loved."

She said: Algiers reminds me of Alexandria. You know, I am going to take you with me to Alexandria—isn't it your darling city?—and drown you in the sea.

What do you say to your beloved who will drown you in the sea? You say, of course: Do drown me. These are the waves in which we all want to drown, without choking with salt water, instead a calm, delicate drowning, or else a rough, stormy drowning in which one loses one's self, loses one's head. You say: No, I'll never drown, when you have already hit sandy bottom, settling with conscious eyes in your tomb beneath layered, unbearably heavy waves?

She said: I am like the phoenix that they talk about. I revive myself in the seawater.

He said to himself: In the waters of passion, in the baptism of fire.

She said: In the sea salt, in its silence and scorching sun, in the delicacy of its moon.

He said to her: Always youthful. You come out of the scorching water in the tenderness of new youth.

He said to himself: This woman will never perish. She herself sets the number of years according to the dictates of her inner needs. The burning pond of passion is the well in which she sees the wheat-colored flower of her face glittering next to the water's surface.

He said to himself: She never goes back to something past; she never mentions it. She never says that this or that has happened and ended. Everything is present. Every moment starts anew, as if the past had never existed. Thus the past is neither forgotten nor remembered, because it never exists in the first place. In fact all her stories take place in present tense. As well, she cannot entertain the future. It simply doesn't exist.

He knew, at a later course of time, that things in her world had many names, also that one name referred to several things and several people too. He learned that differences in her passionate, private convictions faded and disappeared over years, over dreams, people, visions, fancies, facts, challenges, and disappointments.

He said to her: Why are you without your usual dynamism today? I trust this is not a depression cycle?

She said: No, it's just the change of seasons. It always happens in spring. You know, snakes shed their skins in late spring. We used to find their skins in the courtyards during Baramhat, when I was a kid in Sharqiya. You know that I am from Sharqiya province?

He said: And the birds change their feathers?

She said: Ah, the old phoenix.

He said: The ever-renewed, the born daily.

She said: I have no roots. There is no haven for me in my self, and this scares me. I am a reflection of others. I am destined to be a reflection of the ones I love. I dedicate myself to what they love. I love for myself what every new tyrant in my life loves. This removes me from myself. Each time, I know nothing except what the tyrant wants, without his even saying it.

He said: There is a seed in you, which is your essence. This does not change. No one has known this seed in you. Do you know it yourself? I want to see it in your magic ball. I want to reach the heart of this essence. It's not impossible, is it?

266

She said: Our roles have reversed. Nothing is missing from your viewpoint except a broom on which I fly at midnight beside the church tower. So now you've become a seer!

They laughed together: a troubled laughter.

She went on with her stories, sipping her second beer:

He was the first I really loved, after my high school infatuations of course. He was my professor at university. A classic case, it happens repeatedly, but ours was different. He was an American lecturer at university, on loan to us for a year, and a member of the Brooklyn Museum Mission. He was only a few years older than me. Tall, with a face tanned by Luxor sun, a thin but full beard. A potential poet was in him. He taught me how to find the poetic in stones, in amphitheaters, in amulets, in terracotta, in worn out ancient coins, in remains of bones, in potsherds, and in pottery. His book—published only this year—is on the goddess Mut, the wife of Amun, and her magnificent temple, constructed on the same axis as Amun's temple at Karnak. I read the book in manuscript. There was a long review of it in *Time* magazine. Correspondence between us has been over for a long time, but when he first left I received daily letters, sometimes two or three letters—believe me. Recently I went back to them. For a long period of time I couldn't read them. I kept them in a wooden container—no, not a coffin—a big cosmetic box, the jewelry box every woman keeps. As you know, I don't have valuables. A pair of earrings here, a necklace there, suffice; and I keep replacing them all the time. I don't like gold. Somehow my jewelry continuously disappears. I make my bracelets, brooches, and necklaces available to any friend who comes by and admires them. Servants, relatives, friends of relatives—they're all welcome to them. That's why you find my jewelry—of silver, any other metal but gold—constantly changing. Anyhow, Richard asked me to marry him at the end of the year. He was crazy—I was already married. I had separated from my first husband, true

267

enough, but I was still married, and he knew it. The impossibility of our marriage did not occur to him, even though I was an Egyptian, Muslim, married woman in the era of 'Abd al-Nasser, and he was a Protestant American. It's true my first husband had left me and was totally out of the picture. His love had been that of a lunatic youth. I discovered in his radicalism and progressivism a sadism difficult to imagine. I shall not tell you how I suffered at his hands. Don't ask me how he used to torture me physically, spiritually, and emotionally; how he used to humiliate me physically and mentally. I will not speak of it nor do I want to recall anything of it. My mother, of course, was flabbergasted when Richard visited us and asked for my hand. After he returned from his home in Massachusetts, I went to his room. From my youth, I have never been embarrassed by something I believed in, and I didn't care about doing what needed to be done, or about what people said or did. I can face and challenge others, or remain indifferent, without dramatizing. Such matters are beneath my concern. I spent a week with him—the happiest week of my life— a week in which nothing mattered but us. We did not tire from making love; not a moment of lassitude. We used to eat in bed! Can you believe it? This is not simply talk. Love produces miracles, it is true. As you know, the driving power of action is not simply physical exertion, the mechanical, if you wish.

Mikhail was listening with enchantment to this story untouched by vulgarity. It was this first time in a new friendship, between them, that permitted him to listen in admiration, captivated by a measure of temporal distance—both physical and emotional—to a love story not possible to divulge to a lover. Below them, the statue under the large restaurant window was illuminated by a strange light, as if emanating from her story.

She said in a sort of dreamy sorrow: I don't doubt he resents me now.

268

Puzzled, he said: Why?

She said: When he came back, he found everything had turned against him. The activities of the American Mission had ceased, the lectures discontinued, and the authorities had asked him—politely but decisively—to leave the country. That was during the Dulles period, the crisis between us and the United States. I didn't see him after that. Then came my divorce. Events overpowered me. Perhaps they still do.

He said to her: Truly you resort to a beautiful and wonderful trick—trick in the good sense of the term—that calls for admiration. When you love something or someone, the veil is removed and you can see what's in front of you. Haven't I said you're an enchantress? This is your true self. Things with us may become confused and fake, but your trick of vision guarantees the purity of truth.

He asked himself about the difference between two states of things. On the one hand, there is the realm of the covert, where promises seem mysterious, set in a common, diffused, indirect lighting— the state of concealed magic and imperceptible appeal. It is where intentions and projects are begot, where beginnings are created and things appear without even feeling that they are taking shape, becoming, and growing. On the other hand, there is the realm of actual events that have taken place, the relationship with its bonds firmly tied, having developed ribs that can be touched, whose solidity can be pressed against. The strange and foreign thing that came to be—and stood up, definitive, dry, and weighty—has characteristics other than the ones that radiated in its dawn. It has its own laws, its trajectory, its limiting darkness.

He wondered about the gap, the crack, the barrier line, even when invisible, between the dream and the intention, between the intention and the realization, between the project and the trunk pushing its rounded wood in the firm land.

That crack was in everything: in love, in building a wall, in

269

poetry, in political parties, even when reaching the outskirts of a new city and entering its suburbs, or when you bought for yourself a book or a shirt.

That first course of time did not come again.

In the following course of time, she said to him: You are worried and not . . . not sure.

She was trying to find the proper tone, to discover what was on his mind. She came up with a comfortable expression: "not sure."

After a moment she asked him: Why aren't you sure?

He said fervently: I am not sure of you. Tell me, to what extent is this worry about assurance justified?

She said: Surely, there is no room for questioning.

He said: What a response! Please do give up being clever with me for a moment. Let's get down to the heart of things. Does this mean: "Yes, there is no room for a question; you should be assured," or does it mean to the contrary: "No, there is no need for the question at all."

He said to himself: Does it mean "Yes, my love for you is constant, not a matter of questioning," or does it mean, "There is nothing between us to question."

She said: Lack of certainty is an essential ingredient in this relationship. It's normal, isn't it?

He said: No.

She said: To a certain extent, it is, isn't it?

This seemed to him like yielding on her side. She was meeting him halfway.

He said: Not as far as I am concerned. I want certainty, absolute and definitive.

She said: As for me, I'll respond later. With a fundamental answer.

Of course, she never responded. In reality, fundamental issues were not a matter for responding or for questioning.

Later, she said: Certain issues are best left hanging. Certain things should never be said.

And that was indeed the only possible response.

Does saying amount to negation, cruel exposure, cancellation? Does definition imply desiccation, reduction, diminishment? Or does saying signify a causing of pain and an uncovering of illusions?

The wall of this soul crumbles from the inside. Drops from its salty water overflow into a wide, intermittent line—rusty and dull.

She had said to him: I am delighted that you exist, and that I have met you.

But this was not enough for him.

Rama was clearly the star of the small party that took place spontaneously after the waves of day visitors had ebbed and the Auberge calmed down.

On opening the window, Mikhail inhaled the lake's salt odor permeated by the twilight of early evening. Sharp, silver, luminous spearheads of stabbing stars were fixed on the lake's surface. In the light slap of the waves melting away on the sandy shore and in the air saturated with fleeting putrid gusts of decay, a threatening sensation touched gently, but repeatedly, the edge of his heart.

He drove this dangerous calm away from himself, and went and knocked at her door. When she opened the door, he was instantly met with boisterous cries and greetings by the circle of friends in the room. The party had already started. Lamps were lit on the table, next to the bed, in the ceiling, and in the bathroom. There were two bottles of Vat 69, a bottle of cognac shining with a precious, clear amber, and the reddish, highly suggestive liquor of Bisquit. The glasses were of different shapes: elongated ones made of the usual thin glass and crystal ones refracting light. At a glance, he could see the crowded plates, one next to the other, large and small. Slices of *qarish* cheese: a dewy, ribbed, and pressed curd. The deep red thin strips of *basturma*:

jerked meat with white fatty veins. The boiled, reddish, and rounded sausage. The splendor of tender green, comely lettuce. The delicacy of mint leaves like spicy, dark green flowers. 'Abd al-Jalil, stocky and weighed down, the collar of his shirt open, got up. His eyes protruded a little in his Arab-African face. He took her hand to his mouth with its large fleshy lips and said: You, my lady, were the first to teach us to be concerned about the people and to sacrifice everything for humanity. In his voice were the first inklings of tipsiness that come after the first or second drink. He said: Mikhail, do you know that Rama is our mentor? We used to know her under her *nom de guerre*, Fatma. She is the one who taught me revolutionary principles. Who would believe it? It was twenty-five years ago. She was then— allow me, my lady—a young girl, but a mentor just the same. She was most rigorous, precise, determined, and beautiful as well. The Roneo duplicating machine used to be under her bed.

Mahmud said: Let's toast this beauty first and then toast revolutionary rigor.

The seriousness of charged memories was made lighter by toasting and laughter. Samir got up, with his tall athletic figure and the naïveté of his light-colored face, which combined the meekness of a poet with the harshness of a desperado. He emptied his drink in one go and said: At that time, I was a child roaming the streets of Haifa.

The day before, Rama had got up to dance with Samir. They were taken by the music—coming out of the tape-recorder in a hushed rattle—and by a reciprocal and sudden flair of tenderness. Embracing, they went out to the balcony with its dim lights overlooking the lake. The lake looked to have been dashed to death and lying still on the sand. Mikhail was drinking and talking to Samia, the slender-faced one with profound eyes, as he watched them. The noisy clamor of the tape recorder sought him out among the crowded female bare backs on which the arms of dancers settled in formal and traditional poses.

272

The flutter of silk and evening dresses, perfectly surrounding the curves and bulges, opened up loosely and swaying musically at the legs and hems as the women moved closely and elegantly. There was an agitating uproar in his blood from the fierce blows of ice-cold whisky, from the tiny breasts of Samia, exciting in their finesse under his eyes, from the wild tape recorder rhythms, occasionally torrential, and from the obsessive passions and hankering jealousy.

Rama on the balcony seemed as if hurled into the arms of Samir. She pressed her face into his large shoulder. He bent with his mouth on her black hair tied in an elegant blue hair band. Mikhail could feel her ample body embraced by the poet who had run away from Israel, and his masculine blood erupted. Suddenly and without any possible resistance, he felt as if he, himself, was churning in the act of love. He put his drink down, held Samia's hand, and started dancing, slowly and stubbornly.

Now, Rama was again beside Mikhail, her knee tightly next to his leg under the table. Waves of speech and alcohol were flowing within him, hitting him from inside, now lightly and playfully. He was weaving a story with a complicated plot about the adventures of restoring the columns and the steps of the ancient Roman amphitheater and Alexandria's wall in Kum al-Dikka, and how he once led a mass demonstration against Farouk and 'Abd al-Hadi, the Chief of the Royal Cabinet, in practically the same spot thirty years ago, and how he had come up with a slogan for the demonstration—"No colonialism or exploitation after today!"—and how they replaced the Union Jack with the green flag while sporadic bullets were resounding hesitatingly and indecisively from the British barracks that was then at Kum al-Dikka. He was involved in the story, narrating his reminiscences and brilliantly captivating the group. Salwa was round and small like a mischievous duck, jolly with a trembling voice. Following the story, she sang Fairuz's song about Jerusalem in a low, warm, and sensuous voice. Nura, with her oval face and loose blonde hair, spontaneous in her popular dialect, having forgotten the inflections of a voice trained to be delicate and sophisticated, told joke after joke with obscene hints and just that appropriate measure of audacity, without an embarrassing cheapness or cumbersome reserve. Samir recited the radical songs of Sheikh Imam, and said that he had heard them and memorized them in Israel. 'Abd al-Jalil, having become completely drunk, spoke about al-Numairi, 'Abd al-Khaliq Mahjub, and 'Abd al-Shafi. It was clear that he had not visited Khartoum since he was a schoolboy in elementary school. Mahmud spoke of the intrigues among the personnel in the wings of the UN and the corruption of politicians.

The cognac bottle was emptied after the whisky bottle. Mikhail said: Just a minute. I have a surprise for you. I was hiding it for you. He went to his room to bring back a bottle of vodka. When he came back carrying the clear, translucent liquid in the bottle with baffling Cyrillic letters, he was met with applause. He said: This is the best of what they have. They have nothing else except caviar perhaps. 'Abd al-Jalil laughed with them. Rama came back, having washed the glasses under the large tap—the water had not run for a moment then it poured forth in a heavy stream. The location of seats changed for no reason with a sort of spontaneous mobility and liberation. Samia moved next to Mahmud, silent, with her heavy eyes, in her hand an appetizer plate of soaked lupine seeds. Salwa and Nura sat together facing 'Abd al-Jalil and Mikhail. As for Rama, she distributed the glasses and filled them. Her seat happened to be next to that of Samir, very close in fact. She clinked her glass to Samir's, and gazed at him as she was drinking. Her subdued and immersed look gave her away in an instant. Mikhail was drinking glass after glass of vodka and smoking on an empty stomach. The faces and the conversations around him were glowing, at times becoming defined with dazzling

274

precision, then clouding and melting in a sensually soft effect. A pit of pain, the sense of impending loss, was a hard stone implanted in the resilience of such collegial company, storytelling, and drinking. It formed a hump rising above the hushed din of the tape recorder, which was emitting a nerve-straining, forgotten music that no one was listening to. The pit was a piercing piece of shrapnel covered by slippery delay, derision, deferment, and ambiguity.

Following the fatigue of drinking, singing, and laughter, that of jokes, random dallying, and concealed flirtation with hands and legs, the farewell greetings came heavy with satiation and excitement. Steps toward adjacent and facing rooms were quite determined but slow. There were staggering "good-nights and sleep-tights," with hands gesturing and the last of light laughter.

Mikhail was in the final moments of troubled sobriety at the border of intoxication, without having overstepped it. Intuitively and without precision, he sensed now the rest of the night's drama. When he returned to his room, he hurled himself on his bed with his clothes on. He waited in a daze without thinking. He could not estimate how much time had passed before he was dialing her room number. The telephone rang for a long time, seeming to penetrate the night. He put the receiver back, raised it again, redialed, heard the ring again, persisting and stubborn. For a third time, he dialed. Certainty and doubt were equally rising in his mind. She could not have fallen asleep and she could not have gone out. At last the ringing ceased unexpectedly, and her voice came weakly, hesitating and knowing: Hello. He said he had forgotten his cigarette pack in her room—he couldn't go out to buy cigarettes now, could he come and fetch it? She said, having resolved her hesitation in a decisive tone that put an end to the situation: Yes, come. Samir is with me.

Despite that, he did go.

He does not know how he managed to knock on the door and then

275

see Samir opening the door with his youthful body and boyish looks, bare-legged, wearing a light, beige, chamois sport jacket, and nothing else, over his flesh. Samir said in a very calm tone: Come on in.

Everything seemed unreal. Rama was sitting in bed with stubborn features, her back leaning on the bedstead next to the wall, her knees up under the white sheet; wearing her white, short, nylon nightgown that he knows so well. Above her head, a picture with gaudy colors— as if he were seeing it for the first time—of palm trees under the Pyramids and a camel driver watering his camels. The table lamp is the only one lit. Everything is familiar, but his contact with it has been disrupted. In the shock of knowledge and certainty, everything moves slowly, with a special rhythm, and in a way that cannot be stopped, in the trajectory of another world in which he has no place. In the light of the definitive and perfectly clear situation, the blow is not felt, as if the heart, having felt an unbearable weight and having become tightly gripped, has lost the ability to feel. She says to him: Have you gotten your cigarettes? He has lost the capacity to say even a word. He hears her from this strange other world to which there is no connecting bridge. It seems to him that Samir is looking at him and simply waiting with no embarrassment, no sense of triumph. Nor does he feel resentment or rancor toward Samir either. In fact, he does not quite absorb the fact that he is there.

Mikhail cannot know or remember—no matter how much he tries—how he went back to his room, how he took off his clothes. He felt the water gushing on his feverish naked body, shaking with uncontrollable shivers under the shower. He felt the weight and volume of the water, but he did not feel its temperature, whether cool or lukewarm, only its heaviness as it poured down. He did not realize until later that his body had become alien to him. In the bathroom the convulsions of nervous vomiting were mixed with crying fits and water pouring on his body as he strove to withhold the roaring of his intestines heaving up in uncontrollable physical contraction that had a will of its own—repetitive until utter exhaustion. He did not know—in the dizziness of pain and fatigue that brought him down to a profound pit of agitated visions—how he came to his bed and covered himself with a sheet. Flickers of dreadful, fluttering wings that stretched to cover the length and width of the sky embraced him and rocked him until the mercy of dawn arrived without his realizing it. His sleep was a tattered mercy of torn pieces.

In the morning when he freed himself from agitated sleep, escaping worrisome waves of visions, he found on the side table next to him a folded paper under the matchbox, a few small coins, two washed cups from the ones she had used, and a small china plate, old and yellowish on the bottom, with a handful of peanuts in it. The leftovers of yesterday's party. He could not tell what all this was nor could he comprehend it. When he opened his eyes at last in the twilight of morning in the curtain drawn room, it smelled putrid and stagnant with cigarette smoke and bathroom humidity. Pain awakened with him, stabbing him. A hushed stab that had come to stay, blunted, with a heavy grip. A letter from her was on the paper, written in pencil, in her own large script. He did not read it. When did she write it? When did she enter his room and come with these things? Was his room left open? He felt for his watch under the table lamp. The taste of cigarette smoke in his mouth felt bitter and brackish. It was six in the morning. The day had not yet started. Have I slept at all? Two hours only.

Dearest,

When you were talking yesterday, you stood out, and I was overwhelmed by love for you. Your demeanor was lofty, reaching the sky. You were able to make me feel proud of you. So why did you spoil everything? What is the significance of what you saw?

277

We both know it's a trifle. What happened tonight is nothing. Don't you know this? I could not help it. I am not asking you to forgive me. I am not asking for anything. What is between us is stronger and the more lasting.

Your Rama

He didn't feel himself breaking into short sobs: a tremor that shook him up, took him away, then returned him completely empty, as if hollow. An unbearable pain. He felt around for an aspirin, swallowed it as he tore apart the letter.

When he was late and did not come down for breakfast, Mahmud came asking for him. He put his cold hand on Mikhail's hot forehead. Then Rama came along with Nura and Mahmud; she stayed with him for a while. Mahmud told Rama: I'll leave him in your care. She brought him, after insisting on it, a cup of tea without milk or sugar. She smoked a cigarette with him without exchanging words. As if she had become the one who was understanding and forgiving.

Bent over, I am creeping slowly in the dusty narrow neighborhood. All the lamps are off, and the walls are prominent and threatening, as if tilting on me. There is no one in the closed windows, no one behind the walls. Faces have turned away, disappeared. Eyes are silenced, avoiding involvement. Silence is dense, abounding. I creep slowly and on my shoulder there is a bird, which I feel is glued to the base of my neck, light in weight, but with rough feathers. Tightly close to my neck. Firm, not budging. Faceless. I find the points of claws on the back of my neck, with the solidity and smell of iron. I glance at their subtle luster. The claws are gripping my shoulder bones on both sides, a grip I can't liberate myself from. The swan, the roc, the falcon, the phoenix, Braque's white bird, in the jet blackness of nightmare with two fierce wings. Its beak a pointed, wounding lance. It grows bigger on my shoulders, its weight increases without interruption. Its burdensome presence does not cease. I stand up somehow—with difficulty—in the lonesome darkness. The neighborhood is still empty and long, long. No one else is in this night. No succor. I support myself on the floor by my hand, with all my force, trying to get up from beneath the weight that envelops my shoulders with its claws. Its grip can never be removed. It smells pungent, breath-stifling. Its wings are spread out. It plunges its claws deeper into my bones. Painlessly. There is only its weight: hooks plunging into the bones. All hope of getting rid of it is gone, of saving myself from this unbearable burden. I can no longer stand. I creep with desperate insistence. The speed of my creeping on the dust is diminished. My hands scrape against the rough, pure, unpolluted sand. Beneath it lie gravel and pebbles. Resistance diminishes and I am moving downward. There is no use in any resistance. The ground draws closer, I collapse upon it.

An ibis falls toward the cultivated fields of corn, upside down in the sky: meek and steady, soaring without movement, not covering a distance nor taking time. Suspended, his wings are not moving.

The dark inner sky opens up suddenly, rising, illuminated. The fall is complete. It has never taken place at all. Incomparable lightness: every weight has been removed. The stone columns are lofty and elegant in the old southern Egyptian church, ending in a distant dome without light. The jubilant wild flowers of the heart on the colored glass, across the scorching sky, are purple red, flaming with pride. The sun behind the leaded stained glass is calm. The church stones are warmed by skins of ancient lichen. There is a sublime silence of eminent significance. In it peace has overcome all tension.

13

Death and the Fly

I n the end we were conducting love rituals as an act of faith, no more.

We were not making love, nor was love being made through us.

He used to feel an impure, agitated joy when stumbling upon her by chance, on a field trip, amid Greek columns constructed in the pharaonic style in the desolation of the seemingly calm and meek sand. Simply their togetherness, without planning, under the warm stones towering to the sky in this narrow gallery between repetitive, unchanging columns—as if these pillars composed a monophonic tune in some fixed, timeworn harmony—gave him temporary security, though without assurance as to the next moment.

Mikhail used to feel himself unable to focus on one sensation when photographers aimed and snapped their cameras. Or when water flasks opened, gurgling out their reviving drops. Or when feet plunged into soft sand, only to be extracted with difficulty, bestowing vigor to the legs, charging the muscles with vim, constricting the whole body into something new. Or when shoes struck tiny, ribbed fragments of dusty granite, the eyes rolling in darkness, night-blind from the sun's recent dazzle, or as laughter tinkled in the vast expanse, echoing amid the stone columns, the entire group seeming scattered around the small temple and throughout its only open colonnade.

Her short field trip has brought her next to him: they are gazing now at the granite capital with lotus, plaited with sophisticated elegance and excessive beauty, much more dainty than it should be. It does not have the reverence of imposing and timeworn rigor. Seemingly Byzantine in retrospect.

He looked at her in the shade. Her face had a particular beauty, having reached its high-strung perfection then declining. The next moment it might collapse, melting into final decomposition. Although the moment never came, it was always threatening explosion.

They rode in the roaring Volkswagen on the sandy road through vast desert. She told him that she belonged to the cult of moon-worshippers and spoke of divine prostitutes.

But here between the columns, she is in her dark jeans that envelop her full thighs. The two hafts of her heavy, shapely haunches sway slowly when she lifts her feet from the grip of the surrounding sand, time and again. She seems as if her amulets and talismans have dried out and withered away, consecrated by deities who have died, who ceased to possess the energy for impinging on life. Something like the echo of love and apprehension was clamoring in his heart. The opening of her bursting blouse revealed the upper slope of her bosom where tiny, separate drops of perspiration clung to the taut skin, each shining by itself, round and perfectly precise. Her green eyes, after the scorching light, seemed blurred in the ever-changing, dark, humid, stony shade.

He said: I didn't hear from you yesterday at the Center. You didn't call.

She said: I was sick. My temperature was a little high last night, so I went to bed early with an aspirin and squeezed a lemon on my forehead.

As usual, he did not believe her. He said: Hope you get well soon. Somehow I can't see you as sick.

He meant, of course, that she was neither in her bed nor in her room. Yesterday, in the early evening, he had seen—without her noticing him—a concealed smile on her lips, dreaming of a forthcoming and awaited pleasure.

She said in a defensive tone, hostile and challenging: I'm not so sure you intend that as a compliment. You always picture me as some rock, like Gibraltar or the Himalayas; as if I can't be a human being who falls sick and recovers, and who—like everyone else—suffers physically and mentally at times, as if I am not a woman.

He said: A woman you are, indeed, a real woman. You are telling *me*?

She said: Aren't we seeing your usual suave self right now?

He said: I really meant you are a superwoman. There's an element in you that goes beyond the limits most of us know. Haven't I told you that you are an enchantress?

She said: Oh, stop it! At times, I feel especially vulnerable, as if I don't possess certain immunities.

He said: But I don't know how to say it . . . you are immortal. You're not touched by death.

She said: If our car had gotten lost in the middle of the desert, you'd know just how wrong you are.

He said: May you be protected!

Dreamily, she said: When I die I will turn into a red cactus flower in the sand, a prickly cactus blossoming once a year only with a red flower.

He said: Yes. I know the spines of that cactus. I also know its red

283

flower whose beauty and delicacy are incomparable. But only once a year? Your flowers are many.

Mahmud had aimed the camera at them as they were absorbed, leaning on the inner shoulder of the stone columns at the edge of the light. The camera snapped, the picture was fixed in that ephemeral immortality of the photosensitive paper.

Mikhail said: Come let me take your photo now.

Mahmud said: No, my dear fellow. We only serve. We do not want compensations or thanks.

He looked at Mahmud without anger. The others joined them.

They had eaten the cookies and the colored eggs, had finished off the *fasikh* salted fish and the lupine seeds. The casual flirtation and the passing dalliances were done with. They drank and conversed, jumped rope and played cards, had their siesta in the shade of the timeworn stone on the soft sand. Mikhail felt he was floating above the group, meeting with Rama only by random. She was holding on to Mahmud's arm and the two of them walked in the sand, talking, while he was turning the pages of a new translation of *The Book of the Dead*, without interest. Samia had made herself a turban, like those of southern Egyptians, from her white scarf. 'Abd al-Jalil, Samir, Nura, Salwa, Ilham, Butrus, and Suzi were wearing light, colorful trousers and short-sleeved shirts, low-cut blouses, white skullcaps brocaded in the Nubian style and berets jaunty at one side. Cameras, thermoses, handbags, empty Coca-Cola bottles, half-full bottles of Scotch, nylon bags and wrappers decorated with cigarette advertisements. They were moving around, getting ready for departure. The car doors were open, waiting a short distance away in the sands. Mahmud came to them with his slow steps and his dry, longish, triangular face, hollowed by lines. His long fingers had fine bones and his bright, carved eyes glowed at them anxiously as if they were evil portents. He was a poet, and she

284

had once said to Mikhail: He is the picture of Dorian Gray . . . but he is kind.

Get-ready calls, clapping and shouts: Come on people . . . We're late! Gathering up the wrappings, the small bags, and all that was bought: small baskets, primitive straw hats, bead necklaces, dried dates sold by oasis children and adults haggling and bargaining in their obtuse Bedouin dialect; their vehement hands yanking on short sleeves in an effort to draw attention; their wilted eyes, half-closed from successive eye inflammations, and their scrawny bodies.

She said to him: Show me what you bought.

A fake, ornamented, puff-bellied scarab. A frail, ceramic Osiris wrapped in shrouds. A mummy smaller than a hand's palm. Easter had come and gone, but the mummy remained buried in its stone grave. Mary did not come and cry. A bronze Bastet cat with soft cheeks, the length of a finger, alert and confident, lying in waiting position.

She said without being convinced, as if she were casting doubt on his ability to choose and his expertise in the art of bargaining and buying: Yes, it is fine. *Mabruk:* May you enjoy it! Beautiful things. You know of course they are not authentic.

He giggled—burst out with laughter.

In the commotion of departure and the agitation of return, she disappeared from his sight. The sun was about to set. The long road contained nothing but a boredom of repetitive dunes and black rocks, low and pyramid-like, and their non-stop engine wounding the desert calm with its continuous, extended roaring, unrelenting, with no gap. They were now in the long white station wagon. Samir was driving and the transistor rattled away with anonymous classical music. The car was dim; Mikhail had reclined his head on the back seat, letting it sway in rhythm with the running wheels. Alone, incurably depressed. A soundless, repressed bitterness settled in his heart as he saw her from his back seat. She was tired from the trip, also no

285

doubt from her ventures the night before. She propped her head on Mahmud's shoulder and slept against his side. Her fluffy hair—that special, primitive, dynamic, rough fragrance he knew so well was tied by a blue ribbon, away from her forehead—now scattered on Mahmud's dark leather jacket in an intimate, familiar way, a firm physical intimacy with nothing new about it. Dorian Gray's face was reflected in the car's interior light, black and glowing, with engraved lines and sculpted features. Worn jealousy could not move him now, only this slow, steady deterioration taking place in a stupor of disappointment. Exhausting silence prevailed among them all. Heads bobbed agitatedly as the station wagon quivered and rolled along with its seamless roaring. Darkness, chilliness, and desolation were stealing into tired bones.

At the gas station in Fayoum, a single, strong lamp shines above the faint, small light bulbs casting yellowish rays on tin cans, jacks, tools, pipes, and black inner tubes, dangling and mildly smutty, round and thrown one on top of each other like torn off body parts. A heap of dusty blown tires made of rough rubber, also square tiles having traces of irremovable grease could be seen in the light. He brought her a cup of coffee, lukewarm, the last from the thermos. He offered it without words, and she accepted it. The long car with Samia, 'Abd al-Jalil, Suzi, and Salwa had returned to its monotonous din, moving along in the nocturnal darkness through obscure fields falling away peacefully on the sides of the agricultural road between brittle agglomerates of nondescript trees.

Rama woke up, raised her head, and said: Where is Mikhail? I haven't heard his voice for a while. Where is Mikhail?

He did not find the strength in himself to respond. He couldn't trust the tone of his voice. He felt stiff, and he was anxiously silent for a moment as she looked at the back of the car and said with alarm and anxiety: Did we leave him in Asyut? What happened? Did he go with the others in the Volkswagen? Where is he? Several half-asleep voices were raised: But Mikhail is here; here he is . . . with us. Of course, we haven't left him.

Mikhail shook his head. No one laughed. She was silent and everyone went back to their troubled sleep in the stubborn din. Samir was driving with assurance and without moving his head. Mahmud did not speak. Mikhail closed his eyes, painfully awake, seeing her small head swaying on the black leather jacket now.

She had told him how years before she had been on a mission to the Horus Temple at Edfu. The train schedule had gone awry because of an accident in Asyut. When she arrived at the station late at night, she had missed her train. Or it hadn't arrived. The station assistant came unshaven with his wilted collar, without tie, wearing an old official jacket with puffed pockets. He told her the situation. She couldn't find anyone from her group at the station, not the elderly monuments inspector, nor the messenger, nor the foreman. Doubtless they had become convinced that either she'd left before them or hadn't yet arrived. She said to Mikhail that she wasn't helpless, or empty-handed as they say. Instead, when faced with a crisis, she glows with energy and never loses her head. She said that after checking with the station manager, she learned that the archaeological group had returned in the official car to the resthouse, and there was no way now to join them. The one and only crumbling horse carriage couldn't undertake the trip, and there wasn't a telephone at the resthouse. When she asked the station manager about a hotel where she could spend the night until she could catch the morning train, the kind old man laughed and said: My daughter, *you* in a hotel in Edfu? Of course, he was generous and helpful, as he should be. She said that 'Amm Fanus, the station manager, was an old-fashioned, tarboosh-wearing Copt. His white collar was elevated and starched under his official yellow jacket with its round bronze buttons. She said he was

287

over sixty for sure. In those days they did not have birth certificates, and doctors were easy-going when writing down the age, taking into consideration the stipulations related to age for employment. Surely he was seventy, at least. The age lines on his face were soft and his eyes behind the round lenses of his glasses were alert. He carried himself straight and firm. He was a tough Copt, a blue bone, as they say, and terribly kind-hearted.

'Amm Fanus had said to her: You are the lady inspector of monuments? *Ahlan wa-sahlan*. Welcome. You honor us. You go to a hotel, here, at night, alone, my daughter? Has hospitality disappeared from the world? By God, you are just like my daughter. I swear by God's bounty that you should spend the night in my home.

She said she was delighted by him and spent the night with the Coptic family. She had remained a family friend ever since. She said the house was directly behind the station, as was typical of railway workers' houses. 'Amm Fanus sent the only porter in the station—a boy with bruised shoulders and black, rough, pock-marked face, who limped a little—with the news home. She said that when she entered the house, his wife came out of bed to warm up dinner for her, *mulukhiya* with duck's wing, from the day before. She apologized, would not end her apologies, saying she was keeping these leftovers for 'Amm Fanus, that they were as fresh as Arabian jasmine, and she kept urging Rama for God's sake to eat. She offered her fresh, home-made bread, sun-baked that morning. She brought her the nightgown of her daughter Matilda, a medical student in Cairo, and wished her good appetite, saying that a blessed mouthful is good for a hundred. She added: My poor thing, you travel at night for your work. May safety accompany you at every step. Rama said that she spent the night with them, tears of joy and gratitude in her eyes. She had never slept better than that night at their place.

As for him, all he had was a lukewarm cup of coffee from the thermos, which he poured into its plastic cup in the gas station between two sections of a long, exhausting trip during which she laid her sleeping head on the shoulder of their common friend—his and hers—putting her arm around his in the darkness of the station wagon where sleep and fatigue prevailed.

He said to himself with faint sarcasm, which he knew was out of place, a sarcasm he could ill afford: From three fishes and two loaves of bread, five thousand ate and were full, and there were even leftovers.

All day long, he searched her for signs of love's turbulence and desire's anxiety. Somehow she seemed content, in fact satiated and self-sufficient, in a hushed physical flourish in the heart of softly rounded, fresh, green leaves. Her flourish neither sharp nor glowing; its thorns neither breaking nor cut off.

She told him that the night when her father died she woke up whimpering, but she didn't sob. It wasn't possible for her to sob, even her mother's tears couldn't get her started. He was lying on the bed, a life full of adventures, love, and fortune ended and the energy that swept like a storm stopped. He had once raised the slender, bony, little girl, with her long braids, between his arms and tossed her toward the ceiling, as if he were granting her the sky. She would touch the ceiling with her little hands. The push of his hands surrounding her waist controlled and released her, sending her lightly up, then grabbing her in a tight embrace while her fluttering, plain dress flew about and air blew between her bare legs. Suddenly his gay, adventurous, and excessive flings with beautiful women—radiant and magnificent as if they were from another world—came to a halt. All his glories and victories fell silent. The incredible legend had arrived at this stillness: motionless, in front of her in a room lit by a single faint lamp. The door of the room was open, leading to a dim hall, while her mother whimpered. His closet was slightly ajar, not properly closed.

289

His pictures hanging on the walls: in complete military outfit, in masterly control, his eyes self-assured, with a rigorous face, yet having a meek touch. His tight trousers pressing his long legs and giving them a robust look. Here he is with the old-fashioned flying helmet, as if he were in control of the skies, with his smile—both daring and timid—offering the photographer and the world the profile of a pale brown face. His lips, thin like hers, firm. Beneath them is indicated a slight shudder about to manifest itself at the slightest emotional reaction. She knows the touch of his lips on her cheeks and their long, light, firm, tight pressure. His hazel green eyes—with which he gazed at what no one else saw—are tormented and stern. They exude tenderness and enfold secrets that used to shake the entire country—secrets that he will never divulge to anyone now. And here he is riding his horse as if he were about to come out of the frame. Here he is fencing, extending his arm with a long, slender, tip-shaking sword; on his face a mask of wires with a slender-thread net. With her as an infant in his lap, proudly showing her off to the photographer, to the whole world, vaunting the dearest in his world. He had said to her, when she went to him, childishly crying: Don't ever forget that you are my daughter!

No one could take her out from the room of his last slumber. Calm, relaxed in his yellow bronze bed with its back stand, its round slender posts and gleaming balls atop its four corners. She spent the first night with him, staying up, just the two of them. She kept a kind of night vigil praying sensuously with her hands crossed, though without rites and cults. But he had already departed—no words, no movements from him. Her lonesomeness was not that of loss and solitude; it went much deeper. Now that he was dead, he was with her alone, truly, for the first time. She didn't doze, couldn't recall how the night passed. Did it pass? The bounty shrivels in front of her eyes, and love—all of it—will never respond to her heart-rending call, escaping endlessly from her flat childish chest, the chest of a girl

290

waking up hungry in front of a cooking fire for food she will never taste. The rough sea has come with its last wave, passed over her, and drowned her. Its water dwindles away in the thick firm sand—the world's flesh—as it recedes and dries out unable to offer anything. She remembers only a tiny black fly that keeps buzzing in the stifling room. It is taken aback by night, light, and death. It moves in quick gyrations straining the nerves, then descends suddenly and alights on his fair, wrinkle-free forehead. It settles there, and no one shoos it away. An ugly fly with a sticky round small body moving its wings and its many minute hairy legs; secure, turning its head on the sole sun that had not set and will not set. Standing on his forehead, he who burst with fire and flood, who could not bear ugliness in the slightest of things. It moves slowly on his forehead and he leaves it alone. He does not shudder in anger with his husky voice that makes the four corners of the world shake. Her eyes are glued to the fly. She falls into the grip of unconscious and misty fascination, yet very alert, awaiting some miracle, but nothing happens.

At the bottom of this fixed, dark enchantment that does not partake of time, neither night nor day, she said she knew in a definitive way that he had died. She was shattered from within, soundlessly and without tears. Dry-eyed, she was carried out, putting up no resistance.

This is what she told him.

She never ceases to look for the love that died in her long, ever-changing dream, the love she'll never find again.

My child, your childish body will never be lifted again. The power and tenderness of that first grip are not of this earth.

He said to himself: This is a classic case.

She said to him in the morning: All's well that ends well.

He said to her: Do you want to say that everything has ended?

She said sharply: Nothing has ended; probably it hasn't even started.

291

The last bouts of that which is between us, like the last stages of a fever, attacking, retreating, drowning me then ebbing off—they aren't over yet?

This epistle of mine to you is nothing but the cry of a lonely solitary. It is natural, familiar, ordinary: just another loner in this ship sailing without end, teeming with loners who fill highlands and lowlands, roads and flanks of the earth. Isn't that so? Amid crowds in the din of travel, in the whirring of cement mixers, in the rattling of reinforced concrete, in the crashing of bricks and the howling of brakes of transportation trucks stopping suddenly. In the midst of commanding cries from the foreman with his long, clean *jallabiya* and the sorrowful, rhythmic singing of southern Egyptians that won't end—their ancient stock resisting extinction—wearing long-sleeved, reddish cotton flannels. On their rags bluish-gray cement spatter has solidified. With them a new clan of school boys wearing long, black, rubber shoes, smoking American cigarettes, applying Brilliantine on their hair, climbing the scaffolding with bare chests and shorts, confidently and proudly earning five pounds a day.

In the midst of this whirlpool of anger and din, when the cries of your flesh, the sighs of your desire and your tormented tears seized me, I used to say to you, I want a response. Never did I mean that I wanted these rational and logical answers, so calculating, taking into consideration future possibilities while evaluating past reflections, analyzing psychological make-ups and social dialectics, such as you give me. This is a favorite game, yet it is trivial and shabby. I can—it was always in the cards for me to do so—play this boring game too, with something akin to sarcasm. But I wanted to find an answer, with you, to this lonely cry, this common, quotidian loneliness, I wanted something to tell me I wasn't totally alone in the end, that someone heard me at least, knew I was here. I found no response. Nor was it logical or natural to find one. But I never accepted such logic, such a reading of nature.

She stood at the door, as if hesitating to enter the room. She was wearing a long evening dress, black with large flowers embroidered in colored threads, the back bare, tightly holding her firm bosom. She said to him: Don't you want to see what I bought? He said: Yes. She said: Come with me. In her curtain-drawn room, lit and exuding a salty breath, she spread on her bed in childish earnestness, and anticipation, hand-woven fabrics in the Bedouin style, a delicate belt from palm leaves, a fired clay jug with a round belly decorated in red, a small gleaming blue pitcher with a slender spout, jewelry in the shape of large yellow crescents with small jingling metal fringes, and necklaces of light yellow amber with their large, lustrous beads. He said: Great, Rama. Most beautiful! She gazed at him thoughtfully and deliberately, radiant with a restrained joy in her eyes, the reflex of one who is waiting in vain. She collected her small treasures, bent down, and shoved them into her large bag. When she stood up, she slowly, cautiously, moved close to him, then kissed him quietly on the mouth—an unexpected kiss, silent, dry, and light, without lingering or eroticism—once and then twice, a kiss of gratitude in a pardon requesting mode without admission of sin exactly, more a kiss of penance in anticipation of what she knew would happen again.

Something hung in the air of the room as if in the aftermath of something, waiting for last rites.

She said to him: You've made up your mind on this? You're not coming to the party?

He said: No, I am not coming, as I told you. I'm exhausted.

She said insincerely, as if she were trying to relieve her conscience: Won't you change your mind? There is still time, you know. He said: No, the time is gone by.

She said: May I ask you for a favor? He said: Please, do. She said: My handbag. I won't need it. I have this small purse. And I worry about leaving my handbag like that in the room, as it is open. The purse was black embroidered with silvery threads, studded with what seemed like tiny pearls, soft and flat, beautifully designed. He said: Yes, it is always open, ready for any newcomer! She said: Darling, you are absolutely right!

She handed him the handbag filled with a thousand and one things, and tried—for the sake of demonstration—to zip the bag. Impossible to do. She shrugged her beautiful shoulders and said: I'll see you when I come back. It might not be tonight. I'll be too late. Tomorrow probably.

She said goodbye to him in a sudden and decisive way, without a kiss, without a word. She had washed her hands of something and was totally preoccupied with something else.

He watched her as she left. Her firm brown back seemed tender and vulnerable as she raised her arm wrapping around herself a black shawl embroidered with silver designs, making a half turn, as she did, that signaled departure. Her bra straps pressed the flesh of her back, behind the soft fabric, making it look plump on each side. The bra's lines were evident, directly beneath the décolleté where the roundness of her slightly protruding breasts in the tight dress was defined. As he came out behind her, there was a non-stinging, light mist in his eyes.

The handbag was in his hands with its expensive, old leather still warm; slightly faded at the folds, having pliable, soft wrinkles; his fingers plunged in its round and full belly. It swelled with things overflowing from its opening, as if about to pour out. The handbag emits her fragrance, that of her skin and of a perfume he knows so well—the perfume that haunts him in tormented nightmares of longing. He did not hesitate, despite the ethical restraint, in emptying the handbag calmly and confidently. His heartbeat was speeding a little, but his wakeful eyes were observing the arrangement of things, with the intention to return them in the same order. Was this a betrayal of a trust? His instant inner response was that somehow he had an

294

indefinite right to plunge into everything related to her, as if they were his own things. After all, what was between his hands was not something strange, but his. He said to himself that he had, in his turn, opened to her himself and everything that belonged to him.

Later, when the shock faded, leaving him in a cruel, bare, raw light, as if numbed between white walls with rough paint, without curtains, no window, not even a nail, it occurred to him that Rama, without being completely aware, also perhaps wanted, and did not want at the same time, to open this dimension of her intimate life. It was as if she simultaneously wanted and did not want him to take with his own hands and see in the light some of her intimate apparel that still had the warmth of her body folds and their concealed traces. Yes, probably she wanted him to know, to pass through some test.

He brought out of her handbag first the postcard that he had sent her on her birthday on which he wrote one phrase, "I love you," and a comic, multicolored lion with gaping jaws made of shiny cardboard; its eyes were two round marbles moving in their sockets. Along with his card, she had received it on her birthday, by post. She had said to him: Look! It's from my cousin in Sidi Bishr, an honest lion that kills you with laughter. A ticket from a soccer game that had on it the autograph of Pelé himself; an elegant advertisement for the Palestine Hotel on glossy paper; a reservation slip for fifteen pounds at the San Stephano dated June 6; a black kohl pencil thick and round in its copper tube, whose sides had rusted and whose luster had faded, its tip sharp as a porcupine quill; a sapphire scarab, a dark red nail-polish bottle with a long neck and a white plastic screwtop, a comb to which a few of her hairs were still attached, a large safety pin, an eyebrow pencil, her pocket dictionary of ancient Greek; and a strange, small, faded picture on a light brown postcard of outmoded size of a girl in her early adolescence, naked and slender, in a royal-style, luxurious marble bathtub—her breasts not yet sprouting.

In the old picture the bathroom walls were made of veined marble, the sink was oval, with different-shaped bottles and boxes of old brands now uncommon, a water tap as if of pure, massive silver. The girl has slight, protruding bones; even the wilted paper of the photograph still exuded a scorching feminine appeal, a very precocious one. Her hair disheveled, slightly ruffled on the sides, the photograph made in an era when hairdressers and hairdryers were unknown. Her face both very strange and very familiar, in her clear eyes a direct and triumphant gaze, which he recognizes.

His heart dropped. His eyes were fixed on a context where time had lost its face.

He saw a love letter on lined paper from a student notebook written in a script of someone clearly uncultivated, with big letters flowing carelessly in a heavy gush of passionate emotions: dense, but not delicate.

My sweetheart, my duck,

This is the first time I travel. My mind is at peace not feeling upset. You are in the immortal splendid memories of our first meeting with affection and love. Do you remember the first time I came to you? The first day of Ramadan? That is we have been together for one year. That time under the Pyramid under the moonlight. Do you remember my duck? You sang to me. Remember? I don't want to put responsibilities on you just ask after me by saying How are you, What are you doing my sweetheart? How can I forget the black and white dress of our immortal night and also the disease of the age you spoke of. Tell me you'll read this book my sweetheart and I will read it too. We want to settle down my duck. I don't want you disappointed in the Zamalek apartment. I know I can depend on you completely. I always say No one is like my sweetheart. I met 'Amm

Fanous yesterday in the train to Helwan, he said about you What a splendid girl! I want to answer saying She is my sweetheart and my love. But in the situation not possible. Your words do not leave me, we should have met before. I wish Ahmad and Madiha for our children, why do you object? God keep us for the other my duck.

Your darling forever

At the end he could make out the letter *M* joined and intertwined with the letter *H*, like the signatures of people who think they are the first and the last in the world, no need for them to clarify who they are.

He read the letter once, twice, three times; then over and over. He returned everything to the handbag in its former order or disorder, without any change, with a solicitude that he knew was total, as if he were a character in a detective story careful not to leave any fingerprints or evidence. He took off his clothes, moved with what he felt to be mechanical and silent moves in his room from which the world had been shut off. He turned off the light, slept instantly, numbed, as if he had just undergone major surgery.

Her arm was on his neck, close to his eyes. The light underarm hair on her brown skin. A somewhat dark spot on the elbow with minute, slightly rough bumps. He raised her arm and kissed her lightly on those bumps. His lips felt the difference in the dry skin at the spot touched. His was a kiss of pure affection, as if in consolation and pity for this blemish in her beauty. Within the smoothness of her skin, this flawed flesh made him love her the more and increased his tenderness toward her. She gave him a furtive and angry look; she did not miss the significance of his kiss, as if it could find no other place and was not therefore strictly necessary. A frown clouded her face, but quickly disappeared. There was no gratitude, anger, appreciation, or pardon in her looks. He had insulted her with this unwanted kiss.

297

When he woke up, his eyes were salty with dream tears that would not tumble down.

She had said to him: I am not the most beautiful of women. That much I know. But I claim I am the most tender of women and the most capable of giving pleasure too.

And he had said to her: For me you are the most beautiful, the most magnificent, the most wonderful, and the most lasting of them all.

She had responded: What a child you are!

He said to himself: "Love"? The word seems meaningless, given the baggage it carries. This double game of love and hate is deep-rooted. Around it bubbles repressed blood and, for it self-esteem is shamelessly sacrificed. Why play such a game in the midst of so many other, truly serious matters? What's the point when there's already so much meanness and ugliness presenting their claws and fangs? I understand the need for work that will lighten this tyranny in a precise, utilitarian way. After all, what is it that pacifies torment and soothes isolation? The black bones of hunger, oppression, and mass humiliation surround us while the electric, glossy instruments of trivial luxuries accumulate, all of them mangling the earth at the same time. And so what do we do? We make love. Sweat perspires from our two bodies attached forever, as if we had no will at all. Consequently, fragmented visions from the larger world sting, then remain to haunt us.

He said to himself: Are these obsessions and anxieties our human lot? Are we fated to strive for pleasures accompanied by lashings from innumerable hands, delivered inside rooms with closed doors?

Mikhail says to her: I have no way out but to conceal my love from you and others. The cycles of longing for you, feeling aversion to you—turns of passion, fervor, repulsion, and ecstasy—I conceal from you and others. You conceal everything about your life from me and I dig with my nail-injured, bare hands into the earth's layers, as

298

if generations that have neither begun nor ended simply accumulated on the surface of your body, your soul, your heart. Since we hate expressions of sentiment, seeing them as trivial, I have to bear in silence and solitude my heart's languishing—a heart that possesses no defenses but the strength of a rigorous delicacy and a spirited, sometimes sarcastic awareness with every beat.

Where have I let you down then? Where have I failed? Why do you reject me? Is it you who are rejecting, or I? Or is rejection a ritual that runs us both? It was not possible for me to reject you, no matter how much I retreated backward. I have not broken our covenant nor infringed upon it. You are the land of my love, the body of my homeland in which I am exiled—no matter how tightly I close my lips on the terrors and torments of silence. You, who welcome all invaders of your bodily sanctums in fresh and sweet acceptance, without condemnation or dissension.

I do not know your intimate rhythms, the puzzling inner fervor, the mysterious way you greet so many mornings after. Speaking with a thousand tongues and never short of words, you divulge nothing. My beloved, you're stubborn and willful. You implement your will— how you settle on it, I have no idea—without ever saying: No, never. You procrastinate forever, then circumambulate situations and wills, slowly, taking an eternity. You never allow for time running out. You take however much time to reach your destination—a destination no one knows—within the continuing presence of that radiant, undying first and last father.

She said to him: I am knocked down by bouts of total immersion in my inner self, in self-inspection and silence, in distance from the entire world. I cling to myself until I reach what resembles a psychological explanation, which I accept temporarily, without conviction.

He said: I want to share it with you.

She said: Sharing is an exorbitant process.

He said: I can forbear.

She said, with silent eyes, neither denying nor accepting him: True. Very forbearing, like me.

He said: Though I am no love-making instrument.

She said: That too I know.

She was wounding him now, intentionally or not.

I have known your seven masks: Rama swan Circe enchantress phoenix cat Amazon Isis; but I don't know you. I have heard your innumerable voices: the childish, small voice dreading darkness. The complaining voice desperately seeking help in the night of your solitude that occupies the entire center of the day with no relief. The strong voice, unbreakable by blows that would cleave flint. The practical voice handling matters among workers, columns, monuments, and papers, self-confident but without concern for self or others. That's the voice of running things, of calculated strokes and tools. The passionate voice exciting manhood in your embrace to stab. The sexy voice dripping pure, submissive femininity having nothing in it but the liquidity of a formless flowing. The hoarse, husky voice. The dreamy voice of a world that is all one wave: gently green, blossoming, lunar. I have held your face while you cried from pleasure and bliss. I have kissed your hair while lightning tracked through my heart, with you crying in pain and ecstasy. Frozen, head bent down, I didn't retreat from your fierce, hostile voice. Bending all of me toward you, I tried to escape through the barrier of your indifferent voice. I have heard your depressed voice and your twittering joyful tones in the rustling of dawn, shaking and breaking from the heart of darkness and arresting isolation. I never believed the voice of contentment and surrender, given with drooping eyes, except when you gave me your hands as if granting me everything. The pleading moans and flowing, stubborn tears I couldn't disregard, so I came to you, again and again, as if I were the one penetrating your oasis effulgent with springs seeping from sands stretching

300

until the end of my years. Your pleasure-cry at the stab of intimate encounter, while I catch between my open palms the suns of your spheres, collecting in my lap the dazzling limbs of the sky.

He said: Just the same, I love you. While you . . . I don't know. I'll continue to love you, even if you aren't there. I'll go on without entering into details. I know I'll bear this all my life. Yes, I might be wild, stumbling in my steps, primitive if you wish, in the fury of this defiant emotion whose harness I hold with my tightest grip though nothing brakes it. All right, immature if you wish. But I'm tired of being mature and balanced. It's not boredom that moves me, but the storm inside that flings me around. I half surrender to the storm, partly want it. Have I been able to say it?

She said to him: You've indeed given up a great deal of your rigid Coptic reserve. It used to be impossible for you to entertain even a simple, spontaneous kiss of encounter or an affectionate, easy-going embrace.

He said: Luckily, I learned from the hands of a master.

She said: It's true you've learned something from me—but most importantly you've learned everything about me. There's nothing left to know. My life's an open page for you.

He said: Nonsense. There's plenty yet to know, probably the most significant part.

She was silent, not wanting to argue.

He said: You still refuse the possibility of being accepted, of being finally justified, despite everything.

Distraught, she said with frustrated wishing: If that could happen, it would be magnificent.

Then she went on hurriedly: But raising the question by itself, alone, is what plants doubt in the heart of the entire issue. In fact, it negates it. Justification is not conditional, hence not an issue for consideration. It exists first, without a question.

He realized at once she was right.

He said: And yet I am not invasive, possessive, or authoritarian. Those things I cannot be.

With a silent gaze, as if she realized that he sensed an awkwardness in moving away from the topic, she said: No. You are right.

His steps before his final appointment with her were taken next to an old red-brick wall, under the shade of dense trees. The last soft rays of sunset were falling as if drawn by a fine-tipped pen, making the wall's bricks look gentle, soft, firmly of one element. Their solidity melted away. And bygone torments ebbed away. They became memories, no longer resented by the senses in anger or bitterness. The veil of timeworn mystery was removed, erasing all clandestine intrigues. Behind this wall they experienced harmony and the peace of a dreamless sleep. The lowly fence stretched until they faced at its end an old house with a small, patchy garden that blocked the way. The sea whispered, though they could not see it. They retreated toward the clamor of trams, trucks, and shops in the process of turning on their lights, one after the other, in Abu Qir Street. They heard the clip-clop of horse hooves on the asphalt amid cars and buses, and suddenly a seashore patrol in khaki uniforms and brown, dry, shaven faces moved past them, the mounted soldiers holding their long, black guns.

His hand was on her shoulder as they walked together; he felt the fullness of her heavy steps. They had washed their hands of trying to guess the future, were now surrendering their dispirited bodies to the mystery of sunset lights.

14

The Ninth and Last Day

She said to him: I received your card—you alone remembered my birthday. I'd forgotten it myself.

He said: How can I forget it? It's the day the war of 1948 was declared, the same day I was detained by the authorities.

She said: Better for you if you'd forgotten it.

He said: Many happy returns. So what happened? I don't understand.

She said: I am sad, angry—above all bored.

There was that concealed dull grief in her face. Her eyes turned navy blue, turbid.

She said: I can't understand their silence. I've never despised them as much as I do today. How could they let him die like that? In cold blood, while they crossed their arms? Why, they shackled their own hands.

He said: In revolutionary work, people do die, you know? The so-called calculated risks?

She said: But like this? Gratuitously? In twenty-four hours?

303

A tragicomic sham trial, then a death sentence? He has been put to death! This is murder.

He said: Yes, but—to be fair—wouldn't he have done the same thing, possibly worse and far more extensive, had positions been reversed?

She said: Maybe, but this is different.

He said: Ah, it is? Why, it's not different at all. Come off of it with your story of ends and means and such talk. It's simply unreal, to put it lightly. Don't ever bring up the story of the people and the dictatorship of the majority, which is the only democracy. All this is childish absurdity at best, and in most cases it is bad faith. No, my dear lady, it is not democracy! Killing a person, even a single one, intentionally and deliberately, for whatever purpose, cannot be justified or compensated by any means. Man is not to be killed at all, and is not to kill. I don't know of a necessity, of any need for it, not even ethical necessity or what is called justice. Man is not to be killed.

She said to him thoughtfully: Yes, your position is clear and declared. You have given up on political work and you did not hesitate in announcing it.

He said: Nothing is left but work from day to day, perhaps making a living, with immersion for sure, with concentration. Submerging oneself, yes. This is everything. Daily work? What is it? What is it worth? Simply crossing from the shore of one day to the shore of another.

She said: You're clear and honest. No secrecy. But those who're involved in the struggle, what are they doing? In light of their work, I am quitting the life you just described. My decision is definitive. Believe me. Don't say I'm emotional and rash. I've studied the question from all sides. I'm leaving everything. I am going back to the underground, as I did so long ago.

Her voice was quivering again, that feminine quiver that he sometimes came across in their passionate and intimate physical encounters.

She said: Like you, I'd left it all. But now it's unbearable. I can't be silent. I can't stand such disappointment. I'll go back, and I won't hesitate to kill. That's my lot: to kill. Yes, kill, demolish, strike with bullets and bombs.

He did not smile, and of course he did not believe her. But the frenzy in her reaction, in her quavering voice was real. The irrationality of the image that obsessed her was clear, very much in evidence.

She said: I won't shut up. What's left to this life? Monotony and emptiness.

He said: You? Your life monotonous and empty?

She said: Yes, yes, yes. What did you think? All this is emptiness or an escape from emptiness.

For a moment, silence joined them firmly in the garden of Le Petit Trianon. But it could not relieve the annoyance in their give-and-take, in her fury and anger.

On the fence of the sunny garden stood pots with small shrubs, trimmed on the sides, excessively cared for. Their green gleamed, as if artificial, because of water spraying. The lightly faded white table-cloths had delicate-lined blue designs. The sun was discrete, the Stella beer in two long thin glasses—its slightly turbid foam having subsided—along with a heap of yellow lupine-seed skins in a saucer.

It occurred to him that she might be serious and she might very well take this plunge, that it was not necessarily a matter of delirium bursting from the anguish of losing an old and intimate relationship, for surely it was not simply a political relationship. It was more than a simple and final honoring of yet another figure fallen in her battlefield. It was more than loyalty, after her own fashion, to a deep-rooted friendship of heart and flesh alike.

He said to himself: How strange she is! Her friendship with the exiled prime minister, the elderly aristocratic gentleman, then this too: the famous working-class communist who's been killed. Both at the same time! How strange her relations are! Perplexing, inexplicable, and as real as if she were Mata Hari or a James Bond character, but neither superficial nor sensational. She has friends—more than friends for sure—on every step in the social ladder and on the psychological ladder too.

She said: We belonged to the same cell. I was his superior. Here in Alexandria on the Corniche we conferred all the time. I came to know his character, his kindness, his courage, his heart-felt honesty. I taught him the dream of justice and victory; then he taught me.

He said to her: Yes. The dream of justice. Leave alone for now the dream of victory. Where have these dreams—liberty and the erasing of ugliness from the face of the earth—gone? How we once dreamt in the infancy of this work, each from his or her distinct angle. A revolution against all oppression, physical and spiritual! Rejection of all oppression and exploitation, all hunger and alienation! But now, what's left of these dreams between our hands? Even the crumbs slip through our fingers. The victims, the martyrs, the sorrows, the enthusiasm that make us soar high and the faith that lights the fire of determination in us, stronger and loftier than all the mountains? We carry it proudly without feeling its weight. Devotion to that which we knew under the title of Struggle, in which the distinctions of day and night disappear, as if the Kingdom of Heaven would arrive on the morrow, just beyond the next corner, right here on earth where we envisioned all its poor multitudes as saints. Nothing carries weight in the midst of this obsession with altruism, self-sacrifice—and world-sacrifice—for the sake of an impossible justice.

She said, as if still dreaming: All the small, practical details that absorb life and are raised above it, when sleeping and when awake— the clandestine pamphlets and newsletters, the never-ending meetings, encounters and proselytizing, the wrangling in discussions as if the future of the world, the future of the human race, or the people's

306

collective death, all hung on a single phrase, on a single word. Organizing sit-ins, managing strikes, moving demonstrations, coining slogans, planning programs, forming committees, distributing tasks, challenging risks, indifferently and without even considering them as risks, but just as trifles of the moment.

He said: Where did all this go? With it went our youth forever, never to return. The shock of falling into silence cannot be described. I cannot even go back and imagine it. After the fall of these dreams, I learned to party all night and drink until drunk. I learned how to smoke, how to strike up amorous adventures. How trivial they were! In the beginning I was actually puritanical. But along with despair, I became more human, like the rest. I used to come home at dawn every day, so I could go to my office in the morning at the Egyptian Contractors Company, here in Alexandria, and I would sleep in the bus for the seven-minute journey, calculated by my inner clock. I'd wake up by myself, precisely, just before getting out at my stop. I used to involve myself in adventures just for the sake of involvement. I neither knew nor cared about what would happen the next day. Mine was a strange recklessness, pleasing in its immorality and sorrow.

She said: I went back to the sofa in my room and lay on it, motionless and speechless, for the totality of nine months, as if it were a period of inverted pregnancy, after which I did not deliver, but arrived at a new death, another one at the heart of life. I would not open my mouth. I was totally and genuinely estranged. I did not care about the world. I was not interested in it. Up till now, I don't know how I came back from this maze. I returned, of course, with a wound or, to say it frankly, with an incurable deformation, and I don't know if it has healed.

He said: Childhood's gone. We've simply grown up. Today we are exiled into our dreams, estranged from our dreams without ever departing from them. What are we doing exactly? You are an

307

archaeologist. So what are you searching for? For some bygone vestiges in the heart of ruins, which your digging will never reach. And I, constructing columns, noting down different styles of architecture, assessing the techniques of ancient engineers no one cares about. Restoration: how useless. What's the utility in hieroglyphs, Demotic, and Greek? What have you read in your inscriptions and your epitaphs? All this sterile absurdity is invariably written down in all languages, at all times. So what is the use? There are more pleasant entertainments, no doubt.

He had said: In these streets, over forty years ago maybe, I obscurely sensed, rather smelled in the air—just like that—the fragrance of frank sexuality, without even knowing it. Had I reached seven? I can't remember. I might have been younger. But I recall the 'Attarin Street and Hamamil Street tram that used to be yellow, clean, and elegant with its wooden seats, gleaming in the early morning sun. The air was cool, humid, gentle. I was walking, possibly running, stretching my steps to hurry while my hand was in my father's. He was holding in his other hand his black ebony cane with its ivory handle, sculpted in the form of a bird's head, a falcon; its eyes a semi-precious gemstone, something green. He towered next to me, all security and love. His long coat flew about in the air over his light brown, *sakaruta* silk caftan and the wide belt. Possibly he was rushing to make an appointment at the *wikala* storehouse in front of Kum al-Nadura. The street was wide, the carriage drivers were showing off, with their red-brown horses lifting their heads in their copper bits, exhaling suddenly from their nostrils and neighing. I would shudder a little in front of their height and awesome dignity. The large wood warehouses with their extended stone fences and massive iron gates wide open, their dark insides, under the arching doorway vaults, ending in vast sunny yards in which piles of newly sawn wood, planed, dark yellow, planks of equal size, rose. They seemed long and immense. How do they carry such boards, raise them up, and arrange them with this geometrical precision? A few shops: in their doors a white marble stand on which there was a scale with two copper trays and a black iron needle, sharp tipped, swaying with refined sensitivity. Do you remember those kinds of shops? Behind the scale, they had shelves lined with cigarette packs—Coutarelli and Matossian, Gazelle tobacco—round glass jars of candy; on both sides of the scale were white mirrors written on in fancy English letters I didn't know and also in calligraphy, the *thulth* and *naskh* styles. In those days, they didn't use the *riq'a* script nor the hybrid scripts common in today's handwriting. Despite myself I read them all with an audible inner voice, as if reading was a duty not to be passed over. I spent my childhood—I still do—reading advertisements, not missing a single letter. The street tiles under my feet were large, black, and smooth, each tile slightly concave, full of strength, attached in geometrical patterns, and gleaming. They must have been sprayed and the water had not altogether dried—it was very early in the morning.

My father said: Let's go through here. I know a short cut that'll get us there in a jiffy.

With my father I entered a long narrow alley with low houses close upon each other, painted pale yellow. Their iron windows and balconies were closed above turned-off lamps of clear curved glass in the shape of inverted bells. The carts purveying liver and pickled eggplant were empty and parked next to the walls; no one beside them. An air of laziness and late sleep clung to the alley. There, on the doorsteps, before narrow wooden doors behind which stood dark staircases, barely seen in the light of the still street, I saw women sitting at ease, right there, on the stony doorsteps in light nightgowns revealing colored underwear. They sat next to each other or faced each other in the alley. Their bare legs stretched on the ground in scandalous relaxation. Heavy black kohl lined their puffed eyelids.

309

Their mouths large and sharply defined, painted pale red, resembled wounds. Was my speeding heart beating from my fast stride and the big strong hand holding mine? Or was it from the sudden wonder at this women's scene, the like of which I'd never beheld? Their surrender on the floor, early in the morning, made it seem as if they were fishing for things, of which I had no concept, from the few passers-by at that early hour—fishing with their dark, predatory eyes. A standing woman gestured from within her low door, as if she were about to enter—a gesture I could not understand, as if she were calling or warning. She smiled, then laughed once only—an extended, penetrating, wounding laugh that had no interest in anything. In my sudden surprise, I didn't recognize to whom she was gesturing nor why such aggressive laughter, since no one was in the alley, in front of her door, but us. A troubling, yet, in a sense, soothing air in that strange narrow alley with its closed windows and balconies. In the exhausted features of these women—lulled, loose, and heedless—and in their strange gesturing was a kind of liberating surrender and enjoyment. It was as if they were playing a game, difficult but pleasant. The game flourished discreetly: cactus plants in the heat of a comfortable and closed glass.

We passed by two women sitting on a doorstep facing each other. I sensed a shudder and a slight fear, in which I found a new taste, not undesirable. Passing through an area threatened by unknown risks, that's how it felt. Anyway, I was secure enough to handle it. I overheard one of the women say to the other, with an exhausted hoarse voice, nevertheless a biting tone, in the context of an intermittent chat: And so my dear, I made a spectacle out of him. Her bosom was big and hanging on her belly without anything supporting it beneath her slip. Her breasts were mysterious, slightly scary too. Her thighs, to the contrary, were slender, well wrought, bronze without the sun ever tanning them, bare almost up to the belly.

310

We passed Saba' Banat Street, where the tram was jingling along joyfully. We passed the roundabout in front of the Labban Police Station, where my eyes glimpsed with pleasure the shop of a European patisserie where we used to buy *harisa* when returning home. The *harisa* was on the spread-out, large, round, dark copper tray with its appetizing light brown color, its surface gleaming, the walnuts and hazelnuts—ivory white lobes planted in the flesh of the sweet dish—slightly protruding on the surface. The early evening before returning home—the day's best moment—was when I had in my hands the cardboard box and felt the warmth of its half pound of aromatic *harisa*, whose honey oozed over the wrapping oilpaper. When we approached Kum al-Nadura, a lot of square, triangular, green, white, and blue flags were fluttering on ropes and masts, and a huge black ball was hanging. This meant a ship was coming from the sea carrying vast, unlimited promises. We moved across agglomerations of houses and a shabby depot of wholesale onions, sack-cloth, chicken cages, vegetable baskets, smithies, *basturma* ropes on which dark round masses of cured meat with their penetrating smell were hanging, the photographer's shop with photographs behind the glass: smiling faces with fixed eyes, plucked eyebrows of women in the shape of very thin arches like black semi-circles, their lips painted in the shape of small hearts; the big merchants in their *jallabiyas* and waxed moustaches, with tarbooshes and long canes. Another world entirely. Nothing left of it now but its debris. Where did it go?

This was his story.

The whole group was enjoying a short relaxing break under the umbrellas. In front of them were small, slender, green, narrow-waisted tea glasses, china coffee cups with blue designs, tall Stella bottles, and short Coca-Cola bottles. Chips of the backgammon game were moving quickly in successive strokes and chess pawns were falling down. The young Nubian waiter with his white *jallabiya*, red belt, and big turban seemed like a schoolboy acting the role of a waiter. Suddenly, for a second, he saw her at a distance, alone, as if she were an empty island amid waves. She brought her hand down from her forehead to her eyes, shutting them and slowly rubbing them. Her lips, tense in a silent lonesome torment—a slice of pain severed from her suddenly, despite herself. That was painful for him. He set out to go to her while his heart was melting. Then his inner motion came to a halt, suddenly and intently.

I was violent with myself, and I have reached a decision and made up my mind.

When it was time to return, he would loiter so that he would not find himself close to her. He glimpsed her looking at him, and he sensed that despite everything, she was calling him. He pretended to be busy. Inwardly he made fun of this infinitesimal, typical maneuver of lovers, until someone else took the empty seat next to her. He sat next to Mahmud, unwillingly but patiently, as if he were not paying attention to anything, and he valiantly engaged Mahmud in a lengthy conversation about difficulties of work and of techniques of monument restoration, of the stupidity of officials and their old-fashioned ideas, their insistence on destructive routine, the shortage of funds, the slowness of implementation, the strange character of archaeologists. Throughout, however, as he turned his head, laughing boisterously and gesturing enthusiastically, he glimpsed the long gaze Rama was casting upon him. Calm and thoughtful, she conveyed a double-edged apology and complaint, both to him and to herself. In his firm determination, there was self-challenge and a slight vengeance. In it was a pain squeezing him into its strong grip, into contractions concealed beneath laughter.

Rama, Rama, my last call, why do I find myself alone as if loneliness were the norm; and if I must find myself alone, why can't I find the power to bear it? There should be such power. Or is this loneliness really a necessity, instead of a typically childish complaint?

312

Either way, it's an unacceptable weakness. Why don't I find the old warmth in your eyes, those eyes I see as both beautiful and harsh inasmuch as they are prudent and reproachful? Even when I said to you that which I never say to anyone, not even to myself—whether awkwardly, gushed, or interrupted, slightly confused and fervent, I was trying to open with difficulty, incompletely—yes, without competence—old doors rusted shut because they have not been opened since their closure. I was trying to decode the echoes in the tone of your voice, of that clamor whose wild noise is heard day and night, the clamor of raw monsters attached to the walls of my self, clinging by nails and teeth, never closing their eyes. I embrace them, despite their deformations, unable to set myself free from them.

Why do I speak to you when my words come out sparingly and with difficulty, when I find in your eyes nothing but a neutral, contemplative gaze which adds to the confusion of my words, finding myself plunging alone, further and further, with motionless hands, into the swamps of this shallow-water desolation?

He said to himself: Why?

Because in you, my old friend, is a fundamental weakness that you claim as a fundamental strength. That is all.

You staunch man of ethics whose measures have been contorted.

Neither weakness nor strength is this thing?

There was, of course, no response.

He had said to her: In all this story there's no dialogue; the dialogue did not take place.

She said: But it happened. It happened indeed.

He said: If it happened, then in an unexpected way, in an unfamiliar way that I missed and didn't recognize.

She said: Yes, it happened.

He said: What a pity!

She said: Don't ever be sorry.

313

He had said to her: You know I am southern Egyptian at heart and still am. Southern Egyptians—all of us—believe in one god, with no double.

All our lives between infertile mountains and the deep and narrow valley, on the shores of our only river with its vast and still surface, able to gush in an uncontrollable flood to the outskirts of desolate desert: solitary, believing in a sole god.

She said: How lucky you are! At least you believe, even if in a solitary, unrepeatable one.

He said: This is what I know. I don't know anything else. I cannot know more than a single entity who can encompass everything. He is everything. My devotion is singular, monastic. As for you, you are polytheistic, as if you came from the African bush, from the farthest frontiers, from the waterfalls of an inner, subtropical area. In this place the cries of deities are dominant and varied. They send out commanding wails from forests of tormenting longings and suffering. Cries of pleasure burst forth, the flaring up of seasonal lightning from rainfall beneath dark, heavy, ripped clouds that look like moving walls of erotic monuments, engraved with thousands of gods in continuous copulation across time.

He said: My desire for oneness, this inclination for the desert, for the monastic, creates in me all this tension you hate, and leads naturally to incompetence. For me, there is only one pole tying down everything in my world.

He said: There is no room for choice, reciprocity, or variation, no place for lessening the power of this unbearable, irresistible enticement toward a single, unique goal.

He said: Had it not been for the mercy of God, I could have become truly a tyrant who sees the world only in one color, in one tone, all poured in one totalizing cast.

She said: I cannot understand this oneness. I might be persuaded intellectually by it, yes, but that is all. The phenomenon of the many and of variety with all its different manifestations, with all types of beauty and risks, attracts me every time. How quickly I surrender to temptation!

He said: No, your surrender is not giving in to temptation. Perhaps you, yourself, first and foremost, are the maker of temptations. Isn't that so? You are a goddess too, among other goddesses, in your own right. Maybe you are all the gods in all their infinite images, but you—yourself—are one, unique.

She said with a contented smile: I don't know. These waters are too deep for me to wade into.

He said: You? You're an excellent swimmer. It's me who drowns in a hand's worth of water.

He said to himself: Does everything happen in this story in closed hotel rooms and in glass-covered train stations? Between windows with drawn curtains and columns of iron and granite?

The railway station at night, the train from southern Egypt is late and the station assistant says that the semaphore has signaled that the train will arrive immediately. Then he says: Wait, no, this is the train from Rosetta. The group has come together on the platform for first-class passengers, sitting on wooden seats, their luggage and packages with them, exhausted and anxious in anticipation. Samia is squatting on the long wooden bench, having crossed, Indian-style, her two slender legs with their bluish-bronze tautness, not minding exposure. She leans her head in its southern Egyptian turban to her hand. She seems as if she has assumed a yoga posture, dozing off in peace. Somehow it appears as if her eyes are open. Mahmud is moving around in the station with his leather sport jacket, made in Berlin, flung over his shoulders, his eyes hollow and gleaming, the skin beneath them loose and arched. 'Abd al-Jalil comes from the buffet with a tray of Turkish coffee cups, their foaming surface having spilled on the saucers—the

315

dark coffee seems light and quivering—along with bottled water, Alexandrian brand. With alert, catlike eyes Nura puts her head on Samia's shoulder, who whispers to her, from time to time, with calm, soft, and insinuating words. The train whistles in the station as it enters the platform on the other side. Its fearful and powerful echo resounds under the glass ceiling. Mikhail has gone for no reason other than to escort the group to the station, as he has decided to spend the night in town, and has managed to implement his decision. This is an indication of separation, of initiating a process that cannot be reversed—decisive, even if not altogether finalized. But something has reached its end. There's no hope of extending its tether. From a distance her gaze hints that she knows.

During the prior evening, in the cafeteria, she had begun weeping uncontrollably. She choked out that she could not stay in town after the group departed—though the two of them had agreed to just that, earlier that morning. After last night's party, she did not return to the hotel until dawn. Neither did Mahmud, Samir, and Ilham. Mikhail had told her, half joking, half bitter, that the phoenix was getting rid of its feathers once again. Her tears—a continuous and limpid outpouring—did not move him. He knew her competence when it came to weeping. He said to himself, this crying is skillfully done, and she easily perfects it. He also said to himself that cruelty to oneself and to the other in the last scenes of this relationship was something to be expected, banal, also a bit too facile.

The train whistled from a distance. It entered from the dark outskirts of al-Hadara's sleepy houses. It passed the sandy, dust-swept platform that lay beneath a second coating of trash and old grass displayed in stark relief under the platform's mobile, dazzling electric light. Mikhail was shaking hands with the group, one after the other, kissing them hurriedly, without too much emotion. They would be meeting up in a couple of days in Cairo, on their way to Edfu and

316

Horus Temple. He came toward her with unhesitating steps, feeling his eyes shining with the decision-making he had taken on, then finished with. She got up from her distraught, seated position. He could see the counter-determination in her body. Everyone's gaze was directed at her—even if furtively. Samia was gesturing, in a way that could hardly be detected, to Nura. Rama shook his hand. Her grip was strong. She shook his hand twice, three times, without relaxing her grip. She did not lean toward him; his lips did not brush her cheeks with the light, customary kiss. He said to her: Goodbye. She said: So long. Her eyes revealed solidity. No bitterness, no anger, no denial, no consent to a decision, implicit or explicit.

His steps to the station gate are steady. He turns around once, waves, while they—including Rama—stand on the platform waving back. He says to himself: With such steps the exiles leave their home-land knowing they will never return.

She had said to him: Nothing, I mean there is no news. Nothing new. Nothing is happening. I want something spectacular to happen.

He had said: Lucky you!

She said: Just like that. Where's the cleverness, the canny judg-ment, the suavity of expression so typical of you? Wouldn't it have been more appropriate to say: Oh dear, what a pity!

He said: Because you are searching for something spectacular, all sagacity—as you say—gets lost.

She said: Pardon me. I didn't mean it that way, and you know it.

He said: I wanted to say, and of course I didn't know how to say it, that you're lucky. You can still hope and search for something spectacular.

There was nothing to distract them from the concentration of their close-lipped, repressed suffering.

He said: Of course this doesn't mean anything. It's just my lack of a graceful way of putting it, as you say.

317

The dance was about to end. The echoes of tormenting, joyful music hit the ancient, solid, bare stones. A skull with its socket holes of two gaping eyes leans against the soft, smooth cheek blushing with merriment and pleasure. Funeral dancers with almond eyes, with youthful agility; small-breasted and naked except for a light belt beneath the belly; their hair, plaited in slim, long braids, bedecked in delicate wreathes of lotus and jasmine. The kiss of displayed teeth clinging doggedly to her without lips, sucking the nectar from her supple, open, warm mouth and from her skillful tongue, fast-moving in its quest. She moves from one bony arm with cracked fingers to another in the flare of the last dance, amid stony, pocked faces and distended, thin, bowed bones. Dark greenish faces with protruding eyes press the faces of the smiling, round-cheeked, angelic Cherubs. Bastet, the cat, squats quietly, neutrally gazing on at what is beyond the old men with their dangling bellies, filled with dangling intestines, swinging to an obscene melody. They move in the prescribed steps of the dance, swaying and hurling their arms to indicate a voiding, a finishing off. Their bare ribs in white, dry, open skeletons press against supple breasts filled with firm creaminess. The raised bones of swinging arms and legs start oscillating. These bones end in long fingers of interlocked joints, smacking and clacking around slender waists and firm, plump haunches under transparent dresses quavering in the ecstasy of a fast rhythmic dance toward the darkness of hollow caves, where salty seawaters roar as they crash against the cave's rock walls, and will continue crashing against those rocks without surcease or hope.

No. Something resembled hope in this dimness, even if lacking comfort.

All that I criticize in her—my Love—is that she didn't really know me. Was her adventure with me—like her adventures with all her men, her conquerors—a matter of knowledge, revelation, some inner triumph that goes beyond me, beyond them? Is it a matter of something that's not related to us, that encompasses but goes beyond? It is a non-personal, non-individualized element in men that refuses to be defined by reference to positive or negative points.

Without blaming himself, he said: I never reached the first category of her lovers. But I occupied a niche in her life. Not the bottom niche either.

No consolation or bitterness in that.

In the final course of time that they knew together, her face appeared strange, as if he had never known it.

He said to himself: But this is what happens all the time. Behind the mask of this estrangement, I have known her body and her soul. I have known both their throbbing beats: bare, open, slaughtered, vulnerable, offering no resistance, dripping blood and yearning.

The music of her voice flowed toward him; she spoke to him as if to a stranger. For the first time, he learned this was not one of the tricks of love. A siren with claws lures ships with an irresistible pull, causing the destruction of sailors' bodies on her rock, generation after generation. In his estrangement, a new group of her friends, unknown to him, surrounded them. She introduced them one after the other to him, and she introduced him to them. Nothing clings to his ruptured memory: not a name, not an image, as if he were disowning an alien invasion, annulling it. In the debris of memory's rubble remains a round face laughing and engaging in a long-winded discussion of projects and plans amid introductions, greetings, handshakes, calls, and small talk. She said to the good-natured face with the narrow and clever eyes behind thick-lensed glasses, in an ordinary tone, passing it off as uncontrived, but fooling Mikhail not one whit: I was late for my bank appointment. Yesterday I had a hundred and fifty pounds of legitimate expenses for the restoration account. Tomorrow I'll return it, or deposit the check. The man with the good-natured face said:

319

Sure, that's okay. She said: Tonight then, as agreed, we'll see Chaplin's *Great Dictator*. We'll have a good laugh. Then she suddenly looked at Mikhail as if she remembered him. From now on, he would be outside her ring. She said: Mikhail, will you join us for the movies tonight? He said: Thanks, I'm busy tonight. Everything seemed to him tasteless, confused, silly, incapable of provoking a response. When he returned to his room, he found under the door a white slip of paper without signature: "Mikhail, if you have time, I would like to talk to you." When he called her on the phone her colorless voice exhibited directness, blankness, and neutrality. She said: Yes. When she opened the door for him, she was wearing a light dress, sleeveless and décolleté, falling on her obviously naked body in a casual and negligent way. She put her hand on her chest: Welcome. Come on in. My apologies. As if she hadn't actually been waiting for him as a result of their phone conversation. She rectified: You arrived sooner than I expected. With your permission—and she hurried into the inner room. He felt in his mouth a slight but genuine bitterness, from the tip of his tongue. He thought to himself, she is apologizing to me now about her appearance as if I were a visitor making a polite call. On another day, not that long before, she reciprocated by laying herself bare physically and spiritually, the heart getting rid of its sediments. Their reciprocal self-exposure used to be practically a pillar of faith, a daily ritual.

She came out wearing her loose-fitting *jallabiya* studded with small, ancient, bronze coins engraved with the sultan's dates and signature in the intricate royal calligraphy of *tughra*. She wore a wrought copper necklace and large, crescent-shaped earrings dangling from under her hair, which she had quickly arranged and pushed to one side of her face.

He kissed her on the mouth. It was an experimental kiss, a kiss of exploration and recalling. The spirit was not stirred. His soul was blocked behind a stubborn inner obstacle, as if fluttering with small wings, tied to threads of confusion and uncertainty, cemented in another dimension unable to reach this close encounter that his lips practiced, as if to perform a ritual without conviction. His sentiments dispersed. His passion still possessed the strength of a firebrand, but he did not know whether it could become a torch while in detention.

After a gesture of favorable disposition and a very short response, she left her mouth for him but without participation. Then she put her hand gently on his arm, lifting his hand from her back. She went on showing interest, as if spontaneously, in recovering the routine of familiar gestures, established by their old ways, but without a goal and without enthusiasm.

She said to him: Mikhail, let's be friends, act like friends. Can't we? I invited you to have a drink. Let's see: I have nothing except the remainder of this Remy Martin, unfortunately or perhaps fortunately. I am not drinking. All I want is to see you for a while, for the sake of the old days. She poured him a glass and gave it to him: Cheers for the old days!

He remembered the first night, how she invited him to talk, spelling out the word talk as if he didn't know it.

He said now: Don't you want to talk a little? Come on, let's go out on the town.

She said: Yes, I dream of sitting with you, somewhere, without conversing, without doing anything, without thinking about anything. Silence with a friend is most conducive for relaxation. I am so tired. I dream of sitting with you alone, silently, in a small bar without drinking; only to relax.

He said to her: So be it, but I have a small surprise.

He brought out of his jacket pocket a round bottle of Napoleon cognac. Its bottle glass green and the liquor reddish brown, with a slender neck on which there was a grand golden logo in bold letters.

She said: Oh, that cannot be resisted! Let's drink here together.

321

She sat barefoot on the floor, having flung her shoes away in a hurry. Her *jallabiya* was spread out around her, its jingling bronze resonating lightly on the round mat with its white and black hair, loose and long. She told him: This is a monkey skin from Addis Ababa. A friend of mine, a specialist in Coptic history, brought it to me as a gift. With a rigid move, he sat down on the soft skin with his trousers and shoes, next to her, silently, half smiling. His trousers were a bit tight at the knees, so he stretched his legs out and reclined on his elbow. They listened, without much interest, to tapes of revolutionary and popular poems, cynical in their rejection of everything, recited by an elderly voice, hoarse from hashish. The tape recorder looked expensive and modern, having a futuristic design and rigor, as if it were controlling an intricate set of functions. He cared neither for the poems nor for the recital in collapsing voice; and he told her that. She was unhappy with his comment and their discussion on this subject led nowhere.

She said to him: I'll prepare something for you to eat. cognac opens up the appetite. I have olives and *basturma*. He said: Don't bother. Cigarettes are my appetizers. She said: Myself, I want something to eat. The cognac has me sweating. I'll shower and get rid of this *jallabiya*. It feels heavy now. Do you know how much it weighs? Smiling, he said: No. She said: Ten pounds! I have in fact weighed it. He burst out with laughter. He knew she was naked beneath ten pounds of cloth and bronze. She came back with a small plate that had on it a few soft, wrinkled-skin, black olives in light olive oil. Her face was washed; she had let her hair down and put on a new nightgown that he did not recognize—brick-red, a light fabric, not transparent, but short, coming up to mid-thigh, its hem ornamented with a very thin border of refined white lace.

He was lying on the large bed with his shoes still on. He had only taken off his jacket. She looked at him with very slight astonishment and imperceptible questioning. She said: I thought you would have

322

made yourself at home and gotten rid of those shoes. He made no response. Their kisses were sensual encounters and juxtapositions. The cognac tingle would not leave him, but that refreshing, glowing wakefulness—where the weight of the body and the world cease to be—was not forthcoming. Her arms around his neck were heavy, her body in her new brick-red nightgown, which he did not know, was slowly moving around his legs in the depths of a difficult dance of the flesh, with meager offering, without music and without words.

She said to him: No, no, not in this way. The limbs relaxed in the exhaustion of the fall and of the disappointment. She slept next to him while he dozed in successive, short, stifled spans, but never losing himself in the peace of fulfillment and redemption. As he embraced her naked waist, her breasts touched the side of his arm, lifelessly. He left her room just before dawn without waking her up.

Her telephone was constantly busy the next evening when he dialed on the old black rotary, time and again, with a persistence he could not fathom. Always busy. She had taken the receiver off the hook. She could not be speaking on the phone without interruption. Besides, telephones in this town were not usually out of order. Was she staying out late while the receiver was off the hook? Surely not. Is it another party or a special rendezvous with a new friend? Or does she know from experience the extent of stubbornness that possesses me at times, so she short-circuits any possibility of communication? Thus his obsessions were turning things over. He went on dialing until every possible rendezvous hour had gone by. Three in the morning and he was suffering a strange, desolate, and fanciful insomnia, teeming with nightmares. At last, he fell into the abyss of troubled sleep. When he woke up, as early morning light was stealing in from behind the shutters and the half-drawn curtains, it flashed through his mind that the number he had been dialing all night long was not hers, but his. He was shaken. Calling himself! Imagine such a thing.

323

Yes, yes, how could he have continued to dial his own number from his own phone? Of course the telephone was signaling busy. He still could not figure out his strange error! But was it an error? Or was it a will that went beyond his will, blocking off every road within himself? Who knows? How easily he discovers now this useless thing in the gray cloudy morning.

He said to her: At times you seem to me like a huge, tree-like boulder with multiple branches and roots. Like those trees that used to be in the old days. Maybe they're still in al-Azbakiya; do you know them? With twisted trunks, and branches hanging down becoming trunks themselves, penetrating the earth, standing as entrenched columns, one next to the other, each having its own roots. I meant something like this tree when I said you were pagan and multiple.

Her mind wandered in contemplation. This image of her has either pleased her or upset her.

She said: Yes, I got married twice and divorced twice. I don't claim to have been a nun. You know this. Even before marriage I had my youthful flings like all girls do.

He said to himself: Now, in this new context I can tolerate this admission and put up with it, as if the ardor of the first relation and the blaze of its flames had reached the point of returning to a stoic calm, ordinary now in the scheme of things.

In the bottom of his heart, he knew that this was, at least, not yet true.

He said: And me? Where is my place on this tree?

She said, as she looked at him from a certain distance, from above: You . . . You remind me of a boy climbing one of the tree trunks with devotion and effort, searching for a fruit, as we used to do in mango season. But your climb on the tree absorbs you and you plunge into the dense leaves, not wanting at times to come down with the fruit.

324

They laughed together.

But a certain penetrating stab took him by surprise as he was laughing. He did not realize that the stab could reach yet a new depth. From frustration to bitterness, from hate to disdain, from aversion to indifference: the classic cycle!

She said: But you have always managed to keep a mask of reserve and seriousness, so I forget sometimes. My apologies.

He said: No, it's nothing.

This is no mask. It is a granite coffin, and what is inside is not a mummy; it is a living entity in the grip of a tormenting monster, in a chaos of agitation and fires. A soul embodied in an imprisoned passionate body, which knows no way out, no outlet through which to steal away into the blueness of cold sky. It explodes under an unrelenting, continuous pressure, but the granite lid never shakes off.

He said to himself: Is it true that the search for oneness, from beginning till end, is what destroyed you? And is the wreckage complete, sealed? This persistent, all-consuming endeavor—that seeks to sharpen the points of the world without scratching them—causes you to fall apart, piece by piece. Isn't that so?

He also said to himself: And at last, even in this fall, as long as it's happening, you won't be a subject for your self-pity. These old tears are not the business of others. You can bear it, too.

He went down from this room and its stifling walls. The pangs of pain had exhausted him. He sensed their essence. It was past midnight and the night had entered into profound stillness. The air hung heavy, enclosed. Before him stretched long days and nights, he wasn't finished yet with anything. In the vast openness next to the sea, on the port's sidewalk, the night in mid-May felt hotter than usual and the water's surface appeared motionless as far as he could see. A strong leaden surface, it was greenish, its waters melting silently on the sword of slight sand, under the boats—boats with protruding

325

bones and proud chests. Their spread nets were drying, dangling without a flutter. In the morning the fishermen would mend them and at evening they would go out early seeking their meager fortune.

Mikhail heard unhurried but determined footsteps behind him. When he looked around, he saw someone approaching. The man reached Mikhail, slowed down, and greeted him: Good evening, *Effendina.*

It was an Alexandrian from the inner city. He wore a shirt and trousers. On his head was a small *lasa* skullcap of white perforated knit. A thin man, his eyes were wakeful at night. It was clear that the sun had tanned his clean-shaven face—still fresh, youthful, taut, not in the least flabby.

Mikhail answered back: Good evening.

He looked at Mikhail without reserve or sense of awkwardness. His footsteps fell alongside Mikhail's. With utter familiarity, he said: Service to you, *Effendina?*

Mikhail said: Not at all. Thanks. I'm just strolling.

The young man said: Stranger here?

He said: A stranger? Yes, a stranger. But I am originally from here. I was born and lived here.

The young man said kindly and generously: *Ahlan wa-sahlan.* You honor us!

Then the young man hurried a little and said: So long. He went his way toward the low, stony houses, one next to each other, behind the royal palace piercing the sea, the mysterious towers and domes, the lamps illuminating only limited round spots in the moonlight. In front of them were a large green garden and Indian palm trees with outspread palm leaves, quiet in the heat, as still as a painting. In front of their houses, men slept on mats. They were gathered together in their sleep, supporting their heads on folded arms. In their surrender to the night sky, there was a kind of haughtiness, which they were not aware of.

She had said to him: Isn't all this somewhat old-fashioned, no more in use?

He had said to himself in a loud voice: Isn't all this very primitive and very naïve?

She said to him: Primitive maybe, but it is not obtuse and it is not—what is the word?—raw, it is not obscene.

He said to her: It is fierce and has no place here now.

She said: And that is why I love you.

He said: And that is why I love you and hate this primitive thing.

She said: That's not true. Or not quite, at least. You may also hate it, but surely you love it too.

He had said: Perhaps.

The ground of the sidewalk under his feet was white, washed with fine cracks. The road in front of him lay empty, though hardly desolate. The unflecked sky hung oppressively near, but he shouldered its difficult burden in a familiar way, as if the sky itself had become part of him. The moon had plunged into the sea bequeathing a pale yellowish redness. The stars were dense, crowded. The stings of their lights clustered in a sea of blueness: dark, luxurious, silky black. The night-hunting kites were flying in large arcs, coming down straight with calm wings then rising up effortlessly, coming toward the sea from the side of the graveyard.

And Mikhail knew there was a subterranean love still in his heart, no one to blame for its presence. Despite all the lies, all the deformations, the flow of life's sap in this love had taught him that there is, just the same, a candor and fidelity that go beyond the sum of things. Her love, her desire was no lie.

As for me, I am surrendering myself to the last of what I have—as far as I know, to the last of what exists. I'll confront this ache until the last day with no armor, with no camouflage, and with no vindication.

327

Modern Arabic Writing
from the American University in Cairo Press